WHEN ANGELS REST

Books by Donald Harington

The Cherry Pit

Lightning Bug

Some Other Place. The Right Place.

The Architecture of the Arkansas Ozarks: A Novel

Let Us Build Us a City

The Cockroaches of Stay More

The Choiring of the Trees

Ekaterina

Butterfly Weed

When Angels Rest

WHEN ANGELS REST

DONALD HARINGTON

COUNTERPOINT

WASHINGTON, D.C.

Library of Congress Cataloging-in-Publication Data
Harington, Donald
When angels rest / Donald Harington.
p.   cm.
ISBN 1−887178−07−4 (alk. paper)
I. Title.
PS3558.A6242W44   1998
813'.54—dc21   98−34795
CIP

Book design and electronic production by David Bullen Design

Printed in the United States of America on acid-free paper that meets the
American National Standards Institute z39-48 Standard

COUNTERPOINT
P. O. Box 65793
Washington, D. C. 20035-5793

Counterpoint is a member of the Perseus Books Group.

10   9   8   7   6   5   4   3   2   1

FIRST PRINTING

For Fred Chappell
old son

PART ONE

· ·

Where children are,
there is the golden age.

NOVALIS

In all the wild imaginings of mythology
a fanciful spirit is playing on the borderline
between jest and earnest.

JOHAN HUIZINGA, *Homo Ludens*

Set in the fictional, quirky backwater locale of Stay More, Arkansas during WWII. A coming-of-age tale for the town's young people and also for a nation whose innocence is sorely tested by the loss of a president and the war events overseas.

CHAPTER

. . . .

1

WHEN I WAS THOROUGHLY ELEVEN, WORKING ON TWELVE, I first met you. You were not part of the gang that beat me up, but you watched them do it. That was the first and only thing I knew about you for the longest time: you liked to watch. Of course you also liked to listen; did you hear it when the bone snapped in my arm? I did. And that was when I suddenly knew you were there. Probably, without even knowing it, I had been waiting for you a very long time.

Now that you were there, I was tempted to introduce my tormentors. I may as well. That was Sugrue "Sog" Alan who slammed the baseball bat down on my arm; Sog was not yet seventeen, too young to be drafted or even to join with his parents' permission, but he was big enough, tough enough, not to have needed the baseball bat; he could've broken my arm with his bare hands if he'd tried. His best buddy, Larry Duckworth, was only fifteen, but already the handsomest man in Stay More since all the best-looking ones had been drafted or joined up. Maybe Larry was vain and even jealous of my nice face, for he chose not to break my arm but to blacken one of my eyes. The only one of them that I might have beaten in a fair fight was Jim John Whitter, who spelled it Witter and maybe was right but whose stupidity kept him a year behind me in school although he was a year older than me. He took advantage of how the other two had already defeated me to do something he couldn't have done alone: kick me in the groin. I wondered if you could even imagine how that felt.

You looked the three of them over and betrayed no disdain, though I am trying to picture them for you as villains, which they were. Then you looked at me, on the ground, whimpering in pain and grunting not your name, which I didn't know yet, but the name of Ernie Pyle, my hero. If Ernie could have come to my cries, even though he was frail and scrawny, he could have trounced all three of them together, he could have obliterated them, with his words, if not his fists. But he didn't come. You did. I liked to think that you felt sympathy for me, if not much knowledge, certainly not yet any affection. I wasn't fishing for your pity, nor did I hope you could rescue me, as I had prayed for Ernie's aid. I wasn't even, as some would argue, simply imagining you out of the desperation of the situation. You were there, as much as I am here. You couldn't do anything. You couldn't protect me from those bullies, but you could, and you did, give me to know that you were there.

That would sustain me for . . . a long time (I nearly said *forever,* but neither you nor I believe in that). You sat beside me when Doc Swain put the plaster cast on my arm. "Can you get out that newspaper of yours with only one hand?" Doc asked me. Sure, I said; it was my good arm, the right one, that peeled the pages from the press. He shook his head. "Who was it got on the wrong side of you, boy?" he asked me.

I winked at you and grinned manfully. "Oh, just some of *them,*" I said. I wasn't going to name any names, except to you.

"Well, if they were out to kill ye, they did a right poor job of it," he

4

said. "I reckon you'll live. But I was you, I'd cross the creek without a footbridge next time I seen them a-coming."

When I was not yet six and had just the faintest idea who you were, not enough to keep me from it, I had run away from home and was lost in the spooky woods of Ledbetter Mountain for some time. Doc Swain had organized the search party—the entire populace, some hundred-odd Stay Morons—but he had not been the one who had found me, and I suppose it had frustrated him. Now that I come to think of it, now that I'd met you and had you beside me, now that I'd speculated inter-minably about just who it was who'd found me, I can only wonder: was it you?

During the exciting days following our first meeting (I was thrilled to see how readily and easily and cozily you shared my bed at night), I searched in vain for a good name for you. At school, the little one-room (white, not red) schoolhouse across Swains Creek from the village, I had sat alone since August at a desk meant for two. I didn't have infec-tious cooties, not that I knew of, and I didn't have B.O., not that any-body had ever told me, and I wasn't the only fifth grader: Sammy Coe was also eleven, but he didn't want to sit with me, or, rather, I didn't want to sit with him, and he knew it. The only advantage of sitting alone was that during air-raid drills when we all had to get down under our desks, it was easier for me to get under the desk without bumping into and getting tangled up with a deskmate. Air-raid drills were ridicu-lous; we had never seen an airplane. Maybe Miss Jerram, a pretty but not terribly bright spinster of twenty-three or thirty-three (who could tell? and besides, any unmarried woman past nineteen was considered a spinster) had not assigned me a seatmate out of spite, because she knew I was smarter than she was. But now I could install you to share my desk, calling you, for want of a better name, *Friend*. Some of the other kids launched admiring glances at the white plaster cast on my arm, which would soon bear their inscriptions of good wishes, all of them except Sog's, Larry's, and Jim John's, whose wishes would be bad. When Miss Jerram said, that first day afterwards, "Dawny, do you want to stand and tell us all what-all happened to ye?" I turned to my new seatmate and said to you, "Friend, why don't *you* tell 'em?"

5

But of course you would not, or could not. It was Jim John across the aisle who blurted, bragging, "That stinkin Jap done went and told on us in that stupid newspaper of his'n, and we whomped the soup outen him!"

Did Miss Jerram understand that? She could not permit herself to believe that I was smart enough to be a newspaper editor, and therefore she refrained from reading my paper. Or if she snuck a glance at it she never told me. But she knew darn well that most of the student body had been divided, for going on four years, practically since the war started, into two factions, rival camps who opposed each other not only in baseball but in war games such as Dirt War and Dare Base and all-out Capture the Flag. With or without her knowledge and consent, these two factions occupied opposing sides of the schoolroom with the aisle as a divider, a demilitarized zone across which spitballs flew.

There were the top dogs, led by fat Burl Coe until he got drafted and by Sog Alan in his absence, who called themselves Allies, from the privilege of feeling and sometimes being superior (most of them came from the "better" families of town, to the extent that the farms in the bottomlands were more productive than those on the mountains), and there were the underdogs, who did not choose to be called Axis but had no choice. I certainly did not elect to be an Axis, let alone a despised Jap, but it fell my lot by default. Most of the girls, except a few chosen as sweethearts or sycophants by the Allied generals, were also Axis by default. Before the war, we Axis had been required to be the redskins in games of cowboys-and-Indians, and bandits in games of sheriffs-and-outlaws. Somebody always has to be the bad guy.

They were the in-group; we were the out-group. Whether one was Ally or Axis had nothing to do with how dumb or smart one was, or even social status as such (in Stay More there were only two social classes anyhow, with hardly any distinction between them: the poor, and the dirt poor—or, from a different perspective, since none of us were starving and all of us were fairly happy, the rich, and the feeling-rich). And just as the Civil War had pitted brother against brother (including two historically famous brothers from Stay More), opposing members of the Allies and the Axis could be found in the same family. For example, early in the war years, when the sides were first drawn, there were the triplet sons, Earl, Burl, and Gerald, of Lawlor Coe, the blacksmith, who, before Miss Jerram organized her War Effort Scrap Drive to remove all of it, had an abundance of waste pieces of iron and steel from which both the Allies and the Axis fashioned their arsenals. Burl was the dominant triplet and thus insisted on being an Allied general, leaving his brothers to be the Axis: Earl the Nazi and Gerald the Jap. Dulcie Coe, the triplets' mother, had given Burl's tousled auburn locks a GI haircut at his request, had slicked and combed Earl's hair into a Hitlerian flap, which he darkened with stove polish, adding a false mustache of horsehair, and she had made Gerald's head look like a parody of the caricatures of Premier Hideki Tojo; when Gerald's efforts to give himself buckteeth by gripping his lower lip with his upper teeth did not do the job, his friends—two of us—fashioned him a false set from a dead cow's teeth.

The two friends of Gerald, including me, empathized with him by wearing cow's teeth also during the battles, or even by slanting up the corners of our eyes with charcoal. The other friend was Willard Dinsmore, the smartest of us all, and when Gerald and Willard and I put our heads together in games requiring strategy, intelligence, and cunning, especially with the brawn provided by our Nazi conspirators, the Axis often routed the Allies. Before long, I'll introduce you to Willard, and I think you may like him best of us all.

But for now, and for a while, it's Gerald we're looking at: pudgy, freckled, towheaded, the least and last of three insufferably identical and homely brothers whose names, you are quick to understand, rhymed, the way we all pronounced his as "Jerl." But no one except his mother called him that. Nearly everyone had a nickname of sorts, as if it were bad luck to speak someone's actual name. Even their pronunciation of my diminutive, "Dawny," turned it into a kind of nickname, but ever since the war started all of the Axis and the Allies called me Ernie rather than Dawny because I had once in a moment of extravagance or enthusiasm blurted that I thought Ernie Pyle was a greater man than Franklin Delano Roosevelt. Likewise, Gerald Coe had once blurted that his ambition in life was someday to become mayor of Stay More. This little town, lost as it was in the remote fastnesses of the Ozark Mountains, had never had a mayor, unless you considered that

in the old days, more than a century before, Jacob Ingledew, who'd
founded the town with his brother Noah, had proclaimed himself
Mayor, mostly just an honorific title. Being least and last always makes
one a little more alert and sensitive than those who are first and fore-
most, and Gerald, or "Mayor Coe" as others began to call him in jest,
perceived that Stay More might not continue its relentless decline and
population loss if there was a responsible civic government to rescue it.
Those who truly knew him, as few did (you and I among them), had
every reason to believe that he might actually run for and be elected to
the post someday, and, further, that he might actually save the dying
town.

Of course *mayor* is pronounced simply "mare," and that is what we
all of us had come to call him, Mare Coe, a name that lent itself to further teasing (a nickname is by virtue of its bestowal a form of teasing)
because of the association with female horses or nightmares or, as Sog
Alan usually called him, Mary. Taunts could be easily made: "Mare
smokes marijuana," or "Stay Mare of Stay More," and, prophetically,
Mare would join the marines.

Despite his pudginess and his flaring freckles and the anonymity
that comes from being identical to two nondescript brothers, Mare had
qualities that not only made him the natural commander of the Axis but
also, had he lived long enough, might actually have elevated him to
mayor of what was left of the community of Stay More. He was smarter
than his brothers. Until he graduated from the eighth grade at fourteen, he was Miss Jerram's star pupil, her pet, and (some of the kids
gossiped) her secret lover. Whether or not there was actually anything
going on between them (and nobody ever testified the two had ever
been seen together outside of school), it is a fact that she was the only
one who could distinguish him readily from his brothers. The triplets
not only looked exactly alike (they didn't dress identically but wore an
indistinguishable wardrobe of overalls and old shirts) but also talked
identically, with the same inflections and only the subtlest differences
in their choice of words, which did not escape Miss Jerram's keen per-
ception: she knew, for example, that Mare's favorite negative was "Over
my dead body," and his favorite affirmative was "Fine and dandy," and
she smiled at him more often than she did at his brothers. Because she

8

was nice to him, he went out of his way to please her, and even after he'd graduated he helped her conduct that great award-winning scrap drive and that great knit-off.

Paradoxically, as far as the War Effort was concerned, the members of the Axis were much more patriotic than the Allies. When the great knit-off began, I was still in the second grade, and a Red Cross lady came from the county seat, Jasper, to show all of us, including Miss Jerram, who didn't know how, the art of knitting. We learned how to click those needles and loop those skeins for Our Boys Overseas. Soon all of us—except the Allies, who thought it was sissy, and refused— were adept at making knitted squares out of the khaki or olive drab yarn from the wool from the sheep of Stay More that had been dyed in advance. When enough squares were finished, they'd be stitched together into blankets, and although these blankets disappeared we'd be told how they'd become part of "Bundles for Britain" and thus warming and comforting to Our Boys Overseas.

The Axis girls, like Ella Jean Dinsmore, whom I secretly was crazy about from the second grade on, graduated from doing simple wool squares to knitting mittens, socks, and even sweaters for Our Boys Overseas, and the Stay More public school, thanks to the Axis, won the Newton County prize for Most Yarn Intertwined, a certificate that Miss Jerram dressed up with a frame trimmed with knitting and hung over the blackboard.

We did even better for her War Effort Scrap Drive, rounding up virtually everything metallic in the whole town, whether it was scrap or not. Mare Coe drove the hay wagon and mule team we used to load up with the collection—wagon-wheel rims, hoes, plow points, broken anvils, shovels, everything. We asked him, "What iffen they're still a-using whatever piece of metal we want?" and he replied, "Jist ast 'em if they kin someways live without it." Somehow we talked the few remaining menfolk out of their hammers, saws, and plowshares, the womenfolk out of their washtubs, pots, pans, and tableware, and all of the children sacrificed their jumping jacks, pocketknives, and any other play-pretties made out of metal. Doc Swain was permitted to keep his essential medical tools, but everything else metallic in the town had to go. As the result of our efforts, it was declared that we'd collected more scrap than any other rural school in the whole state of Arkansas, and Miss Jerram got the privilege of christening in absentia a liberty ship.

Doing things for the War Effort diverted us Axis from our constant battles with the Allies, and allowed us to feel truly superior to the Allies, who remained more interested in games and dirty tricks than in the patriotic activities of the War Effort. The Allies had commandeered as their clubhouse ("Operations Headquarters" they called it) an old house built up in a tree nearly a century before by Noah Ingledew. It couldn't exactly be called a "tree house" because that conjures up an image of a jerry-built hovel constructed by children, and Noah Ingledew's house had been an entire double-wing dwelling erected high up in a sycamore tree. The Allies always got the best of everything, and we Axis were consigned to using as our Operations Headquarters an unused back room in the old Ingledew General Store; nobody knew we were there. The Allies' clubhouse in that sycamore tree was just north of the village, and they had dug foxholes all around the perimeter of it to protect it, and not even Mare Coe could lead a successful assault on those foxholes. Whenever we played War, the Axis usually had to defend the village proper, the main street along which we'd dug so many foxholes that the grown-ups complained. The Allies were usually victorious in assaulting and taking the village from us. The only times we truly beat the Allies were Saturday afternoon baseball games. With Mare's help as pitcher, our Axis baseball team could sometimes beat the Allies, who always after a defeat vowed to get even in the trenches, but even there, hurling the old potatoes that we used as hand grenades, Mare could often defend us against the assault of the Allies. The Allies would rather play any sort of game than expend energy on behalf of Our Boys Overseas.

The only thing the Allies were willing to do to help the War Effort was collect grease, and they had an ulterior motive for that: it was a way to get into the movies. As his own contribution to the War Effort, Doc Swain offered to take whoever could collect a lard bucket of grease to the Saturday night movies at the only movie theater in Newton County, the Buffalo, on the square in Jasper. The Buffalo was our Rialto. Doc not only was one of the few people in Stay More who possessed an automobile, but also because he was a doctor he had a "C" sticker for it that permitted him to fill his tank at Dill's Gas and Service. During the war there was a national speed limit of thirty-five miles per hour, and on the dirt road between Parthenon and Jasper there was one little level straightaway, where, if Doc floored the gas pedal on his old heap, he could get it up to thirty-three or thirty-four mph, almost the speed limit. Each Saturday night Doc took the winners of the grease-collection contest the distance of more than ten miles to the movies at the Buffalo, where the admission for kids was a lard-bucket of grease, meaning usually bacon fat or pork renderings. Often I was in the group of kids who crowded into Doc Swain's car with their grease buckets, and I got to watch the Movietone News before the serial and the feature came on. That newsreel was always full of the latest thrilling shots of how we were winning the war in Germany and the Pacific. And I decided, for the benefit of all of those in Stay More who couldn't go to the movies, to start a newspaper reporting the leading items from the Movietone News. Naturally my main motive was to start giving myself the experience I'd need to replace Ernie Pyle when he retired.

I mail-ordered for $1.98 plus postage (earned from my after-school job as stockboy and general factotum at Latha Bourne's general store) a "hectograph," or gelatin board, which was a simple wooden tray filled with hard purple gelatin on which a master sheet (hand-printed with purple pencil) could be impressed and duplicated up to a maximum of about fifty copies. My little newspaper, never running to more than four pages except at Christmas, had reached a circulation of not more than forty at the time I met you. I had decided to call it *The Stay Morning Star,* a clever play on the town's name. Putting out the newspaper required me to get up before school every Monday and, after giving postmistress Latha Bourne twenty copies to put in the post office boxes, carry the other twenty around to the RFD mailboxes of those who didn't have post office boxes. It was a long hike, up hill and down vale, in bitter weather that past winter, and sometimes I was tardy for the beginning of school and caught what-for from Miss Jerram. Then on Sunday afternoons I had to hike around to each of those places again and, after being announced by their barking dogs or knocking on their doors, I inquired whether any of them had anything to say that was worthy of being reported in the next day's paper.

On these reportorial rounds I never stopped at the yellow house, out on the Butterchurn Holler road, occupied by the strange bearded old man known only as Dan. I wasn't afraid of him, as most of both the Allies and Axis were. His house wasn't scary; in fact, it was quite pleasant and, being painted yellow, was bright and cheerful. But somehow I sensed, or knew, or had once been told, that he did not want visitors, or company, or friends. Although he'd been there longer than I'd been alive, he was still a "furriner," meaning not a native of these here mountains. He lived there with a girl, presumed to be his daughter, who was never seen in the village, who had never attended the Stay More school, who was reputed to be beautiful by those who claimed to have caught a glimpse of her. I left my little newspaper in their box each Monday morning, but I never even thought of stopping there on Sunday afternoons to ask for news. Keeping to themselves as they did, what news could they possibly have anyhow?

For that matter, few others had any news. The most common thing I heard, after all the effort to reach some of those remote cabins and houses, was "Nothin this week, Dawny, sorry to have to tell ye." But occasionally, like fishing for hours without a nibble and then landing a lunker, I got something truly newsworthy: a son had been in the D-Day invasion and survived. A son had been killed on his ship in the Pacific by something called a kamikaze, fiendish, which is where a pilot dive-bombs his plane with himself still in it. A son had been in something called the Battle of the Bulge and was wounded. I reported all of this excitement in a style that Ernie Pyle would have admired, even if he'd have grinned at the way I imitated him. My stories never gave away any troop movements or sank any ships.

But usually my reportage was mild and limited to such things as sports (AXIS TAKE ALLIES 3−0 ON MARE COE'S NO-HITTER) and, the main source of news, visits. Sunday afternoons, the time of my news collecting, were by tradition the time of the week for people to visit one another, and I could usually fill a page with items like WHITTERS VISIT DUCKWORTHS, COES VISIT DILLS, or DINSMORES VISIT DINGLETOONS. But one of the "visits," I discovered, involved a man too old to serve with Our Boys Overseas who was visiting with a young woman whose husband was one of Our Boys Overseas. "She's jist my little niece, didn't ye know?" he said to me, and I reported that fact in my story about the visit, which, however, got me into trouble. When I was hurt and puzzled by the uproar, dear Latha Bourne tried to explain to me, "He's not really her uncle. They're not even any kin to each other, which is unusual for any two people in this town."

The small costs of putting out *The Stay Morning Star* (mostly for the newsprint, in short supply) were borne by the advertisers: Latha Bourne's General Store ("Limited Supply of Post Toasties Just In"), Dill's Gas and Service ("Three Shade Trees, No Waiting"), and even now and again (although I later learned the AMA wouldn't have approved) Doc Swain ("Come in and ask about what streptomycin can do for you"). I was still in love with Latha Bourne, which is what people kept on calling her although she was now Mrs. Every Dill, but I never made a nuisance of myself around her anymore; I worked as her stockboy, janitor, and delivery boy for a little while after school each day, and once a week I took down her dictation for her ad in my paper, for which she paid me another fifteen or twenty-five cents, depending on whether it was a full-page ad or just a half-pager, although I protested that I could just consider those ad costs the rent on the little side room of her store that she let me use as my newspaper office.

No one, least of all myself, considered my newspaper to be in competition with the county's weekly, published in Jasper and printed on a real press, which came out on Thursday afternoons and, to my pleasure, always carried the Scripps-Howard syndicated column of Ernie Pyle, which I read religiously. Ernie Pyle was my first experience of the writer whose life is almost as important as his work, and therefore an inspiration to become a writer, not just to entertain or inform people, not just to reach *you*, but to be admired as a writer. Ernie was just an old Indiana farm boy; like myself, he had been put to the plow at the age of nine, and like myself he had hated it. Now he was on the front lines, living and sweating with the troops, dodging enemy fire, risking his life to report in his homespun, folksy style the doings and dreams and daring of the enlisted men. He made heroes out of common men.

He always identified the soldiers he interviewed by their hometowns, even their street addresses, and I always watched closely to see which ones were from Arkansas. The very week after the Allies broke my arm, he wrote about some of the boys in Ordnance over in France (Ordnance is a branch of the Army, not a town in France), "The soldiers did a lot of kidding as they sat around taking rusted guns apart. Like soldiers everywhere they razzed each other constantly about their home states. A couple were from Arkansas, and of course they took a lot of hillbilly razzing about not wearing shoes till they got in the Army, and so on. One of them was Corporal Herschel Grimsley, of Springdale, Arkansas. He jokingly asked if I'd put his name in my dispatch. So I took a chance and joked back. 'Sure,' I said, 'except I didn't know anybody in Arkansas could read.'

"Gentle Reader, everybody laughed loudly at this scintillating wit, most of all Corporal Grimsley, who can stand anything."

That column was a revelation, in more ways than one. It let me know, for the first time in my life, that the rest of the world thought there was something wrong with the fact that we preferred to go barefooted in Stay More, not that we didn't know what shoes are, but because we didn't need 'em. And there were some of my subscribers who couldn't read *The Stay Morning Star* because they never needed to learn how.

But the main revelation of that column, startling me, was that it gave you a name. Gentle Reader. I had been calling you "Friend" just as a temporary handle until I found a better one. With Doc Swain and the others I had recently seen a movie at the Buffalo called *The Thief of Bagdad*, one of the ever-popular Arabian Nights films, and it had a fabulous genie in it, and I thought of calling you Genie, but there were a couple things wrong with that: a genie does one's bidding, and you won't ever do mine (even though I'll try to make you, farther along); and Ella Jean Dinsmore, my secret passion, sometimes was called "Jeaner" or sometimes just "Jeannie," which sounds just like Genie. So I had to give up that notion.

Gentle Reader, that would do just fine, and it would be many more years before I discovered to my dismay how promiscuous you are, reading not just me and Ernie Pyle but everybody else. Still, I'll always like to remember my first meeting of you, and my first discovery of your name.

So when everyone in school, including Miss Jerram herself, was given the opportunity to inscribe my plaster cast, I remembered you.

Most of them just wrote their names, or some stupid silly little thing like "Roses are red, Violets are blue . . . " or added clever variations, " . . . Sugar is sweet, but you stink ha ha!" Lack of originality was rampant: "When you get married and live like pigs, Don't treat your wife like Maggie does Jiggs" or "Yours till the Statue of Liberty sits down and the ocean wears rubber pants to keep its bottom dry." Some were threatening: "Your leg next time," wrote Sog Alan, "Dry up and blow away," wrote Larry Duckworth, and "Go climb a weed," wrote Jim John Whitter. Miss Jerram wrote "Here's hoping someday you'll discover that others aren't as dumb as you think they are." Ella Jean had little to say, but it was sweet: "Hope you go far with the Stay Morningstar."

There were twenty-five people in the schoolhouse and their writings nearly covered my plaster cast, but I was careful to reserve one corner, where I put a dotted line. The expression "dotted line" isn't quite accurate, because usually the line is dashed, not dotted. But it was for *you*, Gentle Reader:

— —

CHAPTER

2

WHEN THIS STORY REALLY GOT STARTED, I HADN'T YET MET YOU.
One Saturday afternoon the summer before, Mare Coe (who'd never
yet actually done anything about his declared intention to become
mayor) came into my newspaper office at Latha's store and, pointing at
my hectograph, inquired, "Can you print up posters and such on that
thing?" I explained to Mare that the gelatin board could print up to
about fifty copies before it began to become illegible. "Shoot, that's
more than enough, I reckon," he said, and he took from his pocket a
folded sheet of paper that he showed me. I read it with great interest,
because politics ought to be a newspaper editor's first priority, even
more than war news, but there'd never been any political news in the
history of Stay More. "What sort of figure would ye charge me for

printin it up?" he asked. We agreed on a penny a sheet. He counted his pocket change and decided he could afford to have twenty copies printed but wondered if that might not be too many, "just to tack up hither and yon." We discussed the various places that the poster ought to be tacked up: both ends of Latha's store porch, the three big trees at Dill's Gas and Service, near the door of the old Ingledew General Store, the front of the schoolhouse, on the one remaining show window of the abandoned bank building, both sides of the lone pine tree that dominated the intersection of the main road and the road up Banty Creek, various other trees in "downtown" Stay More (there were of course no poles yet for telephone or electricity anywhere in the town), and even on the giant sycamore tree that served as the pedestal for the Allies' clubhouse.

Mare and I calculated that twenty copies ought to be enough; he gave me a quarter and I gave him a nickel in change. I asked Mare if he'd be amenable to a few corrections in his grammar, spelling, and sentence structure. "Do it everhow you like," he consented. I didn't charge him anything for helping him tack up the posters:

COME ONE COME ALL!

Let's Us Start Us A Goverment!

Seeing as how just about all the menfolk has had to
leave town to serve our country against Hitler and
Mussolini and Tojo, and Stay More is just awasting
away on the vine, don't you think we ought to get

organized

and see if we can't do nothing about it! Let's have
a election, and put together a "slate" of town officials
like mayor and aldermen and town marshal and all!

But first, let's have a meeting to discuss what we need
to do to have this election and get it all going!

NEXT SATTERDAY NIGHT, AT THE SCHOOLHOUSE!
EVERBODY BE THERE! RIGHT AFTER SUPPER!

PER: GERALD A. COE
(Candidate for Mayor and I sure
would appresiate your support and
I pledge to do my utmost to serve
you and this here town!)

Well, we tacked those up everywhere, and we knocked on Estalee
Jerram's door, right across the road from the schoolhouse, to ask if we
could put one up on the schoolhouse door and also to get permission to
use the schoolhouse for the meeting. Miss Jerram was delighted to see
her former star pupil, and the way she greeted him like a long-lost star
pupil convinced me that, contrary to rumor, they hadn't actually been
seeing each other since he graduated. "You didn't spell Saturday correct," she pointed out to him. "Also I think you've spelled appreciate
wrong too."

"Dawny here printed that," he said, as if it was my fault we'd mis-
spelled a couple of words. Miss Jerram looked at me as if she were cal-
culating whether to hold me back one grade or two. "You'll come to the
meetin too, I hope?" he asked her.

"Well, goodness gracious, Gerald, don't ye know? That's our knittin
night!" Miss Jerram was the leader of the Axis girls who met every Saturday night at her house to have a knitting bee, fashioning the sweaters
and mittens and socks that were going to Our Boys Overseas.

Mare clapped his brow, and then I clapped mine, not in imitation of
him but because I'd thought of something else too: "It's also the night
Doc Swain is taking some of us to the movies!"

Somehow Fridays didn't seem as important as Saturdays, and Mare
didn't like the idea, but he borrowed a black Crayola from Miss Jerram
and we went around to all the posters we'd already tacked up, scratching out "Satterday" and writing in Friday.

That week's issue of *The Stay Morning Star*, which I delivered to all
those RFD and post office boxes, carried a front-page article about the
big political event under the headline STAY MORE TO FORM CITY GOV-
ERNMENT, and on an inside page I ran a sort of profile of Gerald A.
"Mare" Coe, 18, son of the town's blacksmith, Lawlor Coe, and triplet

brother to Burl, recently sent to Army boot camp in Texas, and Earl, who like Gerald was classified I-A and expected to be drafted any day now. I even included an editorial, "Everybody who is a citizen or who wants to be a good citizen ought to come to this meeting. Besides, it will take our minds off the war." And I couldn't resist including these words, "Here is a good chance for the rival crowds that are called Allies and Axis to bury the hatchet and smoke the peace pipe."

On Friday night after supper I met Mare at the schoolhouse and we waited to see who-all would come. We wondered if any of the Allies actually would show up—when Burl Coe was drafted into the Army his place as leader of that faction had been taken by Sog Alan, the meanest and surliest of all the Allies, who'd have been happy to shoot all of us Axis if he hadn't donated his gun to the scrap drive. The third of the triplets, Earl, although he was one of us Axis (and the hard-hitting catcher of Mare's pitches in our ball games), probably would not come, Mare explained. "I just caint persuade him that government is anything to get excited about," Mare said.

Lots of people felt that way, apparently. We had a poor turnout: of Stay More's grown-ups, the only one who came to the meeting was Miss Jerram. This set me to brooding about whether or not people actually did take the trouble to read *The Stay Morning Star.* Since all of those who did show up at the schoolhouse, except Mare himself, had been a pupil the previous term, the whole lot of us simply looked like another session of school, or, since we weren't all there, like a session of school when many are out with measles, colds, or the flu.

Eventually some of the Dinsmore kids showed up (including Ella Jean!) led by seventh-grader Willard Dinsmore, who was Mare's lieutenant, more or less, as leader of the Axis. "Aint there nothin to eat?" Willard politely inquired, disappointed. Did I say earlier that none of us in Stay More were starving? I'll take that back. Willard, though he got just as much to eat as his brothers and sisters, all twelve of them, in the shack they lived in away back up on Dinsmore Mountain, which is to say, enough victuals to sustain them without making any of them fat, was always hungry. Food was on his mind all the time. This struck me as phenomenal because I myself never gave food a thought. Willard wasn't a conspicuous sort of person, despite looking like a scarecrow, and that wasn't like him to speak up, even mildly and politely. Maybe he wasn't naturally the quiet type, but with six brothers and six sisters he probably never had a chance to get a word in edgewise. And in school, Miss Jerram wouldn't let him talk. There was a rumor that one time back in the fourth grade he'd stolen her lunch, and when she'd accused him of it, he'd given her some back talk, and she'd never forgiven him, although it was hard to imagine Willard giving anybody any back talk, he was so pleasant and gentle. He wore eyeglasses, a cheap pair of wire-rimmed mail-order specs, and he seemed to be hiding behind them. He was tall for his age, fifteen, and so scrawny it was pitiful, although he was a great first baseman on our ball team. I sometimes thought that Abe Lincoln must have looked like Willard when he was that age and doing his reading around the fireplace. Willard didn't have a fireplace, just an old stove to read by, if he read, and I suspected he did. I suspected Willard was the smartest feller in school, smarter even than me. Latha Bourne told me once that Willard probably had been named after an old traveling salesman who'd come to Stay More perennially since the days it had first been founded, but had died here before I was born. Eli Willard was his name, and he was from Connecticut, and while I know little about his personality I picture him as resembling another native of Connecticut (who wound up in Sleepy Hollow, New York), named Ichabod Crane: "He was tall, but exceedingly lank, with narrow shoulders, long arms and legs, hands that dangled a mile out of his sleeves, feet that might have served for shovels, and his whole frame most loosely hung together." Those words pretty well summed up the image of Willard Dinsmore as well as his namesake.

Altogether, we had a poorer turnout at that meeting than we'd have the following afternoon at our weekly ball game between the Axis and the Allies. There weren't enough from either side to constitute the nine needed for a ball team. The three Allied thugs who months later would thrash me sauntered together through the schoolhouse door as if they were three Western outlaws entering a saloon in search of mischief. Each of them was carrying a copy of Mare's poster that they'd ripped down, perhaps as a gesture of defiance, although it made it look as if they were each too stupid to remember what they were doing without the poster. Behind them came two of their girlfriends, and three other members of the Allies, but the Axis still outnumbered them by one, or two if you counted Miss Jerram, who was sort of an honorary Axis since she was leader of the Axis knitters.

From force of habit, each of us sat at the same school desk we'd ordinarily occupy during the school day, Allies on one side, Axis on the other, even though this was summertime and we hadn't sat in those seats for many weeks. This prompted Miss Jerram to stand up and say, "Well, boys and girls, we may as well get started. Since this here is *my* schoolhouse, don't ye reckon I ought to be in charge of this meetin?"

"Nome," said Willard. "Mare's the mare. It's his gubberment, and he orter be in charge."

"Willard Dinsmore, nobody gave you permission to speak," Miss Jerram said, pouting. "And you, Dawny, take off that slingshot." She pointed at my customary summertime necklace, a slingshot made from strips of an old inner tube and a fork of bow wood, without which I was never seen in the summer. Such a weapon was not allowed in school.

"This aint school," I pointed out, setting the tone for the proceedings. "This is a town meeting."

"All right," she relented. "Gerald, this meeting was your idee, so you mought as well take charge of it. But you'd just better lead the Pledge of Allegiance anyhow." She motioned for him to stand, but she did not sit down herself, not even after the Pledge of Allegiance.

Mare the mayor-to-be rose humbly, stooping his shoulders more than was necessary, and even blushing a little. He put his hand over his heart, so we all stood and put our hands over ours, and we faced the flag, furled on its pole and collecting dust in the corner. None of us tried to improve upon the version we'd first recited in the first grade: "Apple legions to deaf leg often knighted states of a merry can to the wee public for witches hands, one Asian in the vestibule with little tea and just rice for all."

Then Mare rubbed his hands together as if to rinse the sweat from them. He coughed. He looked at us apologetically, as if he'd made a big mistake dragging us out here on Friday night. Then he cleared his throat noisily and said to Willard, "I aint the mare yet, ye know." Then he glanced at Sog Alan and said, "First just let me say I'm mighty glad that you Allies was good enough to join us."

"We aint jined ye yet, Mare," Sog Alan said. "We'uns turned up, but we aint *jined* ye."

"I'm just glad you're here," Mare said. "No sense in us being always at each other's throats. The main purpose of this here meetin is to bring harmony to Stay More."

"*'Harmony!?'* " Larry Duckworth snickered, as if he'd never heard the word in his life, and he probably hadn't.

"It means we need to agree with each other more often," I pedantically defined the word for the poor fool.

"That'll be the day!" Jim John Whitter declared. "The Allies won't *never* agree with the Axis!"

"Boys, boys!" Miss Jerram said. "If you'uns aim to fight, I won't be a party to this. I'll march right out of here!"

We waited for her to march right out of there, but she didn't. Maybe it was just as well. At that moment we could have demolished the Allies in a fair fight, outnumbered as they were.

"We don't have to always agree," Mare declared, and glanced at me as if to refute what I'd said. "Matter of fact, to be a government we've got to have opposing parties, like the Democrats and the Republicans, and we'll keep each other on our toes by not agreeing. It's called 'checks and balances.'"

"Fair deal," said Sog, "so what if I was to run for mare myself?"

"Fine and dandy," said Mare. "That's your right and your privilege, in a democracy."

"Just what in heck is a mare anyhow?" Larry Duckworth wanted to know. "I never heared of ary such a bird till you started in to callin yourself one. What town do you know has got a mare? Has Jasper got one?"

As far as anyone knew, our county seat did not have a mayor. There was a county judge, which was an administrative position, not a judicial one, and the judge was in charge of everything.

"Most sizable towns has got mares," Mare said. "Aint that right, Miss Jerram?"

"That's what I've been told," she declared. "But I never saw a mare myself."

"So what does a mare git to do?" Sog wanted to know. "If I win the 'lection, can I boss folks around?"

"Sog, you boss 'em around anyway," Willard Dinsmore observed. "But don't worry none 'bout winnin the 'lection, because you aint got a dog's chance."

"What d'ye want to bet?" Sog challenged him.

"A mare," said Mare, who ought to know, "is supposed to be the principal officer of the town, in charge of good works, and fixin what's broke, and also he does ceremonies like presentin a 'key to the city' to important visitors."

All of us stared at Mare as we contemplated these strange images. Ella Jean, my sweet, was the first to speak. "When's the last time we had a important visitor?"

There was no answer, for not even Miss Jerram, who'd lived here for some years longer than anyone else, could remember any important visitors.

"Heck," Mare protested, "I don't *have* to give nobody no keys. It's just sort of honorary anyhow."

There followed a halfhearted discussion of just what a government might accomplish for Stay More. A few suggestions for civic improvement were proposed, but any idea the Axis offered was disputed by the Allies, and vice versa. One of the Allies submitted that the town could look a little better if we tore down the old gristmill, unused for many years but still towering above the town with its four-story bulk clad in rusty-red tin that had once been meant to imitate brick but never succeeded. But Willard said truthfully, "That'd leave a mighty big hole in the sky," and naturally we Axis were protective of the building because it was part of our defended territory, the village. According to history or legend, Jesse James had once robbed that mill, and the Axis argued that it ought to be left standing just as a monument to the great outlaw.

I raised my hand and intimated that in the interests of beautification, how about painting some of the buildings? Both general stores and all of the houses (except the hermit Dan's yellow house) were without paint, their natural wood a kind of dusty tan, and while I would grow up to realize that that color was absolutely appropriate for the rustic setting of the village, it seemed to me at that time, when my civic zeal was coming on, that we could use some white paint on some of them. We could apply the paint ourselves, if need be.

"Who's gonna buy the paint, Ernie?" one of the Allies wanted to know, and another one said, "I aint never used a brush in my life and I aint about to start in to learnin how."

Mare said, "I don't reckon we want to *change* the town none. But if only there was something we could do to keep the town from gittin smaller and smaller. The way it's shrinkin, there won't be nothin left of it by and by." He said these words mournfully, and, I have to admit, prophetically.

One of the Allied hussies, Betty June Alan, said to Mare, "Silly, the reason it's gittin smaller is Uncle Sam keeps on takin all the menfolks Overseas!"

She had a point, although Stay More's population had been declining long before the war broke out, and the Depression more than the war had probably cost us numbers of our people, lost to the California emigration.

"Yeah, Mare," Betty June's big brother Sog put in, "Just what d'ye aim to do to stop the war and bring all them daddies back home?" It was a rhetorical question, although I was tempted to throw the question back at Sog, if he was also going to be a candidate for mayor. When Mare could not answer the question, Sog said to him, "Aint it about time you went Over There yourself and did your part?"

"Any day now," Mare acknowledged, mindful of his draft status. "But while I'm waitin to be called up, there's a lot to be done to help this town."

"Like *what?*" the Allies demanded, but none of the Axis could answer them.

Mare was moved as close to tears of frustration as I'd ever seen him, and I ached to reply on his behalf, on all our behalves, but I realized that I myself didn't have much enthusiasm for politics. I sat there wondering if Ernie Pyle had ever been required to cover a town hall beat or do any kind of political reporting. He'd been a copyreader and a telegraph editor for the *Washington Daily News* before he'd started writing a regular column on aviation, the first ever. I wished that an airplane would fly over Stay More sometime, but I'd never seen one.

Willard Dinsmore tried to come to Mare's rescue, to mine, to ours. "We could help some of the unfortunates."

"Like *who?*" the Allies demanded.

"Let's us start with the Dingletoons," Willard proposed.

CHAPTER
3

WHEN THE LARGE FAMILY OF DINGLETOONS FIRST CAME TO STAY More and simply took over an abandoned farmstead in a remote and rocky corner of Butterchurn Holler during an autumn early in the war, their reputation preceded them: they were known to have a habit of simply helping themselves to unoccupied real estate without paying rent or making any gesture of acquiring legal tenancy or ownership. They weren't sharecroppers. E. H. Ingledew, our town's retired dentist and mortician, who nominally owned the Stay More land they began to squat on, called them "the Starlings" out of his unwillingness to call them Dingletoons, a supposed corruption of his own family name, and because the starling is a bird who'll move into and take over a wood-pecker's nest. After the woodpecker has gone to all that trouble to hack out the cavity and build a nest in it and call it home, it comes home one morning to find a bunch of starlings have usurped the place.

Supposedly Ace and Bliss Dingletoon had moved their seven children into the crude cabin of rounded logs—not one of the original old-time hewn-log cabins carefully crafted in the last century but one built hastily during the homesteader boom before the First World War and gradually rotting ever since—and had been subsisting there for quite some months before the owner, Ingledew, found out about it and rather halfheartedly accosted the father, Ace Dingletoon, and asked if he intended to pay any rent on the place. Ace tried to tell E. H. a story about how he'd run into an old lady one time who told him that she'd known Ace's grandfather, who had actually been one of the Ingledews, but the grandfather had been a kind of outcast who couldn't read nor write nor even pronounce the name correctly. "Mought we not even be cousins therefore?" Ace had said to E. H. Ingledew.

"Hell," E. H. had observed correctly, "everbody in this here county is cousins anyhow."

"If I was to learn my kids how to say our name correctly, so's it's Ingledew 'stead of Dingletoon, would ye be willin to let us keep on a-tendin this old run-down godforsaken place?"

"Stranger," E. H. had replied, "ever fool knows you folks is always on the lookout for a empty place to move into, and if this aint the beatenest gimmick ever I heared to git yoreselfs another'n!"

The Ingledews had at least collected some token rent from the previous occupants for the forty acres of barely workable land. But Ace and Bliss Dingletoon could pay no rent; they had seven children and one mule and not much else. They had never owned land or property, had never paid rent to use a dwelling, had never cropped on shares or in any manner recognized that the land they used belonged to somebody else. Just where they came from originally was obscure. Just where they were going eventually was equally obscure. Only one thing was known for sure: they wouldn't stay long in any place.

They were here today and gone tomorrow. They moved out as easily as they moved in. They were even known to catch wind that a family was planning to move out, whereupon they were ready to move into the house before the chimney was cool. Ace Dingletoon would check to see if the barbed wire fences were all in place and then turn his mule out to pasture, uncoop the chickens and give them free run of the yard, then check the corncrib and hayloft to see if anything had been left behind that could be fed to some stock. The oldest boy, Joe Don Dingletoon, would be sent to search the smokehouse and other outbuildings, if any; one time Joe Don had even found a good chunk of meat still hanging in the smokehouse. The girl Gypsy would be sent to see if there were any edible potatoes in the garden patch and to dig them up. Her little brothers Billy and Taylor, barely old enough to heft and tote a full pail, would be sent to fetch sufficient water from the well or spring or creek so that the mother, Bliss, could commence redding up the house.

If there wasn't enough left behind on the place to make a meal, the kids would go off into the woods and set rabbit traps, or down to the creek to noodle fish. The whole family was trained to know what to do as soon as they moved in. Even the dogs would take off for the tall timber and have a coon or possum or mess of squirrels treed in time for supper. Their first evening in a new home was always marked by a groaning table at suppertime.

Once they had taken possession of a place, it was pretty hard to remove them without the help of the sheriff. They would get their crops planted as soon as the season allowed, so that they could claim nobody had any right to evict them until the crops were harvested. Or, if the season wasn't right for that excuse, Bliss Dingletoon could claim to be imminently expecting, which she usually was, anyhow. One time they'd even painted all the kid's faces with pokeberry juice so it would appear they had the smallpox and Ace Dingletoon had said to the landlord, "How can you talk about rent at a time like this?"

But if worse came to worst, and the landlord was insistent, and Sheriff Cheatham arrived, the Dingletoons were trained to move out just as efficiently as they had moved in. Legend grew up around their habits of departure, and the loafers at the country stores amused themselves by building upon the legend. When the moving day appeared inevitable, even before Sheriff Cheatham had turned his Ford into the yard, Ace would simply blow a horn and the kids, the dogs, the mule, the cow, would all come a-running. One fellow claimed the Dingletoons kept all of their belongings tied together with a rope so that if the moment of their eviction came, they simply pulled it all together into the wagon. Another said that even the chickens were trained to lie down in a row with their feet sticking up so Gypsy could tie them.

The Dingletoons wouldn't allow their kids to go to school, in order to minimize public awareness of their existence and illegal tenancy. In their wanderings from place to place, the Dingletoon children had not only been denied any schooling but also had never been allowed to form any friendships with other children. They never left the premises except to go fishing, hunting, or, the way that Gypsy Dingletoon and Ella Jean Dinsmore discovered each other and became friends, bathing. Halfway between the place the Dingletoons were squatting on and the Dinsmore place was a spot on Banty Creek where Ella Jean liked to sneak away for a regular soak, weather permitting, and that's how she came across Gypsy one evening. I'll say more about this in a moment, but the point is that I hadn't yet met any of the Dingletoon kids that summer, although Ella Jean and her brother Willard knew them.

E. H. Ingledew periodically sent Ace a bill for the rent, not much, but more than Ace had ever seen in cash money in his life, and E. H. periodically wrote "Overdue" on it, and indicated by how many months it was overdue, and then how many years it was overdue. Finally the accumulated rent was up in the hundreds, and E. H. decided he'd better make an attempt to collect. Braving the ferocious snarls of the Dingletoon dogs, he hiked into their (or rather his) yard.

"I'm afeared I'm a-gorn to have to ast ye to git gone," E. H. told Ace.

"Aw shee-ut," Ace protested. "Iffen I was to git off this place, ye'd never be able to find nobody else to rent it to."

E. H. thought that over a minute before saying, "Wal, I'd as soon rent it for nothin to nobody as rent it for nothin to somebody."

"I hate to tell ye this, sir, but I think my old womarn's a-dyin."

E. H., being only a retired dentist and mortician, not a doctor, decided to take a look at her anyway, and although Bliss Dingletoon had jumped into bed for the occasion and was doing her best to look pale and peaked, she didn't look like a likely candidate for burial. "You folks'll all live to the crack of doom," E. H. declared, "but it won't be on my proppity. Sherf Frank Cheatham will be here bright and early in the mornin to make shore you'uns aint left a trace behind."

But when Sheriff Cheatham did take the trouble to drive all the way out from Jasper to help E. H. execute the eviction, he discovered that Ace Dingletoon had not performed the customary ritual of blowing his horn to round up the kids and the stock and pulling that legendary rope that would load all his possessions into the wagon. The stock, the kids, the possessions were still there. Bliss was still in her kitchen. But Ace had departed.

In an act of either desperation or courage, depending on whose opinion one heard, Ace had joined the service. As I reported it in a small news item in *The Stay Morning Star,* "Mr. Ace T. Dingletoon, 34, joined the army this week. This now makes nine Stay More men who are among Our Boys Overseas. Not many of them have left behind a family the size of his, though. We hope they are okay."

They were okay, for a while. E. H. Ingledew couldn't very easily evict a woman with seven kids whose husband was in the service. "Hail far, Each," his brother Bevis said to him, "that wouldn't be patriotic." And Bevis's wife Emelda even insisted on E. H. leaving a sack of flour and a turn of meal where the Dingletoons could find it (to offer such to them would be an insult; charity was totally unacceptable). Joe Don Dingletoon was old enough and strong enough to assume his father's chores, which had been rather lackadaisical to begin with. Since they had had no income in the first place, nor any money anywhere around the house, Ace's absence didn't have any effect whatever on their cash flow situation. Of course they missed him, and the fact that he was illiterate meant that he couldn't write letters home from the war, but for that matter Bliss couldn't have read them if he had. Gypsy, now fourteen, had taught herself to read with the help of an old blueback speller that somebody had left behind in one of the houses they'd temporarily occupied, her main motive being to learn how to decipher the walls: the walls of that house, like the walls of all the houses they had lived in, had been papered with newspapers, magazines, and pages from Sears Roebuck catalogs. Such wallpaper served also as a primitive but helpful insulation in cold winter. Gypsy wanted to be able to read the comics, and she graduated from those to the feature stories, and from those to the news, and before long she was reading the lavish descriptions in the Sears catalog pages of all the clothes that she would never be able to have. Joe Don, two years older than Gypsy, could not help observing his sister standing for what seemed like hours facing the walls. She was peculiar sometimes, he thought. One day he was finally moved to ask her, "What ye up to, Sis?" and she answered, "Readin," and offered to teach him how.

So she introduced him to that forbidden knowledge he'd never had before. She did not tell him that she'd recently started doing something that had also been forbidden: consorting with a neighbor, a nice girl named Ella Jean Dinsmore. It was June, and the creek was warm enough to use in place of the old tin tub for a bath. Girls somehow need to bathe more often than boys, and a galvanized tub doesn't allow a real soak. With a creek of running water you can do all kinds of things.

Shortly before Gypsy Dingletoon discovered Ella Jean bathing in the creek, I had myself discovered Ella Jean bathing. I'd had a crush on her since the second grade, but she never spoke to me, probably because I'd never been able to get up my nerve and speak to her. One June evening after supper I was hiking along the banks of Banty Creek hunting for things to shoot with my slingshot, just getting target practice by popping dragonflies and wasps. I was real good with that slingshot. Well, there is a spot on that creek, a very secluded spot just down the hill a ways from the Dinsmore shack, where there is this sort of depression in the rock of the creekbed, some call it a "hog scald" because that's what it was used for: filled with red-hot rocks and steaming, it'd scour the bristles off a slaughtered hog. But in summertime when there wasn't any butchering, it made a fine bathtub. At least Ella Jean thought so.

Among all the things that were hard to come by during the war—sugar, elastic, gas, tin, chewing gum, coffee, and so on—one of the most precious was soap. Of course the womenfolk still rendered hog lard and ashes into a kind of crude lye soap that was okay, but not really suitable for sudsing and lathering and bathing. Latha Bourne could no longer stock the good store-boughten soaps—Ivory, Lifebuoy, Lava, not to mention Cashmere Bouquet—which were scarce as hen's teeth. And even if she had, the Dinsmores couldn't have afforded to buy a bar. But Ella Jean, doing some housework that summer for Drussie Ingledew, who still lived in the old house that had once been Stay More's hotel, found in the drawer of a washstand an overlooked cake of Palmolive.

She hid it in her sunbonnet and took it home with her, never telling anybody about it. Twice a month she would permit herself the luxury of going down to that hog-scald depression in the rocks of that secret cove of Banty Creek, stripping naked, getting wet, running that cake of Palmolive over her body, over her swelling young breasts, ever so lightly, just enough of it to swab her skin and to fill the twilight air with the unique scent of that brand of soap, which my nostrils could detect from the distance of some thirty yards away in my hiding-place. What the madeleine was to Proust, that Palmolive was to me. The scent of Palmolive would always say to me: *summertime;* it would say: *gloaming;* it would say: *creekwater;* it would say: *clean;* it would say: *fresh;* it would say: *Ella Jean.*

Gentle Reader, you are saying to yourself, *That Donny sure is a little snoop, a regular voyeur!* But I wasn't really trying to spy on people; it just happened in the course of events. For instance, I just stumbled upon Ella Jean, and I was so surprised to come across her that I wouldn't have known what to say. I certainly didn't want to say, "Hi there, Ella Jean, how's the water?" so I had to conceal myself. Before you judge me too quickly, consider how you are concealing yourself: I shall never see you. You have the privilege of watching all of this, including my most private thoughts and deeds, without ever being seen or heard.

I'm not sure Ella Jean would have minded if she'd known I was spying on her. I'd often wondered: those big families living crowded together in those cabins and shacks, did they ever have any privacy? Ella Jean and Gypsy were ripe candidates for friendship because their families were equally impoverished. The Dinsmores may have been even worse off because there were more of them and there hadn't been any father around since Jake Dinsmore had gone out to California during the Depression to seek his fortune, promising to send for his family after he got rich, but he had never again been heard from, and Selena had been trying to raise all those thirteen kids by herself in a shack of only two rooms. The house I lived in was neither a cabin nor a shack, and I was the only child in it. I could not imagine what it would be like to go to the outhouse with a brother or sister or one of both or six of both, nor could I imagine having to share not only the bathtub but the bathwater with a bunch of siblings. Ella Jean may have felt some need for privacy, now that her breasts were a-budding, and that's why she preferred the seclusion of that spot on Banty Creek for her baths. I had never seen bare breasts before. Not a girl's. I knew what they were. Of course I knew what they were for. Not mine. Mine were just a decoration on my chest, like medals, and nobody cared whether they were showing or not. But a girl's were supposed to be in hiding, as you are hiding. If you were revealed, it would thrill me, as I was thrilled by the revealing of Ella Jean.

Every evening after supper thereafter, I stole away to the same spot, hoping for another glimpse of her, or even for the faintest whiff of that breathtaking Palmolive, but I discovered she didn't want to use the precious soap more than twice a month. When she would not show up, I would roll up my trousers and wade out into the hog scald to the same spot she had occupied and stir the water with my hands, as if trying to stir up a hint of that scent of Palmolive. Once, doing this, I looked up to see her coming down through the forest path that led to her house. She didn't see me, and I got out of there and concealed myself in a dense clump of brush where I could—and did—enjoy nearly a whole half hour of watching her take a bath. It was toward the end of this half hour that Gypsy Dingletoon appeared. Ella Jean did not betray any modesty in the presence of the stranger-girl. They exchanged howdies. From my concealment, I could barely hear their voices as they timidly and warily made known to each other their habitations, their full names, their ages, Gypsy two years older than Ella Jean but that difference not enough to keep them from intuiting, as only girls can grasp through mysterious feeling, that they had enough reasons to like each other to the point of trying to become friends.

At length, Ella Jean held up the white bar of Palmolive and said, "Lookee at what I've got." By this point, Gypsy had hiked the hem of her dress and waded out into the water, so that Ella Jean could hold the bar of Palmolive right up to Gypsy's nose.

Gypsy took a good sniff and said, "My! You must have a lot of money!"

"Aw, I'm pore as Job's turkey," Ella Jean said. "I found this some'ers, and sort of stole it. Do you want to try it out? I don't keer if you was to use it a bit."

Gypsy needed no urging. She simply pulled her dress up over her head, wadded it into a heap, and gave it a toss that landed it on the bank of the creek. It was her only garment. She could have made use of a brassiere, but she'd probably never seen one. If the sight of Ella Jean's little welts excited me, I don't know you well enough yet to tell you what the exposure of Gypsy's bubbies did to me. Also, she had hips, which Ella Jean didn't. She carefully accepted the precious bar of soap from Ella Jean, and with her other hand cupped and splashed water over her front and shoulders and face, and then ever so lightly applied the bar of Palmolive, whose fragrance, rising from both their bodies in aromatic concert with the smell of the creekwater and its traces of fish and of the evening air and its traces of all summer's growing things, transported me out of the dull life in which I was usually imprisoned. I sighed so loudly it was a wonder they didn't hear me.

From that night onward I had the awfullest time trying to decide whether or not I liked Gypsy even more than Ella Jean. In her way, Gypsy was prettier, more grown-up looking, like a movie star is pretty. Ella Jean remained just a beautiful child. Two more years and Ella Jean would be just as sightly but meanwhile Gypsy had all the glamour.

Thus, at that meeting Mare called to try to organize a government, when Ella Jean's brother Willard, who may also have been developing some powerful attraction for Gypsy, suggested that we ought to do something to help the poor Dingletoons, I was the first to take a flying leap onto the bandwagon.

CHAPTER
4

WHEN WILLARD DINSMORE, WHO, AS I WOULD LEARN, WAS EVEN more powerfully smitten with Gypsy than I was (his hormones were four years in advance of mine), made his suggestion about some sort of aid for the unfortunate and now fatherless Dingletoons, the idea inspired little enthusiasm among the rest of the Axis and none at all among the Allies. Some of us, like myself, who were "in comfortable circumstances," that is, weren't living hand-to-mouth, admired Willard for his altruism: if any family in Stay More really deserved public assistance, it was the Dinsmores, who, after all, were native Stay More folk, not outlanders like the Dingletoons. But most of us on the "good" side, the Axis, knew very well that if we did anything for the Dingletoons it would have to be done in strictest secrecy and anonymity, not because the Dingletoons were too proud to accept any help but because it was bad manners even to think of offering help in a land where self-sufficiency was the way of life. Those on the "bad" side, the Allies, weren't capable of charitable works anyhow; the notion of doing something *for* someone else was totally alien to their belligerent, authoritarian selfishness, and they made it clear that their purpose in life was not to help the Dingletoons or anybody else but to gratify their own desires for victory, mastery, revenge, and evildoing.

"But we ort to leastways do somethin to help 'em help themselves," Willard argued.

"Old Blue, their mule, died the other night," Ella Jean informed us of tidings recently learned from her new friend Gypsy.

"You aim to buy 'em a new mule?" Sog Alan asked, not of her or of Willard but of all of us Axis.

"Has anybody got a extry mule?" Miss Jerram put in.

None of us had extra mules, and none of us had any way of buying a new mule for the Dingletoons. "We could steal 'em a mule," Sog suggested. It was the first constructive idea he had come up with, but his motive obviously was to recruit the Dingletoon kids to the Allied cadre.

"Who from?" we asked.

"Ole Dan," Sog said, calling the strange reclusive man who lived in the yellow house by the only name we knew to call him.

"Ole Dan needs his mule, I reckon," I observed.

"Not if he was locked away," Sog said. "He ort to be put in jail."

"For what?" I said.

"All kinds of things," Sog said, and began to count them off on his fingers, naming the various wrongdoings that gossip had laid upon Dan in his mysterious past: escaping from prison; embezzling from some employer he'd worked for, maybe even a bank; killing a patient while a doctor; ruining a client while a lawyer; hiding out from the FBI; or abducting as a child the girl presumed to be his daughter. "But the main thing," Sog said, grasping his big thumb, "is that he's probably a Nazi spy." He glanced around at those of us Axis who were doomed to be Nazis and added, "I mean the real Nazis. The ones in Germany. Hitler's men."

"Now where would you git a notion like that, Sog Alan?" Miss Jerram wanted to know, but there was a slight tremor in her voice, as if it were a distinct possibility that had never occurred to her before.

"Don't you think he's mighty suspicious?" Sog said. "He don't never visit with nobody or nothin."

"But why on earth," Willard asked, "would Hitler want to plant a spy out here in Stay More, Arkansas?" It was just a rhetorical question, but it set us all to thinking. After all, to me and to most of us, Stay More was the center of the world. If I were Hitler I'd want to keep an eye on it.

"If we stole his mule and gave it to the Dingletoons," Mare pointed out, "he'd just think they stole it from him, and he'd get it back."

"Forget the mule," Sog said. "I think if you want to be mare and get anything done for this town before you're called up, the best thing to do would be let's all spy on that spy! Let's keep a good eye on him and if we catch him up to somethin, we could get him put away."

"He aint no kind of a spy!" I said. "He's just a ole feller tryin to mind his own business."

Sog scowled at me as if the idea was already dawning on him to break my arm at some point in the future. Then he looked around at the rest of the small gathering. "Anybody with me?" he asked. "Who wants to do a good turn for this town and help get rid of ole Dan?" All of the Allies automatically held up their hands because Sog was their boss, but even the younger Axis, the littl'uns like Jim George Dinsmore and Troy Chism, first-graders, thrilled by the excitement of the idea, held up their hands.

Miss Jerram, bless her heart, rose to her feet and took a stand. "Boys and girls," she said, "I'd advise all of you'uns to just leave that pore ole man alone. It sure seems to me that if you really and truly want to do something as a play-like government, you could do something more for the War Effort."

"Catchin a Nazi spy would be War Effort," the Allies contended.

"What more could we do?" the Axis asked. We had already collected all the scrap in town as well as stuff that wasn't even scrap yet, we had knitted up the wool of all the sheep in Stay More, and we had collected enough grease to drown the Japs and the Germans in it.

"The milkweed is a-going to pod," Miss Jerram said, smiling. We wondered if her brain was a-going to pod. But then she said, "Haven't

37

you never tore open a milkweed pod? It's got all this white fluffy stuff inside, like cotton, that the War Plants are using to fill life preservers with." The blank looks she was getting from her audience made Miss Jerram explain, "A life preserver is something that a soldier, sailor, or a marine straps around his chest when he's out on the ocean so that it will hold him up if the ship sinks." Enough of us showed signs of understanding that she was inspired to continue, "They call 'em Mae West life preservers because wearing 'em . . . well, I reckon, puttin one on makes ye look kind of busty like her. Anyhow, they're collecting milkweed pods for the War Effort, if you boys and girls would care to go out and get some."

In the weeks ahead, as all of the milkweed of Stay More (*Asclepias syriaca*, or silkweed, cousin to but not to be confused with *Asclepias tuberosa*, butterfly weed) reached maturity, we Axis got organized to hunt for it, each of us equipped with a tow sack (burlap bag) into which we stuffed our gatherings of pods, plucked all along the creek banks and the roadsides. This activity was some small consolation to Mare Coe, who could not hide his disappointment that the effort to organize a Stay More government had not only failed but been dismissed by Miss Jerram as "play-like." In the next issue of *The Stay Morning Star* I dutifully reported, under the headline GOVERNMENT IDEA NOT SUCCESSFUL, that Mare's efforts to organize a town government had met with "mostly indifference," and that the only constructive thing to come out of the meeting was that we, at least the Axis faction, were now engaged in collecting milkweed pods for the War Effort and "if any of you readers has lots of milkweed on your property that we don't know about, please let us know."

Mare wasn't very friendly to me after that, and I wondered if he held it against me for simply telling the truth, that the government meeting had not succeeded. But I also told the truth about the Allies, that instead of helping us collect milkweed pods they were "starting a secret watch to gather information about a suspected undercover agent."

Somebody threw a rock through the window of the side room at Latha's store where I had my newspaper office. Tied to the rock was a message: "Name eny names and your dead." I wondered if Ernie Pyle ever had rocks thrown at him.

Willard Dinsmore suggested that we Axis ought to invite the Dingletoons to join us. The wasteland of the Dingletoon property—or rather
the squatting they farmed—was overrun with milkweed, and they'd be
glad to help us collect the pods. The Axis took a vote and decided to
permit the Dingletoons, all four of the older kids, to become Axis and
to allow them to decide for themselves whether they wanted to be Nazis
or Japs. Ella Jean Dinsmore reported that her friend Gypsy had said
there was a strong possibility, since Ace Dingletoon was in the service
and couldn't stop them from doing it, that the Dingletoon kids might
enroll in school when it started. Not that they wanted to, having never
been to school before. Willard thought that the best thing we could do
as a public service for the Dingletoons, if we couldn't find another mule
for them, was to get them to go to school.

Ella Jean and Gypsy had, since that meeting at the creek when Ella
Jean had shared the Palmolive, become the very best of friends, practically inseparable. They were seen together in the village, walking with
their arms around each other. They spent the night at each other's
house, sharing their play-pretties, such as they were, and engaging in
all manner of girl-talk, such as it was. Of course I did not eavesdrop on
them, as I had snooped upon their bathing at the creek, but I could
imagine, and my imagination, as you have already gathered, Gentle
Reader, was beyond imagining. I could very easily hear the girl-talk of
Ella Jean and Gypsy as they discussed their worries and dreams and
dislikes, and their favorite subject, boys. I knew, from what Latha told
me, that girls did superstitious things designed to identify their future
husbands. They would put live snails in a Mason jar overnight, believ-
ing the snail would leave in a trail of its slime the initials of the man
they'd marry. Or they would eat an over-salted hard-boiled egg before
bedtime and have a dream of their future husband bringing them a
gourd of water to wash it down with. Or they'd have a "dumb supper,"
with a lot of ritual and mumbo-jumbo and spooky goings-on, during
which the phantom husband appeared to take his place at the table beside the girl he'd wed.

But I had to imagine something more interesting that Gypsy and Ella
Jean did as their superstitious divination for determining who their future husbands would be. I had to hope it would be something that

would tell Ella Jean she would marry me some day, and I had to imagine it was an old-time superstition Ella Jean had learned from her grandmother: a girl who wishes to glimpse a sign of her future husband has to wait for a night when it's the dark of the moon, and then urinate on her nightdress and hang it before the fireplace and go to bed all naked. The next morning, when the gown has dried, it will carry the image of the groom-to-be! Better yet, if they do it just right, the essence—not exactly a ghost and not exactly the real substance—of the future husband will visit the girl while she's naked in bed and give her a foretaste of what their sleepings-together are going to be like, after which he always leaves something of his behind, such as a handkerchief or a gallus, as proof that he was actually there! Latha told me all about this.

Ella Jean was sleeping over at Gypsy's house the next dark of the moon when they tried out this notion, not because Gypsy's house had the requisite fireplace—the weather was much too warm for a fire anyhow—but because Gypsy's house, unlike the two-room Dinsmore hovel, possessed an extra room where the girls could set up two pallets on the floor on which to sleep and on which to be visited by the phantoms or essences of their future husbands, if it came to that. According to the tradition, the girl is supposed to sleep alone in her own room, but that was simply a luxury that neither Gypsy nor Ella Jean, in their crowded households, could enjoy.

The two girls waited until everybody else had gone to sleep, and then they carried a couple of kitchen chairs into their room. They took off their nightgowns and spread them out on the floor, and squatted over them. Gypsy had no trouble peeing all over her nightdress, but Ella Jean discovered she had a bashful bladder and couldn't do it, at least not while Gypsy was there beside her. So Gypsy had to close her eyes and turn her back, and even then Ella Jean didn't manage much of a piddle, and lost her balance while squatting, and did a clumsy job of it. The girls draped their wet gowns over the backs of the chairs, and went to bed and, before falling asleep, talked awhile about who they'd really like to see show up during the night or in a two-dimensional image on their nightdresses in the morning. They agreed that the first thing they'd do in the morning, even before looking to see whose imprint was on their nightdresses, was to discuss who, if anybody, had appeared to them in their sleep, so they could match that person's image with whatever image appeared on their nightgowns. Then they fell asleep. And dreamt. And were possibly visited by incubi or phantasma who cohabited with them.

"Well?" Gypsy said to Ella Jean, shaking her awake the next morning. "Did ye see ary a soul?"

Ella Jean was groggy from sleep and from whatever activities had drained her in her dreams, but she managed to blush and to say, "I aint so sure. What about you?"

"I hate to tell ye," Gypsy said. "It was *three* of 'em, but I don't rightly know which one of the three actually done it to me."

"*Three* of 'em?!" Ella Jean said. "Couldn't ye tell 'em apart?"

"*Naw*," Gypsy whined. "What I'm tryin to tell ye, they was all alike. Don't ye know anybody hereabouts who's three all one and the same?"

"Why, Gypsy!" Ella Jean exclaimed. "You don't mean them Coe boys, do ye?"

Gypsy nodded, abashed, as if she'd done something very wrong. The two girls got up from their pallets and went to inspect their nightdresses, which had not completely dried, but were dry enough to bear the faint stains of some kind of design. I wanted to imagine that Ella Jean's was a reasonably clear image of my own face, but it was an indistinct figure that might have been the head and neck of a gander or drake but on closer inspection revealed itself to be simply a large question mark.

But Gypsy's was clearly a face, with freckles, and pudgy. "Sure looks like Burl Coe to me," Ella Jean observed.

"How kin ye tell him apart from th'other two?" Gypsy wanted to know.

"Well, I don't know, I guess. Maybe it's Earl."

"Or Jerl," Gypsy suggested. She pondered, and then offered, "Maybe all three of 'em are gonna marry me, like your sisters done to Billy Bob."

Gypsy was referring to two of Ella Jean's many sisters, Jelena and Doris, who were twins (their names were Jelena Cloris and Helena Doris, but this confused their mother when she was yelling at them), and who had both fallen in love with the youngest of the eligible Ingledew brothers, William Robert, who was living with both of them in a modest shack he'd built on the side of Ingledew Mountain, unbothered by those who frowned upon the sinfulness of this bigamy. The twins had become identically pregnant, and I had recently reported in the *Star* that people were making bets on which of the two sisters would have her baby first.

Gypsy had no intention of marrying all three of the Coes. Any one of them would be one too many, as far as she was concerned. She was so upset by the outcome of her nightdress-peeing experiment that she neglected to pursue the matter of just who Ella Jean might have dreamed about or whose image lurked behind that question mark on her gown. Gypsy did not even report to her best friend a crucial fact: whichever one of the triplets had slept with her in her dream had, in the process of retrieving his britches afterward, let fall his pocketknife, which she had discovered in the bedclothes before she woke up Ella Jean.

Soon after that, unable to banish the memory of how exciting the dream had been (the Coe boy, whichever one he was, had been exactly the kind of lover who had anonymously made love to her many times before in dreams), Gypsy got up her nerve and went to the Coes' house and boldly asked the mother, Dulcie Coe, "Whar's yore boys?" Dulcie informed her that Burl was off in Texas somewhere being taught by the Army how to march and salute and all, that Earl was down to the shop a-helping his daddy, and Jerl—well, Jerl was real scarce these days, hardly even showing up for dinner or supper. Dulcie had no idea where he was. Dulcie winked and giggled and speculated that he might've found himself a girlfriend somewhere, although that wasn't likely. More than likely he'd taken to brooding on account of not being able to start a government for Stay More so's he could be mayor of it.

So Gypsy went down to the Coe blacksmith shop, where Lawlor Coe still managed to find something to keep him busy. Because the War Effort had removed not only all the scrap iron but also all of the in-use iron, there were horses wandering around without horseshoes. Sometimes Lawlor just went to his shop to pound his anvil for the music it made. And Earl, soon to go into the service himself, kept him company there, which is where Gypsy found him and showed him the pocketknife and stared him straight in the eye as if she could tell whether he was lying or not if he claimed never to have touched her before, and she demanded, "Earl Coe, is this here yore knife?"

He turned it over in his hand, opened a blade or two, peered close at the Barlow label on it. "Nope," he said. "This here used to belong to ole Mare. Where'd ye git it?"

It was perhaps the first time she'd ever heard that nickname by which nearly all Stay Morons except Dulcie Coe now called him. "Mare?" she said.

"Yeah, that's what we've took to a-callin him, on account of he thinks he's the mayor of this town." Earl could not suppress a guffaw.

"Him who?" she said.

"Jerl. But let me tell ye, this here Barlow of his'n was donated quite some time back to the War Effort. For the scrap drive, ye know." Every man and boy of Stay More had reluctantly but dutifully contributed his personal pocketknife to that zealous scrap drive, which of course made impossible the traditional pastimes of whittling and mumble-de-peg, not to mention frog-sticking, apple-peeling, and toenail-cleaning. "Where'd ye git it?" Earl said again, more sternly, as if she'd stolen it from the War Effort.

"I found it in my bed," she declared. "I don't reckon you could tell me whar Jerl is off to?"

"For all I know, he's done already gone to Californy." As I had reported in that week's issue of the *Star*, Mare had finally received his notice; he was to report to the marine office in Fort Smith, and would be sent to Camp Pendleton in California for his training. But he had not left yet.

Gypsy wandered around the village, asking anybody she met if they had seen Jerl, or Mare. She didn't like the nickname because it suggested a female horse, and while her phantom lover may have been pudgy, freckled, and homely, there was nothing unmanly about him. He was a real man. The more she thought about him, defending him from his nickname in her mind, the more she liked him. Besides, what was wrong with wanting to be a mayor? She wasn't quite sure just what a mayor was. None of the many, many towns or townships she had lived in during the Dingletoons' peregrinations from one squatting to another had anything like a mayor, nor even a head man. Who, after all, was the head man of Stay More? Doc Swain? Doc was the justice of the peace, a seldom needed position, and he was everybody's friend and healer, but he wasn't the boss. Did Jerl Coe really want to become the boss of the town?

If so, she decided, it might be useful to get to know him better. But hadn't she read something in that little paper that Dawny put out to the effect that Jerl had been drafted and would be leaving soon? And hadn't Earl said something about California? She'd better find Jerl pretty quick.

She did not wash that nightdress she'd peed on, but carried it to bed each night without putting it on, preferring to sleep with the image of Mare beneath her or above her or beside her, as her position in bed may have dictated. I could easily see these positions in my mind's eye.

CHAPTER
5

WHEN FOURTEEN-YEAR-OLD GYPSY DINGLETOON AND EIGHTEEN-year-old Mare Coe actually and spontaneously became lovers, I did not need to use my mind's eye, because I was there. Nor were they the first couple I'd ever watched. They were, however—and this is what excites me most about it—practically strangers. They may have seen each other in the village, but as far as I know they'd never spoken. Apart from watching some of the baseball games in which Mare had pitched the Axis to victory over the Allies, she had scarcely noticed Mare before. Or, rather, since all three brothers were boring and practically invisible, she hadn't seen them. Actually—as she had confided to her best friend Ella Jean when they were making girl-talk about boys—if she had her choice she would have chosen as a romantic interest Larry Duckworth,

not exactly a handsome prince but certainly much better looking than
Mare. Larry was the youngest son of Oren Duckworth, owner of the
canning factory, which had been Stay More's only industry before the
war, shut down now on account of the tin shortage. But Ella Jean had
been constrained to inform Gypsy that Larry, despite being such a
dandy-looking feller, was one of the leaders of the Allies, the despised
mob of rowdies who thought that Stay More belonged to them.

Although Gypsy and Mare were virtually strangers, I knew from
careful observation that throughout the animal and vegetable king-
doms, male and female conjoin on the spur of the moment without
prior intimacy or knowledge of each other. Any diligent student of nature, of the animals as well as the plants inferior to us, knows that mat-
ing happens everywhere from some built-in urge, without preamble or
to-do, and certainly without the fuss and bother, the gifts and cajolery,
that seem required to promote man's fumbling efforts to find release of
his natural inclination and hunger. While Mare and Gypsy were only
the second couple I'd ever witnessed coupling, I had seen it happen
more times than I could count between bull and cow, horse and mare,
dog and bitch, rooster and hen, not to mention stamen and pistil everywhere.

You will prepare yourself to believe that I wasn't deliberately out to
watch any of that, that it all came to me as a passive, accidental spectator,
just as I was not deliberately peeping on Mare and Gypsy, certainly not
the way that the Allies had begun to spy on ole Dan and his daughter.

It just happened. The Dingletoons joined the Axis and began to help
with the milkweed pod campaign. One evening after supper Gypsy took
her burlap tow sacks and went out along the upper reaches of Banty
Creek to gather milkweed pods. Ella Jean had to help her mother, so
Gypsy was alone, except for me. Believe me, I wasn't following her, and
she didn't know I was there. I was just out gathering milkweed pods
myself, which was a patriotic thing to do, and besides I kept thinking of
Mae West, since Miss Jerram had mentioned her. I wasn't trying to
keep myself hidden from Gypsy or anything, she simply didn't see me.
Believe me. She'd already filled a couple of the sacks, her nimble fingers
real good at plucking the pods, and I'd scarcely filled one of my sacks.
Before long, she just happened upon Mare Coe, who was sitting on a

tree stump right alongside a deep hole of water, one of Banty Creek's best fishing spots. He wasn't fishing, though, nor had he been collecting milkweed pods. He was just sitting there, lost in thought. From a distance I couldn't hear what she said to him, so I had to try to creep up closer.

When I found a good spot where I could hide and listen, I could see that she was holding out that pocketknife to him, and I wondered if she had been carrying it around with her all the time just in case she came across him. Girls don't have pockets. Like all the girls of the time, she was wearing simply a dress, a plain, faded gingham dress, with a hem just above her knees.

She was saying, "I found it in my bed when Ella Jean and me was havin a little magic test the other night . . . " Although these were the first words she'd ever spoken to him, she had seen him so often in her dreams and on that nightgown that he must have seemed to be an old friend of hers, or, better yet, a long-standing lover.

"Why, this here's Ole Stickum!" he exclaimed, turning the knife over in his hands. All of us had given affectionate names to our pocketknives, which made it even harder to sacrifice them to the War Effort. I sorely missed Ole Dirk. "Where'd ye say ye found it?"

"In my bed," she said. "You must've dropped it that time you came and slept with me."

He stared at her as if she were demented. I knew his mind well enough to know that he was wondering, since he didn't know any of the Dingletoons, if the whole family might be retarded. "Well, gosh," he said. "That wasn't me who done that." Then he added, "I mean, I couldn't've dropped a knife I never had no more, but besides that, I couldn't've dropped it even if I did have it in a bed I wasn't never in, to start with! So it must've been somebody else, but I don't know how he got ahold of my knife."

"Are you certain, Gerald Coe?" she said, staring him in the eye. And although his eyes were kind and gentle, they were not totally innocent. The truth of the matter was that Mare had actually had a dream or two, or maybe half a dozen, involving an activity with pretty Gypsy Dingletoon that he had never experienced in waking life.

"Not that I rightly *know* of," he hedged. The times he'd lain with her in his sleep had never been on an actual pallet in the actual spare room at the actual Dingletoon house.

She put her hands on her hips and drew back her shoulders. "There's only one way to find out," she declared boldly. "I reckon you better jist love me, Gerald Coe, and I can see if you do it jist like ye done it in my dreams." And she reached out and put her hands on his shoulders.

"Right *here?*" he needed to clarify a point. There was no misunderstanding just what she meant: "love" in these here parts, alas, invariably was a transitive verb referring to intercourse, not a noun or verb of grand passion.

"Right here and now," she said.

The very day after Gypsy and Mare had consecrated the sandy banks of Banty Creek, she went to Ella Jean to report that indeed he had done it the exact same way that her dream lover had done it. Ella Jean listened eagerly to her best friend's account of the whole episode. She had to know all the details. When they did it, did they do it standing up with him behind her in order to keep from having a baby? No? Well, were they lying on the actual sand at the water's edge? Or was it gravel? Did it hurt any? What did they talk about, if anything, during the act? Did he say sweet things to her? How long did the whole thing take? Did she have shivers and jerks and goose bumps? Afterwards, what did she do to keep from getting pregnant? Jump up and down repeatedly? Drink some ergot? Or take a douche with sody pop?

For three days running, Ella Jean kept thinking up new questions to ask Gypsy. When Gypsy had answered all the questions about the act itself, she began to narrate the hours afterwards, just *hours*, long after she'd finished jumping up and down to prevent pregnancy, when they had talked and talked way into the night, so that they had to find their way home by the light of the moon. By then they had told each other everything about themselves. He had talked at length about his wish to one day become mayor of the town, and his great sadness that the meeting to start a town government had not accomplished anything. She had talked about her wish that she might never again have to keep moving from place to place year after year but could settle down for good in a nice little town like Stay More. When they finally parted, it was almost

48

a spontaneous agreement of theirs—at least neither of them could remember who proposed the idea first—that they ought to join forces,
unite against time and the world and fate, and enjoy forevermore that
closeness and pleasure they'd just had on that creek bank.

"But I have to tell ye, Gypsy hon," Mare said to her, "I'm due to light
out for Californy next Monday to start boot trainin for the marines."
He said that it would make him a little money, which he never had before, and when the war was over and they had licked the enemy and he
could come home, he'd have a nest egg to get him started as the town's
mayor . . . and as her husband, if she'd have him. Oh, she'd have him,
all right, she said.

"No tellin, though," he observed, "how long it might take me to git
back home."

Gypsy's nocturnal dreams were not all erotic; like all the children of
Stay More whose fathers had gone Overseas, she had recurrent nightmares involving monstrous mayhem and the weapons in action, things
she had never actually seen: howitzers, cannons, missile launchers, airplanes dropping bombs and cannonballs and elephants, catapults and
crossbows and constant explosions mutilating the men who were falling
down everywhere with their heads missing or huge holes in their chests.
Now she had a synoptic flash of all that destruction, and she could not
help but ask, in alarm, "But Gerald my darlin, what if ye don't come
back?"

"That," he declared, "is percisely how come I caint ast ye to marry
me afore I go, like all them other fellers is doing." Mare referred to the
fact that everywhere across this great land of ours the brave boys of our
armed forces were wedding their sweethearts *before* they went into combat, just to be sure the girls would be waiting if they came home from
the war. Hearts were breaking everywhere, and Mare Coe had the
gumption to realize that his failure to come home would break enough
of her heart without breaking the whole thing if he left her a widow.

As Gypsy narrated it to her, Ella Jean understood this part easily. A
woman without a man is not a woman. She had been fatherless from
her earliest memory, at the age of three, when Jake Dinsmore had just
briefly paused at her bed to kiss her good-bye before running away to
California, his last words to her "Gimme a li'l kiss, sugar." She was just

barely old enough to sense, if not to understand, that "Pa" means the pucker of the kiss to father. Just as everywhere "Ma" (or mama or mater or mutter or mère or madre or mother) is the purse of the mouth to suck the breast, everywhere "Pa" (or papa or pater or pai or père or padre) is the peck of the puss to put on Paw's profile. For nine years since, Ella Jean had been looking for a man to kiss. Her brothers, though there were many of them, would not suffice. Her doll—well, each of her four older sisters had owned it and used it before it came down to her, and although she renamed it Johnny and made pants for it, it no longer had a head, and she could only imagine Johnny's face and Johnny's mouth, which, however, she often imaginatively kissed. There had been a lot of men in Stay More, but now, with the war, one by one they had all been taken away. Ella Jean could not share the nightmares of monstrous destruction that all of the kids whose fathers were Overseas were having, because she had lost her father not to the service but to California. But she had an exceptional longing for males (which led me to have hope for myself), and when one of them came of age, like Mare Coe, and kissed not her but her best friend, and not only kissed her but also. . . .

It was almost as if Mare belonged to Ella Jean too. Thus Ella Jean had to have Gypsy tell her everything that he had said and did on that creek bank that night.

But there was one thing Gypsy could not tell Ella Jean because Mare had made her promise to tell no one. Even though Ella Jean was not only Gypsy's best friend but the only good friend she'd ever had, and even though you can prove your friendship to somebody by keeping nothing secret from them, Gypsy knew that her beloved had told her how awful it would be if anybody found out what he was telling her.

He had told her this, it seems, as a way of consoling her, or reassuring her that he would come home. He confessed to her that he harbored no animosity toward the enemy. He didn't have a bellicose bone in his body. He explained to her the history and existence in Stay More of the Allies and the Axis, and how the latter were divided into Nazis and Japs, all for the sake of contests, baseball, war games, the play by which we find ourselves in the process of finding each other.

And then he said to her, "I been a Jap for years." And waited to see if she would frown or scowl or pout or maybe even run away.

But she just smiled and said, "Then I'm one too, I reckon. Didn't ye know us Dingletoons has joined the Axis? We aint decided whether to be Nazis or Japs, though. My brother Joe Don wants to be a Nazi. But if you're a Jap, then I'm a Jap."

"What I mean, though," he said, "is I aint a bit sure I could kill a real Jap if they tole me to. Don't you never tell a soul I said this, but I reckon Japs has got as much a right to this earth as anybody else. They may be smelly and slant-eyed and mean and yellow and caint talk plain, but that aint no reason to hate 'em. I used to have me a ole dog who was smelly and slant-eyed and mean and yellow and couldn't talk atall, but me and him was the best of friends, I'm tellin ye, I never liked ary creature more than him . . . until I met you."

"You're a good man, Gerald Coe," she said. "Maybe if you don't kill any Japs, they won't kill you either. And then you can come home to me." She kissed him once more.

CHAPTER
6

WHEN MARE COE LEFT STAY MORE FOR CAMP PENDLETON TO
be inducted into the marines, the Axis were without a leader and in
danger of ultimate defeat by the Allies. Joe Don Dingletoon, Gypsy's
Nazi brother, was a pretty fair pitcher but he couldn't shut out the
Allies, let alone pitch a no-hitter the way Mare could do. And he wasn't
very good at all in war games, in defending the village against the
sneaky attacks by the Allies. Gypsy herself learned to play third base
and would've been a great fielder except that occasionally she'd start
crying and a ball would escape between her feet. Maybe I was the only
one who observed that she'd start crying *before* she committed the error;
everybody else supposed she was crying because of the error.

Ella Jean knew why Gypsy was crying, and I did, of course, but nobody else knew. The secret of her romance with Mare remained locked in her heart and his (Ella Jean and I had keys to the locks). Nobody else really cared why she was crying, except when she'd make a fielding error that would cost us a run or two.

Ella Jean's big brother Willard was the natural candidate to take over as commander of the Axis, at least in terms of military strategy, if not baseball, where he remained our best slugger. But he was a reluctant leader. Not only did he lack the charisma that leaders must have (albeit Mare himself had none of it) but also he was not able to convince himself, let alone anyone else, that it was his destiny to replace Mare as chief of the Axis. In all his fifteen years, Willard had not yet encountered a sure manifestation of whatever was supposed to be his portion of fate, although for at least a dozen of those years he had known that he was foredestined to certain completions or closures that would represent his purpose in life. He knew for example that in three or four more years, somewhere around 1947 or 1948, he would be drafted into the armed forces to join Our Boys Overseas and help bring a conclusion to this bothersome war. But was that his destiny?

Willard had not shared Mare's notion that Stay More needed a civic government, although Mare had offered to appoint Willard as vice mayor. Willard believed that government was a form of meddling. Government was the imposition of unnatural controls over things that ought to be left to their own devices. If you just leave everybody alone, they'll somehow manage. No point in trying to manage them *for* them. If they wanted any help, they'd ask for it. Let well enough alone. Live and let live. "I reckon I don't keer whether school keeps or not," he told me when I interviewed him for a *Star* story about Mare's replacement as chief of the Axis, and I quoted that in my story, but he wasn't referring to school so much as to life itself.

The way to Willard's mind was in a straight path through his stomach. If there was one thing that preoccupied Willard more than his destiny, it was his appetite. When he was three years old, Willard got into serious trouble stealing cornbread from the dogs. He had been doing it for some time before he was caught. Selena Dinsmore always made plenty of cornbread, cooking it in her one big black iron skillet at every noon dinner, where her man Jake and her ten kids enjoyed sopping their gravy with it and pouring honey or sorghum molasses over it for dessert. Often that was the only lunch they had. Corn at least was plentiful, if nothing else was, and there was always enough cornmeal left over after Jake took the most of it to his still to be converted into whiskey. Selena always made enough cornbread to feed not only the twelve people in the family but also the baby chicks, the pigs, and the dogs, who gobbled it with gusto.

Willard begrudged the dogs their share. After all, he said to himself at the age of three, observing the speed and ferocity of the dogs, a dog is capable of foraging for wild game or even tame sheep, but a three-year-old kid can't forage for anything except poke salat. It wasn't fair that the dogs got all that good cornbread. So Willard, whose chore was to throw the cornbread to the dogs and be rewarded by the entertainment of watching them leap in the air for it and swallow it in one gobble before landing, began covertly eating one piece for each piece he threw to the dogs. This almost cured the hunger that had ravaged his body since the day he was weaned.

But Selena, whose absentmindedness was the only reason she'd been so late in weaning him, began to wonder why the dogs continued to fidget and whine around the back stoop after they supposedly had been fed. "Willard, did ye feed them dawgs?" she would ask him, and "Yes'm" he would reply, and this went on for a long time before she decided to check up on him and see if he was really feeding them, and thus she discovered that he was bolting a chaunk of bread for every chaunk he tossed to the dogs. She not only took a switch to his little hide, but made him sleep with the dogs (the boys' bed was becoming too crowded anyway, with Hubert, Tommy, and Vann getting bigger). The dogs were smart enough to know that Willard had been pilfering their cornbread ration, but, being dogs, they could just silently begrudge his sleeping with them. Willard, hearing the growls during the night, thought the dogs were complaining about his theft, and he was slow in realizing the growls came from his own stomach.

The chore of feeding the dogs was taken from him and given to one of his sisters, and Willard was appointed to the job of hoeing the corn and potatoes, although he was scarcely big enough to hold a hoe: the hoe-handle was simply too long for him. Jake Dinsmore suspected unknown pests were grubbing some of the potatoes and getting into the corn and gnawing bites out of the ears, until he caught Willard eating a raw potato. Willard was relieved of this duty and exempted from any chores involving foodstuffs. They made the mistake of not thinking of milk as a foodstuff, and allowed Willard to start milking Rosemary, the cow. Willard hid a gourd dipper in a hollow tree near the milking spot, and thus managed to assuage his hunger and his thirst. Rosemary was a free-ranging cow, not limited to the pasture but allowed to roam the woods, and on her wanderings she discovered Jake's still and helped herself to the still-beer until she could hardly stagger home. Nor could she stand still while Willard milked her, so that he had the awfullest time trying to fill the pail, and Selena Dinsmore suspicioned that he had been drinking from it, her notion confirmed when he began tottering, reeling, and slurring his words. He was never allowed to go near Rosemary again.

That early experience with an altered state of consciousness may have been part of the reason that Willard began to think too deeply and freshly about the meaning of life, and to reach the conclusion that each of us has a position in the scheme of things, and each of us has a destiny. He never came to doubt free will, because he was never deprived entirely of the opportunity to exercise his, but he began to believe that he was foredestined for something, he knew not what, but *some*thing, perhaps something important or at least worthwhile enough to make life worth enduring.

Willard did not fully grasp that life is hard. But he knew it had to be taken, withstood, and survived. Born with the birth of the national Depression, he never had a chance to discover that there had been better times. He took it for granted that everybody's breakfast consisted of soakies: crumbs of biscuit crusts sopped in coffee and milk. And that a great feast was when you could get your beans flavored by a piece of sowbelly. It was not the quality of the fare that was lacking, just the quantity of it. Willard could never get enough to eat. He was always hungry. His many brothers and sisters never seemed to suffer the way he did. Other kids at school didn't suffer the way he did. I certainly didn't, because I could go for days without a hunger pang. School dinners seemed sufficient for all but Willard. His older sisters Doris and

Jelena, the twins, had the responsibility of packing and toting the school
dinner, a galvanized tin pail holding sufficient cornbread and roasting
ears and sometimes possum or rabbit meat or at least hard-boiled eggs,
and Willard got the same share as his other brothers and sisters, but it
was never enough, and that was why, once, in the fourth grade when he
couldn't stand it, he noticed that Miss Jerram's dinner pail had in it two
sandwiches, one of them made with real bacon, so. . . . But once again
he was found out in his attempts to still his hunger, and when Miss
Jerram asked him why he was eating her sandwich, he could only reply,
"I figgered ye didn't have need of the both of 'em." She said he ought
to have asked her first. He replied, "You're kinder hard to ask." She
made him write on the board a hundred times, "I will always ask before
eating somebody's dinner."

He had never eaten anybody's dinner since then. Nor their breakfast
or supper. But he had gone to great lengths to fend for himself. He ate
anything he could find that didn't exactly belong to somebody else. It
wouldn't have been so bad if he had learned how to cook, but like everybody else in the Ozarks, he felt that cooking was something that women
and girls did. Men and boys didn't cook. So Willard had to search and
forage, and to eat his scroungings raw. But after all, most fruit and many
vegetables are meant to be eaten raw anyway.

The remarkable thing about Willard Dinsmore, it almost goes without saying, is that somehow he managed, despite stuffing himself at
every opportunity, to remain so skinny. Older people made jokes about
it that filtered down to us, and the Allies used the jokes as taunts: not
only the usual similes such as calling him skinny as a rail or a snake or a
skeleton, but more extravagant likenings to the leg of a milking stool or
the shadow of a hair and, now that the scarcity of elastic in the war required any of us who wore underclothes to use garments with draw-
strings that were usually tied in a bow, "Willard has to double-knot his
underpants to keep 'em from slippin off."

Maybe it was sheer metabolism that kept him thin. He worked hard,
he played hard, he fought hard in the battles and games against the
Allies, and he thought hard. I never saw Willard with an empty mind.
He was always thinking about something. If I had known him better, I
would have yielded to my constant impulse to ask him, "What are you

thinking about?" But the only one who knew him well enough to ask such a personal question was Mare.

Although Willard was Mare's lieutenant in all the activities of the Axis, and the two spent many of their idle hours together (to the extent that Willard was ever idle: even when he and Mare went fishing, rather than recline on the creek bank with his hat pulled down over his face waiting for a bob of the cork that never came, he was constantly in motion, whipping his cane pole as if it were a fancy rod), Mare never confessed to Willard, as Gypsy confessed to Ella Jean, that he and Gypsy had become lovers and tacitly betrothed. Thus, when Mare was called up into the service and made into a marine (I liked that alliteration and even used it in the *Star:* "Mare the Marine"), Willard went on dreaming about Gypsy without any notion that such dreams were betrayals of his best friend. Not just involuntary night dreams but daydreams too. You could glance at Willard whenever Gypsy was around, on the ball field or in the trenches of warfare, and you could tell just by imagining what he was thinking that he was deeply taken with her.

Just in time for the cane harvest, when all of Stay More's sugar cane would be collected and ground into sorghum molasses (we'd been doing this for years before the sugar shortage of the war), Willard got Gypsy a mule . . . or rather, he procured one for the Dingletoons to use. Nobody—except me, of course—knew exactly how he did it. He didn't steal it, I can tell you, and of course he couldn't have afforded to have bought it. He didn't exactly borrow it, either. One morning the Dingletoons woke up and found a mule tethered to a tree beside the shed that passed for their barn. Bliss Dingletoon insisted that Joe Don and Gypsy canvas the town to ask if anybody was missing a mule. Nobody was. Somebody suggested to Joe Don that the Allies had proposed stealing ole Dan's mule to give to the Dingletoons, and Joe Don, not knowing any better, actually went to ole Dan's yellow house and asked the hermit if he was missing a mule. All of us were awestruck with admiration for Joe Don that he had bravely done that, and even after we'd tried to explain to Joe Don that ole Dan never had nothing to do with nobody, and that the Allies were investigating the possibility that he was a German spy, Joe Don was not fazed or even impressed. "He didn't try to bite my head off," Joe Don declared. "He gave me a real cigarette—well, he'd rolled it hisself but it was real tobacco and real cigarette papers. We had us a good little talk."

Our mouths collectively gaped open and we insisted that Joe Don tell us everything that ole Dan had said.

Dan's yellow house was up above the road that goes to Butterchurn Holler, the same road the Dingletoons' place was on. So they were neighbors, almost, out there in the wildest part of town—well, not jungle-wild, but lush with growth, big trees with vines hanging from them and dense thickets of brush and all manner of wildflower and weed and bush: shady places further shadowed by the mountains. It wasn't exactly spooky up in there, but whenever I was out on my rounds, delivering the *Star* or collecting news, it always gave me the fantods to hike along the Butterchurn Holler road.

"Well sir now," Joe Don related, relishing the expectant reverence in our attitude toward him, "he jist ast me was I fixin to go to school now that time a books was nigh. And I 'lowed as how I'd never been to school afore but was hankerin to." Without going into a detailed family history, Joe Don had explained to ole Dan that the Dingletoons had never "held still long enough" for any of them to go to school, but now that they seemed to be pretty well settled in Stay More, they were giving serious thought to it, even though Joe Don was unsettled by the idea, and worried about the competition.

"He tole me that when he'd been my age, he'd been a schoolmaster hisself, off up in a place called Vermont, and he tole me the story of that." So already Joe Don was raking up information about the strange old man that we didn't know. He hadn't been a bank embezzler or a doctor or an escaped convict but just a schoolteacher! But starting at the age of sixteen? "Seventeen," Joe Don said. "And he hadn't never even finished school hisself. But it seems like this place where he was, Five Corners, was kind of hard up for schoolteachers. And in that day and age, he didn't need a license or nothin to teach."

Anyhow, Joe Don said, the point of all this was to reassure Joe Don that he wouldn't have any trouble with school, as long as he could do what ole Dan had done: always stay a lesson ahead of everybody else. Joe Don grew musing and repeated this as if he'd have his mother make him a needlepoint of it to hang up as a personal motto: *Stay a lesson ahead of everybody else.*

We were eager to know if Joe Don had caught a glimpse of the hermit's legendary daughter.

Joe Don's eyes bulged. "Boy howdy, aint she a looker? I mean, did ye ever see such a scrumdoodle?"

We were obliged to confess that none of us had ever got a close look at her.

"Didn't she never go to the school or nowheres?" Joe Don wanted to know. We shook our heads solemnly. "Well, heck, maybe there wasn't no need? Him bein a schoolteacher hisself?" He thought for a long moment, and added, "Or maybe she was just too shy and afraid of folks?" Joe Don told us her name was Annie but said that Annie hadn't been able to say a word to Joe Don.

When school resumed, the Dingletoon kids were there, all four of them. Joe Don was good enough at reading, and at sums, which he'd mastered on his own, to be placed into the seventh grade despite never having been to school before. Miss Jerram didn't want to make such a big boy sit at desks with little kids. As long as Joe Don followed that new motto, and stayed a lesson ahead of everybody else, he deserved to sit with Willard at the seventh grade desk on the Axis side. And Miss Jerram figured that since his sister Gypsy was two years behind him in age, she should be two years behind in school, so she was placed in the fifth grade, my grade, but to my great disappointment she wasn't assigned to my desk but to that of Sammy Coe, my only coeval and rival.

The fall term passed quickly. I continued to publish *The Stay Morning Star* without fail every week, with news taken from the newsreels at the Buffalo and from whatever was worth reporting around Stay More. Paris was liberated, and Miss Jerram explained to us that it wasn't Paris, Arkansas, but a big city Overseas, the capital of France. The Allies thought they had liberated downtown Stay More but they were mistaken; with the help of potato grenades, the Axis drove them out of the three foxholes they'd captured. The U.S. Army invaded German soil for the first time. The Allies reported that they'd discovered a nocturnal visitor to ole Dan's yellow house: none other than Doc Swain himself. Was Doc Swain also a German spy? The Axis tried to tell the Allies that they were full of beans, that possibly Doc Swain was visiting ole Dan either out of friendship or in order to fix something that was wrong with him. I did not report any of this in the *Star*. The Japanese (the real ones, not those among us Axis) had begun using suicide pilots, called kamikazes, at the Battle of Leyte in the Philippines, and Boden Whitter of Stay More, 19, a sailor on one of the ships hit by a kamikaze in that battle, was killed. Miss Jerram excused from school for two days his kid sister, Tildy Whitter, and his kid brother, Jim John. Jim John declared, looking at me, "I'm gonna kill all you dirty Japs." Even though he was a member of the filthy Allies, we felt very sorry for him, and with Miss Jerram's help the Axis made a card of sympathy lavishly inscribed with sentiments of sorrow and left it in the Whitter's post office box. A few days later Stay More had a pie supper, a fund-raising auction of girls' and women's pies and their companionship during the eating of them, to raise money for a War Memorial in Boden Whitter's memory, and I reported all the bids and the resulting visits in the *Star*. I lost fifty cents on a pie that I was certain had been baked by Ella Jean but had actually been made by Rosa Faye Duckworth, an Ally, and I could hardly speak to her—not that I would have been able to speak to Ella Jean either.

In one issue of the *Star* I gave the front page to the reelection of Franklin Delano Roosevelt and wrote an editorial, "He's One of Us," about the man newly elected to be his vice president, Harry S Truman, who came from a place up in Missouri not too far from the Ozarks and therefore we ought to be proud of Senator Truman, even if he wasn't much to look at. The Allies reported that Doc Swain was often a visitor to ole Dan's house, and that Doc wasn't treating ole Dan for anything. The two men were just seen sitting together on the porch in the autumn chill talking to each other. On the front page of another issue of the *Star*, first asking myself, "What would Ernie Pyle have done?," I ran a story under the headline, ALLIES STAKEOUT INNOCENT HERMIT UNDER SUSPICION AS NAZI SPY. And I named names. Willard himself was not happy with that, since I'd violated the policy that we never tell any adults about our activities. I protested that I hadn't told any adults. "Your newspaper tells everbody, don't it?" he pointed out, rightly. What was worse, three of those names I'd named ganged up on me and beat me up, breaking my arm. But I discovered you. I made true friends with you, Gentle Reader.

Joe Don reported to us about another visit he'd had with the hermit.

This time ole Dan had offered him not only a cigarette but a glass of homemade dandelion wine. "Mighty fine stuff," Joe Don boasted. He said that he and ole Dan had enjoyed a good laugh together over the idea that the Allies were reconnoitering ole Dan under suspicion of being a German spy. Ole Dan had often seen some kids sneaking around his property, but just figured they were either nosy or they were trying to get a look at Annie, "Who doesn't like to be seen," ole Dan said. Joe Don had explained to ole Dan how all the kids of Stay More were divided into the two camps, Allies and Axis. "Heck, I'm a Nazi myself!" Joe Don had told the hermit. And ole Dan had given him the Nazi salute and said *"Sieg, Heil!"* and Joe Don had returned the salute and said *"Sieg, Heil, mein führer!"* and the two had nearly died laughing.

"But then," Joe Don related, "but then he also says, '*Was man nicht kann meiden, muss man willig leiden,*' and I says I'm sorry but I don't know that'un, and he said it in English, 'What one cannot avoid must be borne without complaint.'"

We stared at Joe Don. We stared at each other. We waited to see who would be the first to comment. It was Willard. "Maybe he really is a German."

"He was born in a place called Connecticut," Joe Don said. "Is that in Germany?"

"Connecticut's part of America somewheres," I informed them. "Maybe ole Dan just learnt the German language. Maybe his grandmother was German, or somebody."

"I got to remind you," Willard said to Joe Don, "we'uns has taken a solemn vow, Allies and Axis both, never to tell the grown-ups what we're doing. You shouldn't ort to've told ole Dan you was a Nazi."

One day while my arm was healing in its cast, autographed by everybody including you, Latha told me I had a letter. In the tier of glass-fronted post office boxes inside her store/post office, she had reserved a box for *The Stay Morning Star,* but there was rarely anything in it, never a letter. But now there was a piece of what Latha explained was called V-mail, thin blue paper folded into its own envelope. It was from Mare Coe. He enclosed twelve three-cent stamps. The letter said: "Dear Donny, Here's 12 stamps so you can send me a prescription to the newspaper. I sure do miss Stay More and everbody and even you, ha ha. They have sensors for the mail that black things out, so I can't tell you where I am, or why, or what happens or anything. But I'm a 'leatherneck' now and I'm supposed to shoot the 'enemy' any day now. Say hi to everbody for me. Your pal, Gerald."

I was so happy to have his letter that I ran a front-page story under the headline MARE OF THE MARINES ENTERS PACIFIC CAMPAIGN, even though there was nothing specific I could tell about his activities.

Ernie Pyle himself, I learned from his column, had entered the Pacific campaign. The war in Europe was almost over, and they didn't need Ernie Over There as much as they needed him Way Out There in the Pacific. In my reply to Mare, enclosing the latest issue of the *Star,* I told him to keep his eye out for Ernie, and if he saw him to be sure and tell him he was from Stay More, Arkansas, which Ernie would of course mention in his column, and then we could all feel famous for just a little bit. I also told Mare about my broken arm, but pointed out that in general the Axis were conquering the Allies, thanks especially to Willard, and we even anticipated that the Allies might soon surrender. I told Mare how Willard had got a mule for the Dingletoons, but that nobody knew that he was the one who'd done it. "Gypsy named the mule Old Jarhead," I wrote. I didn't tell Mare that Willard was nuts about Gypsy.

When Doc Swain finally removed the cast from my arm, I wrote Mare and told him all about it.

I don't know if Mare ever caught a glimpse of Ernie Pyle. The ship Ernie was on, the U.S.S. *Cabot,* was also the base for Captain John Henry "Hank" Ingledew of Stay More, who was in charge of all radio operations for the Pacific Fleet (even though back home in Stay More we still hadn't seen our first radio). Hank Ingledew, the lucky dog, shook hands with Ernie Pyle, but as far as I know Ernie didn't put his name and hometown into any of his columns.

If Ernie had met Mare, what would he have written about what happened to him? Of course, to tell Mare's story, Ernie would have had to know Mare as well as I did. So what if Ernie and I had collaborated on Mare's story? We would have needed a little help from you.

CHAPTER
. . . .
7

WHEN PUDGY, FRECKLED GERALD "MARE" COE FIRST CAUGHT
sight of what was left of the village of Motoyama, it seemed to him that
he might be foreglimpsing what his hometown of Stay More, Arkansas,
could become if people didn't take care of it and kept leaving it, and nature herself stripped it of its trees and grasses. It was an awful sight. He
knew that this fighting had harmed it beyond repair. Before all the
women and children had been evacuated back to the mainland, Motoyama had been a little town with a dusty main street like Stay More's, a
general store, a school, a geisha house, a beer hall, and about fifty of the
flimsy, single-story houses, a foot off the ground, that the Japanese typ-
ically built. The people had mined the sulfur that gave the island its
name, Sulfur Island, Iwo Jima, but they had also grown a lot of sugar

cane and milled it into sugar, which was what people in Stay More still did. Now the village was reduced to rubble, denuded of even the coarse grasses and gnarled bushes and trees that had struggled for existence, and pocked with the pillboxes and foxholes from which a steady barrage of machine gun and rifle fire, artillery and grenades, filled the air with blasts and hisses and pops and sizzles and screams. There were even cockroaches all over the place, waiting to inherit what was left of the place after all the shelling and killing. These weren't the same kind of cockroach that Stay More had, but cockroaches all the same.

To the best of his knowledge, Mare Coe had never killed anyone before, except of course in play. In the assault on Mount Suribachi, several days earlier, he had actually fired his rifle in the direction of an enemy soldier, and the man had fallen, hit not by Mare's bullet but by several bullets from Mare's comrades. Mare wouldn't have pulled the trigger in the first place had not a friend yelled into his ear, "My damn gun's jammed! *You* get the Nip!" But Mare, an expert marksman, had carefully aimed to miss.

In the early years of the war, before he was drafted, back home in Stay More, playing war games with his triplet brothers, Earl and Burl, he found himself delegated to be leader of the "Japs." It was all in fun and play, and the "Allies" were always victorious in their games, except their baseball games, where Mare, pitching for the "Axis," was unbeatable, almost as compensation for suffering defeat on the "battlefield" and ignominy as a despised Jap.

But Mare (who got his nickname from his aspiration to become "mayor" of his little town) had a thick hide, and the same altruism or goodwill or whatever fellow feeling that made him the first member of the rival gangs of "Allies" and "Axis" to become political rather than simply militaristic also made him somewhat sympathetic with the people whose representative he had been appointed and whose leader, Tojo, he had been impersonating. The kids of Stay More, like all Americans, despised the Japs, even more than the Nazis, because at least some Stay More families might have had remote Germanic ancestry or in any case they spoke a language that had largely derived from Anglo-Saxon, whereas the Japs were yellow-skinned, slant-eyed, smelly, and the most vicious bloodthirsty soldiers in the history of warfare, and what they uttered bore no resemblance on earth to anything that anybody could understand.

"Atama ga okashii!" exclaimed Hisao Fujida from his bunker as he watched Mare Coe rise up from his sniper's crouch and begin to walk erect and casually into the village of Motoyama, or what little was left of it. What Hisao said may be translated as the equivalent of Mare's having said "His head is plumb peculiar," or "That feller has shore got nobody home upstairs." Hisao added, not without admiration, *"Ban-yu!,"* which means foolhardiness. Mare's act was not bravery or recklessness but sheer brazen determination, although Hisao on reflection had a suspicion of the unthinkable goodwill that could have lain behind it.

Mare took off his helmet, all that preserved his consciousness from the hail of bullets and shrapnel that zipped and zinged all around him, and he began gently to sweep the path with his helmet as if trying to drive a herd of cows. So many of the watchful enemy were astounded by his behavior that they repeated Hisao's exclamation of *"Ban-yu!"* and the machine gunner exclaimed *"Yu-ki!,"* or bravery, and took his finger off the trigger and one by one the others too ceased firing, so that enough of the raucous din had died down that they could hear him.

"Saw bossy," Mare was saying, with the same mild and gentle ease with which he walked. His audience discussed among themselves the possible meaning of his words. In Japanese, *"saw—"* is a common prefatory or introductory expression, like our "Well—" as in "Well, how about that?," or indicative of upbeat determination, as in "Well, let's get going!" But *"bossy"*? Some of them thought he might have said *"boshi,"* which just means hat. But "Well, hat?" No, it was more likely he'd said *"basshi,"* which means youngest child. Was he therefore being insulting? Taunting them as babies? "Well, kiddo"? They looked at each other and repeated his expression among themselves, as they repeated Hisao's *ban-yu* or the machine gunner's *yu-ki*. But, one and all, they stopped firing.

Mare wondered if any of these hidden soldiers were actually natives of this town of Motoyama. Were they defending their own village, as he had defended the village of Stay More against the attacks of the "Allies" in their war games? There was scarcely anything here worth defending, but for that matter there hadn't been much left of Stay More to defend.

Just because he had been required to take the part of the enemy in those war games, to become a Jap in play-like, did not mean that Mare Coe was still taking sides with the enemy. He was not lacking in patriotism. It had been he who, after the successful assault on Mount Suribachi and the raising of the first small flag, had gone back down the mountain to the beachhead and boarded a landing ship and saluted an ensign, and had said, "Sir, lookee up yonder," and had called his attention to the small Stars and Stripes atop the mountain. Mare had been out of breath from running, and the ensign had had difficulty understanding him when he requested, "D'ye reckon ye mought have a bigger flaig than that'un hereabouts, that ye could lend us the borry of?" After Mare had repeated himself and had attempted a paraphrase, the ensign had understood. "Must be pretty rough up there," the ensign had observed, and Mare had said "Yessir, it shore is, but we didn't have a awful lot of trouble a-taking the mounting." The ensign had fetched a folded large flag, which, by appropriate coincidence, had come originally from the salvage depot at Pearl Harbor. Where the first flag was a mere four feet by two feet, this new one was eight by four. Mare had thanked the ensign profusely for it, then had taken off at a dead run, back up the mountain. When he had reached the summit, he had had just enough breath left to lurch forward and place the folded flag into the hands of another marine, who attached it to a makeshift flagpole and, with the help of five other fellows, had begun to struggle to shove the staff of the flagpole into the rubble. Mare had wanted desperately to help them raise Old Glory, but he had been so tuckered out from his errand that he could only sit panting on the ground while the other six marines raised the flag as a photographer took their picture. By all rights, Pfc. Gerald Coe ought to have been in that picture. If he had, his image would eventually exist in a gigantic bronze sculpture in Washington and lesser replicas at Quantico Marine Base and elsewhere. As it was, there would be only a small bronze plaque in Mare's memory on the wall of a hallway of the high school at Jasper, Newton County, Arkansas.

For his pains, Mare got to keep the first flag, the smaller one, and he now intended to plant that flag in the village of Motoyama, just as the boys had done in the game of Capture the Flag back home in Stay

More. He did not see any Jap flags flying in the village, but if he found one, he would capture it.

Hisao Fujida began to laugh. It was the only sound except for the far-distant gunfire elsewhere on the island, as faint as a Ford way off up on the Butterchurn Holler road a-backfiring in the summer night. All of the enemy entrenched in Motoyama town had stopped firing. Like Hisao, like Mare himself, they had a touch of combat fatigue and needed a moment's rest. They watched with amusement and interest as the pudgy, freckled American, perhaps possessed not so much with *ban-yu* nor *yu-ki* but with the *atama ga okashii*, dementia, put down his carbine and took from his backpack a folded red-white-and-blue flag, and began to look around for a pole of some kind to attach it to. All the trees and branches and shrubs had been reduced to splinters and flinders. Mare's best hope was a length of the drainpipe that all the houses had had to catch the precious rainwater, which was the only source of fresh water. But all of these appeared to be gone.

Hisao Fujida's superior, Lieutenant Toshinosuke Kaido, did not see any humor in the situation, and was seething over the implied insult in "Saw bossy." He was tempted to shoot the American himself with his Nambu automatic, but the American had put down his carbine and was thus unarmed, and a gentleman does not shoot an unarmed man. So Lieutenant Kaido took his ceremonial sword, inherited from a samurai ancestor, and approached the American, ready to decapitate him. Hisao Fujida winced, and grieved.

Mare saw the Japanese lieutenant coming and said in his mild fashion, "You'uns had all best jist pack up and git on out. I aim to raise our flag over what's left of this here town." But as the lieutenant raised the sword overhead with both hands, Mare had the sense to back away from him. Backing, he tripped and fell into a shell crater.

Back behind the lines, where ninety other marines of Alpha Company, the Second Battalion, Twenty-eighth Regiment, Fifth Division, were watching with even less amusement than Lieutenant Kaido possessed, and where Mare's platoon sergeant was cursing Mare's sister and mother and all his ancestors because Mare had not waited for the "Move out!" command and was thus insubordinate, a sharpshooter stood up and fired at Lieutenant Kaido just at the moment that the lat-

ter raised his sword over Mare Coe's head. The lieutenant fell, whereupon the air everywhere once again was filled with pows and pams and
booms and bings and chattering pops. Mare did not dare lift his head
above the rim of the shell crater and attempt to retrieve his carbine. He
could only lie there, realizing that he might have lost the chance to raise
Old Glory in Motoyama town. "Who'd want the place anyhow?" he
said to himself, as if in consolation. In fact, the entire Twenty-eighth
Regiment desperately wanted it, and had been trying all day to take it.

Pinned down, Mare could only lie there and reflect upon the town
that he had wanted to be mayor of, and, while he was at it, allow his
thoughts to drift to the girl he'd left behind, a lovely thing he'd met not
too long before he had shipped out. Her name was Gypsy, appropriate
for a girl whose family was always nomadic and had not been in Stay
More very long. At fourteen, she was the oldest daughter in a large
family of hardscrabble squatters who lived up in Butterchurn Holler.
Mare had never had a girlfriend before, and it was almost by accident
that he met her one night on the banks of the creek, and a passion hit
them both, not because he was soon leaving to join the service but because of the chemistry of some old country superstition that made a
pretty young vagabond girl fall in love with a pudgy, homely, awkward
but infinitely kind young man. It must have been one of the quickest
consummations of a courtship anybody had ever heard, seen, or dreamt.

Not long afterward, at Camp Pendleton where he trained for the
marines, in his barracks the other guys talked about girls as if screwing
and humping and balling and banging and plowing was the wickedest,
nastiest, meanest, dirtiest thing a fellow could do, but that old time on
that old sandbar with old Gypsy had been the nicest old thing that Mare
could ever have imagined, the loveliest thing in all God's thoughtful
creation of this world. Even now, when the grenade came rolling alongside him, he was able to give himself over almost entirely to the memory of its beauty.

But he had the presence of mind, even while re-creating the vision
and sensation of his first and only experience of a woman, to reach for
the grenade and to give it a fling that sent it back whence it had come.
His thoughts still lost to Gypsy, he did not have time to decide con-
sciously just where to throw the grenade. Almost by accident, even

though he had an accurate arm that could pitch a mean fast ball or a wicked curve ball, the grenade lobbed into a foxhole and destroyed its inhabitant. It was the first person Mare had ever killed. He had no time to reflect upon having killed a Jap before another grenade fell into his lap. By now he could no longer think about Gypsy. Having killed one man, he might as well kill another. He wound up and pitched the grenade into the vent of a bunker and annihilated its five occupants. Gypsy evaporated like dew on the sunstruck grass; had he actually told her that he would never kill the enemy? He began to give his full attention to the job before him. The third grenade exploded halfway back to its sender without hurting anybody. Then the enemy craftily delivered the fourth and fifth grenades simultaneously, one to his left, the other to his right. But he had two hands, didn't he? And while the fourth grenade also detonated before completing its return journey to the enemy, the fifth, thrown with his good left arm, his pitching arm, landed in a machine gun nest and obliterated three of the enemy as well as their machine. The sixth grenade he actually leapt up and caught in the air, like a fly ball, and was thus able to aim, like a pitcher trying to throw a man out at third, and to impart such an unerring focus to its trajectory that it went through the gunport of the largest of the pillboxes, wreaking considerable loss of life and property therein.

One wonders why the Japanese were wasting so many grenades trying to kill an unarmed Ozark hillbilly whose only talent, apart from helping his father blacksmith while daydreaming of becoming the mayor of a town in its terminal demise, was pitching a pretty fair game of baseball, seldom losing. Hisao Fujida asked himself that question, or, rather, since he knew nothing of Mare Coe's background, he wondered why his comrades were not saving their grenades for the imminent onslaught of the ninety other members of the Twenty-eighth Regiment, who were even now setting up mortars, bazookas and a 37 mm cannon in order to shell the daylights out of any Japanese who escaped the grenades returned from Mare Coe, a soldier possessed of *ban-yu, yu-ki,* and quite possibly *atama ga okashii,* but perhaps crafty enough to feign his eccentric behavior in order to lull the Japanese into a momentary but dangerous dropping of their tight security. In other words, this weird American had quite possibly been part of a clever scheme, a decoy, if you will, to trick and thus disarm the defenders of Motoyama. Back home in his own village in Shikoku, playing war games as a boy, Hisao had been similarly tricked. This thought somewhat disturbed Hisao, and whatever benevolence he had felt for the American vanished. His wits returned to him, and he used them.

Hisao Fujida calculated the amount of time it took the American to receive and return a grenade, and Hisao deliberately, after pulling the pin on a grenade, allowed three seconds to elapse before throwing it, counting aloud to himself, *Fujibachi One, Fujibachi Two, Fujibachi Three.*

When Mare Coe caught Hisao's grenade, and started to throw it back, it exploded in his hand, taking off his arm, most of his face, and all of his life.

CHAPTER
8

When Miss Jerram saw Doc Swain's old car pulling into the schoolyard that March morning, she wondered if one of us had took down sick that she didn't know about. She looked around the room at all of us, but we all looked reasonably healthy. Maybe Doc Swain was coming to vaccinate everybody, she decided, but wondered why he couldn't just do it at his office. Quickly she grabbed her purse and got out her compact and snapped it open and took a close look at her face. She already had on enough powder and rouge and lipstick and all to disguise her identity from anybody except her dog. She put some powder on her nose and had time to re-edge her mouth with the lipstick before Doc came into the schoolhouse. We all turned to look at him, a man in his middle sixties, thirty or more years older than Estalee

Jerram, as if she cared—he was a man, wasn't he? and there weren't many of those left in Stay More. He gave us a forced smile, as if he had nothing to smile about. Then he crooked his finger at Miss Jerram, motioning her to come outside the schoolhouse so's he could talk to her in private.

"You'uns keep yore seats and don't go to chitterin and chatterin. I'll be right back," she said, as if she knew for a fact that she would.

But she didn't come right back, and when she finally did, Doc came with her. He had his arm around her, which made us giggle and snicker and titter, until we all saw the reason he had his arm around her was not romantic but just sympathetic: she was sobbing and shaking. I whispered to my seatmate, you, to help you understand: nobody, in the history of her seven or eight years as a schoolteacher, had ever seen her betray any emotion before, any feeling of any kind—not humor, not anger, not sorrow, not anything.

"I reckon ye'd best let me tell 'em, Esty," Doc Swain said to her. "You just sit down there at your desk and let me say it." He helped her into her chair, where she buried her face in her hands and went on blubbering, and then he turned to face us. "Folks," he addressed us, and I admired him for not calling us "boys and girls," which we were, "I've got some sad news to tell ye. Lawlor and Dulcie Coe has just received word from the U.S. government that their boy Gerald has—" Doc, who betrayed emotion a good bit more readily than Miss Jerram but never wore his heart on his sleeve, began to moisten up a bit around the eyes. "Gerald, as most of y'uns know, was servin in the marines in the Pacific, and his outfit was involved in the American attempt to take Iwo Jima, a Japanese stronghold. The American effort has been victorious, and that island has been taken at the cost of over four thousand American boys' lives. You heared me correct. Four thousand, five hundred marines killed dead. Don't hardly seem worth it, does it? All that many for just a little ole sandpile out in the ocean. But Gerald Coe was one of 'em, I'm sorry to have to tell ye. He died a hero. He gave his life after slaying dozens of the enemy. We ort to be proud of him, I reckon."

Doc, who'd pulled baby Gerald and his two brothers into this world nineteen years before, stopped then and waited for our response. Most of us were too shocked to see straight. When Boden Whitter had died in that kamikaze attack back in October, some months before, the news hadn't been brought to the schoolhouse, and besides, Boden hadn't been a member of either the Allies or the Axis. But the first to speak up was Jim John Whitter, Boden's brother. "Goddamn you Japs all to hell!" He shook his fist at each of us.

"Don't forget Mare was a Jap," I pointed out.

Joe Don Dingletoon protested, "Not our Japs. Them *real* Japs."

The two students most affected by the terrible news happened to be deskmates: Mare's kid brother Sammy, my age, who seemed to be paralyzed with disbelief, and Gypsy Dingletoon, who, perhaps not even remembering that her deskmate was the deceased's own brother, elbowed him so she could reach the aisle. She ran down the aisle and out of the room, slamming the door behind her. I wanted to suggest that you run after her, and help her, but you couldn't have done that. So I got up to go after her myself.

"You, Dawny!" Miss Jerram hollered, having raised her soaked face to see who'd slammed the door, futile, since whoever had slammed it was already out. "Where d'ye think you're off to?"

"Somebody better see to ole Gypsy," I said. "Somebody ort to see if she's okay." It hit me that my fellow students were perhaps just as mystified as Miss Jerram about why I'd want to check up on old Gypsy. I glanced at Ella Jean, and she alone seemed to know why I was leaving. She obviously wanted to go with me, but couldn't. I left.

Gypsy was out in the schoolyard, leaning against a tree, crying her heart out more eloquently than Miss Jerram had been doing. I didn't know for sure what to say to her. Come to think of it, I had never spoken to her before, although of course she knew who I was. But come to think of it, I had never spoken to any girl, not just Gypsy. Although I had a great attraction to older women, I was not having much success understanding girls. Gypsy was three years older than me but she was still a girl. I couldn't tell what girls wanted. They never could make up their minds. They were always changing their minds, and, worst of all, nothing ever seemed to please them. Nothing anybody could do would make them happy. Girls, I guess, were born to be sad, with or without a good reason. But now Gypsy Dingletoon had a very good reason. She had all the reason that anybody would ever need.

She didn't know that I knew she had a good reason. She probably didn't know I was standing there behind her, watching her drench the bark of that elm with her tears. I decided I had better speak very quietly and gently. "Gypsy," I nearly whispered, but still it made her jump out of her skin so I even put my hand on her arm as if that magic might make her climb back into her skin. "He was my friend too," I said. I wished I could cry too, but I couldn't.

She stared at me and her whole face screwed up as if an invisible giant's hand had twisted it, and she bawled harder than ever. Finally she mumbled, "Just leave me be." And she motioned for me to exit her life.

It wasn't a good situation to be in, for me as well as her. For something even as momentous as my first conversation with a girl, let alone something as dramatic as a pubescent boy trying to console an older girl on the death of the soldier who had been her boyfriend and lover, we needed a backdrop more spectacular than that drab gray March morning, although the first fragrances of springtime were already full in the air. What we needed was a gentle rain to match her tears, no, what we needed was a downpour to dramatize the awfulness of death, and to remind Gypsy that there were founts of water that could make her tear ducts seem like mere seeps. Friend Reader, could you help? Maybe a little thunderstorm, just enough to drown out her sobs with the crashes and peals, and to commence splattering us with big drops of rain? A well-controlled effort. Thank you.

When the rain hit, Gypsy glanced back toward the schoolhouse, as if to gauge the distance and to realize it was too far to make a dash, even if she could stand to return to her classmates, and then she glanced at the girls' outhouse, right handy nearby, and started to leap for that, but stopped, stared at me forlornly as if, despite my impudence in following her in her misery, I was all she had in this sad world at this sad moment, and she reached out and grabbed my hand! Friend, are you still helping? *She took my hand!* And she led me into that outhouse with her. We did not close the door, which despite your possible preconception of it, did not have a crescent moon carved into it. (You should know that the Stay More school didn't have a boys' outhouse. The boys, like males

74

everywhere in these parts, just preferred to go off into the bushes or woods somewhere.) Gypsy and I stood there in the shelter of that shed, watching the rain come down—perhaps it was getting even harder— and listening to the thunder, and smelling the rain-drenched fragrances of March grasses and weeds and the earliest flowers that obliterated the stale smells of girls' body functions that pervaded the privy. By and by, Gypsy seemed to realize that her tears couldn't compete with that rainfall, so she hushed her crying. And when she sat down, so did I, our posteriors not positioned over the two holes as if we were using them but on the wood beside them.

"How come ye to foller me out of the schoolhouse?" she asked quietly. "How didje even guess that it jist kills me to know pore Gerald's dead?"

"You were his sweetheart," I said. "I just wanted to see if I couldn't give ye any comfort."

"But I never tole nobody we was promised!" she said, then remembered that she had. "Exceptin Eller Jean. She didn't tell ye, did she?"

I couldn't help snorting. Whenever I laughed, I tried to avoid snorting, but it was involuntary, like sneezing. "Course not, silly," I said. "What reason would Eller Jean ever have for even lookin at *me*, let alone tell me anything?"

My grumbling lament made Gypsy look at me as if she couldn't quite remember having seen me before. "Why, Dawny," she protested, looking me over, "I reckon Eller Jean has cast ye a glimpse or two. I've looked at ye. And ever week I've read that paper ye put in our mailbox. Cover to back."

I was flattered because not many people in Stay More admitted to regular scrutiny of the *Star*. Gypsy's acknowledgment of it made me realize that I might have had an ulterior motive for following her out of the schoolhouse: in the next issue of my newspaper I'd have to run a front-page story about the heroic death of Pfc. Gerald Coe in the taking of Iwo Jima, and it wouldn't hurt if I could interview the girl he left behind, and possibly publish a few words of her feelings about the matter. Ernie Pyle taught me that reporters must be objective, cold, and even cynical during emotional moments.

"Gypsy," I requested, bravely, "would ye mind too awful much if I jist tole in the next issue of the paper how you was fixin to marry Mare—Gerald—if he came home?"

My simple question set her to bawling again, and I could only sit there and wait it out, as we were both waiting out the storm. I stared through the open door of the privy at the schoolhouse. Then she abruptly quit crying and stared hard at me. "Was it Gerald tole ye? Was it? Did he go and tell on us?"

How could I answer, without revealing that I'd been prying and peeking? I decided I'd better lie, which I'm very good at. I nodded my head, and said, "I tole ye, he was my friend too. But he made me promise I'd never breathe a word of it to nobody else, and I never did."

Gypsy sniffled and wiped her nose on the back of her hand, but she didn't go on crying. We stared at the mountains that rose before us. Those hills seemed a kind of tangible metaphor for our condition: the hills cut us off from the outside world, the hills surrounded us and sheltered us and hugged us, but most of all they kept us private, they kept us privy to ourselves, our own deepest secrets which we need not ever reveal. But I needed to tell my newspaper subscribers the truth about our hero and his girl. Would it have been ghoulish of me to insist on it to her?

When we had been sitting in the shelter of that outhouse for what seemed a long time, Gypsy announced, "I gotta go."

But it was still raining in buckets, and I pointed out, "You'll git wetter'n a dog."

She stared at me as if I'd insulted her. But then she understood that we weren't talking about the same thing, although I didn't understand. "Naw, I mean, I gotta *go*," she said.

"Well, go on, then," I said. "I'm gonna wait till the rain stops."

"Silly, I'm tryin to tell ye I've got to mail a letter."

"A *letter?*" I said. "The post office is way over yonder." I gestured toward Latha Bourne's store, where the post office was.

"Don't you know nothin?" she said with exasperation, and sighed. Then she took a deep breath and said, "I've gotta go to the outhouse."

"But you're already *in* the outhouse," I pointed out.

"Dawny, you are *real* dumb. Don't ye know what this outhouse is *for?* Wal, I've got to *use* it!"

"Oh," I said, and must have blushed at my slowness. I am told I blush readily but I've never been able to verify it by blushing in a mirror.

"Just to wee-wee," she said. "That's all."

"Do ye want me to step outside?" I asked, over the sound of the thunder crashing and the downpour pounding the roof of the shed.

"Naw, but shet the door," she requested.

Was anybody in the schoolhouse looking out the window? Doc Swain's car was still in the yard. Was he still trying to comfort Miss Jerram? Or was he talking to all of them about heroism and devotion and sacrifice and all those fine things? Wouldn't anyone who really did look out the window and see the outhouse door closed wonder what in tarnation we were doing? I pushed the door shut.

"Don't turn around," she requested. "Jist keep yore back turned till I tell ye."

With the door closed and the sky totally beclouded, it was fairly dark in there, I couldn't have seen her anyhow, but I kept my back to her, and could only imagine what she was doing, raising her dress and sitting over a hole. Minutes passed. When it seemed to me that she'd been sitting there long enough for number two too if she wanted to, I said over my shoulder in a gentle undertone just loud enough to reach beyond the crash of rain and thunder, "Aint ye done yit?"

"Yeah," she said. "I was done a while back. I'm jist a-sittin here, thinkin about pore Gerald. I just caint believe we won't never see him ever no more."

The image of them together on that creek bank that night came back to me. I wondered at the truth of the rumors I'd heard that girls actually *enjoy* doing that. Was Gypsy going to miss that? If she really *needed* that, couldn't some other boy do it with her for her?

Almost as if in response to these licentious and false-hearted thoughts, the door opened, and there was Ella Jean. She quickly entered, dripping wet from her dash through the downpour, the droplets falling from her hair and the hem of her dress. "Miss Jerram tole me to run out here," Ella Jean said, "and see what become of y'uns." Gypsy and Ella Jean hugged each other tightly and immediately the two of them began crying together.

"He aint never coming back!" Gypsy wailed.

"Never coming back!" Ella Jean sobbed, like an echo from the distant mountain. They wailed and sobbed. Again I wished I could cry too. I felt like it, but I just couldn't do it. I wasn't a girl, even if this was the girl's outhouse. It was crowded in there, three people in an outhouse meant for two at most. "How come you're here, Dawny?" Ella Jean asked me.

Her simple speaking of my name, which I don't believe she'd done before, thrilled me. I told Ella Jean, "I just came out here to see if I couldn't comfort her."

"How did ye know she needed any comfort?" Ella Jean asked.

"Gerald told him," Gypsy said.

"He never," Ella Jean challenged me.

"Yeah," I claimed, "I knew they were supposed to get married."

"So you're gonna put that in your newspaper?" Ella Jean wanted to know.

"I'd sure like to," I admitted.

"Gypsy," Ella Jean counseled her older friend, "ye mought as well git used to the idee. Folks is gonna know about it, one way or th'other."

"I don't want them Allies to know it," Gypsy said. "They hated Gerald. They suspicioned it was Gerald who somehow got ahold of Old Jarhead for us."

"But Doc said Mare died a hero," I pointed out. "Nobody hates a hero." That casual remark set the two girls to weeping again and holding each other, and I wished one or both of them would hold me too.

"Them Allies hate everbody who's not Allies," Gypsy observed. "And I'd as lief they never learnt me and Gerald was promised. So don't go sayin it in your paper, Dawny."

Ella Jean put in, "Miss Jerram's gonna take the hickory to all three of us, lessen we git back in there soon."

When we returned to the schoolhouse, Doc Swain was gone, taking Sammy Coe with him, excused because of the bad news about his big brother. Miss Jerram had regained her composure. Although the mood was still somber, as I went to my seat the Allies had fits of giggling, snickering, whispering, eye-bulging, mouth-twisting, cheek-popping, and catcalling, which required a reprimand from Miss Jerram, although she also reprimanded me for leaving without permission. "Dawny, do you want to stand and tell us all what-all you was doing in the girls' outhouse?" That question set the Allies to guffawing and slapping their sides.

What to say? "Nome," I refused.

"What do you mean, 'nome,' anyhow?" Miss Jerram said. "I'm tellin ye to get on your feet and declare what you ran out after Gypsy for."

I stood. "She's one of us," I said. "Axis. We watch out for each other. It looked to me like she took sick or somethin."

"Are you sick, Gypsy?" Miss Jerram asked.

"I was, but I'm okay now, I reckon," Gypsy said.

Miss Jerram studied Gypsy for just a moment longer than was necessary, and I suspected she might have guessed the source of Gypsy's sickness: her heart. "It's a awful sad day for us all," Miss Jerram observed.

CHAPTER

9

WHEN THICK MARCH HAD NOT YET BEEN GIVEN A FAIR CHANCE to take off and bud and breathe, a pall fell upon Stay More, and with it the impossible rains. News traveled fast without any help from *The Stay Morning Star,* which I wanted to shut down, not only because everyone—except possibly the hermit Dan and his daughter—already knew that Mare Coe was dead, but also because I didn't know what I could possibly print about the tragedy. Anything coming from me would be juvenile, meddling, and futile: it couldn't have done anything to help the mood of the town. The shaggy mountains wanted to fluff with green; it was time for them to, but our dismal grief seemed to stun nature herself into dark, black, gray withdrawal. And then the impossible rains began.

What good were words, anyhow? I did not have, and could not get, an interview with Mare's main survivor, Gypsy, nor could I even reveal that she was his main survivor. Besides, in the midst of this gloom, during a thunderstorm, another rock came crashing through the window of the *Star* office, with another note tied to it: "Youl wish you had of staid in the girls privvy if we catch you." Whichever Ally had thrown it must have got awful wet for his pains. I told Latha I'd pay for a new piece of glass to put in the window (it wasn't a big plate glass window, just an eight-light sash with small panes), but I didn't show her the note.

Those rains, which may have started when Gypsy and I ran into the outhouse at the school, never let up but grew gradually harder in their intensity. Not even the oldest kids could recall ever having seen such rainfall; it lasted for days and days, as if—Gypsy said—the skies were going to have themselves a good long cry over Mare's death. Later all of that toad-strangling downpour seemed only a rehearsal for the day of the big storm.

The day of the big storm was a sound-and-sight show of such intensity that we feared the noise itself would wipe us from the face of the earth if the deluge of water failed to sweep us away. I got caught at Latha's store, where I was still trying halfheartedly to put together an issue of the *Star* that would say something about Mare's heroic death. The storm was so terrible that Latha decided we'd better make a dash for her fraid-hole.

Everybody else in Stay More took refuge in their fraid-holes. Each house in town had a storm cellar in the back yard, an excavation roofed over with boards or bricks or rocks or sod, depending on the builder or the sense of architectural aesthetics, and large enough to contain the whole family in the event of a tornado, an event which had never happened hereabouts. No one could remember when anybody had ever been afraid enough actually to use the fraid-holes before. In the back of our minds, we knew the fraid-holes could now be used in case the enemy, the real Nazis or Japs, ever flew their bombers over us and dropped bombs on us, but just as we had never seen a tornado we had never seen a bomber or any other kind of airplane. Thus the fraid-holes were strictly for insurance: contingencies, possibilities, peace of mind.

But into the bargain they provided storage space for the larder, the pantry: the fraid-holes were lined with shelves and shelves of each season's garden produce put up in glass Mason jars, as well as jams and jellies and preserves made from peaches and grapes and muscadines and strawberries and blackberries, as well as bins of Irish potatoes, sweet potatoes, apples, and such.

Latha'd had the presence of mind to snatch up a loaf of bread from her store shelves, and thus during our long stay in the fraid-hole waiting out the storm we had plenty of jelly sandwiches. She had also snatched up a parcel post package that she identified simply by saying, "It came today." When we had eaten the sandwiches and night was coming on, and she had reassured me that my Aunt Rosie probably assumed that I was safe and sound in this fraid-hole, just as Latha's husband Every Dill knew that she herself was probably here for the duration of the storm, I asked her what was in the parcel post package, and she just said, "Oh, it's just for when we get restless or bored."

I laughed and said, "Aw Latha, you know I'd never get restless or bored with *you!*"

She laughed too, and said, "In that case, I won't open it."

If there is either a quizzical or restless expression on your face, it may be because you are wondering why I have never before mentioned, in this story, my Aunt Rosie, with whom I lived. And I will never mention her again, if I can avoid it. Her house was just up the road a ways from Latha's store, and I spent as little time there as I possibly could. I won't even mention at all the man she was married to. The only thing to be said about Uncle Frank Murrison is that there were still rumors he had once upon a time been "carrying on" with our schoolteacher, Miss Jerram.

"Open it," I said to Latha. "This storm won't ever stop."

When Latha finally opened the package, slowly, not as if she were teasing me but as if she were opening a present and deliberately teasing herself, it contained a thing made of plastic, looking very modern, with some knobs and a dial on it, and a name, Philco. And there was a large thing—"battery," Latha said—which had to be put into it and attached to it. The importance of this moment was such that you may have decided to calm the thunder so that we could listen. Thank you. I may need to have you stop all the waterworks soon.

"What is it?" I asked. "And where'd you git it?"

"Sears Roebuck," she said. "It's a home radio."

Of course I had heard of radios, although I'd never seen one. I knew that in the cities, where they had electricity, everybody had one. There was no electricity in Newton County, but apparently you could make a radio operate with one of these big batteries.

Latha got it to working, and my mouth must have fallen open. There were human *voices* coming from it, and then some kind of strange music! And then a lot of noises that Latha said was "static." She played around with the knobs, turning the dial, and almost as if somebody was trying to tell her what to do, a guy said, "Ah! Ah! Ah! Don't touch that dial! Listen to Fibber McGee and Molly!" She quit touching the dial. Then for a whole half of an hour, a story took place involving this man called Fibber and his wife. If you listened carefully, it was a funny story, but it wasn't nearly as good a story as the ones Latha could tell, and I told her that, and she started crying. "No, really," I said. "I like your stories a lot better."

But if Latha was upset because the radio was going to be her competition at storytelling, I discovered that I was going to have some serious competition in the area of journalism. A program of world events came on, and there was instant news, right out of the man's mouth, as if somebody were putting it easily into your ear instead of making you try to read the words. My newspaper couldn't compete with that.

The biggest world event was about the firebombing of Tokyo, in which two hundred and seventy-nine B-29s dropped napalm all over the city, killing 140,000 people. Latha started crying over that too. "Women, children, and old folks," she said.

But even though I was a Jap, and could identify with Latha's pity and sorrow, I felt a kind of elation too, and I asked, "Won't it hurry up the end of the war?" And she had to admit that it would.

A loud pounding came on the storm cellar's thick wooden door, and, opening it and holding her lantern high, Latha discovered the Whitter family: the mother, Jim John, Tildy, and a littlun whose name I couldn't recall. Yes: it was Suke. All of them were wet as dogs.

"Our fraid-hole is a-fillin up with water!" Ora Belle Whitter cried to Latha. The Whitter place was just north of Latha's, but lower, closer to the creek, which must have begun overflowing its banks.

Latha invited them to share our fraid-hole, but Jim John, pointing at me, said "I aint a-gorn in thar, Maw! I din't know *he* was here."

"Boy, he aint got no disease I heared tell of," his mother said.

"He's a *Jap!*" Jim John said. "A *dirty* Jap."

Ora Belle Whitter snorted a laugh. "Stay out in the storm then!" she said to her son, and ushered the rest of her family into the shelter.

But Jim John relented, and, being sure that I had a full view of every mean face he knew how to make, he came on in. I whispered to Latha, "I don't want the Allies to know about our radio! Turn it off and cover it up." She smiled, either at the conspiracy of it or her amusement at my hostility toward the Allies. Or maybe she liked, as I did, my referring to "our" radio. Hers and mine, though I hadn't contributed a cent to its purchase. She put the radio back in its box before Jim John even got a good look at it.

Before long, there was another knock at the door, and there was the whole Alan family, who lived up above the Whitters but also along the creek, and their low-lying fraid-hole had also filled up with water. But we simply didn't have any room for them. Latha's storm cellar couldn't contain any more people. She suggested that they try the Coes: Lawlor and Dulcie Coe lived nearby, up on the hillside above the village, and all three of their triplets had gone into the service, one of them killed, leaving only Sammy, so their fraid-hole probably wasn't crowded. I was glad to see the Alans go. I might've been willing to share a fraid-hole with the despicable Jim John Whitter, but if Sog Alan had come into our fraid-hole I would've had to brave the storm and go elsewhere.

During the course of that night, the Duckworth family also showed up seeking shelter, and had to be turned away, sent along to the Coes. Their fraid-hole, they said, was completely under water, and the creek was lapping up against the front porch of their house.

It thus occurred to me, having seen in the space of a short time the three guys who'd broken my arm, that all of the Allies lived in the bottomlands of Stay More, while we Axis inhabited higher elevations. This set me to reflecting philosophically upon the fact that all of us Axis were not only outcasts but also upcasts, in the sense that all of our houses were up in the hills and on the ridges and in the mountains. The Allies were practically lowlanders! Or at least their domiciles were situated along the meadows in the floodplain of the creeks. What did this signify? That good people, that is, *us*, prefer elevations, while bad people, that is, *them*, would rather avoid the heights? No, probably all that it meant was that the better-off families of the town were those who owned the fertile fields along the watercourses, while the poor families had to content themselves with the rocky uplands. But it clearly revealed to my contemplative mind that there were actual geographical differences between Allies and Axis that I'd never even considered before.

Thus, when the sun actually appeared for the first time in a week, and I was able to wade to my little newspaper office, I began work on a special issue of the *Star* that would have *three* big stories on its front page. I'd never had that many before. The storm news, of course, and the fact that the village proper and all the roads were still under water. (It never occurred to me that I wouldn't be able to deliver the paper to many of the subscribers without a boat, and nobody in Stay More had a boat.) But the two other main stories on the front page, side by side, were GERALD COE DIES A HERO ON IWO JIMA ISLAND, and 140,000 PERISH IN TOKYO FIREBOMBING, the juxtaposition of the stories making it look as if all those Japanese were killed in retaliation for Mare's death. There wasn't much to say about either event apart from the bare facts, as I had heard the former from Doc Swain and the latter from Latha's radio, which, I realized, was going to keep the *Star* in business. Latha let me listen to her radio anytime I wanted to, although she said, "If that battery wears out, you may have to find me another one." She herself decided to tell no one else about "our" radio. "We don't want everybody and his neighbor down here listening to Fibber McGee." From what I'd heard on the radio, I knew the war in Europe was practically finished. I drew a map of Germany for a page of the *Star*, fanciful but fairly accurate, showing big arrows moving like pincers across Germany, closing in on Berlin. The war Over There was so close to being settled that my model and champion, Ernie Pyle, had already been removed from that theater of operations and was even now heading out onto those Pacific islands like Okinawa, the same kind of places where Mare and thousands of other American boys had been killed. "It don't look to me," Willard observed, when I gave him an advance copy of that issue of the *Star*, "like the war will last long enough for me to get drafted."

I didn't need a boat. By the time I had hand-lettered the text of all the stories and got the paper "put to bed" on my little gelatin press, the waters began to recede, revealing that not only all the low-lying fraid-holes had filled up with mud but also all the foxholes of the Axis. We called a meeting at our headquarters in the back room of the old Ingledew store in order to plan the laborious task of re-digging the fox-holes. Willard suggested that a more worthy expenditure of our energy might be to volunteer to help the Allies clean the mud out of their fraid-holes. The Allies' mothers had shackled all of the Allies with the big job of removing mud from the thousands of Mason jars of food, and shoveling mud from the floors of the fraid-holes. So we took a vote: five of us wanted to get the foxholes rebuilt; seven of us (I voted with Willard) wanted to help the Allies clean their stinking fraid-holes.

We had to invade them in order to do it. The Allies didn't want us, at first. We made a whole exciting new war game out of pretending that the Allied fraid-holes were bunkers and pillboxes, and we combined the work of "liberating" the fraid-holes from their mud with the play of make-believe assault. Since so many of the stored apples, sweet pota-toes, and suchlike had been ruined in the mud, they became hand grenades that the Allies tossed at us, and we, without knowing it, dupli-cated Mare's fantastic deeds on Iwo Jima.

All of this work and play in constant proximity to the Allies had an effect on Sammy Coe. Or maybe his experience of the night the Coe's fraid-hole had sheltered the two Allied leaders, Sog and Larry, with their families, had made him begin fraternizing with the enemy. What-ever the case, one day Sammy, who had emulated his big brother Mare in being a fierce Jap, announced that he didn't want to be a Jap anymore. "I'm gonna jine th'other side," he declared, defiantly. That was un-heard-of. Nobody ever switched sides. Being Allies or Axis wasn't a matter of choice, like being Republican or Democrat. It was more like being Baptist or Methodist: you didn't choose your religion, you were born with it, not that any of us Axis were born Jap or Nazi, but we were born outcasts, born as members of the you-group as opposed to the lordly we-group.

My recent theory or observation that the Allies were bottomlanders while the Axis were uplanders didn't apply very well to the Coes. They were in-between, the Coe house neither up the hill nor down in the dell, and thus the founders of both the Allies and the Axis, Earl and Gerald, had been Coes, and now Sammy wanted to switch.

We argued with Sammy, of course, trying to get him to see that there wasn't any connection between our Japs and the Japs who had killed his brother. We also tried to get him to understand that the Allies probably wouldn't be willing to accept him as a "convert" to their junta of the chosen. But Sammy's mind was made up. "Any of you fellers tries to stop me," he threatened, "will git knocked on your head." One day he was seen climbing the wood rungs that made a ladder up the tall sycamore tree that led to the Allies' aerial fortress. Since he was alone, they did not repulse his ascent. He entered into the house where Noah Ingledew had lived a century before, high up there in the twisting branches. The next school day, he requested of Miss Jerram permission to move from the desk he shared with Gypsy to sit at a vacant desk on the Allied side of the aisle.

One night we were sitting around in our headquarters grumbling about having lost the superiority we'd thought we'd gained over the Allies, and the distinct possibility that Sammy could reveal all of our military secrets to the enemy. If not that, there was the distinct possibility that, now the mud had dried in our baseball field and we could commence a new season of ball games, Sammy, who had been our able shortstop, would be playing for the Allies. With his help in the field and at the plate, they could beat us badly. Ella Jean could play shortstop but she simply wasn't a hitter.

These lamentations were interrupted by a knock at the door: it was the code knock, four shorts and a long. We counted heads: there was nobody missing. Who could be out there? Maybe, we thought, the secret code knock had been given away to the enemy by Sammy, and the enemy was outside the door, ready to attack our headquarters! "Don't open that yet!" Willard said, and he went to the door and asked, "Who's there?" A voice answered "Sammy" but it wasn't like his voice; too high and shaky. "Are ye alone?" Willard asked.

"Yeah, please let me in," said the voice that didn't sound like Sammy's.

"If it's all of 'em," Joe Don said to Willard, "we'll fight 'em man for man!"

We opened the door. It was only Sammy. We couldn't let him in, because he was the enemy. He stood there in the doorway, whining, "Lookee at what they done to me," and he pulled up his shirt to reveal the red welts on his chest: he had been branded. He told us what had happened. In an initiation ceremony, solemnizing his rite of passage into the Allies, because he had been a part of the enemy for years, he had been required to sit still while they took a nail, embedded in a long stick and held in the fire until it was glowing hot, and made three small marks in the skin of his chest in the form of the letter A.

"What's the A stand for?" Willard asked Sammy.

"'Allies,' of course," Sammy declared.

"Why, them Allies aint got the sense to pound sand in a rat hole!" Willard observed. "They couldn't find their way to first base if there was signs all along the way." He looked around at the rest of us to see if we also understood his estimate of the Allies' stupidity, but, I'm ashamed to say, we were rather slow in getting it. "Hell's bells," Willard demanded of us, "caint you'uns think of anything else that A could stand for?"

"Arkansawyer?" I offered. Others suggested a variety of possibilities: "Angel?" "Adolescent?" "Asswipe?" and such.

"Lord have mercy," Willard said in disgust.

It was Gypsy who offered "Axis?" and then the rest of us were saying, "Yeah!" and "That's it!" and "She got it!"

Ella Jean was the only one who was mindful of poor Sammy's condition. She touched him gently on his chest near the burns and asked, "Does it hurt real bad? Maybe you ought to have Doc Swain look at that."

Sammy shook his head twice. Whatever pain he was still feeling was eased by Ella Jean's touch and her solicitude. I would have gladly endured a branding like that to get her finger on my chest. Even though Sammy and I—same age, same size—had been rivals more than friends all our lives, I felt genuine compassion for him.

"Aint you told your folks?" Ella Jean asked.

"Heck *naw*," Sammy said. "Paw would butcher 'em."

"They need to be butchered," I declared.

"But we don't want nobody's folks involved in this," Willard said, reminding us of the long-standing policy that neither Allies nor Axis would ever inform any of the town's adults—except possibly Miss Jerram—of any of our activities. Willard declared, "If the Allies ever get butchered, we'll do it ourselfs."

"Then let's do it!" I said, and had the rare satisfaction of hearing all the others second the motion.

CHAPTER
. . . .
10

WHEN SAMMY HAD ANSWERED ALL OUR QUESTIONS (E.G., WHICH one of the Allies had actually applied the branding tool? Sog Alan), the business of the meeting focused upon Sammy's request to be permitted to return to the fold, to forswear his defection to the enemy, renounce his apostasy, and become an Axis again. "I'll be *both* a Jap and a Nazi if you'll let me come back," he offered.

After discussion, Willard suggested, "I got a better idea. Instead of you pullin out of the Allies, you could still pretend to be Allies but be a . . . one of them . . . Dawny, what do ye call them fellers?"

"Double agent," I offered.

"Yeah," Willard said. "You could be a double agent, and find out for us all their plans and secrets, and that way we'd always beat 'em." Our night meetings were illuminated only by the light of a single-wick kerosene lantern, and in the light of that lantern Sammy's face—all our faces—took on expressions of wicked anticipation. Willard concluded, "If they're so dumb they don't know that mark on ye could stand for us as well as them, you won't have no problem."

Thereafter, to our pleasure, and to the gradual erosion of the power of the Allies, Sammy pretended to be a steadfast member of the enemy and even ingratiated himself to the inner circle of tyrants—Sog, Larry, and Jim John—to the extent that he became not just an Ally but a member of their inner council. His undercover activities were subtle: in baseball games it looked like an honest error when he allowed a ball to miss his glove and score an Axis run or when he looked at a called third strike that just edged the plate and put him out. In trench warfare, the Allies could not understand how we knew beforehand their troop movements, or why none of their sneak invasions were truly sneaky.

The Allies, it goes almost without saying, were foul-minded and immoral. "Let me tell y'uns some of the *real* nasties," Sammy said to us, and reported on various of the debaucheries that went on in the tree house, principally involving Betty June Alan, who was rather wayward and no better than she should be, even with her own brother, Sog. But all of the Allied girls, apparently, were required to participate in acts that Sammy had the decency not to describe in the presence of our good Axis girls. Learning all these things about the Allies' private goings-on didn't give us any advantage over them except a chance to feel morally superior to them. Certainly we had our own appreciation of risqué humor and the usual sexual braggadocio as only the inexperienced can spout it, but we never *did* anything.

Sammy's greatest performance of double-agentry was when he learned of the Allies' plan to abduct our Gypsy. It was a daring scheme hatched privately by Larry and Sog, and Sammy just happened to have been in the second of the two pens of the double tree house, and eavesdropped on Larry and Sog talking in the other pen. The essence of their conversation had been that they had become jaded with the charms of their Allied girls. Perhaps Betty June Alan was too readily available and had lost her mystique. They decided that capturing the prettiest of the Axis girls would not only be a coup for the Allies but would afford them some "fresh meat," as Sog had been heard to express it.

Gypsy had developed such a fondness for Old Jarhead, the mule that Willard had mysteriously provided for the Dingletoons, that she had taken to using it as a riding animal whenever she went to visit her friend Ella Jean or even to "pick her up" for a ride to school. Not that any of us needed riding animals to get from one place to another; everything in Stay More, even the outlying hollers and districts, was within reasonable walking distance. Nobody had to walk as far as I did when I was on my rounds delivering the *Star* or collecting news for it, but everybody did a lot of walking. Gypsy wasn't lazy by any means. She just grew so fond of Old Jarhead that she liked to ride the mule, bareback, no bridle, up the steep trail that was a shortcut between the Dingletoon place and the Dinsmore place, and there Ella Jean would climb up behind her and the two girls would ride Old Jarhead to school. Miss Jerram had a strict rule: *no mule at school,* but Gypsy would tether it out of sight along the bank of Swains Creek.

Gypsy was still in mourning for Mare, of course; she still would be, for months or even years or even forever. Nobody but Ella Jean and I knew that she was. She did her best to conceal her occasional crying spells. Willard Dinsmore was crazy about her, but a bit too shy to let her know. He was always polite and pleasant to her and doing little things for her, but he assumed that such a pretty girl wouldn't be interested in a scrawny bespectacled plain and homely guy like him—not knowing that her only lover, Mare, had been even plainer and more homely. It was all I could do, sometimes, to keep myself from taking Willard aside and telling him the true facts of the matter in order to give him a goad to pursue his infatuation with her.

Sog Alan and Larry Duckworth planned to waylay Gypsy on the trail up to the Dinsmore house, before she was within earshot of the house in case she hollered. Sammy heard them talking about just how they'd do it: Sog would pull her off the mule, Larry would stuff a gag into her mouth, they'd tie her up with rope, leaving her legs untied, and make her walk off through the woods to the bluffs that rise above Banty

Creek, low bluffs with ledges leading into caverns where the ancient Bluff Dwellers had made shelters.

Sammy reported the conversation between Larry and Sog, when Larry had wondered aloud, "But then what? How long d'ye aim to keep her in the cave?"

"As long as we wanter," Sog had said. "Until we caint think of nothin else to do with her."

"And then what? Just let her go? She'd be sure to tell on us."

Sog had pondered this, as if it hadn't occurred to him. "Maybe she'd like us so much by then," he had boastfully suggested, "that she wouldn't want to tell nobody."

"What if she hates us instead?"

"Then I reckon we'd just have to do away with her."

"You mean *kill* her? That'd bother some folks."

"Naw, wouldn't nobody miss her."

But Willard, you can be sure, when he heard Sammy's tale, was one person who would miss her. He was furious, and I thought he would lose his self-control and reveal to the others his true feelings for her. He had to take a while to calm himself down and plan a course of action.

First he had to make sure that Sammy had done his listening in secret, without any detection from the conspirators. He didn't want to get Sammy into trouble if they knew who had tipped us off. Then he had to decide whether or not to tell Gypsy, and he decided not to tell her—not because he was too shy to talk to her, but because if he told her, she might not want to go through with our plan to foil the abduction. We kept the whole operation a secret from all except the inner council of the Axis: Willard, Joe Don, Sammy, and myself. We were each armed with a cane spear, and of course I had my slingshot. In view of the enormity of the crime we were going to foil, it would have been nice if we'd had firearms, but all such had disappeared in the War Effort Scrap Drive, even our trusty BB guns. We had a complete arsenal of wooden rifles, wooden pistols, wooden machine guns, wooden mortars, wooden flamethrowers, wooden bazookas, wooden bowie knives, wooden bayonets, and even a wooden howitzer, but while all of these were essential to our warfare with the Allies, they wouldn't do any harm in a "real" situation. I did, however, prepare myself for the mission by filling my overall pockets with some good smooth stones for my slingshot. I was never allowed to use actual stones in my slingshot during our battles with the Allies, but had to content myself with stale biscuits, various berries, or peanuts.

Sammy could not find out for us just what particular morning the conspirators were planning to kidnap Gypsy. All we knew was that it would be a school morning. Willard recruited one of the Axis littluns, his kid brother Jim George, only seven but fleet of foot, to begin hiding out at the foot of the trail as it turns up the mountain from the Butter-churn Holler road. Willard himself would be concealed at the top of the trail, Joe Don and me spread out along the middle of the trail at strategic intervals. Whichever one of us caught sight or wind of the Allied captors would alert the others by the whistle of the bobwhite, which we practiced in advance to make sure that even Jim George knew how to pucker and whistle it. I had been hearing the same notes on Latha's radio as part of a commercial for a soap, "Rinso White, Rinso Bright, Happy Little Washday Song." Of course there actually were a good many bobwhites (*Colinus virginianus*, or quail) in our purlieus, so we hoped that no real bobwhite would be a-calling at the time we had to broadcast the signal. I hoped that I would have the privilege of being the first to use it.

Day after day we staked out that trail early in the morning before school, and had whatever fun there was in watching Gypsy atop Old Jarhead climbing the trail each morning on her way to pick up Ella Jean. We began to wonder—or Willard and I exchanged speculations—that Sammy might have either got his facts wrong or had made up the whole thing as some kind of hoax or even—dared we say it? Sammy might have been doubling back in his double-agentry, and was concocting the whole thing as part of an Allied plot.

Joe Don told us that Gypsy might soon have to stop riding Old Jarhead, because the Dingletoons would need the mule to do their spring plowing, a job that would fall mostly to Joe Don and leave the poor old mule too tired to furnish transportation for Gypsy and Ella Jean. We were just about ready to give up the vigil when, one morning, the bobwhite whistle came from the post of Joe Don himself, and we gathered up our spears and sneaked to his post, where he announced, pointing, "Sog and them are a-hiding right down yonder."

"Let's get 'em!" I said, excited.

"No," said Willard. "We have to catch 'em in the act. We caint just take for granted they're gonna do it." He turned to his kid brother Jim George and asked, "Did ye see her yet?"

"Yep, she's on her way."

We got as close as we could to the Allies' ambush, and waited. We could see Sog and Larry hiding behind trees alongside the trail, Larry holding some rope and some cloth to gag her with.

She came into view, lazily perched on the slow mule. Gypsy was one beautiful girl, and the way her dress was hiked up her legs as she sat astride that old mule made her an easy temptation to a couple of lechers like Sog and Larry. They saw her and we could almost detect their evil drooling and panting.

We waited. Willard was going to give us the signal, and we couldn't move until he did.

Sog and Larry jumped. Sog reached up and pulled Gypsy off of Old Jarhead, and Larry hit the mule with his rope to make the mule take off. But Old Jarhead just stayed there, wondering what was going on. Gypsy began cursing, and I was surprised she knew some of those words. I had a good rock in my slingshot, but Sog was holding Gypsy tight while Larry cut off her cursing by stuffing the rag in her mouth, and I could-n't get a clear shot at either of them without hitting her. Half a dozen other Allies came out of the woods, armed with cane spears, but I was too busy to notice just who they were . . . except Sammy.

Willard made his signal, then sprang for Sog and pulled him away from Gypsy and threw him to the ground. Joe Don hit Larry on the face with one hand while plucking the gag from his sister's mouth with the other. Then he hit Larry again, hard enough to knock him down. "Git Old Jarhead and git gone!" he said to Gypsy. She tried to climb back on the mule, but Sog shoved Willard down, and grabbed her. Willard got to his feet and pulled Sog away from Gypsy and wrestled him to the ground.

The other Allies rushed us, and even Sammy made a show of being on their side, and gave me a harmless poke with his spear, and grabbed for my slingshot. I remembered all the times when as much younger kids he and I used to throw rocks at each other. We were never friends. So I hit him on the shoulder with a mighty swing, pulling my punch at the last instant, the way I'd seen actors do in Western movie barroom brawls. I wasn't a fighter, anyway, not for real, at least: in the play-like battles of the trenches and foxholes I could sham an affray with the best of them, but, as befits a newspaperman preferring the power of the pen over the sword, I didn't have much experience with real fighting.

The Axis were outnumbered. While Willard was holding his own against the older and bigger and tougher Sog, and Joe Don was having little trouble with Larry, the Axis couldn't handle those man-to-man combats when they had a bunch of Allies surrounding them with jabbing spears. Willard could only swat at the spears with one hand while trying to hit Sog with the other, and it wasn't good enough: Sog knocked him down repeatedly. One of the Allies actually punctured Joe Don's arm with a spear, and it was bleeding, and Larry was getting the best of him.

Two of the Allies were holding me on the ground while Sammy pretended to kick me. I lay there as if I were witnessing the whole thing from a distance, imagining a description of it in a news item for the *Star:* ALLIES FOILED IN KIDNAP PLOT BUT WIN FIGHT WITH AXIS. Gypsy had not succeeded in remounting Old Jarhead but was instead joining the fight herself, slapping any Ally who came within reach of her roundhouse palm. Four Allies had to use their spears from the four directions of the compass to keep her at bay long enough for Larry, who had conked her brother cold with a rock, to stuff the gag back in her mouth and tie her up.

Willard had lost his glasses and couldn't see too well without them, and got his face in the way of a haymaker swing from Sog, which knocked him out. Little Jim George and I remained the only Axis still conscious. "Git help!" I urged him, and he took off up the trail, but two Allies ran him down.

It was all over for us, and for poor Gypsy, who was now bound and gagged and about to be taken off to some cave and subjected to unspeakable molestations.

"Leave her alone!" I said from my horizontal position on the ground.

Sog took time out from his preparations for departure to step over and kick me in the face. It hurt like hell, and I think his toenail gouged my cheek. "Hey Ernie," he said to me, "didn't that broken arm not learn you *nothing?*"

He drew back his foot to give me another, more vicious kick. The proverbial stars exploded in the blackness of my skull.

CHAPTER
11

WHEN I CAME TO, I WAS STARING UP AT GYPSY'S PRETTY FACE. She was no longer bound and gagged, and she was smiling at me. She was holding the reins to her mule, who was beside her. Joe Don and Willard were also sitting up, staring at her while they slowly got their bearings back. She waited patiently while the three of us regained consciousness, but it was clear she was bursting to tell us something. "The marveloustest thing happened!" she said. And finally she told us the story.

When the three of us had been rendered unconscious by the goons, who had then started off with their prize, Gypsy, a rifle had fired. Gypsy hadn't known what it was at first, because it had been a long,

long time since any of us had heard the sound of a rifle. But it had sounded right nearby, and then the owner of the rifle had appeared, standing in the trail with his feet planted as if he dared anybody to get past him, looming like some giant above mere mortals and mischievous kids, his long beard making him look like one of the Greek gods if not Zeus himself. Gypsy had recognized him from her brother Joe Don's descriptions: he was a certain privacy-preferring old man known to the Allies as a Nazi spy.

"Howdy, boys," he had said pleasantly to all of them, and had added, glancing at Gypsy, "and you too, young lady." He had continued to stare at her, and at her friends flat out on the ground, including one, her brother, who was his friend also. He had continued speaking to Gypsy, "I don't reckon ye could answer me with that rag in your mouth."

He had pointed the Winchester at Larry and had said, politely, "Kindly take the rag out of her mouth, and undo those ropes."

When the gag had been removed from Gypsy's mouth, and Larry had been untying her, ole Dan had asked her, "Are you okay? Have ye been harmed any?" She had nodded her head to the first question and had shaken it to the second.

The old man had tickled Sog under the chin with the barrel end of the Winchester. "*You,*" he had said. "I reckon you're the one started this whole mess, aren't ye?" Sog had glowered at the old man but had said nothing. "I asked ye a question, boy," Dan had told him, and had traced his Adam's apple with the tip of the rifle.

"Yeah," Sog had said proudly, "I started it."

"You're the same one," Dan had observed, "who's always snooping around my place, because you think I'm a Nazi spy. Aren't ye the one?"

"That's right," Sog had said. "That's me."

"You've invaded my privacy," Dan had said. "And my daughter's privacy. Do you know, I could easily have shot you? If you weren't careful, you could discover a bullet hole right there between your bushy eyebrows, and wonder how ye got it. So I'll tell ye here and now: I have done had enough of you! I don't want any more of you! Get gone and don't let me see ye again."

Sog had sullenly taken off, and his Allies had gone with him. And ole

Dan had waited just long enough to see that the three of us were beginning to revive before he had bid her good day and disappeared himself.

When Gypsy finished telling this, I exclaimed, "It sure is great to have him on our side!"

"He aint on our side," Joe Don corrected me. "He just aint got no use for no foolishness, no matter which side it comes from."

Willard said, "Well, they'll think twice before they try a stunt like that again."

The Allies began to behave themselves, comparatively. At school that day Miss Jerram could not help noticing that all of us were dirty, scuffed, and disheveled, and that those of us on the Axis side of the aisle seemed to have gotten the worst of it. "Have you Armies been fighting again?" she asked.

"Yes'm," Jim John Whitter admitted. "And we won, this time!"

"That's a lie," I yelled at him. "You *lost*, on account of—"

"Hush, Dawny," Willard commanded me.

But the Allies smugly refused to accept the notion that the Battle of Dinsmore Trail, as we came to call it, had been an Allied rout. Just as other battles of ours had been inconclusive owing to forces beyond our control—baseball games had been rained out, or a crucial engagement in the trenches had been interrupted by mothers calling their children to do chores or to eat supper—the Battle of Dinsmore Trail had been suspended by divine intervention in the form of a Zeus-like god who sided with the Athenians against the Trojans. The Allies believed—and rightly so—that they had already won the battle until he came along.

But the Battle of Dinsmore Trail had differed from all our other battles in that the stakes were much higher, the spoils of war more serious. The only spoils of a ball game is the final score. The only spoils of trench warfare is a bit of territory that is given back sooner or later. But the spoils of Dinsmore Trail was the living, breathing, lovely body of a girl, who was spared from untold assault of a lascivious nature. Thus, the divine intervention was not only necessary but morally right.

Satisfied that they'd won the battle if not the outcome, the Allies behaved themselves only long enough to permit some very important things to happen outside our control, outside our world, things that would change our own little lives—or at least mine—forever. The first of these was revealed to us when Latha came into the office of the *Star* late one Thursday afternoon, carrying her radio, which was running, and said, "Dawny, listen here to the radio! The president is dead!"

"Which president?" I asked.

"Of our country," she said. "President Roosevelt died."

She fiddled with the dial, and picked up a station, but all of the stations were announcing the same thing: Franklin Delano Roosevelt, aged sixty-three, had died of a cerebral hemorrhage at Warm Springs, Georgia, while sitting to have his portrait painted. Harry Truman of Missouri was going to be sworn in as the new president.

"What's a cerebral hemorrhage?" I asked Latha.

"I think it's where your brain just bursts from all the blood in it," she said.

"And it *killed* him?" I asked incredulously, not willing to accept the fact that our president no longer existed.

"He's dead," she said.

Time stopped. Somehow it seemed as if this was the end of the world. I would learn that most other people felt the same way, but for me, who never had a father nor a grandfather, at least not worth mentioning, it seemed a personal loss beyond measure. THE PRESIDENT. He was the president when I was born and I was nearly twelve years old and expected him always to be president. I started crying, which I rarely did. I looked at Latha, and she was crying too, and then she reached out her arms and held me, and we both had a good long cry.

Upset as I was, I wanted to just take off running across the hills until I found a place where nobody ever died anymore. But I had the presence of mind to remember my duty: as a newspaperman, I had to bring out an Extra. *The Stay Morning Star* had never had an Extra before, not even when Mare died. But here it was late Thursday afternoon, and the next issue not due until Monday morning. Latha wanted to rush out and spread the news, but I asked her kindly to give me a chance to get my Extra out first, and I went right to work on that hectograph, penciling the magic purple master copy as fast as I could, with a headline that covered practically the whole front of the page: F.D.R. NO MORE. On the back side of the page I transcribed all of the meager facts that the radio was offering about the circumstances of his death, and I even in-

cluded an editorial, "Much as we like our neighbor Harry Truman, we
don't see how he or anybody else could possibly know how to be president." Then at the top of the first page I wrote "*1¢*" and drew a circle
around it, and put the pages to bed in the gelatin, quickly printing fifty
copies. I gave some to Latha to sell to anybody who came in the store,
and then I said, "Go ahead and tell whoever you want."

"We ought to ring the school bell," she suggested. I looked at her as
if she'd suggested we ought to fly to the moon. Nobody ever rang the
school bell, certainly not for school. We knew there was an old bell up
there in the little wooden cupola atop the ridge-pole of the schoolhouse,
but I couldn't remember ever having heard it ring. "If we ring the bell,"
Latha offered, "everybody will come a-running, and you can sell the
paper like hotcakes."

"I never sold hotcakes," I said. But she had a great idea, and we put
it into effect. Without even stopping to ask Miss Jerram's permission
(she probably wouldn't have granted it), we went into the foyer of the
schoolhouse and I climbed the crude ladder nailed into the wall that led
to the bell's cupola, where an old rope was coiled. Latha explained that
the rope used to be hanging down so you could just reach out and pull
it to ring the bell, but the rope hadn't been needed for years so it was
stored away up there. I got it and pulled it, and Latha helped pull it, and
sure enough that old bell commenced a-pealing, crashing these big
round gongs that sounded like "BOMB!" and "DOOM!" depending on
whether the clapper was hitting one side or the other as the bell swung
from the rope's tug.

As Latha had predicted, people came running, starting with Miss
Jerram, from just across the road. "Dawny!" she hollered. "That bell
don't *never* ring!"

I held out a paper. "Extra!" I hollered back at her. "Extra! Read all
about it!" She took one of the sheets, and I added, "One cent only."

"Do ye want me to have to run back over to the house to get a penny,
or can you just extend my credit until the next time I see ye?" She took
a look at the paper's oversized headline, and asked Latha, as if she didn't
trust me, "Is this *true?*" and when Latha nodded, Miss Jerram burst
into tears.

Other people were running up to see why the bell had been ringing, and I was collecting pennies right and left. All in all, I made twenty-eight cents that day, probably the most I'd ever earned in one day in my life, and I was beginning to believe that I was destined truly to follow in the footsteps of Ernie Pyle.

Miss Jerram canceled school for one day in Roosevelt's memory. She had never missed a day of school before. Since that day was Friday, we didn't meet again until Monday. It was a long weekend. Folks wanted to know how I had picked up the news of the president's death so quickly, and while I refused to tell, Latha finally admitted to Doc Swain that she had a radio. Naturally she offered to let him listen to it, as her husband Every Dill was already doing, and their daughter Sonora, whose husband Captain Hank Ingledew was in the Pacific, and Sonora's friends Doris and Jelena Dinsmore, whose husband Billy Bob Ingledew was fighting in Germany . . . and before long there was a huge crowd at Latha's store wanting to hear the radio and listening not only to all the follow-ups and tributes on the death of FDR but also to the symphonic music and, after a while, the return to regular programming, with *Let's Pretend* and *Grand Central Station* and *Meet Corliss Archer*, and even all of those endless commercials for Rinso and Lucky Strike and Wheaties. I realized the radio could very easily put my newspaper out of business, and I was sorry that the rest of the town knew that Latha had a radio and was willing to share the sounds coming from it.

But she had to impose restrictions. When folks started trying to hear shows by Jack Benny or Edgar Bergen that went on past her usual hour for shutting up the store, she told me to post in the next issue of the *Star* an announcement to the effect that the radio would be available for listening only for two hours before and after the usual time that the mail truck came in the morning and the mail was put up in the boxes. Even so, for four hours a day people crowded into the store to listen, and while they were there they often bought something from the store, particularly soda pop and candy when it was on some rare occasion available, and Latha realized the radio was good for business. Her restrictions didn't apply to me: if I wanted to hear *Captain Midnight* or *Hop Harrigan* or *Terry and the Pirates* after the regular listening hours, she would let me, and I gladly donated the twenty-eight cents I'd earned from that Extra to the cost of helping replace her radio's battery. Some of the other listeners chipped in also, and we began buying her a new battery pretty often.

Latha opened the store every morning (except Sundays) at six-thirty, as she had been doing ever since she'd bought the store from Bob Cluley back in 1932. Since the mail truck came about ten o'clock, she would-n't turn on her radio before eight for the benefit of any customers, and by then I was usually in school. But the Wednesday morning after the president's tragic end, as I was on my way to school Latha came out on the store porch and said "Dawny" and beckoned to me. I climbed the porch. "Come inside," she said, and held the door open for me. There weren't any customers in the store yet; it was too early for the radio to go on. But the radio was on. "Sit down," she said. I sat on one of the straight-backed chairs that were scattered here and there around the store. "I was listening to the news a while ago," she said. "You know, sometimes before I unlock the store of a morning, I catch the six o'-clock news." She paused, took a deep breath, and I waited. "I don't know how to tell you this, Dawny. If it breaks your heart, I'm going to hate myself for having to be the one who told you."

"Please tell me, whatever it is," I said. "I can take it."

"Not this," she said, shaking her head sadly. "This is going to keep you out of school. This is going to lay you lower than I've ever known you to be."

"Am I going to have to bring out another Extra?" I asked, wondering what it could be. Had Harry Truman died too? Or been assassinated?

She smiled wanly and said, "Maybe you'll want to, if you can."

"Well, I'm a newspaperman. I'm brave. Like Ernie Pyle, I can put up with anything."

Latha sobbed. She buried her face in her hands, and when she could finally raise her blurry eyes to me, she said, quietly, "That's it. Ernie Pyle has been killed. On some island in the Pacific. The Japanese shot him."

"Don't tease me, Latha," I said sternly.

"Oh, Dawny," she said. "I wouldn't tease you." And she began fid-dling with the radio, trying to find a station that might be broadcasting news. But unlike the day Roosevelt died, the stations apparently didn't feel that Ernie Pyle's death was worth constant announcement.

I was too stunned to have any immediate feeling at all. I had no feeling whatsoever. My mind couldn't even manufacture some disbelief. I waited while Latha changed the dial from one station to another. There weren't very many stations that could be picked up during the daytime. It was better at night. "Did they say if they checked his dogtags to be sure it was him?" I asked. She shook her head. "Did they say if he had any last words or anything?" I asked. She shook her head. "Did they say what the soldiers thought about it?" I asked.

"No, they just told what happened," she said.

"Did they get the Jap who did it?" I asked.

"They didn't say," she said, fiddling with the dial.

Soon it was eight o'clock and people were wanting to get into the store to hear their favorite morning shows on the radio. Latha did something I'd never known her to do before during store hours: she turned the OPEN/CLOSED sign so that CLOSED was facing the world. People stood outside looking through the windows, and some of them knocked on the door, but Latha wouldn't open it.

Finally, during the commercial break of some show, an announcer said, "This news bulletin came from Blue Network Correspondent Jack Hooley broadcasting from Ie Shima, four miles west of Okinawa, where at ten-fifteen A.M.—or last night U.S. time—Ernie Pyle, America's greatest frontline war reporter, was killed by Jap machine-gun fire.

"Pyle was riding in a jeep with Colonel Joseph Coolidge of Arkansas, commanding officer, when a burst of fire sent them scrambling out of their jeep into a roadside ditch. After a few minutes they peered over the edge of the ditch, and the Jap machine gunner, concealed on a ridge, opened fire again. Colonel Coolidge ducked back to find Pyle dead beside him, shot three times through the temple. 'He never knew what hit him,'" Coolidge said.

I yelled at the radio, *"Did they git the Jap?"*

"Just before Pyle had left to join the invasion of Ie Shima, he had told another correspondent that he didn't want to go. But he said the GIs didn't want to be there either, and that he was going along until the shooting was finished.

"Admiral Nimitz called him 'one of the greatest heroes of the war,' although Pyle never fired a shot. This message just in from the White House: President Truman said, 'The nation is quickly saddened again by the death of Ernie Pyle . . . '"

I demanded of President Truman, *"But did they kill the Jap that shot him?"* And I began crying in frustration that I did not know. I would never know. For the first time, I was greatly ashamed to be a Jap. I didn't want to be Jap any more. I didn't want to be anything, I didn't want to ship out across the Pacific and take Ernie Pyle's place on the front lines. I didn't want to run a newspaper. But it was as if two ghosts were returning from the dead to give me orders: Mare telling me that I had to be Jap for his sake, and Ernie telling me that I had to keep on putting out the newspaper for his sake.

"Thank you," I said to Latha. "You might as well open the store." And I went into my newspaper office and cleaned my hectograph and took my magic purple pencil and began hand-lettering another Extra. Out of respect for the late president, the letters of the headline weren't nearly as large, but still they took up a good deal of the front page: ERNIE PYLE IS KILLED. My editorial was tearstained and blurry, but legible: "He died as he lived, with his boots on, in the front lines. Soldiers everywhere lost a buddy. Young newspapermen everywhere lost their finest ideal." In the news story itself I further editorialized: "We should be proud that the person with him when he died, the last person he saw on this earth, was an Arkansawyer, Colonel Joseph Coolidge of Helena, commander of the 77th Infantry Division."

Before I put the Extra to bed, another bulletin came in on the radio and Latha summoned me to listen to a transcription of an interview with Colonel Coolidge describing Ernie's last moments. The Arkansawyer felt that the Jap sniper might have detected a glint from the antenna of the colonel's radio and assumed this meant a commanding officer, and thus opened fire at the jeep after letting other vehicles pass. Colonel Coolidge reported that after they had ducked into their ditch, Ernie had raised his head and smiled and asked, "Are you all right?" The Jap fired again, and those were Ernie's last words, directed to an officer near him but symbolically meant for me.

For the rest of my life, I would hear Ernie Pyle occasionally asking me, "Are you all right?"

I didn't need Latha to go with me to ring the bell. School was still in session when I got there, and I was tempted to explain to Miss Jerram why I was absent, but I just went ahead and started ringing the bell. Miss Jerram was at the head of the pupils as they all rushed into the foyer to see who was doing it, and Miss Jerram hollered, "You again, Dawny! Now who's the Extra for?"

I gave her a copy, and then, since I wasn't going to give away Extras that were worth one cent each, I announced to all my classmates, "Anybody got a penny? Here's another Extra." But nobody had a penny on them. So I let them have one copy free, suggesting, "Pass it around."

"Dawny," Miss Jerram said sternly, "you can't just go a-ringing the bell anytime you take a notion. This Pyle feller may not be as big a man to the rest of us as he was to you."

"What do you know?" I demanded of her. "Just what in hell do *you* know?"

"You go stand in the corner!" she commanded me. "You caint talk to me like that!" She held out a long finger pointing to a corner of the schoolroom.

But the first customers summoned by the bell were arriving in the schoolyard, and I ignored her in order to peddle the Extra to them. They were, I was disappointed to discover, disappointed. The ones who paid a penny demanded their money back after finding out the reason for the Extra. Others had to know the reason for the Extra before making payment, and then refused to pay. Later I discovered that the dozen copies I'd left for Latha to sell in the store remained unsold. All told, only four copies of my second Extra were eventually purchased, not enough to pay for the paper it was printed on.

I don't know which made me feel worse, Ernie Pyle's death or the fact that nobody cared. It was hard for me to distinguish the two reasons for feeling miserable. I didn't go back to school for the rest of the week. Latha didn't mind me hanging around the store, and she even gave me a few chores to keep my mind and hands busy, but no doubt she was getting tired of the sight of me moping around all over the place.

Two days after the Jap killed Ernie, although it wasn't on the radio and we wouldn't know about it for another week or so, William Robert

Ingledew was killed in the siege of Berlin. Billy Bob was Hank's kid brother, a carpenter by trade, who was the husband of either Jelena or Doris Dinsmore, Ella Jean's and Willard's twin big sisters, or maybe the husband of both, and the father of a baby girl, Jelena, that one or the other of them gave birth to. It was ironic that the war in Europe was practically over—if it hadn't been, Ernie Pyle would have still been there instead of on those stinking Japanese islands, but in one of the last battles necessary to take the German capital, Billy Bob, like Ernie, had been killed by sniper fire.

When the War Department notified us of Billy Bob's death, there was pressure on me to bring out another Extra. But I had learned my lesson with the failure of the Pyle Extra. Some folks and kids thought that I was prejudiced against Billy Bob because he had been a member of the Allies before he'd taken up full time husbanding with Jelena and Doris. I didn't hold his Allied views against him. I just had never known him very well, certainly not as I had known Mare, and I argued that since there hadn't been an Extra for Mare Coe, there shouldn't be one for Billy Bob.

As a concession, I devoted one regular issue of the *Star* to Billy Bob's death, with his obituary and announcement of the memorial service, and stories about the collapse of Berlin and the way those Italians had killed their dictator, Mussolini, and his mistress and strung them up upside down. That regular four-page issue had gone to press and was waiting for delivery on Monday morning when, as I was delivering the copies for Latha to put in the post office boxes, she told me the six o'-clock news had reported that Adolf Hitler and his wife Eva Braun had committed suicide in Berlin. Now that *was* cause for an Extra, but there I was with a regular issue about to go out, so I just folded an extra Extra sheet inside of it with a big headline HITLER QUITS. I sold a few of those, too, in addition to all the ones that went to all the subscribers anyhow. And most people didn't know that the Extra wasn't for Billy Bob.

All of these Extras, and all of this constant news coming from Washington, Europe, and the Pacific, gave all of us in sleepy, tranquil Stay More the sense of being caught up in some cosmic storm of events that threatened to stir each of us out of our ordinary selves and make us feel as if we were participating in history. History was a subject in school that bored most of us to death, no fault of Miss Jerram's, but now we were eyewitnesses to it, learning how to live with the fact that history kills—it takes from us our heroes and our neighbors and our friends, and it takes from each of us that self who had dwelled in a Golden Age of innocence and idyllic harmony.

The onrush of that history thundered into our own little world of make-believe warfare and snatched us up. Whatever angels had been watching over our play decided they needed a vacation, a break from the chore of guardianship, and they went to sleep. The Allies, so-called, taking revenge upon Gypsy for their failure to kidnap her, kidnapped instead her mule, Old Jarhead, and drove it into the woods, and cornered it, and speared it, and beat it until it died.

CHAPTER

. . . .

12

WHEN THE RUSTLING, THE CHASING, THE TRAPPING, THE STABBING, and the brutal cudgeling of Old Jarhead were reported to us by Sammy, he was in a state of shock himself and had decided to quit the Allies forever. "If you'uns need a spy to find out their doings and their secrets, you'uns will jist have to git somebody else!" he declared, beginning to cry. "I don't want nothing to do with them no more."

Eight boys and four girls, ranging in age from seven to seventeen, committed felony criminal mischief by terrorizing and beating to death an innocent thirty-year-old mule, who had worked hard all its life for its human masters and had trusted them to be kind to it. Larry Duckworth had opened the mule's gate in the Dingletoon shed and attempted to capture the animal, which had escaped and fled into the woods, where all the other members of the heinous gang called "Allies" pursued it, piercing it with their cane spears, driving it ultimately into a barbed wire fence where it became entangled and broke its leg. The Allies then proceeded to hit the mule with baseball bats and sticks. Jim John Whitter even stuck a stick up the mule's nostril, inflicting such pain that one of the Allied girls, Rosa Faye Duckworth, fainted. Two other girls helped put the mule out of its misery by clubbing it upon the brain, causing the mule to lose consciousness.

Nobody ever put out an Extra of a newspaper over the death of an animal, but I was tempted. That was my reaction, and the editorial was already writing itself in my head. Gypsy's reaction to the loss of her mule and pet was greater grief than she had shown over the death of Mare; she was nearly hysterical in her sorrow and anger. Ella Jean's re-action was to suggest that we ought to go to Jasper and get the sheriff and have all the Allies arrested and locked up—which, come to think of it, would probably have been the wisest legal course. Willard's reaction puzzled me. He who had obtained the mule somehow somewhere in the first place as an anonymous act of charity for the Dingletoons, and who was seething with controlled rage not only because of that but because he was crazy about Gypsy and sharing her grief for her mule, said that we should leave the sheriff out of it, leave all of the grown-ups out of it, in accordance with our policy. I expected Willard, as commander of the Axis, to declare that we were now officially at war with the Allies. Never mind that we had been "at war" with them for years. All of that had been fun and games. We now existed in a state of *real* deliberate serious all-out wide-open take-no-prisoners War. But Willard just said, "Let's not be hasty."

"Hasty, hell," Joe Don swore, and went off to see the old hermit Dan and request the loan of his Winchester, the one serviceable firearm in town. I think Joe Don actually intended to inflict bodily harm upon each and every one of the Allies. He was upset not so much over the loss of an animal necessary for the Dingletoons to earn their livelihood—al-though spring plowing was long finished and they really wouldn't need a mule again until first haying, and they could borrow someone's mule for that—as over the senseless cruelty of the mule's murder.

But Joe Don returned from ole Dan to report that the hermit, after asking for and listening to Joe Don's reasons for wanting to borrow the rifle, politely turned him down, arguing, quite rightly, that shooting any of the Allies would be criminal and would make Joe Don liable to imprisonment. And apart from the old saw that two wrongs never make a right, it wasn't the best way of dealing with the matter, ole Dan counseled. "He just tole me," Joe Don reported, "that his best advice was for us not to think about revenge but some kind of 'victory that could be had through peace rather than war.'"

"Huh?" Sammy said.

"He tole me what ole Ben Franklin said one time," Joe Don reported, "which is, 'Whatever is begun in anger, ends in shame.' He thought the best thing to do would be for us all to just cool off for a few days. He said that if we let our hatred make us violent, we sink below those we hate. We'd be worse than the Allies."

"So what are we supposed to do?" I asked. "Just pretend nothing happened?"

"For a few days, anyhow," Joe Don said.

"I'm for that," Willard said, "but I reckon we'd best take a vote on it." We summoned all the Axis together and spent hours arguing the advice of ole Dan. Some of us still wanted to go around to the houses of each of the Allies and drag them bodily out of their houses and string them up. Some of us, however, were impressed with the wisdom of the old hermit, and argued that there could be a greater victory through shaming the Allies instead of destroying them. Finally, the vote was not in favor of Peace rather than War so much as it was in favor of Patience rather than Immediate Bloodshed. I could live with that, and didn't need to bring out an Extra to announce it.

"Just remember," Willard concluded, "that the Allies don't even know that we know about it. Not yet anyhow. Let's not get Sammy in trouble by telling anybody we know."

But apparently the Allies expected us to have found out about Old Jarhead, and they were expecting our instant retaliation. The next day, all the Allies came to school equipped not only with whatever weapons they could lay hands on—their spears, their slingshots, their baseball bats, and the same sticks they'd used to kill Old Jarhead—but also they came to school equipped with Sog, who was no longer a pupil, having graduated. As everybody took their seats, each of the Allies cast anxious glances across the aisle at us, but we tried our best to look innocently ignorant of whatever they'd done. It was hard, because we held all of them in such contempt.

"Well, Sugrue," Miss Jerram said to the despot of the Allies, "I thought we got rid of you last year. To what do we owe the pleasure of this visit?" Her voice dripped with such sarcasm, particularly on that word "pleasure," that I immediately suspected somebody may have told her about Old Jarhead.

"I'm just here to watch out for my friends," Sog declared, and gestured expansively with both hands at his fellow Allies.

"How come you and all your friends is armed?" she asked, and stepped down from her platform to snatch up one of the sticks that an Allied littlun, second grader Troy Bullen, was carrying.

"Just to pertect us from our enemies," Sog said.

"But looks to me like not none of your enemies is armed," Miss Jerram observed. And for once in my life I had to admire the lady's intelligence. She commanded, "I want each of you Allies to take your sticks and stones and such and pile 'em on my desk." There was considerable hesitation and reluctance among the Allies, so she suggested, "You first, Sugrue. Put that ball bat on my desk *now!*"

"I aint your scholar no more," he declared. "You caint boss me around."

She narrowed her eyes at him, "Sugrue Alan, you never were my scholar! You never had the sense to be in school in the first place. But you're in my school*house,* and I'm giving ye a choice: put your ball bat on my desk or git out of here!" She pointed to show him where the door was, as if he were too stupid to find it on his own.

Sog took his baseball bat and not-so-gently banged it down on top of her desk and left it there. One by one each of the other Allies deposited their weapons there, until they were spilling off onto the floor. I decided I'd had a secret crush on Miss Jerram all these years.

Then a strange thing happened. Rosa Faye Duckworth, Larry's thirteen-year-old sister, who supposedly had fainted during the torture of Old Jarhead, stood up and requested of the teacher, "Ma'am, could I move to the other side?"

"Rosa Faye, you may," Miss Jerram said, without meaning to rhyme. "Sis!" Larry Duckworth hollered as she collected all her stuff and came across the aisle. "You jist wait till I git you up to the house!"

Miss Jerram informed him, "Larry, you have spoken out of turn without permission. Go stand in the corner." Rosa Faye accompanied his progress there with the sticking out of her tongue at him.

The only empty place on the Axis side was at my desk. You were sitting there, but you gladly stood because you knew I didn't mind her sitting with me. Rosa Faye wasn't much to look at, and I wasn't accustomed to having a seatmate, but I scooted over a little bit so she could sit here. "Hi," she said to me, and I returned the greeting. She had gathered up all her stuff from her desk—books, thick pencils, Indian Chief tablet, her homework, a yellow chiffon scarf, a broken chain necklace with a heart locket, a comb with broken teeth, a moldy apple, a length of licorice, a piece of broken mirror, a red plastic hair barrette, a rose shade of lipstick in a beat-up tube, and a tiny empty coin purse with a snap fastener—and we opened the top of my desk so she could crowd all that stuff in among my stuff.

Two Allied littluns, Troy Bullen and his girl deskmate Suke Whitter, stood up and Troy said, "Ma'am, we'd like to move to the other side too."

"Well, your desk is screwed to the floor," Miss Jerram observed, "and we won't take the time to unscrew it just now. But you can sit temporary at the recitation bench."

So two more of the Allies defected. There were only nine of them left. "Heck," Sog belittled the abandonment. "They aint nothin but two sissy gals and a yellow momma's boy."

Sog's sister Betty June, the former slut, stood and said, "Ma'am, there's one more sissy gal wants to step across the aisle."

Sog grabbed her by the wrist and snarled, "Juner, you jist do that and I'll kill ye."

She did that.

He didn't kill her.

But there weren't any empty seats on the Axis side. Since Sammy Coe had already returned to his desk on our side, Betty June had to sit

The ones formerly called Allies scouted around and found some rocks that were concavely shaped for scooping, and began digging. Those of us formerly called Axis pitched in and helped, taking turns. It was slow, and a lot of work. Ordinarily it would have been time for morning recess, but we didn't take recess. We were hoping we could have it all done by noon dinnertime.

A mule requires a pretty big grave, to get its legs and all underground. The mound of gravelly earth grew higher and higher beside the hole. The grave didn't go down six or eight feet or whatever depth they bury people; it was just deep enough to bury a mule and cover it up good.

Then came the tricky part. "Who will volunteer to help push the remains into the tomb?" Miss Jerram asked, and while she was trying not to discriminate between former Axis and former Allies, she directed these words primarily to the latter. But it required all of us—all who could bear to touch the infested corpse—to push and pull on that body until we got it up to the edge of the hole and needed just one more concerted shove and tug to get it into the grave. Three boys were standing down in the hole pulling the mule's legs, and when Joe Don shouted a warning, "Here she goes!" two of them scrambled out in time; the third, who was Sog himself, did not get out in time, and the mule's body toppled into the grave, knocking him down and landing on top of him. The weight of that mule nearly did him in. I wish it had. He lay there screaming in pain for help.

"Let's just bury him too," Joe Don suggested.

But after a struggle, and prying up parts of the mule's body with poles, we managed to extricate Sog, who was as ugly as his heart: covered with dirt, maggots, some abrasions, sweat, and guilt.

"Are you all right, Sugrue?" Miss Jerram asked, and those were the first kind words she'd ever spoken to him. They were exactly what Ernie Pyle's voice sometimes asked me. The gentle, caring tone of her voice tipped him over the edge, and he began crying uncontrollably. His own sister, Betty June, had to hold him until he could stop. I have never been able to decide whether Sog was crying because of the unexpected sympathy from Miss Jerram, because of his accident and the pain and chagrin of falling beneath the mule, or out of delayed remorse over killing the mule. Maybe it was an accumulation of all those plus a lifetime of being a holy terror. His fellow former Allies looked greatly embarrassed on his behalf, or, rather, they tried not to look.

When Sog finally ceased sniveling and whimpering, Miss Jerram said, "Now class, I think we should each and everyone take a handful of dirt and each and everyone say something fitting to the occasion and then sprinkle the dirt atop the remains. I'll start off." She reached down and filled her hand with fresh earth and held it over the grave. But she stopped. "I'm sorry," she said. "What was the departed's name?"

"Old Jarhead," whispered Gypsy.

Miss Jerram turned back to the grave and said, "Old Jarhead was a beast of burden but not a dumb beast. I never had the privilege of living with a mule but I hear tell they are just about the smartest animal there is. Smarter even than pigs. For all what we might know, Old Jarhead might be smart enough to go on hearing us as we say some words over him. If he can hear us, I want him to know how very sorry we are about what we've done to him." Miss Jerram sprinkled her handful of dirt into the grave.

"Her," Willard said. "Old Jarhead was a female. Not that it makes no difference." He reached down and got a handful of earth and held it out over the grave. "Mules is sterile, male or female. Mules can't breed, maybe that's why they're such good workers. She was smart enough, like all mules, to know what she could do and couldn't do. On a real hot day of work when a horse would wear itself out, a mule will just coast and become lazier to save itself. Mules may seem lazy but they know what they're doing. Old Jarhead would never've fought with other mules the way horses fight among themselves. Mules has the sense not to fight." He opened his hand and dropped the dirt into the grave.

Joe Don stepped up. "I never knew a horse as smart as you," he said into the grave. "Horses will pull a load for all their might; mules'll only use as much of their strength as they have to, and not a pound more. A mule will quit if the load is too heavy; a horse won't have the sense to. Mules do everything the easy way. Old Jarhead, I wish I could be as easy as you."

Joe Don's sister Gypsy was beside him with her handful of dirt, although the tears were streaming down her face. "Good-bye, Old Jarhead," she said. "I sure did enjoy having you as long as I could. Your little feet were handy in the garden 'cause they never trampled the plants. You got your small feet from your daddy, who also gave you your surefootedness and your long ears and skinny legs and that silly bray of yours I could hear a mile off. Your momma gave you your shapely body and shapely neck and hard muscles and your height. When your daddy the jackass and your momma the mare got together, they never could've imagined that we'd be here right now pining over your death." Her dirt fell into the grave.

"Anyone else?" Miss Jerram asked. I wanted to say something, but I felt it had all been said. Miss Jerram let her expectant glance fall upon the ringleaders of the Allies and then called them by name. "Larry? James John? Sugrue?" Larry and Jim John hung their heads and avoided her eyes.

Sog's jaw and lip were still trembling, but he managed to say defiantly, "I never done nothin in my life that I was sorry for." He looked around at all of us as if challenging anyone to defy that assertion. Then his voice broke. "Until now," he added. "I wish this hadn't never of happened. I wish I hadn't let my pure meanness get the best of me. I wish that mule was still alive. But since she aint, I hope she will excuse me for what I done." He reached down and lifted a handful of earth to scatter into the grave.

"Thank you, Sugrue," Miss Jerram said. "Now class, how many of you'uns know the words to that good old hymn, 'Farther Along'?"

Most of us raised our hands. We had recently sung it at the memorial service for Billy Bob Ingledew. People had been singing it at funerals in Stay More for as long as anybody could remember. So now we sang all the verses and repeated the chorus at the end of each one:

> *Farther along we'll know all about it,*
> *Farther along we'll understand why;*
> *Cheer up, my brother, live in the sunshine,*
> *We'll understand it, all by and by.*

There was something about the words and music of that hymn, about its rhythm and accents, even apart from its message that promised us some ultimate comprehension of all these senseless deaths, that was truly of the country, truly rural, even pastoral: death too thrives in Arcadia.

The last "by" of that chorus is held, it endures almost *in fermata:* you can sustain it as long as you like. All our voices, charged with the emotion of the scene and the moment, were still holding the sound of that final note when suddenly its prolonged hum was overridden by another sound: from somewhere high up in the air, far off, came a peculiar drone.

Our mouths still open in the holding of that note, we turned our faces upward and beheld the first airplane that we had ever seen.

PART TWO

· ·

What a piece of work is a man!

How noble in reason!

. . . in action how like an angel!

HAMLET

> War and everything to do with it remains fast in
> the daemonic and magical bonds of play. Only by
> transcending that pitiable friend–foe relationship will
> mankind ever enter into the dignity of man's estate.
>
> JOHAN HUIZINGA, *Homo Ludens*

CHAPTER

· ·

13

WHEN WE HAD DETERMINED THAT IT WAS INDEED AN AIRPLANE and not just one of the several buzzards circling overhead, it was Ella Jean who first voiced what we were looking at: "There's *two* of 'em! And one's chasing the other!"

"Lord have mercy!" Miss Jerram commented.

"Hot ziggety!" said one of the littluns.

"That front'un's a B-29!" said Sammy Coe, who, like many of us, had seen those superfortresses in the newsreels at the Buffalo movie house, or in one of the movies we'd seen there, like *Aerial Gunner* or *Practically Yours*. But the many of us present who had seen those pictures shook our heads.

"That aint no B-29," Larry Duckworth declared. "That's some kind of a Jap bomber!"

"Is it Americans a-chasing him?"

"I sure hope so."

"What if he drops his bomb before the Americans shoot him down?"

"Heck, if he was a Jap he'd have one of them big zeroes on his wings."

"I don't see no zeroes."

"Looks like some kind of a star to me."

"Hot ziggety."

We stood, craning our necks, shielding our eyes with our hands, secretly hoping that the pursuit plane would catch the big plane and blow it up before it could drop its bombs. But again it was Ella Jean who first voiced what we had suddenly detected: "That second'un aint a-chasing the first'un! It's just a-follering it."

I had a chance to put in my two cents. "Look!" I said. "The second one doesn't have any engines!" The first airplane had two big engines, as opposed to the B-29, which everybody who had seen one knew had four engines. The first airplane looked like a whale, with a sleek, rounded body. Not that I had ever seen a whale, either. But the second plane, though smaller, and not sleek at all, but clumsy, like a wooden crate, had much longer wings, huge wings, and no noticeable engines at all. It looked almost like a boxcar. Not that I had ever seen a boxcar, either, since there weren't any railroads running through Newton County.

"What's holding it up there?" someone asked.

"Maybe it's one of them newfangled jet planes," someone else speculated.

"Goodness gracious," observed Miss Jerram, "I do believe the first airplane is *pulling* the second airplane."

Sure enough, she was right. The second plane was not a jet. The whale was pulling the boxcar. There was a towrope strung out between them. I had once seen a newsreel of airplanes refueling in the sky, of a bomber attached by a gas line to a tanker, and I was about to offer that as a theory, but neither of these planes was a bomber or a tanker.

No sooner had we detected the towrope than it broke. Or rather the end attached to the boxcar-like plane became unattached. The whale-like plane kept on going, but the boxcar-like plane banked and began to circle. It slowed and drifted.

"It's gliding!" said Ella Jean.

"It's a *glider!*" said Sammy. "I've heared tell of them."

"It caint go nowhere but *down*, now," Willard observed.

"Where's it gonna land?"

"Right *here*, maybe!"

"No, it aint. It's fixin to try to land down in the valley."

"Hot ziggety!"

"Boy-oh-boy!"

"Will wonders never cease!"

"Maybe it won't land in Stay More. Maybe it'll decide there aint nothin here worth landing for."

"But it caint go nowheres else! It's got to land, because it don't have no engines!"

"Probably," offered Miss Jerram, "it will have to land in that field above the schoolhouse."

"Let's go watch it land!"

We scattered ever which way. Some of the littluns took Miss Jerram's hands and they started off at a trot back in the direction of the schoolhouse. Miss Jerram was a pretty good runner.

But some of us formerly called Axis did not follow, because our leader, Willard, wasn't following. "I got a hunch," he said to Joe Don, "that it aint a-lookin for a meader down in the valley. It's lookin to land somewheres up high, maybe right over yon hill."

"Yeah," Joe Don agreed, "he'd need to land at a high place in case he ever took a notion to take off again." None of us disputed the logic of this; a glider won't ever take off again without a tow.

The group formerly called the Allies had a different idea. The glider would land in the vicinity of their sycamore tree clubhouse, the meadow known as the Field of Clover, now part of the hayfields of the Whitters. Jim John was convinced that no other field in Stay More would accommodate the landing of an aircraft, and he wanted to be there when it did, and he persuaded Sog and Larry to light out in that direction.

So the funeral cortege was split up into three or more groups, each heading in a different direction, everyone keeping their eyes on the sky, where the big glider endlessly circled over the whole countryside from edge to edge. Sorry to tell, we forgot all about Old Jarhead and never finished her funeral. "Thataway," said Willard, and five of us followed him—Joe Don, Gypsy, Ella Jean, Sammy, and myself. He led us not far away from the funeral site, up over the next hill, through a thicket of trees to the edge of a long but narrow meadow that ran along the ridge of the mountain. "Here," Willard said. "If I was lookin for a good place to land that thing, this here's where I'd do it." I trusted Willard but I was uneasy. What if his hunch was wrong? I didn't want to miss the landing of the glider. I was already rehearsing my interview with the pilot for an Extra to appear this very afternoon.

The glider continued to make several slow circlings of all of Stay More, as if it knew that we were waiting for it at several possible landing sites and it wanted to decide which group of us was most favored. Then the big crate with its enormous wingspread began to lose altitude, and sure enough it looked as if it were straightening out to land in our meadow. "Told you," said Willard, not boastfully but matter-of-factly. But as the glider began to descend toward us, we suddenly realized that a forest of tall trees was blocking the approach. Suddenly the glider nosedived, and we gasped and held our breath in anticipation that the plane would crash headfirst into the ground. The speed of its acceleration, however, enabled the pilot to use gravity to give the plane the extra push necessary so that, by yanking back on whatever yoke he was steering by, the pilot was able to hedgehop over the highest trees and set his course for our meadow. The big crate was close enough that we could see how it was covered not by aluminum but by some kind of fabric, and it did indeed have painted on its side a big five-pointed star inside a circle, an insignia of the United States of America. "Well, it's one of ours, that's for sure," Joe Don remarked as it came in for its landing.

It was quite a show. The huge glider had two small wheels on struts sticking out from its belly, and another wheel on its nose, and this tricycle didn't seem to be large enough to support the landing of that heavy body. The problem, though, was stopping the whole thing before it reached the end of the long meadow and the thick trees beyond. The glider touched down, hopped a few times with decreasing bounces like a rock skipped across the creek, and then kept on skidding down the meadow-runway. Did it have brakes?

"Aint it got brakes?" Willard wondered, using one foot to pump an imaginary brake pedal.

Whether it did or not, the glider couldn't stop short of the treeline. Some of us (not me) covered our eyes with our hands as the big blunt front end of the glider smashed into the trunk of a walnut tree with a terrible rending, crashing sound, and the plane twisted so that one of its long wings slammed into other trees and splinters flew everywhere. The shuddery sounds of the crash were over in a second, but they seemed to explode on and on as the fragments settled and dust cleared. Those of us who had covered our faces (not me) slowly peeked through our fingers (not mine) to see if anything was left of the aircraft.

The nosewheel had been driven up through the fuselage, which was totally wrecked, and the flat floor of the plane was crumpled and buckled. There was a huge gaping hole in the side of craft, where the fabric had been torn asunder and the wooden structure splintered, and through this hole tottered the pilot, dressed in a shock helmet and a strange outfit, holding one arm as if he'd broken it. After him stumbled another man. And then another. And another. These men, each dressed in full combat uniforms with helmets and shoulder packs and bedrolls and gas masks and rifles and everything, were so formidable that the six of us as one dropped to the ground in the tall grass and tried to hide ourselves from their sight. The leader of the group made some motions and silent commands to his men, and two of them set up a machine gun pointed in our direction, while two others dropped to the ground with their carbines aimed our way, and two more stood beside the opening of the glider through which, one by one, more and more of these soldiers came lurching and limping out with their carbines ready for firing.

One time before the war I had gone to Jasper with Doc Swain and some others, not to watch a movie but to see the circus. A traveling circus had come to the little county seat, two nights only, and among all the other wonders of the spectacular show had been the unforgettable sight of a little automobile driving into the ring and no less than a dozen clowns climbing out of a vehicle that couldn't possibly have held that many.

Now there were not merely a dozen clowns emerging from this glider, but, all told (as a newspaperman relishing the thought of the next Extra, I took the trouble to count with my finger), counting the pilot, there were *thirteen* combat-ready soldiers aboard that glider. And the last of these was leading a mule. I'm not kidding. A four-legged mule.

It was the handsomest mule any of us had ever seen. It was not old and gray like Old Jarhead—not until this moment did we realize how casually we had abandoned the funeral back down the hillside in Butterchurn Holler—but young and powerfully built, and if, as the eulogists at that funeral had claimed, the mule is the smartest of all animals, this mule was ready to graduate from college. Maybe he had already graduated from a service academy. He was wearing a bright brown horse blanket that said US ARMY on it, and he looked as if whoever was in charge of him had to spend a lot of time brushing and grooming him. Or even as if, like a good soldier, he was in the habit of keeping himself neat and clean and kempt.

For a moment there, some of us must have thought that this was Old Jarhead returned from heaven, or Old Jarhead reincarnated, but if so, she had been reincarnated as a male, for that was clearly what he was. This mule was the only creature on that plane who had not been shaken up by the crash. The twelve soldiers and the pilot looked as if they couldn't believe their good luck in still being alive, and they could hardly stand straight, but the mule acted as if this whole experience were just another joyride, and he looked around at the terrain as if he didn't really mind being here or at any rate was ready to take whatever orders were given him.

But as soon as the soldiers got their heads cleared and their bearings straight, the leader made some more sign language with his hands and pointed our way, and some of the soldiers ran out across the field in our direction, then dropped to their bellies in the grass with their carbines constantly pointed toward us.

"Maybe we ought to surrender," Willard whispered. "Anybody got a white handkerchief?"

No one did. "Do you want my panties?" Gypsy whispered. I knew it was a rhetorical question; she didn't wear panties.

Willard blushed scarlet. I was sure his color would give us away if any of those soldiers were looking directly at the clump of tall grass in which we were trying to conceal ourselves.

"I aint skeered," declared Ella Jean, and she suddenly stood up. A rifle fired, and she dropped to the ground again, unhurt but terrified.

A voice yelled, "It's just a girl, you fatheads! Hold your fire!"

The leader came running very close to our hiding place. We could see the silver bar on his collar. "Where are you, sweetheart?" he called. "Come out. We won't hurt you."

But Ella Jean had the sense not to show herself again. The leader was still holding his rifle as if he might want to use it. Two of his men came up beside him and those three began stomping around through the grass until they were right on top of us. Willard raised his two hands in surrender, so the rest of us imitated his gesture, and then the six of us got to our feet with our hands behind our heads.

"They're all just kids," the leader said. Then he asked Joe Don, perhaps because he was oldest, "Did we land in your pasture?"

"If you can call that 'landing,'" Joe Don said.

The men laughed. "You can put your hands down," the leader said. "You're prisoners, and you won't try anything."

Willard pointed east and said, "Germany's a few more miles thataway. Aint you fellers in the wrong place?"

The men laughed again. One of them said, "We're not bound for Germany. We're getting ready to go to J—"

"Knock it off, Polacek!" the leader said to the soldier, then he said to Willard, "It's just about all over in Germany. Haven't you heard?"

"We've heard," I said. "We've got radio, you know."

"Shouldn't you kids be in school?" the leader asked. "This is Wednesday, isn't it?"

"Teacher let us out," Gypsy said. "Matter a fact, she *took* us out. To bury a mule."

"To what, pardon me?" the leader asked.

Two other soldiers joined us. "Perimeter's secure, sir!" one of them said, saluting. "Sir, I think Lieutenant Bosco broke his arm in the landing."

"I'll look at it, Sergeant," the leader said, and then he called toward the glider, "UNLOAD, DEPLOY, AND TORCH IT!" Then he pointed at us and said to the soldiers behind us, "Segregate 'em, search 'em, and silence 'em." The men saluted him and he took off at a run.

The soldiers separated us, making us stand several feet apart with our hands raised on tree trunks while they patted us over, as if we'd have any weapons, which of course we didn't, not even pocketknives. Two soldiers argued with each other over the privilege of searching Gypsy. I was brooding about the officer's last command: I knew that "silence" was a euphemism for "put to death," and I wondered if they could really get away with it, destroying innocent country kids.

"Do I look like I've got anything on me?" I demanded of the soldier who was patting me.

"Hush, kid!" he snapped. "No talking." Then he fished the pencil out of my shirt pocket and asked, "What's this?"

"A ray gun," I said. "Deadly."

He twisted his fingers into the collar of my shirt. "Don't get smart, punk."

"It's my tool," I said. "I write for the newspaper."

The officer was back. "Private, didn't I say 'silence'?"

"Yessir but this squirt was giving me lip."

"Son," the officer said to me, "we're going to ask for your full cooperation from now till our bivouac is fixed."

I gave him a good military salute and said, "Yes *sir!*"

He looked at me kindly but a bit quizzically. "Do you know what a bivouac is?"

"You fellers is a-fixin to camp out," I said.

He chuckled. "That's right. And we can't do it *here*." He turned and spoke loudly enough for everyone to hear him, "Let's MOVE OUT!" He gestured northward.

Those guys were efficient. The poor mule was loaded up with packs and packs and boxes and boxes of stuff that had to be all roped together, and then the mule was led away. I didn't see how the mule could carry all that stuff, but he kept his head up like a good soldier. Then a corporal with a flamethrower set the glider on fire. In no time at all the big crate was cinders.

"What kind of airship was that?" I asked the officer, walking rapidly beside him as he headed north.

"It was a Waco CG-4A," he said. "It did its job. Now excuse me."

He trotted away from me, to the head of the column of men and mule. Four soldiers marched ahead, behind, and in between us six Axis, keeping us apart from each other and hurrying us if we slowed down on the march. For some reason I was in front and the others behind me. Gypsy and Ella Jean were having a rough go of it, especially because of the way the soldiers were ogling them as if they hadn't seen a female in months . . . and maybe they hadn't.

I was thirsty and, I suddenly realized, very hungry. It was past time for what would've been our noon dinner at school, where my dinner pail and everyone else's was still in the foyer. And poor Willard, always obsessed with his stomach, was visibly wilting from hunger.

We came out of the forest at the road that dissolves into a woodland trail not far up above the old dogtrot house, the Dill family place, where Latha lived with her husband Every Dill. As soon as we reached the road, the officer halted the column and silently made a bunch of hand gestures that strung his men out into two files along both sides of the road. The officer dropped back and asked me, "Where does this road go?"

"Well, pretty soon it comes to an old cabin where an auto mechanic lives with his beautiful wife who's the town's postmistress and store-keeper and—"

"What about the other way?" he asked.

"Oh, it just sort of peters out, up that way. There's a deserted old house maybe half a mile up in those woods."

"You know the country pretty well, don't you?" he said with admiration.

"Lived here all my life," I said. And then I couldn't resist adding, "I have to know all the roads real well in order to deliver my newspaper."

"Are we keeping you from your paper route?" He pronounced it "root," not "rowt."

"Well, I wanted to bring out an Extra this afternoon to tell all about your landing and all, but it don't look like I'm going to get a chance to do that, does it?"

He stared at me a while. Then he said, "Oh. I get it. You're not just a paperboy. You *publish* a paper."

"Yes, sir, and I sure would appreciate an interview."

He smiled. "We call it 'interrogation.' And your turn will come. Now show us that deserted house."

CHAPTER
14

WHEN WE CLIMBED TO THE DARK HOLLER OF THE MOUNTAIN forest containing the abandoned farmstead, one of several in the environs that were so run down that not even the squatting Dingletoons would have cared to use them, the first thing the officer wanted to do was test the water in the well. The well housing was of crumbling rock masonry, but its cap was a huge cement slab with a hole in it large enough to accommodate a bucket. There was no bucket, and only the frayed remains of a well rope dangling from the rusted iron pulley, but of course *they* had a bucket, possibly made from the very metal of our War Effort Scrap Drive, and they lowered it and brought up some water, and tested it with some kind of chemical strips. Then one of the men was told to step off the distance from the well to the outhouse, a teetering shack without its door. "Ninety-two and a half feet, sir," he reported.

I understood what they were doing, and I spoke up. "I don't believe anybody's used that outhouse for a dozen years."

"Were you here a dozen years ago?" the officer asked me.

I was not, but I could have assured him that the water in that well was perfectly potable, and I was dying for a few gulps of it. Still the officer had to be sure that some kind of tablets were dropped into the water before he could let us have any. Then he had the first drink himself, either from the privilege of seniority or perhaps he figured if he didn't drop dead at once it would be all right for the rest of us to drink it.

When we'd all slaked our thirst, Ella Jean spoke up on behalf of our hunger. "Mister," she said to the officer, "we'uns aint et our dinner yit."

"Hoo!" said one of the soldiers, "'We'uns aint et our dinner yit.'"

"Polacek!" the officer snapped at the soldier. "This young lady would probably think your Bronx accent is hilarious if she got a chance to hear it. Why don't you say something for her?"

"Sorry, sir," Polacek said.

"Say it to *her*, Polacek!"

"High big department, miss," Polacek said to Ella Jean. Or something like that.

The officer said to us, "Isn't it kind of early for dinner? We haven't had lunch yet."

"Hereabouts," I told him, "the noon meal is always dinner. And it's way past noon, I think." The high sun had moved past its zenith, and was getting hotter.

"My mistake," the officer apologized. "Well, let's all have dinner, then! Rucker!" A soldier came up and saluted. "Rucker, give these people our best bash."

The officer had a sense of humor. His idea of a bash was to let us share the soldier's rations, an assortment of canned meat products, two types of biscuits, canned cheese, fruit bars, and chocolate bars. Willard astounded Rucker and the other men by consuming enough of the biscuits to feed the whole platoon. But the officer didn't eat with us; he was too busy reconnoitering the farmstead and giving instructions to the men for the setting up of the bivouac.

"What do you think they'll do with us?" I asked Willard.

"I don't rightly keer, as long as they feed us," Willard said, grinning. Then, more seriously, he said, "I reckon they're bound to turn us loose directly."

Corporal Rucker said, "Hey, you guys pipe down. Lieut says you gotta keep quiet till he's finished."

"Finished what?" I asked.

Rucker held up five fingers, and named each one. "Search. Segregate. Silence. Speed. Safeguard. That's the rules. Doesn't say feed. Says, 'Do not give them cigarettes, food, or water.' We've given you guys plenty of the last two. You need a cigarette?"

The officer, whom Rucker had called "Lieut," returned to us. "Okay," he said. "I guess I'll take you one at a time in order of seniority. Who's oldest?" The officer took Joe Don and they disappeared into the old house, whose floorboards, I knew, were mostly rotten. They were gone a while. What was happening to Joe Don? Gypsy and Ella Jean attempted to exchange nervous speculations, but Rucker silenced them. We waited anxiously to hear a scream.

Finally Joe Don returned. He was smiling as if he knew something the rest of us didn't know. "I reckon you're next," he said to Willard, and Willard got up, belched, and went into the house.

"What was that all about?" I asked Joe Don.

"Kid!" Rucker yelled at me and wagged his finger. Joe Don simply made a gesture of crossing his lips with his finger as if to say they were sealed.

We sat in silence as, one by one, Willard, then Gypsy, then Ella Jean, and then Sammy, were interrogated, or regaled, or raped, or whatever was going on in there. I was terribly impatient, and increasingly nervous. As the youngest and last, I had to endure the waiting and wondering and not one of my friends—or fellow Axis, if they weren't exactly friends—could give me even a hint as to what to expect.

It was midafternoon before my turn finally came, as Sammy emerged from the house, giggling. At least, I told myself as I entered, whatever was going on in there had some redeeming comic value. I exchanged glances with Sammy in passing, but he just rolled his eyes.

Inside the house, the officer had found a spot in what once must have been the kitchen where the floorboards weren't completely rotted through, and he had set up two canvas folding chairs, the kind that movie stars and directors and Civil War generals sit in. The two chairs faced each other, closely; he gestured for me to sit in one, and then sat in the other himself.

"So," he said to me, and then called me by my full name (I assumed any of the others could have told him my name). He held out his hand for a shake, and I shook it. "I have the honor of being interviewed personally by the editor-in-chief of *The Stay Morning Star*." There was no sarcasm or condescension in his voice.

"Yessir," I said. "I guess *they* told you all that."

"Lieutenant McPherson at your service, sir," he said. He took a real cigarette from a package in his pocket and then offered me one. "I don't suppose you smoke?"

"Not yet," I said.

"Good. Don't start. It's too hard to stop." He lit his own cigarette with enormous pleasure, took a deep draught from it, and exhaled, careful to tilt his head so that the smoke didn't come into my face. "How long have you been putting out the *Star?*"

"A year or so," I said.

"Mimeograph?"

"Hectograph."

"Ah!" he smiled. "I had one of those."

"Really?" I said, warming to him. "Did you edit a newspaper?"

"Not when I was your age," he said. "I wasn't nearly as bright as you."

I probably blushed. "I'm not very bright."

"None of your friends," he pointed out, "knows the meaning of 'bivouac.' Where'd you learn it?"

"I read a lot," I said.

"So, in a way, you already know why we're here, and I won't have to answer any questions along that line."

"Yes, you will," I said. "Stay More isn't enemy territory. Why are you *here*, when you ought to be invading Japan?"

He stared at me as if he might even have been asking himself the same question. Then he said, *"Sore yori kore-ga yoi to omoi-masu."*

"'Scuse me?" I said. Polacek's Bronxese I could figure out, but not this.

"I said I think this is better than that, that being here in Stay More is better than being in Japan. I said it in Japanese."

"That's funny," I said. "You don't *look* Japanese."

He laughed. "Nor do you, Donny. But I'm told you're the skibbiest of all the local Nips." I must have screwed up my face in puzzlement, for he took the trouble to explain what "Nipponese" meant and to say, "I'm teasing. 'Skibby' is derogatory slang, originally meaning a Japanese prostitute who consorts with Occidental men but by extension it now means any Oriental man or woman."

"What's an 'accidental man'?" I wanted to know. It sounded daring, like a man who couldn't control all the exciting episodes that befell him.

"*Oc*cidental," Lieutenant McPherson corrected me. "Means the western hemisphere, means *us* as opposed to the Orientals."

"So *they*"—I gestured in the direction where my friends were waiting—"must have told you all about the Axis and the Allies."

"I couldn't get a word out of Willard Dinsmore about it," the lieutenant said. "He's a brilliant commander and strategist. If the real Japanese had a few generals like him, they wouldn't be losing this wretched war."

"So who told you?" I asked.

"I can't answer that."

"Okay. Did whoever told you also tell you how our schoolteacher, Miss Jerram, this very morning put a stop to us being Axis and Allies?"

"I know about Old Jarhead," he said sympathetically, "and I'm sending a detail with shovels at nightfall to finish the burial."

"That's nice. What's a detail?" He explained that word to me. I was expanding my vocabulary by leaps and bounds. "You're not keeping us till nightfall?" I asked.

"I hope not," he said. "It depends on you."

"*Me?* How come?"

"Samuel Coe showed me his mark, his brand, his 'A.'"

"How'd you get him to do that? And what's it got to do with me?"

"I could require you to strip naked right now," he said, with assurance. "And you'd do it. But I'm not going to. I don't think you're hiding anything, except your feelings. You really are inscrutable, you know? That's good for a newspaperman . . . but not always so good for a young boy. So tell me. Why didn't you report the Allies' branding of Sammy in your little newspaper?"

"It wasn't none of *their* business," I declared.

"Who is 'they'?"

"All the grown-ups," I said. "Sammy's daddy would totally exterminate the Allies if he knew about that."

"So you exercised your prerogative as editor to censor the news?"

"Yeah."

"And likewise you did not give any coverage to the attempted abduction of Gypsy Dingletoon in the Battle of Dinsmore Trail."

"Wow. You know a lot!" I couldn't conceal my admiration for his interrogative skills.

"And might I presume," he went on, "that you aren't even going to report the funeral of Old Jarhead?"

"Maybe not," I admitted. "I haven't really decided."

"So it's time for you to make some decisions," he said. "I'm going to ask you to make a real big one: to honor my request that no news of our landing gets into your paper."

"Heck," I protested. "Probably everybody in town saw you come down." I did not mean to make a poem, and the rhyme embarrassed me.

"But only *you* and your friends out there know that we survived the wreck and burning of the glider."

"Why does it have to be such a big secret?"

"Himitsu to himitsu-ni suru," he said. "If you will promise me to keep our presence here strictly a secret, I will tell you one or more of our secrets."

"Such as? You could start off with telling me why you picked Stay More to invade."

"We didn't pick it. We don't even have terrain maps. My men out there"—his hand swept the area—"don't even know where we are. But I assure you we are *not* invading Stay More. We are not hostile."

"Then how come you-all fired at Ella Jean when she stood up?"

"Are you ready for the first of the many secrets I'll swap you for your secrecy? Will you promise me not to print anything in the *Star* about us?"

"Not *ever?* Not even after the war is all over?"

His expression became wistful, as if I had suggested the possibility that the war *would* eventually end, but he might not even be around to see it. Then he spoke quietly, "Donny, there will come a time, soon, I can't tell you when because I don't know myself, when you can have an exclusive on a really hot story. You can scoop the big dailies. And I'll help you all I can with that, in return for your promise to keep everything quiet until I tell you."

The prospect excited me. He was talking my language, journalism. I wanted to ask him what he thought of the late Ernie Pyle, but that could wait. "Okay," I said. "Sure. I promise. Nothing in the *Star* until you tell me." I offered him my hand, and we shook on the deal. "Well?" I said, waiting. "So what's the first secret you're gonna tell me?"

There was nobody anywhere near earshot, but he scooted his chair closer and feigned a conspiracy between us, hiding his mouth behind his hand and lowering his voice. "The bullet fired at Ella Jean," he said, "was a blank. Each of our rifles, *shoju*, is Japanese, and is not loaded with a *shojudan*, bullet, but with a *kuho*, blank. The machine gun, *kikanju*, is a Japanese 7.7 mm copy of the French Hotchkiss, or *hochikisu kikanju*, loaded with blanks. The BAR, or Browning, which they pronounce *burauningu kikanju*, is loaded with blanks. Our mortar, a Japanese Stokes, which they pronounce *sutoku-shiki kyokusha hoheiho*, won't hurt anybody. And of course all our hand grenades are just *shuryudan* training grenades without fillers or fuses: they will shatter on contact and leave a blob of red paint on whatever they hit. We have quite a lot of antitank rifle grenades, *juyo tekidan*, that are projectiles which will hit the target and cover it with the red paint. Our flares, *shomei*, will light, and our radio, *musen tsushinki*, has working batteries, but all our ammunition is fake."

"Oh," was all I could say. I think I was beginning to understand, but all I could think to ask was, "Do your men know they're shooting blanks?"

"Of course," he said. "Do you want to know another secret in return for your promise never to tell your parents about us?"

"I have no parents," I said.

"Oh? You live with—?"

"My aunt."

"Okay. She'll want to know where you've been all afternoon and you can tell her—"

"She never asks me anything."

"Okay. I see. You probably spend all your time with Latha Bourne."

I was stunned. "How do you know about her?"

"You yourself told me that she and her husband are our closest neighbors down the mountain. Willard told me her name. Joe Don told me how nice she is. Sammy described her store and post office. Ella Jean told me how beautiful she is. Gypsy told me her store is where you have the office of *The Stay Morning Star*."

"Why do you need to know all those things?"

"It's called intelligence. Not *this* kind of intelligence," he reached out and touched my cranium, "but the accumulation of information one needs to know, including but not limited to secrets." He smiled. "Later you can tell me all the secrets about Latha Bourne. Right now I need your promise never to tell her about us. Not a word."

That was a tough request. If I couldn't tell Latha, who could I tell? But as long as I was making promises to this very sharp and kind army officer, I might as well keep on making them. "Okay," I said. "I won't tell her anything. So what's your *next* secret?"

"Good," he said. "Let's shake on that promise too." When we had shaken hands for the third time, he patted the pistol strapped to his belt. "This Nambu automatic, *jido kenju*," he said, "is *not* loaded with blanks. It has real .7 mm cartridges in its clip. But don't you dare tell a soul." I shook my head solemnly, a bit honored that he was sharing with me intelligence known only to himself. He laughed. "Maybe," he said, "if we run completely out of K rations and have to shoot a cow for food, I'll have to use my pistol!" I laughed with him. "No," he said, "I'm not going to shoot any cows. But the time might come when I'll have to ask you to buy some grub for us at Latha's store."

"Sure," I said. "Any time."

"Well, I guess that's about it, for now." He stood up, and I stood also. He put his hand on my shoulder. He was a tall man, and I really had to bend my neck to look up at him. "One more little *himitsu to himitsu*," he said. "And perhaps this one will hold us, for the nonce. Do you know the word *nonce?* English, not Japanese. No? It means the present, for the time being. Okay? Well, I need you to promise, for the nonce, that you will not discuss any of this even with your friends, your fellow Axis, let alone your enemies, the Allies. I know you will be curious to learn from each of your friends what I talked about with them, but each of them has already promised me not to discuss our presence here with each other, and therefore none of them will be willing—or should not be willing—to discuss it with you."

"Did you have to bribe them with *himitsu to himitsu?*" I asked.

He laughed. "No, actually, it was threats more than bribes. But don't even ask them about *that*."

"Okay. So all of us Axis will just have to pretend that this whole day never happened."

"Excellent! Can you do that? And give me your word?"

We shook hands for a fourth time. Shaking hands standing up was somewhat different from shaking hands sitting down. Our hands weren't on the same level. I had to reach up. "So what's the last secret?" I asked.

"You and your friends have been required to think of yourselves as Japanese, right? Even those of your Axis who have been Nazis, such as Joe Don, will now have to change into Japs as Germany surrenders." He began walking me toward the door. "You know, your General Willard Dinsmore managed the tactical coup of guessing where we'd land, even though, I can tell you, our pilot, Second Lieutenant Bosco, who broke his arm in the process, was trying his best to land on a remote mountaintop where we wouldn't be found." We were at the open door, and I could see my fellow Axis waiting for me, sitting in the late afternoon sunlight as it filtered through the second-growth timber that grew up like dank weeds around the old farmstead. I doubt if we were close enough for them to hear these concluding words of Lieutenant Mc-Pherson: "What a coincidence, or accident of destiny, that we should land in the midst of a fine group of boys and girls who, like ourselves, have been given the role of pretending that they are Japanese!"

CHAPTER
15

When the six of us were safely out of sight of the bivouac, marching down the mountain trail back toward the village, I couldn't stand it any longer. "Wow!" I said to them. "How about that guy?"

"What guy?" said Willard.

"Lieutenant McPherson," I said. "Aint he something else again?"

"McPherson?" Willard said. "That don't strike a bell with me. You, Joe Don?"

"Never heared tell of nobody of that name," Joe Don said.

"Hey! Come on, you-all!" I complained. "Caint we even say what we thought of him?"

"Him who?" Sammy said.

"The lieutenant!" I turned to Gypsy and appealed to her. "Didn't you think he was the best-looking man you ever saw?"

Did I detect a faint spark of agreement in Gypsy's eyes? But she just said, "Dawny, you're the only good-lookin feller I've seen lately." I would have blushed if I hadn't known she was just teasing me.

It took courage, but I spoke to my secret sweetheart, Ella Jean, "Didn't *you* like him?"

"*Hush*, Dawny!" said my sweetheart.

So I hushed. I was dying to learn what prices he had paid to buy each of their silences, but it was obvious they weren't going to talk, and I even grew abashed at myself, as if my attempt to make them talk was a violation of my promise to the lieutenant.

Walking past Dill's Gas and Service, which of course wasn't a conventional service station but just a shack with a gas pump out front and a yard in which the owner tinkered with cars, we casually waved at Every Dill, who was working on Doc Swain's car under the big maple tree. "Howdy," Every called to us. "Any of you'uns find where that gliding machine come down?"

Willard spoke on our behalf. "Howdy, Ev. Nope. Reckon it must've been over towards up yonder back around in there somewheres."

We came to my house, or rather Aunt Murrison's, but I didn't see her, and I didn't stop there. I might or might not show up for supper. We went on into the village. There we encountered a group of what was left of the former Allies, sitting on the porch of Latha's store. We couldn't just pass them by, and that store was my destination anyhow, regardless of whether I could say anything to Latha about our adventure.

"Any luck?" asked Jim John Whitter, who couldn't hide his disappointment that the glider hadn't come down in the Whitter meadow, the Field of Clover. All the Allies looked like they hadn't been invited to somebody's big birthday party.

"Nope," said Willard, our spokesman as well as our general. "Didn't it land down here in the bottoms?"

"Nope," said Larry. "Looked like it landed somewhere back up thataway where you'uns was."

"Saw it drift over a few times," Joe Don said, "but couldn't make out rightly just where it took a notion to light down."

We sat in silence on the store porch for a while, as the afternoon waned. It was a situation for getting out our pocketknives and doing a little whittling of useless sticks, just to pass the time, but we didn't have any pocketknives anymore. Gypsy and Ella Jean said they had to go help start supper, and they left together, their arms around each other. I was jealous, not of their arms, but of the almost sure chance that they *would* compare notes on their experience. After a time, Jim John said, offhand, "Don't look to me like we'll be able to put a ball game together this Saturday, since you Axis has got us so bad outnumbered now."

"We aint Axis no more," Willard said. "But we'll make ye the loan of a few players, enough to help ye play us." Sog, the former warlord, said glumly, "Aw, shee-ut, us Allies might just as well show the white flag, lay down our arms, and call it quits."

"Yeah," Larry agreed, "we might as well pull in our horns. But then it sure is going to get real dull and slow around this old town."

The former Axis, the four of us, couldn't help exchanging looks, and in their looks I caught enough to convince me that I hadn't just been dreaming what had happened during this long day.

"Too bad," Willard said sorrowfully. "It'll sure enough just get real dull and slow hereabouts." Even he, with his great strength, had to bear down and concentrate to avoid cracking a grin.

The next day in school, Miss Jerram declared that since we were no longer divided into Axis and Allies, she might as well reassign all of our seats, so that the aisle would no longer be the division between opposing factions. "But we don't have only a short time left before school lets out for the summer," she observed, "so we might as well just stay put where we are until next fall." Then she conducted a postmortem on the hunt for the glider. Representatives of each of the parties who had scattered all over creation as the glider was landing were invited to report on their success, or rather their lack of success, and various speculations were made about just where the glider might have landed. Several students—not us—had seen the smoke billowing up from the mountain ridge where they assumed the glider may have crashed in flames. "Joseph Donald," she said, "didn't your group go up in that direction?" Yes'm, Joe Don reported, and they tromped all over the mountain a-lookin for that durn thing, but all they found was a pile of ashes. "Then whoever was flying it must've burnt to a crisp!" Miss Jerram said. "That's just awful. Maybe we ought to notify the sheriff or somebody." Willard suggested that if the Army Air Force or whoever had sent the glider was missing one of their men they'd probably be sending somebody out to look for it. Miss Jerram used up a good chunk of our "time o' books" for the discussion of the glider, which was just as well with me, because I had no enthusiasm or patience for the day's lessons in geography, history, mathematics, or even English. Then Miss Jerram said, "I hate to say it, but all of us got so wrapped up with that glider yesterday that we forgot all about the poor mule's funeral, and we didn't finish filling in the grave."

Gypsy said, "That's okay, Teacher. I went up there last night and saw to it."

"Saw to it?"

"I filled in the grave," Gypsy declared. Was she wearing a touch of rouge? Had she painted her mouth too?

"By yourself?"

"No'm," said Gypsy. "Ella Jean went with me."

"What did you use for a shovel?"

"Well, uh—" Gypsy struggled, and for a moment there I thought she might say, "A folding U.S. Army shovel made from the War Effort Scrap Drive," but she said in fact, "We just sort of kicked a lot of that pile of dirt back into the hole, ye know, and then we just sort of drug the rest of it in with sticks and rocks, ye know."

I couldn't wait for recess. At recess, the divisions had never been Allies on one side of the schoolhouse yard, Axis on the other, but rather boys on one side, girls on the other. I crossed over, and grabbed Gypsy by the arm, and asked, "Did you run into that detail that McPherson was sending to finish the burial?"

"What's a 'detail'?" Gypsy wanted to know.

"One or more troops of soldiers sent out for a particular duty," I defined it for her.

"*Soldiers?*" Gypsy said, and I thought she was doing a splendid job of pretending she'd never heard that word either.

"Didn't some men help you and Ella Jean fill in the grave?" I insisted. "Or didn't you help some men do it? Or watch 'em do it? Or anyhow take 'em to show 'em where the grave was, which they wouldn't've known to begin with?"

"Dawny, have you been readin them comic books again?"

I was exasperated. It was true that I sometimes read comic books, when I could get them, and I was partial to the military activities of the various captains: *Captain America, Captain Marvel, Captain Wings, Captain Midnight,* and *The Captain and the Kids,* but even my thorough familiarity with those comics would not have goaded my hyperactive imagination into fabricating the adventures I—and Gypsy—had just had. Or would it have? Needless to say, the rest of the school day was agony for me. Whatever fondness I had discovered I had for Miss Jerram was reversed when she sent me to the blackboard to do some arithmetic problems and then jumped on me. "Dawny, you're not marking up sums. You're drawing pitchers of airplanes!"

The minute school was out, without so much as a word attempting to coordinate the agenda with the other former Axis, I took off lickety-split for the bivouac, not stopping at Latha's store, not stopping at my house, not stopping period. My bare feet were red and sore and my lungs were trying to leave my chest when I arrived panting at the old farmstead in the dark holler up above the Dill place.

There was nobody there. There was no trace of anybody having been there. I mean, there were no footprints in the dirt nor prints of a mule's horseshoes. Nothing. I went inside the old house, walking carefully on the rotting floorboards, to the place where Lieutenant McPherson had set up the two director's chairs for my interview or interrogation or whatever it had been. I found the place where the chairs would have been and where our feet would have touched the floor, but the dust and debris were thick and untouched. Nobody had sat there. Or not for a dozen years. I stepped my foot into that dust, and it left a clear print, which seemed to mock me, as if to say, "I'm the *only* footprint in all this dust." It occurred to me: why would anybody have bothered to bring *director's chairs* into this place?

I was reeling. I went back outside the house and yelled, "HELLO?" My voice, higher and less manly than I'd thought, traveled way up into the dark holler and faintly echoed back to me. Pleading, I yelled, "WHERE IS EVERYBODY?" Some birds flew up from a distant tree, and that was all.

I sat down on the edge of the porch, alone except for you. I needed you to tell me that I had not lost my mind. I needed you to forgive me for not paying much attention to you except in times of need. More than anything, I wanted you to help me sort through my head about the day before in an effort to discover where I had gone off the track. Even if you could not explain to me why there was no trace whatsoever of anybody having been at that house for twelve years, perhaps you could explain what actually had happened yesterday.

I was certain that I had gone up into the mountain forest with my friends Willard, his sister Ella Jean, Joe Don, his sister Gypsy, and Sammy, kid brother of my only local hero, the late Mare Coe. I had thought that we were hunting for the place where a glider would come down out of the sky. I had thought that we had actually seen the glider come in for a crash landing, and that everything as I have written it for the past many pages actually happened. But—and this was my first new thought—was it possible that I, having lost all of a heap my local hero Mare, my national hero President Roosevelt, and then my all-time hero Ernie Pyle, was driven to create a wonderful new hero, Lieutenant McPherson? Okay, granted that I did that. So why couldn't I *keep* him? For pity sakes, if McPherson was only the product of my pubertal fancy, like a mental image of a voluptuous but impossibly tantalizing woman summoned up to promote the most extravagant erotic thoughts, why couldn't I make him come back again? When I dreamed of Ella Jean, either at night or whenever my conscious reveries needed her, the loss of her at the end of the episode was always softened by the thought that she'd return whenever I wanted.

Could *you* let him come back again? Gentle Reader, one thing I know about you, if nothing else, is that you possess certain powers, even a kind of magic: you could snap shut this book right now and obliterate me, just as you opened it in the first place to create me. Could you kindly let the soldiers come back again? Or, if they had to leave and go into hiding somewhere else, could you help me find them? If you will, I promise you the most exciting story you've ever read.

I stood up. I remembered one little thing that had happened here yesterday: the business of the well water. A soldier had been required to step off the distance from the outhouse to the well, to make sure that the former could not have contaminated the latter. I went to the well, where the old fragment of rope still hung from the rusted iron pulley, untouched. The soldiers had produced their own rope and bucket and pulled up several bucketsful of good clean pure well water, and refilled their canteens with it, and everybody had had a good drink, but there was no trace of this activity around the well. I looked up at the out-house, and walked slowly toward it, bent over, studying the ground closely, until, finally, halfway to the outhouse, I spotted in the dirt the unmistakable imprint of the heel of a soldier's boot. There was just that one, but it was clear, and it was enough. "Ha!" I exclaimed, with exultation.

"Very good, Donny," you said.

"Thank you," I said to you. Thank you for restoring my faith and convincing me I wasn't crazy. I even looked around for you, but you weren't there. In your place was simply a bush, speaking, not unlike that burning bush that spoke to Moses. The bush spoke again, repeating the same words, "Very good, Donny." And then the bush raised one of its limbs and brushed some leaves away from its head, and I could see the face. The bush was my new hero. The bush turned its head and spoke louder, "Rucker!" Another bush appeared before my bush and its limb snapped up in a salute. "Goddamn it, Rucker! You missed a spot! Look! Is that a heelprint or isn't it?"

"Sorry, sir!" Rucker said, and the bush fell to his knees, and with his bare hands began scratching at the dirt around the heelprint until it was obliterated.

"Otherwise, wouldn't you say?" McPherson asked me. "We covered our traces pretty well."

"You sure did," I said, beaming to find him again. "Where are you?" I asked, and realized it sounded as if I couldn't even see *him* inside his bush when there he was, right before me! and the other bush Rucker still groveling in the earth. But Rucker finished the job and got to his feet and began looking for other places where he hadn't covered his tracks. "I mean," I clarified, "where is your bivouac?"

"Where are we?" McPherson repeated my question with a chuckle. "We're all around you. See if you can find us." He swept the grounds with his hands as if challenging me to find the bivouac. I looked all around, and saw nothing. The lieutenant took my arm and guided me, and we walked until we came to the first tent. The tent was covered with branches, totally concealed. The second tent also. At each of the tents, bushes turned into soldiers before my eyes, grinning at me. All the tents and soldiers were virtually invisible from a distance.

"*Camouflage,*" I said.

"That's it, Donny," he said, and showed me where several foxholes had been dug and carefully covered up with shrubbery, and even the excavated soil, lighter in color, had been evenly distributed and covered with topsoil. He showed where emplacements had been constructed for mortars, machine guns, and antitank guns, each concealed in a foxhole covered with branches that looked like natural bushes or weeds.

"You guys have been busy," I remarked.

"What else is there to do?" he said. "But when you were hunting for us, just now," he said, "you forgot something. You forgot one of us."

I thought and thought. Then I remembered. "The mule! Where'd you hide the mule?"

"Where would you hide something as big as a mule?" he asked.

I looked around, and saw the old barn. It wasn't actually a barn, not one of those gambrel-roof warehouses for storing hay but just a dilapidated cowshed with a rusty tin roof. It looked as if it hadn't been opened in years, and there were still spiderwebs all over it, but, as McPherson showed me, it had a mule inside it. "Young Jarhead," McPherson declared, grinning. "Formerly known as ASM147, Army Special Mule. GI Moe, the men called him. Gypsy let us rename him." He gave Young Jarhead an appreciative pat on the head, and Jarhead looked as if he wished he could raise a hoof in salute. "Speaking of which, the others will be here soon. Let's see how they take it. Here, let's get you ready."

McPherson gathered up some assorted vegetation and netting and made me into a bush, and then we covered our tracks. His bush and my bush stood side by side near the old house, waiting, and sure enough before long Sammy Coe showed up. Sammy's mouth dropped open in astonishment at finding that the bivouac had disappeared, and he began looking wildly around him, almost in panic. I wondered if my own face and attitude had conveyed such desperate surprise and disappointment minutes earlier. I started to giggle, but the bush next to me clamped its limb end over my mouth. Sammy looked up as if he had heard the beginning of my giggle and stared right at me for a brief moment before

his eyes continued to wander all over creation in search of the bivouac.
Sammy went inside the house, just as I had done, and I knew he might
find the prints of my bare feet in the dust but nothing else. Soon he
came back out, looking as if he were about to cry. Had I looked so for-
lorn and tragic? Just as I had done, he sat down on the edge of the
porch, with his head in his hands. I knew he did not have the advantage
I'd had, of being able to appeal to you. To whom then was he appealing?
Maybe he was praying.

Soon Gypsy and Ella Jean came up the trail, arms around each other
as usual. But their arms fell to their sides as they saw the place and then
saw Sammy sitting in dejection on the edge of the porch. Gypsy
shrieked and cried, "Lord have mercy! They've all done gone and *gone!*"

"It caint be!" Ella Jean cried. "They couldn't've just cleared out dead
and gone without no word!"

I had to raise two limbs to cover my mouth.

Sammy said woefully, "They aint nobody ever been here to begin
with!" And I had a wave of fellow feeling for his sense of having dreamt
it all.

Willard and Joe Don weren't far behind. "What in the Sam Hill!?"
said Joe Don.

"I'll be jig swiggered!" said Willard, who glowered at Sammy as if
Sammy had scared them all off, and demanded, "Where in tarnation is
everbody?" I knew that Willard was smart enough to do what I had
done: search for any remaining footprint on the path to the outhouse.
But before he could think to do that, it was Gypsy who thought to call
out for her new friend.

"JAARRRHEADDD!" Gypsy hollered.

And from the old barn came the loud bray of a mule.

Gypsy laughed and started for the barn.

But a bush stood in her way, and behold, the bush decreed loudly,
"FALL *IN!*" And behold, twelve other bushes, thirteen if you count me,
lined themselves up in formation before the commanding bush. We
stood at attention, like good bushes. "AT EASE, SHRUBS!" ordered Mc-
Pherson, and we not only relaxed but broke up in laughter.

CHAPTER
16

WHEN ALL OF US WHO HAD BEEN WOODLAND PLANTS SHED OUR vegetation and looked like human beings again, McPherson said, "Something will have to be done about Jarhead. He gave us away."

"If you don't want him, I'll take him," Gypsy said, and, I swear, batted her eyelashes at the lieutenant.

"No, I'd rather you had a talk with him and explain that he can't just sound off whenever he wants."

"He was just answerin me when I called him," Gypsy said.

"Well, I hope the enemy doesn't try to call him," McPherson said.

"Are ye a-fixin to take him to Jay-pan with y'uns?" Joe Don asked.

"Joe Don," McPherson said sternly, dropping his jovial tone, "you don't *know* that we're going to Japan."

"Naw, but I can sure *guess*," Joe Don said.

"Maybe that's not the enemy he's talkin about," Willard said to Joe Don, then he said to the lieutenant, "Maybe the enemy is the one that you're a-fixin to hide out from, right here. The play-like enemy."

"Good boy," McPherson said.

Willard bristled at the "boy." He asked, "How big do they grow men where you come from?"

McPherson studied him as if trying to determine if Willard was being insubordinate. Or, since Willard wasn't his subordinate and he couldn't put him on KP duty or whatever you do to punish a soldier, he was trying to analyze the note of unfriendliness. It suddenly occurred to me: Willard was jealous of McPherson because Gypsy had developed a powerful attraction toward the lieutenant! Why does it take me so long to realize these things?

The lieutenant knew the way to Willard's heart. "Would you people like a snack?" he offered.

While we were sitting around munching the fruit bars and chocolate bars, and Willard was working on his second helping, the other lieutenant, the one with the gold bar on his collar (and thus just a *second* lieutenant, although I couldn't understand why gold was considered inferior to silver), came up and said "Mac, I'm sorry but this damn thing is killing me." He was painfully clutching his arm, which had been broken when he piloted the glider to its crash landing.

I spoke up. "I broke my arm just like that not very long ago, and Doc Swain put a plaster cast on it, which I had to wear for several weeks, but it's good as new now." I held up my arm and twisted it every which way to demonstrate its flexibility and soundness.

McPherson addressed not me personally but the group at large. "You have a doctor in this town?"

Sammy said, "Doc Swain can fix anything what's wrong with man or beast."

I nodded, in rare agreement with Sammy, and added, "Besides, he's the justice of the peace," as if that helped matters.

McPherson was thinking. Finally he asked, again not of me personally, "What would he charge to set Bosco's arm and put it in a cast?"

"Heck," I said, "oftentimes if you can't pay him, he'll take produce or livestock or something in trade."

McPherson smiled. "Would he take Jarhead?"

"You just better not, mister!" Gypsy said.

"I was teasing you, Gypsy," McPherson said. "I could pay the good doctor whatever he wants. But the problem is, of course, we don't want any of the adults to—" he hesitated, realizing that he might be hurting our feelings by implying that we weren't adults. "It's crucial we keep our presence here a secret from all but you good people."

"Doc won't tell nobody, if we ask him not to," I affirmed.

"He'll tell his wife," McPherson said, "and she'll tell a friend, and that friend will tell—"

"Doc don't have a wife," I said. "He don't have nobody. He lives all alone. He's an old man," I added, as if being old is a guarantee of being either alone or not gossipy.

McPherson was addressing me now instead of the group at large. "Would Bosco have to visit his office? Or could the doctor come out here?"

"He makes house calls," I said, "if you got a house." I grinned and pointed at the deserted building.

"Okay. Volunteers for a detail to go after Dr. Swain?" All six of us held up our hands. "Hmmm," McPherson said. "We don't need that many. You do it, Donny." I saluted, and turned to go, pleased with the assignment. He called after me, *Himitsu! Shikyu no himitsu!*

I ran all the way to Doc Swain's. He was sitting on his porch, no customers . . . or rather no clients . . . *patients* is the word. Patience. I was all out of breath. "Doc, there's another broke arm needs fixed!"

"Didn't I tell ye to play hide-and-go-seek from them Allies?" he said.

"It's not mine," I said. I looked up and down the main road of the village. Old Lola Ingledew was sitting on the front porch of her store, but she was too far off to hear us. "It's a Army Air Force lieutenant. Can you keep a secret?"

"If I don't have nothing better to do, I can," he said.

"You know that glider that come down yesterday?"

"The one that burnt all up?"

"Yes, but the pilot lived. His arm is broke, though. He needs you."

"His arm or his leg? Caint he walk? Why don't he come to me?"

"That's part of the secret," I said.

"Let me get my bag and all," Doc Swain said. He went into his house and returned quickly, carrying his bag and whatever plaster and stuff he needed to set and cast an arm. "Where's my damn car?" he demanded, as if I'd stolen it.

"Every's still workin on it, I reckon," I said.

So we walked. Passing Dill's Gas and Service, Doc called to Every, "Don't tell me if the news is bad."

"Piston ring is shot," Every said. "You need it right now?"

"I can walk," Doc said. "It will do me good."

"Who's ailing?" Every called.

"Nobody you know, I reckon," Doc said. "Nor me neither."

We walked on. Lieutenant Bosco wasn't going to die before we got there. I wondered how much I could tell Doc about everything, but decided that any talking ought to be left to McPherson. At least I could say, without sounding too self-important, "This is all very secret."

"You done told me that," Doc said.

The last half mile was hardest for him, uphill and slow. We arrived at the old farmstead. As before, everything was camouflaged. There was no one in sight. "They're hiding," I said. "But they're here."

"Or else you got the wrong house, Dawny," he said. "This is the old Stapleton place. Aint nobody lived here since—howdy!" McPherson came out of the house, and approached us.

I introduced them. "Doc Swain, Lieutenant McPherson, United States Army."

"Should I salute or shake hands?" Doc Swain asked. "Not if it's the broken one."

McPherson laughed and shook Doc's hand. "It's not me. Could you come inside? Donny, the other Axis are out behind the barn, learning judo, if you'd like to join them."

While McPherson was taking Doc Swain to fix Lieutenant Bosco's arm, I moseyed out behind the barn to see what judo was. I'd heard of it. In the pasture, the soldiers were sitting on the ground in a circle with

Gypsy and Ella Jean, watching Sergeant Harris and Corporal Rucker demonstrate the holds and armlocks and takedowns and strangles of elementary judo. They motioned for me to join them. I removed my slingshot from my neck. "Let me hold that for you, Scout," one of the sitting soldiers requested, but he didn't merely hold it; he tried it out, with pebbles. I didn't mind. Harris and Rucker were experts at judo, and before having Willard, Joe Don, Sammy, and me try something on each other, they demonstrated. I could see why Harris outranked Rucker: there wasn't any sort of stranglehold that Rucker could make on Harris that Harris couldn't break loose from, and not only break loose from it but in the process trip Rucker up and throw him down and disable him. It was fun to watch, but not such fun to copy. Willard and Joe Don were paired off, and Sammy and I were paired off; Sergeant Harris would demonstrate an armlock on Corporal Rucker, and then Sammy would try to do it to me. Although Sammy and I were about the same size, he was tougher, I guess. There's something about being a newspaperman, using one's wits and one's words to report a world, that keeps one from being athletic. I was embarrassed to have Gypsy and especially Ella Jean watching me get thrown and twisted and clobbered. But they never giggled, and after a while Sergeant Harris suggested that they ought to start learning these things too. "Women are better at judo than men," the sergeant said, "because their arms are limber and they have a natural talent for pulling hair." He started them off with all the various finger holds: wrist press, thumb lock, counter, and rear hammerlock with wrist pressure, but they graduated quickly from those simple holds to the various armlocks and then to "hacking." Their hacking, the sergeant said, had to be mostly play-like, because they could easily hurt each other.

"Judo is serious business," the sergeant told us. "It's not a game of sportsmanship and play. Its purpose is to keep from being killed by killing. So you have to be careful in practice, because you could gouge an eye out, choke your opponent, make him deaf, paralyze him, give him a blackout as well as a black eye."

We got so caught up in learning judo that we forgot what had been going on in the house. At one point when Sammy had thrown me over his back and I landed on mine, knocking the breath out of me, I looked up to see that our audience had increased: both lieutenants and Doc Swain were watching us. Lieutenant Bosco's arm was in a plaster cast almost identical to the one I'd had. I wanted to tell him that as soon as the plaster hardened we would all sign our names on his cast.

"Somebody could get hurt, doing them things," Doc Swain remarked about our activities. He stepped forward and grabbed Joe Don's hand as he was strangling Willard and said, "You've got your thumb right smack on his sternoclavicular joint. You could kill him."

"I'm jist doing what I was learnt, Doc," Joe Don said. "But I wouldn't do it real enough to kill him."

From that point on, Doc's kibitzing took some of the fun out of our judo practice. We got a whole lesson in anatomy from his intrusion. He showed where my kidney was located and warned against causing it pain. He said if Ella Jean hit Gypsy above her belly button it would make her puke. He pointed out the solar plexus and the carotid artery and larynx and cautioned against any blows to these vulnerable parts.

Eventually McPherson said to him, "Doctor, we need to talk," and led him away. I assumed he was simply trying to remove him from interfering with the judo lessons, but that wasn't it. McPherson needed, I eventually realized, to give Doc Swain the same kind of little chat he'd had with each of us the day before, to impress the need for secrecy on him, perhaps even to bribe Doc Swain to keep this bivouac a secret. But what would he bribe him with?

It was getting on to suppertime but we were having so much fun with judo that we didn't want to go home to eat. At least I didn't, and I was probably having less fun than my more athletic friends. Eventually McPherson returned to us. Doc Swain was gone. Speaking on our behalf, Gypsy said, "Captain, can we just stay for supper?"

"I'm not a captain, Gypsy," he said. "You can call me Mac if you like. We'd love to have you for supper, but our supply of rations could run out, especially in view of Willard's fondness for them."

"Could we just come back after supper, then, Mac?" she asked sweetly. And added: "Like last night?" I was jealous. I hadn't come back the previous night.

"Don't you think your mothers are going to wonder what you're doing?" Mac asked. He grinned. "Where I come from, a good girl wouldn't be out after dark."

"How do you know I'm a good girl?" Gypsy said.

"Where do you come from?" I asked him.

He didn't answer either of our questions. "After supper," he declared, "my men have to practice their night movement and their night fighting."

"Couldn't we watch?" Gypsy asked.

Mac laughed. "The whole point of our exercises is to be invisible!"

So we had to wait for another day. It was impossible getting through school Friday, not simply because it was Friday but because we were impatient to return to the soldiers' bivouac for more judo lessons or, as it turned out that afternoon when we got there, not simply more judo lessons but also what the lieutenant called "mass combatives" and his men thought of as "taking a break": rough-and-tumble games. These games were even more dangerous than judo, and Gypsy and Ella Jean weren't allowed to participate in some of them. The lieutenant explained that jungle fighting and Japanese trickery had been the mother of the invention of many of these free-for-all and team games. Only one of these games had we ever played before, Foxhole Fight, when Allies had tried to pull the Axis out of our foxholes and take our place. At the end of two minutes the winner was whoever had the most foxholes. But the way these soldiers played it, using their actual "official" foxholes excavated in the yards and fields of the old Stapleton place, there was a lot more pushing, shoving, pulling, and general hand tricks than we Axis or Allies had ever imagined.

One of the funniest, as well as the most fun, was the Crouch Bout, wherein we formed a circle and each of us hunkered down with our hands on our hips. The object was to push each other to the ground without rising up from the hunkered squat. Whoever touches the ground with his hands or gets pushed outside the circle is eliminated, one by one until only one is left. We looked like a bunch of ducks fighting, and the girls laughed constantly. Sergeant Harris usually was the last one left hunkered.

Then there was Climb the Trees. We divided into two groups of eight each, arbitrarily called Allies and Axis: Willard and Sammy were Allies while Joe Don and I were Axis. (Lieutenant McPherson himself joined the Axis, but Lieutenant Bosco, disabled, had to sit with Gypsy and Ella Jean and watch, so he served as referee, giving the command CLIMB THE TREE and blowing his whistle after ten minutes). Each team tried to prevent the other team from getting up in the tree. When the whistle blew, the team with the most men up in a tree was the winner.

For other games the "Allies" and "Axis" turned themselves into "horses" and "riders" with we younger or smaller guys riding on the shoulders of the larger ones, and I had the privilege of having Mac himself as my horse. One game was called "Pickaback," which was the way Mac pronounced piggyback, and involved starting twenty feet apart, and when Bosco gave the signal, the horse-and-rider teams would try to get to the opposite side without being knocked over by the other horse-and-riders. It hurt like hell to get knocked off my "horse" (his shoulders were just as high as a horse's back) but the more we played this game the better I became at jousting and the better Mac became as my trusty steed, so that eventually we were unbeatable.

Saturday there was no school, so we could look forward to a whole day at the bivouac. Unfortunately, the other Axis (of the town, not of the rough-and-tumble soldier's games) wanted to go with us. Or, rather, since they didn't know where we were going, they wanted to know why we were abandoning them on Saturday, the best of all play-days. How could we tell them that we'd discovered a new kind of play that was far more fun than anything we'd ever done before but that we couldn't allow any more Axis to join us there? How could we get away from them? The littluns, especially, were pathetic, and a problem. And those who had defected from the Allies, like Rosa Faye Duckworth and Betty June Alan, had assumed that their defection would allow them to become members in good standing of the Axis and to participate in all our activities.

"I got to make hay while the sun shines," Willard gave as an excuse, but later some of the other Axis had gone to visit the Dinsmore hay field to volunteer to help him with haying, and he wasn't there! Where was he?

"Maw's feeling porely, and I got to stay home and keer fer her," Gypsy gave as her excuse, and Betty June Alan took a casserole of food to the Dingletoon house as a get-well gift, and found that Gypsy wasn't there! Where was she?

"I got to work real hard on next Monday's *Star,*" I gave as my excuse, and later Latha reported that several of the Axis had brought in news items for me, but I wasn't there! Where was I?

"Aw, I've just been out tracking down a news story," I told her. "Turned out it was a false alarm anyhow." I hated to lie to Latha, but it wasn't exactly lying.

Still, without being able to ask my close Axis colleagues how they felt about it, I felt rather guilty, having such fun to the exclusion of all the Axis except us privileged few. If the situation was dull for the Axis left behind, it was even worse for the Allies, who had no one to play with, no one to fight with, except each other. I heard that Jim John and Larry had actually got into a fistfight with each other. I wished I'd been there to watch it, but I was watching—and participating in—far more interesting spectacles.

All of that activity in those judo practices and mass combatives was leaving us drenched with sweat and sore all over, but the worst was yet to come. On Saturday Sergeant Harris put us through what he called "calisthenics," which sounded like some kind of disease, or something taken for a disease. He said we needed it because we "weren't worth diddly squat" in the rough-and-tumble exercises. I think "diddly squat" was a euphemism for something nastier. Sergeant Harris often chewed us out. Ella Jean cried. Both she and Gypsy eventually dropped out of the calisthenics, but, as I discovered, not because the exercises were too strenuous for them, nor because Sergeant Harris chewed us out, nor even because the sergeant called his men, and us, "ladies" when we didn't do something right. The reason Gypsy and Ella Jean had to drop out was that all of us were becoming too gamy for them to tolerate. I mean, all of us smelled really awful. For that matter, Gypsy and Ella Jean didn't exactly smell like roses, but at least they could run down to their secret swimming hole on Banty Creek and smear that wonderful Palmolive all over themselves. These soldiers hadn't had a bath and needed one in the worst way. Well, they were each given a daily ration of one helmetful of well water for cleaning, but they had to shave, and brush their teeth, and if there was any left over they just sort of dabbed at their armpits.

"Could we rent a washtub from anybody?" McPherson asked us. I told him that I could get ahold of one rent-free, and I volunteered to go get it. That was characteristic of my desire to leave a constant good impression on the lieutenant. There was a good galvanized tin washtub on the back porch at Aunt Murrison's that had somehow escaped the War Effort Scrap Drive because, after all, my aunt and uncle needed it for a monthly bath and they made me use it for a weekly bath. It was time for my weekly bath, which I usually had on Saturday afternoons anyhow, before getting ready to—. I suddenly realized that tonight, as usual, Doc Swain was going to take some kids to Jasper to see the picture show. I'd forgotten all about that, but I guess it wasn't going to hurt me to miss one of them, even though I wouldn't be able to use the newsreel as source material for my—. I suddenly realized that I had done nothing to get Monday's issue of the *Star* ready for press. Oh well, I could work extra hard on Sunday, couldn't I? Then I realized Doc Swain wouldn't be going to Jasper anyway, because his car was still in the shop at Every's.

I had no trouble sneaking around the back way to my aunt's house and stealing that washtub off the back porch. I had no trouble carrying it, one hand at a time until that hand got tired, for most of the way back to the bivouac. But for the last stretch of the trail, uphill and rough, I had to try carrying the washtub upside down on top of my head, staring at the ground and oblivious to whatever was around me.

Thus I didn't see the sentry until he stopped me. The soldiers usually posted a sentry, hiding in the brush, near the place where the trail arrives at the bivouac. This one rapped me on top of the tub, and I quickly took the tub off my head and looked up at him. His name was Private Crowder.

"You know me," I said. "I'm just taking this tub so everybody can have a bath."

"Yeah, I know you," he said. "But I don't know *her.*"

He pointed. There, close behind me, was Rosa Faye Duckworth.

CHAPTER
17

WHEN MCPHERSON FINISHED WITH HER AND CAME OUT OF THE house, he summoned me into the house. He did not send Rosa Faye back to town. He sent her off to join the others.

"Is there another girl you'd like to invite?" he asked me, with clear exasperation, as we sat down in the director's chairs. "One more girl, and then you'd have an equal number of boys and girls, four of each."

"I didn't invite her, sir," I said. "She must've just been following me."

"Yes, I know what she was doing. She had been sitting on the front porch of your aunt's house, waiting for you in hopes of being able to tell you in her own way, I suppose, that she'd like to become better friends, that she'd like to work for the *Star*, that she'd like to do anything if only you and the other Axis did not exclude her from whatever you've been doing lately. When she saw you come and make off with the washtub, she followed you, trying to find out where you were going. And sure enough, you led her right into our lair."

"I'm sorry, sir," I said. I had learned from the other men that you always put "sir" into whatever you say to him.

He sighed. "Are you interested in her?"

"Oh no!" I said. "No, sir. She has to sit with me in school because she's now on the Axis side instead of the Allied side. Heck, she's at least a year older'n me, sir. And besides, sir, the only girl I'm interested in is Ella Jean. But she's just not interested in me, sir."

He smiled. "You want to bet?" And then he dropped the smile. "You needn't call me 'sir,' Donny. Rosa Faye's brother remains a chief of the enemy, the Allies."

"But she's on our side. When the Allies killed Old Jarhead, you see, she switched over. I'm sure she wouldn't tell Larry anything. Not if you talked to her the same way you talked to the rest of us. You could talk a kid out of a piece of cake. Heck, you could even talk Willard out of *wanting* a piece of cake."

He laughed at the compliment. "I'm not sure I was totally successful in my little talk with Rosa Faye. But there's no way I can keep her from joining us—unless I banish the whole lot of you."

"She'd probably be real good at learning judo," I suggested.

"You've all had a lot of fun with judo, haven't you?" he asked. "But it isn't a game. As Sergeant Harris tried to tell you, it's meant to kill. These men are all killers. *I* am a killer." He said these last words almost threateningly, as if I were going to be his next victim. I couldn't help trembling. "Sometimes I think that I've been incredibly derelict in my duty, letting a bunch of kids hang around with a pack of coldhearted killers, and even showing you how to kill with judo," he went on, as if he were talking to himself, severely criticizing himself. I wondered if being licked by a deer was some kind of folksy talk where he came from, wherever that was. "You don't *need* to learn judo. But we've enjoyed your company, and you've helped our morale: you've been a nice diversion for my men while we sit out this stupid wait, but—"

"What are you waiting for?" I interrupted his conversation with himself, in my newspaper-reporter voice.

"There's a war game about to begin," he said. "That's all I can tell you. I don't know when. I wish I did. That's one little thing they forgot to tell me."

"Do you mean the 'enemy' could show up any minute?" I asked, continuing my reportorial questioning.

"Or next month," he said. "But yes, maybe any minute. Maybe they're on their damn way right now. Who knows?"

"Could we help you watch out for 'em?" I offered.

He thought about that, and smiled. "That could be very helpful, but probably it wouldn't be kosher, because in a real situation we wouldn't be getting any such cooperation from the natives."

After I got his definition of *kosher* and in the process learned that he wasn't a Jew himself, I asked, "How do you know you wouldn't get any help from the natives? When you land in Japan, you might discover that all the country people are sick and tired of the war and they want to help you beat the Jap army."

McPherson really cut loose with a laugh that must have carried out to all the others, who probably thought we were sitting around telling our favorite jokes. Then he said, "What a dream, Donny! But you might even be right. We're not counting on it, though. Not one of us expects to come out of that mission alive."

"There!" I said. "You just admitted that you *are* going to Japan."

"Apparently all of you kids have already guessed that," he said, "and it's one more of our secrets you'll have to keep to yourselves."

"Are they just going to drop you there in a big glider the same way they did here?"

"Don't pester me for troop movements, Donny," he cautioned.

"Okay, but there's just one thing I don't understand. When they drop you there, you'll be out to kill the Japs with judo and guns and whatever, right? But *here*, for this war game, you've got to pretend you're the Japs? That don't make sense."

"Maybe it doesn't. But the 'enemy' that's coming to get us is a crack battalion of armored troops whose ultimate mission will be to drive their tanks into the mountain country of Kyushu. That's mainland Japan, or the southernmost of four main islands of the country. Supposedly the terrain of their objective is very similar to your mountains, which is why these maneuvers are being inflicted upon you people."

"So you-all have to play like you're their target, and in reward you get to go and help 'em do the real job and get yourself killed doing it."

His smile was wan. "That's about it. My men have been trained in *senjutsu*, a Japanese tactical doctrine that will allow us to expose the tank battalion to the same tactics they'll expect in their invasion of Kyushu. I like to think of my men as *samurai*, the ancient warrior class, who possess the seven virtues of *Bushido*—but I'll bore you with those some other time."

"These guys of the 'enemy' are coming to Stay More in *tanks?*"

"All kinds of tanks. There will be really big M-10s, and M-4 Shermans, and a thing called the M-7, open at the top but mounted with a 105 mm howitzer," he said. "It has anti-aircraft defense in the form of what they call the 'pulpit,' a mount with a .50 caliber machine gun in it, but they won't be able to try that out against actual air assault during the war games. All of the assault will come from my men on the ground, each of those different tanks will require a different method of destroying it."

"And you're supposed to *lose?*" I needed his confirmation of my suspicion.

"Ultimately, yes. We're Japs, remember? But there will be an umpire, and my men are the pick of the lot, crack troops chosen from the Army's best, selected for their wits and their strength as well as the seven virtues of *Bushido,* and also for their willingness to give up their lives for the cause, and I haven't given them any instructions to lie down and surrender."

"So you're really going to fight?"

"Not to kill, *this* time," he said. "But it will be a fight. And you'll have a ringside seat. You should get a press card to stick in your hat."

"I don't have a hat."

"Behind your ear, then," he said, and reached out and gave me a little swat on my ear. "Now let's go join the others. Sergeant Harris has chosen an activity that will allow the girls to remain out of nose-shot of our stinky bodies, until we have the privacy to use your washtub." He put his hand on my shoulder and led me to where the others were. Sergeant Harris was in the process of explaining to the kids the General Alertness Drill, which involved developing instantaneous responses to spoken commands, for example, everybody freezes when he says STOP! He was explaining that this is what'd you do if an enemy flare caught you on a patrol in no man's land: if you tried to duck or make any movement at all you'd get shot, but if you just froze completely you'd either not get noticed or be mistaken for a tree.

McPherson and I both joined in the alertness drill. I learned how to respond properly: not just to STOP but also to SIT DOWN, STAND UP, GET OUT OF MY SIGHT, JUMP IN THE BUSHES, ROLL ON YOUR BACK, and SCATTER. Some of these were almost like playing hide-and-go-seek, and Rosa Faye participated in all of these, and she didn't even seem to have to keep her distance from the men the way the other girls were doing. None of the movements in this drill required a lot of exertion, so we weren't getting any more stinky than we were to begin with. After we'd practiced the alertness drill for an hour, and had come back from the SCATTER command, the lieutenant made a motion to the sergeant and then gave a command of his own—FALL IN—and we all lined up in front of him. Rosa Faye was just a little late because she hadn't heard FALL IN before and her first reaction to it was to fall down. But she quickly got up, blushing, and stood at attention in a line with the rest of us.

"Now it's time we rehearsed a few situations," Lieutenant McPherson said. "Supposing we're down behind enemy lines, and taking assessment of our condition. Straighten up there, Coe!" Sammy had lazily allowed himself to get into the at-ease position instead of attention. Then when the lieutenant snapped "Bosco!" poor Sammy thought at first that we were being told to "boss" or something.

"Sir?" Sammy said.

But "Sir?" said the other lieutenant, stepping forward smartly and clicking his heels as he came to stop at rigid attention. I still didn't quite understand this rank business, why Bosco would be subordinate to McPherson and why silver was more important than gold. But then as I stared at Bosco standing there with his arm in a cast suspended from a cloth triangle around his neck, I realized that the bar on Bosco's collar was not gold but brass. Also I got a good look at the wings over his shirt pocket: a pair of brass wings on either side of a large letter "G." That wasn't *his* initial. What did it stand for?

"Eyes front, Donny!" McPherson said to me, and I aped the other men, who were rigidly at attention, staring straight ahead. Then McPherson addressed the brass lieutenant. "Bosco, you are useless to this mission," McPherson declared. "With your broken arm, you're just holding us back."

"Sorry, sir!" Bosco said, even if he wasn't required to say 'sir' to a fellow lieutenant.

"Since we are behind enemy lines, your job of piloting the craft to a landing is successfully completed, but you are incapacitated and therefore a liability to the mission. Do you understand what we have to do to you?"

"Yes, sir," Bosco said. "They shoot horses, don't they?" He said this matter-of-factly without any intended humor.

McPherson unfastened the strap of his Nambu automatic and drew the pistol out. "If you fell into the hands of the enemy, they could torture you and you'd give away our secrets." He slowly raised the pistol and pointed it at Bosco. I hoped he remembered that it was loaded with real bullets.

"I realize that, sir," Bosco said. "My only regret is that I didn't get everybody to sign my cast." He lifted his arm. The cast had been signed by a few of the men, but I hadn't had a chance to inscribe it.

"Sorry about that," McPherson said. "Thanks for landing us." Then he fired. It was a terrible burden of knowledge, to be the only one who knew that McPherson's automatic didn't have blanks in it, and I must have jumped a foot or two. McPherson fired a second time, and then a third, and Second Lieutenant Bosco, glider pilot of the Army Air Force, clutched his stomach with his one usable hand and crumpled up on the ground. I looked around bewildered at the other men. Not one of them was betraying any emotion! Each one of them continued to stare straight ahead like zombies, as if this were something they hadn't even noticed, or as if it were something they did every day right after breakfast. By contrast, Gypsy and Ella Jean and Rosa Faye were screaming their heads off and dancing around like they had to go to the outhouse badly, and then they were holding each other. Willard was trying to copy the impassive attention of the soldiers but he was doing a bad job of it, and was shaking like a leaf. Joe Don was the only one capable of speech.

"Hey!" he yelled at the lieutenant, "now what did ye have to go and do *that* for?"

"Can it, Dingletoon!" McPherson snapped at him, and pointed the pistol at Joe Don. "Do you want to be next, for making so much noise? You're giving away our location."

I was about to protest, myself, because I was the only one who *knew* the bullets were real. But I was too scared to speak.

McPherson put the pistol back in his holster. "Well, you men passed that drill. You kids flunked it. Why don't you go back to town and play your Allied buddies in a game of baseball or something? My men want to use the washtub after they've buried poor Bosco."

The girls didn't need to be told twice, and they scampered away from there. But before they got very far, here came Doc Swain, carrying his black doctor's bag. "Finally got my car fixed," he said. "So I can take the corpse for an autopsy." He gave the body a kick like kicking a car's tire. "Looks like he's pretty dead. Are you dead completely, son?" he asked the corpse.

"Yes sir," Bosco replied, motionless. "I'm dead as a dodo."

All the men started laughing. "FALL OUT!" McPherson said. Bosco got up off the ground, and some of the men started hugging him.

"Anybody else want to see the pitcher show?" Doc Swain asked.

"Doctor Swain has kindly consented to drive Lieutenant Bosco to the county seat, Jasper," McPherson announced, "where he can catch a bus and eventually get back to Camp Chaffee. So any of you who want to sign his cast had better do it now."

"I can take two or three more to the pitcher show tonight," Doc said. "It's *The Mummy's Curse* with Lon Chaney."

All of the men raised their hands. None of us Japs did. I personally couldn't stand movies with Egyptian mummies who moved around, and anyhow I didn't want to go to Jasper when there was more to watch in Stay More.

Gypsy said, "Us gals wants to sign Bosco's cast, and then we're gonna go fix a nice supper to bring for all of you'uns."

Doc Swain said to me, "Dawny, you'll miss the newsreel."

"Those things are weeks old anyhow," I said. "I'll just use the radio."

"Sorry, men," McPherson said. "Jasper is off-limits to anybody ex-

cept Bosco, and he's dressing in civvies, thanks to the good doctor." He
turned to Gypsy and said, "We appreciate the offer of supper, especially because our supply of K rations is very low, and we're sure that
you girls are wonderful cooks, but I don't see how you could slip some
food past your mothers."

"You just leave that to us, captain!" Gypsy said.

The girls each signed Lieutenant Bosco's cast, and then they each
gave him a kiss on the cheek, which caused the other men to howl and
whistle and make remarks, and Rucker said, "Hey, Doc, my arm is broken too!" After the rest of us had signed the cast, mostly with expressions of "Good luck" and "Nice knowing you," Bosco gathered up his
gear and Doc Swain drove him away.

"See you in Okinawa!" McPherson called after him.

The girls each returned to their homes, where Gypsy told her mother
that all the Dinsmores had took sick, and Ella Jean told her mother that
all the Dingletoons had took sick, and Rosa Faye told her mother that
both the Dinsmores and the Dingletoons were laid up with something
awful, and the three girls got busy with their mothers' help cooking up
three large pots of, respectively, pork and beans, boiled greens (mixed
turnip, mustard, collards, and poke salat), and enough chicken-and-
dumplings to feed an army (or a small part of one).

Their efforts were hugely appreciated by the soldiers, six of whom
proposed offers of marriage on the spot to the three girls, who declined
on the grounds they couldn't decide which one to marry. We had a real
banquet. The soldiers had each taken a good bath in my washtub, and
put on fresh clothes, and spruced themselves up a bit. After we'd made
pigs of ourselves, and Willard was obviously in paradise, Sammy Coe
furnished the dessert: he had persuaded his mother that he needed to
take blackberry cobbler to both the Dinsmores and the Dingletoons,
families with a total of thirteen sick members, all of whom would need
seconds, and thus he needed enough to feed 'em all. Polacek claimed
he'd never had chicken and dumplings before, which we found hard to
believe, but I don't think any of those men had had blackberry cobbler
before. Willard brought the cream, and had three helpings himself.
There wasn't a speck of food left over.

The soldiers offered their cigarettes to us, and we accepted—or rather Ella Jean declined, so I declined too, but Gypsy actually smoked one, and so did Rosa Faye. By the time I had changed my mind and wanted one, it was too late to ask. We lighted a nice campfire, which helped a little to keep the mosquitoes away. All of these men had known mosquitoes before, but they hadn't learned that there's only two things you can do about mosquitoes, if the smoke doesn't keep them off: one, you can be so alert, as in the General Alertness Drill, that as you soon you detect the faintest touch of one of them lighting down on your arm and hear the STINGER! command, you slap down and kill the bastard; or, two, you can be so tough that all those stings don't bother you at all.

Stuffed as we were with all that good food, most of us didn't mind the mosquitoes. We sat around as it grew dark talking about anything, even mosquitoes. Joe Don remarked, "Back when we'uns had our guns, it used to take two of us to have a squirrel hunt, one of us to fire off small shot to clean away the skeeters so th'other'n could see to shoot the squirrels."

After the men had stopped laughing, Willard said, "Shoot, I never could get that far on a squirrel hunt, because three or four of these here skeeters would rassle my dog down and suck all his blood until he was dead."

"I heard from Latha Bourne," I contributed, "that when they finally got window screens on the houses, it got the skeeters flummoxed. But then the skeeters started in to carrying little bitty skeeters that they could push through the mesh, and then when the little skeeters got through and sucked the blood of those in the house and grew and grew, they'd come and unhook the screen door so the others could get in." This little windy drew such appreciative laughter from my audience that I started racking my brain for other stories. But all I could think to add was, "Have you-all seen any lightning bugs yet? Well, those are just skeeters with flashlights!" This crack didn't get quite as much response, and I decided maybe most of these men didn't know what a lightning bug was, or hadn't seen one.

"My Vermont grandfather," McPherson himself put in, "used to tell one about being caught by a swarm of huge mosquitoes, and he shot three or four with his revolver but had to crawl under a big iron wash kettle to get away from the others. But the mosquitoes began drilling right through the sides of the kettle. So he took his pistol butt and clinched over the beaks of any that penetrated. That held them for a while, but after a few more had been riveted to the kettle like that, they just flew off with the kettle!"

"Vermont grandfather?" said Sammy. "Heck, I heard the same story from my grandpa, only it wasn't no kettle, it was a tent, and after he'd clinched ten or twelve of the skeeters, they just put too much strain on the tent-pegs and flew away with the whole camp."

"Vermont grandfather?" said Joe Don. "Are you from Vermont?"

I had been wanting to find out where McPherson was from; in fact, I had asked him once but he'd ignored me. Was he ashamed of his birthplace or did he just want to keep it a secret?

McPherson nodded but we couldn't see him in the dark. We waited, and eventually Joe Don said "Sir?" and finally McPherson said, "Yes, my hometown is Brattleboro, Vermont."

"What do ye know?" Joe Don said. And then he told everybody about the old hermit Dan, who lived in the yellow house down the mountain, and everything he knew to tell about him: how he was a legendary fiddler and renowned marksman with a rifle, how he knew German even, how he'd stopped the Battle of Dinsmore Trail and everything. "He's an old man now," Joe Don said, "but when he wasn't hardly no older'n me, he was a schoolteacher in Vermont."

"Really?" said McPherson. "I wish I could meet him."

"I'd be mighty glad to take you," Joe Don offered. "His house is right down through the woods yonder, probably not more'n a mile. If you're from Vermont, he'd likely hanker to talk your own language with you."

"You know," McPherson reminded him, "we can't have any contact with the population."

"He prowls these hills all by hisself," Joe Don said, and looked all around in the growing darkness. "For all what we know, he's right out there watchin us, right now."

CHAPTER
18

When the Germans surrendered and V-E day was declared, Tuesday, May 8, it was a day too late for that week's issue of *The Stay Morning Star,* which I had managed to bring out at the usual time on Monday morning by forcing myself to stay away from the bivouac all of Sunday. I thought of bringing out an Extra for V-E Day, and later learned that all of the other newspapers in the world except mine had brought out Extras for the occasion, but at least I had already, in the regular issue the day before, had a story, GERMANY SURRENDERS, which, while it didn't exactly predict V-E Day, made it pretty clear that victory was at hand. That was my lead story; I deliberately played down on the back page a small article, FLYING CRATE'S LANDING NOT CERTAIN, which said, "Reports of some kind of flying apparatus floating down to the ridges east of town last Wednesday have not been confirmed. No one has been able to say they actually saw any landing, while others say they saw only some smoke which indicated the machine may have crashed and burned." The rest of the issue was pretty dull. I hadn't had time to get out on my usual rounds to gather news, and while eager Japs had left a few items about visits in my basket at Latha's store, there wasn't much of real interest to report. Thus, I wasn't too happy about showing this issue of the *Star* to the soldiers as an example of my talents, but I printed up an extra dozen copies anyhow, and on my early Monday morning delivery rounds before school I gave the copies to the sentry at the camp and asked him to be sure the lieutenant got one.

"I'm proud of you, Donny," McPherson said the next time I saw him. "The *Star* is a splendid little piece of journalism." Maybe I got kind of damp around the eyes. It had been a long, long time since anybody had said they were proud of me. "I like the clever punning way you've in-corporated the town's name into the name of the paper," he went on. "And of course I'm terribly appreciative and admiring of the way you handled—or deliberately mishandled—the news of our landing."

I didn't know what to say. "Thanks," I said. "I figured you'd like that."

"Have you thought about a career in newspaper work?" he asked.

"Sure," I said. "I've always wanted to be the next Ernie Pyle."

His expression saddened. "A great man," he said. "A *very* great man."

"All you soldiers loved him, didn't you?" I asked.

"I loved him not as a soldier but as a fellow journalist." When I lifted my eyebrows at this statement, he said, "I haven't told you I belong to the same fraternity of Fourth Estaters that you do."

"You're kidding me."

"I don't suppose you've heard of the *Columbia Spectator?*" It sounded like the name of a ship, but I knew he must be referring to some news-paper. I shook my head. "It's just a college paper, but one of the best. I had the privilege of editing it a couple of years ago, but then when I went into graduate school I switched from journalism as a major to Japanese literature, because one of my friends at Columbia—" He stopped and chuckled and said, "I'm boring you with all these things about me." I shook my head vehemently, but he said, "Let's talk about your career. For college, you ought to go to one or the other of the Two Columbias. Columbia University in New York City, where I went to school, has a top-notch journalism department, but the University of Missouri in Columbia, Missouri, which would probably be easier for you if you couldn't get to New York, has one of the best. So one or the other."

I had never given a thought to the fantastic idea of going to college, and I told him that. I was just in the fifth grade. Nobody in Stay More, as far as I knew, had ever been to college. Anyhow, I said, I did want to hear about him and what he'd done. "Why did you get interested in Japanese literature?" I asked.

He made a dismissive gesture with his hand. "Oh, there was another Donald in my life then, Donald Keene, my classmate at Columbia, who was a fanatic about Japanese writing. Don introduced me to the work of a fabulous seventeenth-century novelist named Ihara Saikaku, and when I read his *Koshoku ichidai otoko*, which might be translated as *The Man Who Spent His Life in Love*, I was hooked. It was the first of a whole new genre of fictions called *ukiyo-zoshi*, or tales of the floating world, which are bawdy, some would say pornographic, yet more irresistible than sex itself. . . . But I'm rambling. Back to you. Do you keep all the back issues of the *Star?* You should. Don't ever throw anything away. You'll regret it when you get older. Anyway, I'd appreciate it if, next time you come up here, you bring me the back issue that has your story on old Dan, the hermit in the yellow house." I told him I'd never written a story about ole Dan. He expressed great astonishment. "Possibly the most interesting person you could ever have interviewed!"

And then he told me some unsettling news: the evening before, while I was slaving to get out the issue of the *Star*, Joe Don had taken McPherson to the yellow house! Joe Don had first stopped at the hermit's house to ask the old man if he would care to meet a fellow Vermonter and had tried to persuade the old man to go with him up to the bivouac. That was against the rules for Joe Don. He wasn't supposed to tell any adults; he wasn't supposed to show the bivouac's location to anybody. But it didn't matter, because the old man had said, politely, that he didn't want to "intrude." The old man revealed that, just as Joe Don suspected, he had known about the bivouac all along, and had covertly watched from the woods, and had even been present Saturday night for the banquet. Joe Don had asked the old man if it would be all right if he brought the Vermont lieutenant to meet him, and Dan had graciously agreed. Of course McPherson was rather put out with Joe Don when he heard about all this, but he really was so homesick for Vermont that he was eager to meet the old man, especially after Joe Don assured him that it was possible to hike through the woods from the bivouac to the yellow house without crossing any roads or trails or passing any other houses. In other words (as I knew myself), there was a kind of direct link between the yellow house and the bivouac, topographically, and now there was a direct link between the two Vermonters, who had gotten along famously together.

"Good Lord, have you seen his *daughter?*" McPherson asked me. No, but I'd heard about her, I said, and I explained how she'd never been to school. "Yes, I know," he said. "But she's just as bright as you are!"

"Well, at least you don't have to worry about either one of them telling anybody about you," I said, "because they don't talk to folks."

"They talked to me," he said. "Both of them."

I began to suspect that the lieutenant, like Joe Don himself, had become infatuated with ole Dan's daughter. There was nothing wrong with that, and I enjoyed the fantasy of Stay More providing a girlfriend for this smart, handsome hero of mine. But if McPherson was going on a suicide mission to Japan he didn't want to leave any broken hearts behind. It was already bad enough that Gypsy was so goofy about the lieutenant that she seemed to have forgotten Mare.

There was another thing I had to ask McPherson. Apart from the thought of his hitting it off with the old hermit, I was dizzy from the discovery that he had been a journalist himself and a fellow admirer of Ernie Pyle, and I liked him more than ever, but sometimes he puzzled me. "When you shot Bosco," I wanted to know, "did you want me to think that you had real bullets in your pistol? You told me you did. You said it was a secret just between you and me."

"That was a *situation*, Donny," he said. "I was testing your reaction, and I was testing my men."

I pointed at the Nambu pistol in his holster. "But now you've put the real bullets back in?"

He nodded. "You never know when you might need them. These woods have bears and wolves and panthers in them."

I shook my head. "Nobody has seen any of those for many years. I've never seen one. I saw a coyote once, but you don't need to worry about coyotes."

"Well, there are some strange creatures out there. Last night we saw some sort of snout-nosed animal that looked like an overgrown rat with a long tail. He had real sharp teeth."

"Sounds like a possum," I said. "They're harmless. They're real good to eat, though, if you want to shoot one."

"But then this morning we saw the same creature again, and he had put on a suit of armor!"

I laughed uproariously, but self-consciously wondered when was the last time I had really laughed. "Oh, that wasn't the same creature. That was an *armadillo*," I explained to him. "Come to think of it, they *do* sort of look like possums with armor." He joined in my laughter. "There's no telling what kind of weird creatures you'll find when you get to Japan."

"Oh, they've prepared us for *that*," he said. "The Japanese wolf was exterminated in 1920, but we'll see the wild boar with monstrous tusks, and sika deer, and the macaque, most northerly of all monkeys, the same creature who illustrates the Buddhist wisdom, 'See no evil, hear no evil, speak no evil." McPherson demonstrated with his two hands. Then he said, "But they just didn't prepare us for Stay More, for possums and armadillos. My men joked about the armadillo, wondering if that was the best tank the Sixteenth Armored Division could send to attack us." After he had quit chuckling over that, his expression grew serious and he said, "It's good they can still joke. Good for morale. But I know they're bored, and tired, and a little scared. They can't have leave, and they can't get mail, and they feel cut off from the world. They're getting kind of starved for women, if you know what I mean. Hell, so am I. But I think we all understand that we may never have a woman again. Some of the men have developed this horrible red rash they're scratching all the time, and at first I wondered if it's some kind of venereal disease, you know, from sexual contact. But I got a little of it myself, and I haven't had a woman in a very long time."

"Is it around your . . . *thing?*" I asked.

"Some. Mostly around my calves and ankles." He rolled up his trouser leg and showed me.

"Those are chigger bites," I said.

"Chiggers?" he said.

"They don't have chiggers in Vermont?" I explained to him just what a chigger was: a fierce little red mite that usually doesn't start appearing until late May or early June but was early this year because of the heat. In its larval stage it attacks anything that moves—man, mouse, bird, or reptile. They don't burrow, like ticks, or jab, like mosquitoes, but inject something that makes you scratch like mad and thereby do the digging for them. Then after you've scratched a little hole with your fingernails, they crawl in and have a feast.

"It sounds like the Japanese mite," he said, "which causes *tsutsugamushi,* or Japanese river fever, often fatal."

"Nobody has ever died of a chigger bite that I know of," I said. "But it sure causes a lot of torment." I explained that, as with mosquitoes, there were only two things you could do about them, but neither one involved smacking 'em or ignoring 'em. One was, you could pick some pennyroyal, a common little mintlike ground cover, and crush it up and smear it on your skin, and that would keep them off; they couldn't stand the smell of pennyroyal. Or, if you've already got 'em, and already scratched 'em, you can kill 'em by dabbing a little bit of Chism's Dew on the spot. Chism's Dew was a locally manufactured whiskey; Luther Chism, the proprietor, lived just beyond Butterchurn Holler. No, I couldn't buy some for McPherson and the soldiers, because I was underage, but Luther would probably be willing to sell a jug to Joe Don, who was his closest neighbor. Joe Don wasn't of a legal age either but he wasn't just an innocent kid like me.

Whatever displeasure McPherson may have felt for Joe Don because of his violating the rules in order to introduce the lieutenant to the old hermit was forgotten by Tuesday, when Joe Don showed up after school at the bivouac with a demijohn of Chism's Dew, which the men (being the pick of the Army's brightest) discovered was not only good for treating chigger bites but had another, livelier use. It was V-E Day in Europe, and the soldiers made a kind of celebration/ceremony of converting Joe Don from being a Nazi into becoming a Jap, like all the rest of us. We made a hilarious game out of it. Joe Don was given a Hitlerian mustache with charcoal and sent off to hide as in a game of hide-and-seek, and each of us, armed with a *shoju* (loaded with blanks of course), went out searching for him. Whoever found him would have the privilege of "shooting" him in the ceremony. It was such fun that I wasn't too jealous that Sammy was the one who found him. Joe Don was marched into camp, holding his hands up in surrender, while we yelled whatever taunts we could think of—"Kill the Kraut!" "To hell, Heinie!" "Farewell, Führer!" "Futz to Fritz!" "Junk the Jerry!" Sergeant Harris then boomed at him, "ANY LAST WORDS, ADOLF?" and poor Joe Don struggled to say something appropriate, finally coming up with, "Mein only regret is I got just one ball to give for mein country!" Then he was blindfolded and the firing-squad-of-one, Sammy, was allowed actually to fire the *burauningu* at him. The Japanese BAR made a lot of noise, and I wondered if it carried all the way to the Dills' house. Joe Don, having watched the convincing death throes of Bosco a few days before, attempted to duplicate them. Then Corporal Rucker took over for the resurrection and transformation, presenting Joe Don with an actual Japanese soldier's uniform, and the girls were required to turn their backs while Joe Don took off his clothes and put on the uniform. Rucker explained to us that Joe Don was a *gunso*, sergeant, and he pointed out the *erisho* on his collar that indicated his rank. He now outranked all of us, including Gunso Harris, but not of course the *chui*, McPherson. The latter delivered the main speech in Japanese, not bothering to offer a translation for our benefit, but I could assume from some of the grins and smirks on the faces of his men that he was saying something funny. Then Joe Don saluted, but Chui McPherson had to show him how the Japanese salute is different from the American. I really regretted that I would not be able to write a report of the ceremony for the next issue of the *Star*. At least I would be able to report that henceforward the former Axis would now be called Japs, and the former Allies could call themselves Yanks.

In the final part of the ceremony, Willard, acting on behalf of Mare Coe as vice mayor of Stay More, presented to Lieutenant McPherson a "key to the city," made of wood but looking like a big key, with a red ribbon on it, and he explained that Mare had always wanted to present a key to the city to an important visitor, "but we never had none afore." Who was this Mare Coe? McPherson asked. Willard said to me, "You tell 'em, Dawny," so I proudly told the story of Mare Coe and Iwo Jima.

Throughout all this ceremony and celebration, I noticed the demijohn of Chism's Dew circulating from hand to hand, and the men were pouring more into their cups than they needed to put on their chigger bites. Before the day was over I came as close as I ever had to actually sampling the stuff myself, but I was chicken.

On Wednesday after school as I was rushing to get to the bivouac, Latha came out on the porch of her store and stopped me. She said she hadn't had much of a chance to speak with me lately. Not that it was so important, but I hadn't swept the store in over a week, and that was part of my job. Nor dusted the merchandise. "Every day after school, you rush right home," she pointed out. "Is your Aunt Rosie punishing you for something?"

"Aw, I'm not going home!" I said. And realized too late that perhaps I should have used that as an excuse. Why else would I be heading in that direction? "I mean, yeah, I've got to go home but not because she's punishing me. I've just got a lot of stuff to do."

"Oh?" she said. "I've never known you to spend so much time at home." I felt real bad about lying to Latha, and I tried to think of a more innocent lie to replace it, but I couldn't. "I couldn't help but notice," she went on, "that your Axis friends have also been going that-away pretty often. The older ones, at least. The younger ones just mope around my store or Lola's, and complain like the Allies do, 'I aint got nothin to *do!*' Well, why is it, I wonder, that they don't have anything to do and you've got so much to do I never see you anymore?"

I hung my head in remorse, but couldn't even think of a proper apology. "I'll go in and sweep the store," I offered.

"It can wait," she said. "You go on and join your friends in whatever mischief you've cooked up."

"I'll try to come around more, I promise," I said. And I escaped from her just in time to catch up with Gypsy and Ella Jean and Rosa Faye, who were on their way.

There was no way of knowing that I'd see Latha again sooner than I expected. When we got to the bivouac, and the others showed up, Lieutenant McPherson called us all together with his men. He didn't yell "FALL IN" or anything, he didn't make us stand at attention, he just got us all together and said he had some things to say. "The party's over," he said, and I was afraid he was about to announce that the bivouac was off-limits to us kids. But it was his men he was talking about. They'd consumed that whole demijohn of Chism's Dew, and even with a little help from the older kids that was a lot of dew. They were happy to be relieved from the itching of their chigger bites but they were suffering the notorious aftereffects of too much alcohol. But that wasn't what McPherson was concerned about. He announced that their K rations were exhausted. A whole week had gone by since their landing, and they hadn't anticipated they'd have to wait that long for the damn exercise to begin. Since each package of K rations also included four cigarettes, a stick of chewing gum, and a candy bar, they were also out of those things, and starting to die for a smoke. Their training had included some wilderness survival lessons but they did not really know how to forage for food. "I shot that opossum last night," McPherson said, "but what do we do with it?" Even though it was just a rhetorical question, Gypsy and Ella Jean each offered conflicting recipes on how to cook a possum. Rosa Faye said that of course she'd be glad to raid the Duckworth fraid-hole and bring up a lot of jars of canned goods. Sammy said he'd raid the Coe fraid-hole too. McPherson had to wait patiently for an explanation of what a fraid-hole is, and then he said he didn't want any of us robbing our family larders. "You people have a struggle just to feed yourselves, don't you?" he asked, again just rhetorically, but Willard insisted that it was a struggle that had been going on so constantly for so long that it never bothered him any more; he took it for granted as a way of life. Joe Don, whose experiences moving from place to place and living hand-to-mouth had qualified him as an authority on the subject, said that there was no reason why anybody with any wits or sense should ever have to go hungry. "Friends," McPherson said, "listen. We can *pay* for our food. You say there are *two* stores in town? All right, but how we do *shop* at those stores? We can't go down into the village."

I spoke up and said that I'd be glad to go get anything they wanted at Latha's store. "And how do you explain to her where you got the money?" McPherson asked. "Or why you're buying enough of every-thing to feed a dozen hungry men? And she's not going to sell you cig-arettes, is she?"

"She don't sell cigarettes anyhow," I said. "Just the makings. Duke's Mixture and Prince Albert and Bull Durham and papers."

"If I did have the makings, I wouldn't know how to—Harris, what's the expression?"

"Twist a dizzy, sir," Sergeant Harris offered.

"I wouldn't know how to twist my own dizzy," McPherson said. "Even if I did, Latha's not going to sell tobacco in any form to you, Donny."

"She'd sell 'em to *me*," Joe Don said, "if I had the money."

Gypsy said to her brother, "Joe Don, if you had any money, she'd really get suspicious!"

"Same here," Willard admitted. None of us, really, except possibly Rosa Faye, whose dad owned the canning factory even if it wasn't run-ning anymore, might have had any money of our own to spend in the stores. Then Willard asked of the lieutenant, "Couldn't you use your radio to reach somebody at your camp and tell 'em to send you some more K rations?"

McPherson sighed. "Apparently the signal won't carry that far. We can pick up some distant stations, but we can't make contact with Camp Chaffee. If we could, you may be sure that I'd give 'em hell for strand-ing us out here in the middle of nowhere! I asked Bosco to tell head-quarters of our situation, but I'm not sure he could tell them how to find us."

Although my feelings were a little hurt that he thought of Stay More as "nowhere," I was about to offer the suggestion that each of us kids could put extra food in our dinner pails for school and bring it after-wards to the soldiers, which would be better than nothing. But before I could say this, the sentry Private Crowder came up and saluted McPher-son and said, "Sir, there's a bunch of ladies out there."

"*Ladies?*" said McPherson. He turned to Harris and snapped, "Sergeant, you didn't go through with your harebrained scheme to find some prostitutes, did you?"

"No, *sir!*" Harris said. "We were just drunk when we said that."

"These aren't whores, sir," Private Crowder said. "They're mothers, mostly. These kids' mothers. And the lady who runs the store."

C H A P T E R

19

WHEN THE DELEGATION OF WOMENFOLK CAME INTO THE BIVOUAC, my favorite woman addressed my favorite man. "Excuse us if we're interrupting anything real important," Latha said. "But we just had to see what all these young'uns have been up to lately." She looked all around her—the other ladies looked all around them—there was Willard and Ella Jean's mother, Selena Dinsmore; and Joe Don and Gypsy's mother, Bliss Dingletoon; and Sammy's mother, Dulcie Coe; and Rosa Faye's mother—I was sorry I couldn't remember what Mrs. Duckworth's first name was. I guess I was happy my aunt wasn't there. What they saw looking all around them was only an old abandoned farmstead temporarily populated by soldiers and kids. There was no sign of the bivouac.

Selena Dinsmore wagged her finger at Willard and Ella Jean.

"You'uns told me a big fib the other evenin, when ye said all them greens was for the pore Dingletoons. And Bliss says she wasn't sick atall!"

Bliss Dingletoon said, "And these two o' mine used the same story on me!" She grabbed Joe Don and Gypsy by their ears.

And Dulcie Coe said, "So this is where all my blackberry cobbler ended up!"

"It sure was good, ma'am," said Corporal Rucker.

"Best dessert I ever had the privilege of sinking my teeth into," Sergeant Harris said.

"Those chickens and their dumplings," said Polacek, "were positively de-*lish*, believe me."

And all the other men made murmurs of "Mmmm-mmmm!" and "Oh, man!" and "Whatta life!" and a few of them began drooling in the memory of the banquet . . . or the expectation of further dishes.

The women of Stay More were temporarily charmed out of their anger, but Mrs. Duckworth said, "Aw, Rosa Faye made them chick'n dumplins all by herself!" and each of the other mothers protested that her daughter had done the cooking.

"But surely," Lieutenant McPherson said, "they learned how to cook from their mothers, didn't they?"

And the women allowed as how they might have learnt the girls a lesson or two in the kitchen.

Selena Dinsmore, making polite conversation, asked, "Where are you fellers from?"

The men looked at one another, as if waiting for someone else to name his hometown. "We are all stationed at Camp Chaffee," McPherson said. And when he got blank looks, he explained, "That's an army base near Fort Smith, here in Arkansas. Individually we come from all parts of the country. Sergeant Harris here is from Wisconsin. Corporal Rucker, Oregon. Corporal Quigg, Virginia. Private Polacek, New York. Private Crowder, California. Private Keough, Pennsylvania. Private Rogalski, New Jersey. Privates Nilson and Hewes are both from Michigan. Private Macklin, Florida. Private Lambert, South Dakota. And myself, Lieutenant McPherson, from Vermont. At your service, ladies." Mac saluted, then bowed from the waist. Then he said, "I forgot someone. Gypsy, get Jarhead." Gypsy ran to the mule's shed and returned riding atop the animal. "And this is Corporal Jarhead," McPherson concluded. "From Tennessee, I believe." When the ladies had stopped laughing, McPherson looked at them and said, "And you are—?"

The women of Stay More introduced themselves, and I relearned Mrs. Duckworth's name. Gladys. I would remember all these names, because they were going into my next big story in the *Star.*

Latha said, "It's not every day we get even one visitor to Stay More, let alone a dozen soldiers. Did you boys somehow miss the main road to Fort Smith?"

I blurted, "They came on that glider!" Then I looked sheepishly at McPherson, cringing in anticipation of his frown or his reprimand. But he was just smiling.

"So," said Latha, "why have you boys been hiding up here in the woods for a week?"

McPherson sighed. I had known him long enough to know that his sigh meant, "I hate this, but I guess I have to." Then he took a deep breath and glanced at Sergeant Harris and said, "Our orders are to pretend that we are a hostile force in a training exercise. The training has two purposes: we serve as sparring partners—or as punching bags— for a select armored battalion on maneuvers, and, in the process, we sharpen our skills as an elite corps of commandos, rangers, marauders— we prefer to call ourselves *samurai.* Collectively and individually, we are a mean bunch of dogfaces. Each man is a sharpshooter with a rifle, and an expert at judo. Some of the men are the Fourth Army champions in the use of certain weapons: Corporal Quigg with the Browning Automatic, Corporal Rucker with the 81 mm mortar, Private Crowder with the 60 mm mortar, Sergeant Harris with antitank grenade, Private Polacek with machine gun. Privates Nilson and Hewes with the bazooka can hit a target a mile away."

Latha pointed her finger at him and asked, "And what are you the champion at?"

McPherson grinned. "Shooting off my mouth, mostly."

"Lady," said Sergeant Harris, "the tank hasn't been built that he can't destroy."

"*Sergeant,*" said the lieutenant.

"So when is this contest supposed to start?" Latha asked.

"Who knows?" McPherson shrugged. "I expected it to begin soon
after we landed, but our opposition may have lost their way trying to
find us."

"Well, there's no sense in you boys starving to death up here and
making all these kids into storytellers," Latha said. "Come on down to
our fair hamlet and get you some decent food."

McPherson glanced at his men, each one of whom was eagerly nodding his head. Jarhead the mule was nodding his head. All of us kids
were nodding our heads. McPherson sighed again. Then he said to
Harris, "All right, Sergeant."

"FALL IN!" Sergeant Harris said. We all lined up. "DIS!" added the
Sergeant, "MISSED!"

Everybody headed for town, Gypsy riding Jarhead at the front of the
column. The mule seemed happy to get away from the confines of the
bivouac, and his step was lively. The soldiers weren't marching at all,
but sauntering. McPherson carried the large wooden beribboned "key
to the city" that Willard had given him, as if he might be able to use it
to unlock something in town. He walked not as if he were the commander but just one of us, and from time to time he would walk alongside one of us, talking to us. When my turn came, he simply said that we
ought to continue to keep the location of the bivouac a secret. Later he
might need my advice on a new location for a bivouac. I said I knew he
was going to like Stay More.

The first house we reached down the mountain road was Latha's
own, and she pointed it out to the soldiers and told them that was where
she'd be serving supper as soon as she got the store closed. Dulcie Coe
said she was awfully sorry but the supper this evening was going to be
at *her* place, whereupon Gladys Duckworth, Selena Dinsmore, and
Bliss Dingletoon each claimed that *they* were each going to serve the
supper to these soldiers. McPherson solved the dispute by suggesting
that the men could be divided into groups of two or three each to dine
at the available eating places.

At Latha's store (which she hadn't bothered to lock up, trusting anyone during her absence to help themselves and leave the money for
it), she sold the soldiers smoking tobacco and cigarette papers. Most
of them twisted a dizzy and, Latha's post office still being open, they

bought postcards and V-mail stationery and composed notes or letters to distant mothers and lovers. Then they sat on the edge of the porch to loaf and smoke and take a good look at the town. They were glad to be looking at architecture again after looking at nothing but trees. I appointed myself tour guide and I indicated the empty stone building across the road and explained it had been a bank that had never reopened since being robbed many years before. I thought it best not to get into the complications of just how it was that the robber of the bank was the same Every Dill who years later would come back and marry Latha. Next door to the old bank, I pointed out, was Doc Swain's house and clinic; directly across from it the house and clinic of Doc Plowright, who was retired. Just beyond Doc Plowright's was the big old Ingledew General Store, still in business, but losing most of its business to Latha's. That woman yonder sitting on the store's porch by herself was Lola Ingledew, who kept it open. Behind the Ingledew store rose the hulk of the old gristmill, four stories of red tin in imitation of brick. Behind that, across Swains Creek, was the old sawmill and wagon-bow factory, where they used to make bows for the Conestoga wagons that had headed west. I pointed out the little canning factory, shut down for the duration of the war's tin shortage, and, in the far distance, the schoolhouse. That was all of Stay More, not counting the Jacob Ingledew house across from the Ingledew store, which had once been a hotel, and in a sense still was, because it had rooms that were never used. Up the hill behind the hotel was the Coe blacksmith shop.

"What are those pits or craters all over the place?" McPherson asked, gesturing here and there.

"Those are *our* foxholes," I said proudly. "The Jap foxholes. We have to defend the village from the Yanks. You ought to see *their* foxholes."

One of the soldiers pointed and asked me if that river was safe for swimming. I told him it wasn't a river, just a creek, which emptied, miles downstream, into the Little Buffalo River. The soldier and a few others asked McPherson for permission to run down there and take a dip.

"When we're off the bivouac," McPherson said, "you don't need my permission for anything." He himself abandoned the others and took a stroll down the main road, looking at the houses and buildings and our network of foxholes and other defensive emplacements. I followed, telling him if there was anything he wanted to know about anything, just to ask me. He said he thought it was a nice little town, although it was much smaller than he had been thinking it was. He said that the town and the countryside reminded him a lot of Vermont. He told me that the old hermit Dan had told him that was one of the reasons Dan had settled here, because it reminded him of Vermont. He asked me if it was true that Dan and his daughter *never* came into the village. I said I'd never seen them here.

Our stroll and conversation was interrupted by an encounter with a group of the Yanks, who surrounded us but kept a respectful distance from the man in a lieutenant's combat uniform. I wasn't about to introduce McPherson to Larry or Jim John or Sog; I simply whispered to him that those were Yanks, formerly Allies, and he nodded his head as if acknowledging that I had pointed out a species of poisonous snake. And they weren't going to introduce themselves. They scattered in three different directions, probably to alert their friends and families to this "invasion" of Stay More.

In pointing out the various parts of town to the soldiers, I had neglected to identify Miss Jerram's little cottage, across the road from the schoolhouse, within sight of the very place on Swains Creek where the soldiers had chosen to go swimming. Of course none of them had bathing suits, and they seemed oblivious to the woman standing on her back porch observing them as they frolicked naked in the water, diving and bullfrogging and splashing.

News traveled faster than the *Star* could ever do, and before nightfall everybody in Stay More knew that we had a dozen soldiers in our midst. At school the next day, Miss Jerram practically canceled the usual order of lessons in order to have everybody who knew anything report on whatever was going on. Ella Jean told about the soldiers who went home with her and Willard so that Selena Dinsmore could feed them. Gypsy told about the three who went to the Dingletoon house, Rosa Faye reported on the three who came to the Duckworth's, and Sammy on the two, Lieutenant McPherson and Sergeant Harris, who ate at the Coes. I suspected they hadn't chosen Sammy's house out of favoritism toward him, nor because his late brother had been an Iwo Jima hero, but because the Coe house overlooked the village and was more centrally located. Still I was jealous, and I considered asking my aunt if she would be willing to feed a few soldiers that night, or the next night. None of the Japs reporting on our affiliation with the military (of which the Yanks were obviously insane with envy) revealed that the soldiers were Japs like ourselves or that they were destined to invade mainland Japan. But it was made clear that "our" soldiers were going to be involved shortly in a simulated battle with an invading force that would include big tanks and artillery and maybe hundreds of additional soldiers. Miss Jerram said she wanted to remind us that there were just a few days of school remaining and that she hoped none of this warlike activity would distract us from our studies.

I never did learn (as if I could have used it in the *Star* anyhow) just how Miss Estalee Jerram, our nice schoolteacher, met Sergeant Rodney Harris of Eau Claire, Wisconsin. Most people thought it probably happened at the pie supper, but at least I did know that they had already met somewhere, somehow, before the pie supper, and that it was a sheer accident of destiny that the pie that Sergeant Harris successfully bid on was the pie that Miss Jerram made. Some folks said that the idea for the pie supper started with Miss Jerram herself, but I know it was Latha's idea.

Pie suppers didn't happen very often, and we'd had only two of them since the war started, both as fund-raisers for a War Memorial when a Stay More boy was killed, most recently Boden Whitter in that kamikaze attack on his ship. Pie suppers always appeared to be for the purpose of raising money for some worthy cause, but the real purpose is to promote friendship between male and female, who pair off together (not *too* privately) for the eating of the pie. Each of the women and girls of the town would bake a pie, their favorite kind, and wrap it fancifully, in a pretty box or a woven basket (some girls could even make baskets out of cornstalks in the shape of log cabins), and these would be auctioned off to the highest bidder among the men and boys. Whoever bought your pie had the privilege of sitting with you while he ate it; he would give you a piece, or two, or three, but you were supposed to flirt with him or at least listen sympathetically while he courted you. It was

chancy, because there was no way of knowing in advance which girls
had done which pies. That was the reason I'd been stuck with Rosa Faye
Duckworth in the previous pie supper.

A pie usually went for not more than fifty cents, but with all these
soldiers bidding on them (Doc Swain agreed to serve as auctioneer),
the winning bid sometimes got as high as two or even three dollars!
Sergeant Harris paid two seventy-five for Miss Jerram's pie. None of
us realized that she even knew how to bake pies. Did he betray any disappointment when he discovered that the baker was not one of the
younger ladies but a schoolteacher? No, maybe because Miss Jerram
had for the occasion dolled herself up so much she looked like, as Willard put it, "a ten-dollar whore," although I doubt Willard had ever seen
a whore of even five dollars. Anyhow, Miss Jerram and Sergeant Harris
went off to sit on a rock together and eat that pie, and that was the beginning of their beautiful romance.

McPherson pestered me in advance for tips on how to identify or
even guess the baker of the pie, but he didn't tell me his motive: his
heart was set on making the successful bid on a pie by hermit Dan's
daughter Annie. I could have told him there wasn't any chance in the
world that Annie would show up. And she didn't. Everyone nodded in
sympathy and understanding when McPherson's pie turned out to have
been made jointly by the twins Helena Doris and Jelena Cloris, Ella
Jean's older sisters, just recently widowed when their joint husband
Billy Bob Ingledew was shot in the siege of Berlin. Come to think of it,
according to the stories, Doris and Jelena had first met Billy Bob when
he had bid on and won *both* their pies at the War Memorial pie supper
held when the first Stay Moron was killed early during the war. Now,
the town was divided between those who thought Doris and Jelena
ought to remain in mourning and seclusion during this pie supper, and
those who felt it would help them overcome their grief to get out and be
sociable. Willard had already told McPherson the story of his twin sisters. McPherson had suggested to me that I ought to start keeping a
journal to record such stories for future reference, and I had got myself
an Indian Chief tablet from Latha's store, writing on the first page "Article Ideas," and had already recorded two: (1) an interview with the old

hermit Dan; (2) the strange story of Jelena and Doris Dinsmore. I knew very little about either of those subjects, and was determined to find out more.

Whatever gods there be who manipulate our luck and our lot were having themselves a party the night of the pie supper. Not only did Sergeant Harris wind up with Miss Jerram, but Gypsy, who was nearly overcome with disappointment when the lieutenant bought Jelena's and Doris' pie instead of the egg custard pie she'd hoped he would bid on, wasn't too unhappy when the lucky bidder on her egg custard was Willard, who, according to rumor (I didn't see them), got not only a pie but eventually a kiss for his money, thirty-five cents. Best of all, I myself had not bid on any of the pies until a certain one that had been wrapped or concealed inside what appeared to be a girl's nightdress still bearing a faint stain resembling a question mark: "?" I don't know what made me bid my quarter (which was all I had) on that pie. Destiny maybe. I wouldn't have got the pie in competition with the soldiers except for the fact that all of them had already obtained their pies. My pie turned out to be a sweet potato, of which I was not awfully fond, but the baker of it turned out to be Ella Jean Dinsmore, of whom I was uncommonly fond.

It was a good thing I had taken to carrying that Indian Chief tablet with me everywhere because Ella Jean, once we both had overcome our shyness toward each other and had eaten that pie (or at least a piece apiece, perfunctorily), began to talk about her sisters Doris and Jelena, and I needed to take notes. We watched them sitting on either side of the lieutenant, who was doing all the talking, and we imagined that he was charming them just as he had charmed us, and Ella Jean was happy about this, because her sisters, she said, were totally heartbroken over Billy Bob's death. She did not see them much, since they kept to themselves in the house that Billy Bob had built for them, where they were raising the baby, named Jelena too. Ella Jean herself did not know which of the twin sisters was the actual mother of Jelena the baby. But every time Ella Jean had stopped by her sisters' house, she had found the gloom to be so thick it frightened her.

"How come you're a-writing down ever thing I say?" Ella Jean asked me.

"Every word you say I want to keep," I said. There wasn't any coy flirtation in this, and I went on to explain the lieutenant's recommendation that I keep a journal of ideas for articles.

"Would ye care if I worked on the *Star* for ye?" she offered.

I was overcome with joy. "I haven't never had nobody helping me with it yet," I pointed out.

"I caint write stories," she said. "But they's bound to be some ways I could help ye."

"Oh, I'm sure there is," I said.

Before the evening was over, we had, ever so briefly, held hands. I don't mean shook hands over my decision to hire her as assistant editor of the *Star*, but *held* hands in the romantic sense, if only for a few seconds. I had got up my nerve and asked her to explain the wrapping the pie had been in. Was that really her nightdress? What was the significance of the "**?**" dimly stained into it? In answer, Ella Jean took my Indian Chief tablet, and on the page where already I'd written down ideas for stories on ole Dan and on Jelena and Doris, she wrote: "(3) What's the picture on Ella Jean's nightie?" And left me to think about that.

The next issue of the *Star* was an Extra, you may be sure (McPherson told me that in Japan for years the newspapers liked to bring out Extras, and *"Gogwai! Gogwai!"* was the cry of newsboys). The masthead had a new name, the only one after my own. There was even a little story on a back page, *"Star* Staff Doubles," with the announcement of her taking on the responsibilities for "society news," "births and deaths," "page layout," "punctuation," and "drinking water." The latter was her idea: she kept us both supplied with cups of cool well water while we worked on the paper. That Extra, with her help, was twice as long as usual, what with the full story on the soldiers, the pie supper, and so on. I cleared the copy with McPherson, who made only a few minor changes to censor information on the soldiers that he didn't want revealed; he thought I was very clever to write "their bivouac is in a farmyard, and since the word 'farmyard' encloses the word 'army' they are safely enclosed there," but he didn't want even that much given away about their location. He also objected, in my story about the pie supper, to my sentence, "The lieutenant cheered up Doris and Jelena enormously." He said he hadn't been able to cheer them up at all.

I was glad later that I had cut any mention of Doris and Jelena from that Extra of the *Star*. Private Macklin, on a detail to reconnoiter the terrain west of Swains Creek, came upon their bodies lying together holding hands on the blood-stained earth hundreds of feet beneath the crag known as Leapin Rock.

CHAPTER
20

WHEN WE BURIED DORIS AND JELENA DINSMORE, AN AIRPLANE flew over. Much later, I would ask McPherson if there wasn't some kind of word or expression for such a thing happening that seems somehow to have already happened. He would tell me the words, which I would have occasion to use again and am using now: "day shave you" it sounded like, not Japanese, meaning "already seen." The only time an airplane had ever flown over Stay More previously, we had been burying a mule, and we hadn't finished the job. Now the job was not only finished, but had honors: McPherson's seven best riflemen lined up smartly at the graveside and pointed their weapons at the sky and fired. Blanks, of course, or else the volley might have hit that airplane.

193

McPherson told me that military funerals are often accompanied by aviation, but this airplane wasn't part of the plan. He said it was a Piper Cub, and it was "obviously a scout, for aerial reconnaissance." It could fly very slowly, around and around, so that the cameraman could take many photographs.

McPherson was plunged into disconsolate sorrow by the suicides of Doris and Jelena, feeling (wrongly!) that he might even have said something to them that drove them to it. I couldn't say anything to make him feel better. Even though I put in my Indian Chief another article idea: "(4) The History of Leapin Rock," and interviewed Latha on the subject and tried to explain to McPherson that Jelena and Doris were by no means the first persons to avail themselves of that crag's lofty lethality, he was not comforted. Sweet Ella Jean, even though racked with sorrow over her sisters' deaths, tried to explain to McPherson the circumstances of her sisters' having already been plunged into hopeless despair by the death in Berlin of their joint husband Billy Bob Ingledew, but her words could not relieve McPherson of whatever horrible guilt he was feeling. At the funeral, when everybody usually sings "Farther Along," wherein we try to tell each other that we'll understand it all by and by, Doc Swain (who had signed the death certificates and listed cause of death as "broken heart") stopped the singing before it could begin and protested, "Farther along, hell! We done already understood it." But McPherson did not understand it, and farther along he was still so disconsolate that the situation, according to Sergeant Harris, had degenerated from a SNAFU into a FUBAR (Corporal Rucker offered a translation, from "Situation Normal All Fucked Up" into "Fucked Up Beyond All Recognition"). His men became concerned that McPherson was ready to call it quits, to abandon the bivouac and "resign" from the forthcoming maneuvers, and maybe even go AWOL (which Rucker claimed stood for "Absentmindedly Walking Out Legless"). All pretense of being in an orderly bivouac was dropped; the men were permitted to come and go as they pleased, and it pleased them to feel that they were on some kind of furlough, free to go fishing or just to loaf, free to pursue the girls or women whose pies they'd eaten and whose hearts (and beds) were emptied by the all the able menfolk going overseas to fight the war. There was a rumor that Sergeant Harris was even staying overnight at Miss Jerram's house! The discipline of the daily calisthenics under his direction was lost, and the men began to get fat from what they were fed by the ladies.

Nobody's life returned to "normal" after the lives of Doris and Jelena were ended. Doc Swain withdrew into a kind of depression that no one could explain other than speculating that in his long experience of signing death certificates he had signed one too many. I wrote in my Indian Chief: "(5) The History of Doc Swain" but when I tried to get started on that, Latha just said, "Now why would you want to be thinking about that at a time like *this?*" I didn't see my new assistant editor for several days after the funeral, so I assumed she had withdrawn into some kind of depression too. Each evening after supper I made a pilgrimage to that sacred hidden spot on Banty Creek where she took her bar of Palmolive for baths, but she was never there. Perhaps she and Gypsy had used up all of that bar of Palmolive. Gypsy too had tried to cheer up McPherson, but he had said to her irritably, "Gypsy, will you please stop calling me Captain?" And she had withdrawn into her own kind of depression. Her brother Joe Don somehow persuaded the hermit's lovely daughter Annie to invite the lieutenant to dinner, and Joe Don personally carried the invitation to McPherson but, since Joe Don himself wasn't invited, we had nobody to report to us on the success of that endeavor.

Miss Jerram was the only person who seemed to be not unhappy, and that must have been because of Sergeant Harris, who was waiting for her every day after school and was seen walking with her on the roads and sitting with her on her porch, and, according to the rumors, not coming out of her house after suppertime. She canceled school for the day of the funeral, and the next day too, and the following week was the last week anyhow, so she gave all of us some tests and then said "Have a happy summer," and that was the end of school.

A postcard came addressed c/o General Delivery to McPherson, and Latha let me deliver it to him. Of course I read it first: "Hey, Mac! Hope I didn't get your Irish up telling them your coordinates. They tortured the info out of me. Figured what the hell, they couldn't get any good pix of your installation anyhow. Stoving and those chumps in the tank corps can't even find the place! They want me to show 'em. See you in Okinawa, hell. See you in *Staymore!* Bosco." When I gave this card to McPherson and he read it, I was happy to see him smile for the first time in days.

In fact, he not only smiled but laughed over the thought of just what those reconnaissance photos would reveal to the "enemy." They would show the soldiers firing their funeral salute, of course, but not their well-concealed bivouac up on the mountain. They would show a hundred-odd (some *very* odd) Stay Morons surrounding the grave (there was but one, and only one coffin, in which the sisters lay enfolded). The sleepy, decaying village, with numerous *foxholes.* A double-pen house high up in a sycamore tree in a broad meadow, surrounded by *foxholes.* McPherson said those photographs were going to be "our best possible ammunition."

"You know those wings he wears?" I asked McPherson, realizing the question made Bosco into some kind of angel. "I just wondered what that 'G' stands for, between the wings, you know?"

"Guts," said McPherson. "Sheer guts. I hope when our glider lands on a mountain in Kyushu that Bosco will be at the controls." Then McPherson picked himself up out of his gloom and summoned his men to him and said, "Time to get ready." Later he clapped me on the back as if I'd written the postcard myself and said expansively, "Good job, Donny. No, the 'G' just stands for 'glider' because Lieutenant Bosco is an Army Air Force glider pilot. But you can let it stand for anything you like."

The postcard was just a day ahead of its author. We heard the trucks and the jeep long before we saw them, coming up the twisting road from Parthenon. By the time the trucks and car arrived in the village, a good crowd of us were assembled on and around the porch of Latha's store. None of the soldiers were there. Miss Jerram was abandoned. It could have been any early summer's afternoon on a country store porch, except for the absence of menfolk. There were a lot of boys, Yanks and Japs both, and several girls. Ella Jean and Gypsy had both emerged from their sadness, at least enough to pay attention to what was going on in the world. Gypsy had given up on her flirtation with McPherson and had started spending time with Willard, which of course left poor Ella Jean feeling lonely.

The jeep and the trucks came into view and pulled to a stop right in front of the store. The jeep wasn't black like all the cars I'd seen but a kind of greenish brown. So were the trucks, three of them, but the trucks had tops of canvas. Then three more trucks came in behind, one of them with metal sides and top and two flatbed trucks carrying a bull-dozer and road grader.

The driver of the jeep was a private first class, and sitting beside him was Second Lieutenant Bosco. Sitting in the back seat were two men with officer's service caps on their heads, and on his shoulders one man was wearing the double silver bars of a *real* captain (did Gypsy realize?) and the other some kind of gold ornament in the shape of a leaf.

Lieutenant Bosco turned in his seat and addressed the latter, "This is it, sir."

The gold-leaf man looked at us. "Who's in charge of this burg?" he asked. When no one answered, he looked around at the village, the de-serted bank across the road, a vacant house north of Doc Plowright's, whatever he could see. "This town," he said. "This place. Is there a headman or somebody?" When this too was met with silence, he asked, "You people do speak English, don't you?"

I spoke up. *"Hanashimásu Nippon-no. Kore-wa yoi hon-de su."*

"What?" said the gold-leaf. "Is that some kind of redskin lingo?"

"Japanese," said Willard. "He's trying to tell you that we're Jap-anese. But I reckon you caint speak it."

The gold-leaf turned to the captain and said, "I thought all the Japs in Arkansas were kept at Rohwer or Jerome."

"I think they're just kidding, sir," the captain said.

"Bosco?" the gold-leaf said. "You said they were just hillbillies."

"Yes sir," said Bosco. "But they're real *smart* hillbillies, and for the duration of this exercise they are Japanese."

Larry Duckworth spoke up. "I aint no Jap! I'm two hunurd percent American." And the rest of the Yanks nodded their heads in agreement. "Three hunurd," Jim John added.

"Well," said the gold-leaf, "which of you can tell me how to find a squad of soldiers who are camping out somewhere around here?"

None of us answered, until finally Larry said, "I don't rightly know but they're some'ers hereabouts, I can tell ye. I *seen* 'em."

"Bosco?" the gold-leaf said. "Why don't *you* just take us and show us their bivouac?"

"Sir, I agreed to bring you to the town," Bosco said. "But I don't have any obligation to show you where the bivouac is located."

"Are you disobeying orders, lieutenant?"

"If this were an actual situation, sir," Bosco said, "my loyalties would be with the aggressor force."

"Goddamn it, Bosco!" the gold-leaf said. "We're not the strike team. I'm the *umpire,* for godsakes, and Captain Billings's men are the *engineers.* I assume they're just as neutral as I am, right, Billings?"

"Yes sir," Captain Billings said. "We're not taking sides in this fray. Or rather, we're working for both sides."

"Okay, Bosco!" the gold-leaf yelled. "So why don't you show us the fucking bivouac?"

Lieutenant Bosco, whose arm was still in a cast, crooked the finger of his good hand at me, and when I approached, he said, "Donny, how about you go down the road *that* way"—he pointed in the opposite direction from the bivouac—"and see if you can't find Mac, and tell him that Major Evans, the exercise umpire, is here?"

So the gold leaf indicated a major, which was a cut above a captain. Major Evans said, "So the kid doesn't really speak Japanese, huh?"

"As much as he pals around with McPherson," Bosco said, "he could probably talk Hirohito into surrendering. Well, Donny?"

I saluted and took off, running down the main road until I was around the bend beyond Banty Creek and then leaving the road and cutting back through the woods, along a trail that would return me to the road that led eastward from the village up the mountain to the bivouac. I knew all these trails like the palm of my hand. And in no time at all I had reached the bivouac.

To my surprise, my hero had changed clothes. He was dressed in what I quickly supposed was the combat uniform of a Japanese *chui,* or lieutenant, complete with ceremonial sword. Or maybe it wasn't just ceremonial; he probably knew how to use it.

"They're here!" I said. "Bosco is back! And a whole bunch of others. There's a Major Evans, who says he's the umpire. And a Captain Billings with six trucks full of engineers and stuff."

"I heard trucks. I didn't hear tanks," he said.

"No tanks. These guys say they're all neutral," I said. "The strike force comes later, I guess."

"Harris!" McPherson summoned his top noncom. "If I don't come back, if I'm taken prisoner, you know what to do."

"Yes *sir!*" The sergeant saluted.

But McPherson was not taken prisoner, and all of those other soldiers really were neutral. Captain Billings and his company of engineer corps were already establishing their bivouac near the same place where the WPA boys had camped out back in 1939 to build their little cement bridge over Banty Creek, and some of them were already taking measurements of that bridge. To make sure it would support heavy tanks, McPherson explained, as we approached the village from the same circuitous direction I had left it.

Major Evans had set up his headquarters at the old Ingledew hotel, and was sitting in a rocker on its broad front porch. McPherson saluted him, but with the same Japanese salute he had demonstrated to Joe Don.

"Cut the crap, McPherson!" Major Evans said, with a dismissive American salute. "You don't have to *be* a Jap, for godsakes!"

"You want realism, we got realism," McPherson said, and added, "Sir."

"If that's the case, why can't you do a better job of digging foxholes?" The major swept his arm to indicate all of our pits and craters.

"Those aren't ours, sir," McPherson said. "We didn't invent war games, you know. The local kids have been playing War for years." He smiled at me.

"Oh? Well, I can't tell you anything about your opponent's strategy, but I *can* tell you that they are expecting you to defend the village."

"Defend the village?" McPherson said. "That wasn't discussed. I don't have the personnel for that. I've just got one platoon, you know, and the enemy is supposed to find us, and they won't find us anywhere near this village."

"But if they 'take' the village," Major Evans said, "I've got to score points for them. You can't expect to win in the ninth inning if the score is already impossible."

"I'd need to lay a minefield, sir," McPherson said. "We weren't issued mines."

"We can give you mines," Major Evans said. "Tell the engineers what you want, and let's get ready."

"*We* will defend the village," I said. The thought of laying a minefield around Stay More, even with fake explosives, made me angry. The Japs could keep the tanks out without any mines.

Both men looked at me, McPherson with pride, Evans with annoyance. "Get lost, kid," the latter said.

"Sir," McPherson said, "this gentleman is the editor of the local newspaper, and I would watch my tongue if I were you, sir."

"Oh, shit, lieutenant," the major said. "And you've taught him how to speak Jap too, huh? Well, listen, your job was to make a beachhead here, not to civilize the natives. You and I have a few things to discuss in private and I'm asking the kid to beat it."

"Donny, would you mind?" McPherson said.

"Okay, I think I'll go watch those guys trying to blow up our bridge." I turned to go, but said one more thing to McPherson, a thing I'd heard around the bivouac: "Don't let him pull rank on you."

I went to watch the engineers measuring the WPA bridge, which I had watched the construction of in the summer of 1939. It wasn't much of a bridge, six concrete tunnels just large enough to let the water of Banty Creek flow under the roadbed, and often not large enough for that because already the annual floods had jammed driftwood against the side of the bridge so that the cement crenelation along its side had to be sledgehammered away. But one pier of that crenelation remained, with its cement stamped like a tombstone forever: BUILT BY W.P.A. 1939.

I went up to Captain Billings and asked, "Think it will hold an M-6? Or just M-4 Shermans?"

"Oh, hi, Donny is it?" he said. "Where'd you learn about tanks? From McPherson?"

I quoted Sergeant Harris, "The tank hasn't been built that he can't destroy."

The captain laughed. "That's what I hear. But you're a Jap, right? So the strength of this bridge is classified information."

"You said you're working for both sides," I reminded him.

"That we are, son," the captain said. "And we're also working for you people. We aren't going to let the tanks tear down your bridge if your bridge won't hold 'em."

"You're going to lay mines all over," I said.

"We are? I haven't heard that yet. But if we lay mines, they won't hurt anybody when they blow. Might scare a few dogs and cats and cows." He chuckled at the image, but I didn't think it was funny. "Our main job is bridges, though. We may have to get up into those hills and put some bridges across the brooks and streams." He was pointing toward the south.

"Is that the direction the tanks are coming from?" I asked.

"Now there you go!" he said, quickly sticking his pointing hand into his pocket. "Trying to get information out of me. No, as far as I know, the tanks might come from that way." He took out his pointing hand and pointed it toward the west.

"How will they get across Swains Creek?" I asked. It was my turn to point, at the water that separated us from the schoolhouse, the road that went westward up to Sidehill. There had never been a bridge across that creek other than footbridges.

"Guess we'll have to put a pontoon on it. No trouble at all." But he shook his head. "That doesn't mean the tanks are coming from that direction."

They put a pontoon bridge across Swains Creek, which was just a temporary floating bridge, on the tops of boatlike things, but mighty enough to support at least an M-3 if not an M-6. The Japs and the Yanks revived our neglected pastimes in order to stage a battle over that pontoon bridge, with the Japs attempting to prevent the Yanks from crossing it. Since we outnumbered them so much now, our defense of the bridge was successful. We generously allowed the Yanks to run back and forth across the bridge after we had secured it.

The grown-ups of Stay More congregated on the porch of Latha's store to talk about the forthcoming invasion of the town, or, as far as most of them were concerned, the invasion that had already occurred— although the engineers and the umpire's staff were polite, respectful of property, and eager to have our goodwill. Doc Swain came out of his

funk to serve as "headman" of the village for discussions with Major
Evans, although Oren Duckworth, father of Larry and Rosa Faye and
the town's lone industrialist when his canning factory was operating
before the war, felt that he ought to be considered the headman, and insisted on participating in the discussions. Of course all of us Japs felt
that Willard, who was vice mayor when Mare was still here and therefore now the mayor since Mare's death, ought to be considered the
headman, but he wasn't quite yet a man, and he didn't insist on participating. It was Oren Duckworth who grabbed the privilege of reporting
to all of us on the discussions, of telling us not to be alarmed by the
presence of all the soldiers or the coming of the tanks, to stay in our
homes and not get in their way, to understand that all of this activity
was intended for a good cause, the training of U.S. soldiers, and to remember that if any damage occurred the U.S. Army would reimburse
us. He didn't say a word about defending the village.

I told Willard and Joe Don that McPherson's samurai might have to
defend the village and we ought to do whatever we could to help, starting with this: we would find out just which of the roads leading south-
ward or westward out of the village were being "improved" by the engineers, with bridges or grading or widening or whatever, and we'd let
McPherson know. Spying on those roads, the three of us determined
that the enemy was definitely coming from the south, from the old road
that meandered through the forests to Demijohn and Swain along the
upper course of Swains Creek.

It took the engineers several days to get that road ready to support
tanks.

CHAPTER
21

WHEN THE ROAD TO SWAIN WAS READY, WE WERE READY TO TELL McPherson, and the three of us reported to him at the bivouac. He said it stood to reason that the invaders would come from the south, since that was the direction, at a great distance, of their base, Camp Chaffee. But since Major Evans and all the engineers and their convoy had arrived from the north, and McPherson had requested a minefield be laid with the northern direction in mind, the mines weren't going to help anyhow. "Who needs mines?" Sergeant Harris asked.

We Japs volunteered to patrol inconspicuously that "improved" road to the south, and to notify McPherson the instant we saw or heard any approaching tanks. There was one lofty spot on the Swain road known as Piney Gap where you could not only see the road as it continued a mile farther south but you could hear any engines coming along that road for miles away. This patrol gave me another sense of deja vu, reminding me of that time we'd staked out the Dinsmore trail to prevent the Allies' abduction of Gypsy. But like that time, day after day went by without any sign of anybody coming on that road. I took advantage of the lull to consider bringing out an Extra of the *Star*. Ella Jean, my assistant, urged me to. But I realized that when the actual battle began, we might have to bring out an Extra every day. In an inspired stroke of genius, Ella Jean and I decided that for the duration of the "occupation" of Stay More, our newspaper would become a daily, and we even put that into the title: *The Stay Morning Daily Star*. I couldn't have done it without her, and I was pleasantly surprised to discover that she was better at lettering the copy onto the master sheets than I was, because her hand was neater. She also lettered for me a card that boldly proclaimed PRESS and I took to wearing it pinned to my shirt everywhere I went, especially when I was interviewing engineers for stories. Just as Ernie Pyle would have done, I made a point of finding out those engineers' hometowns and even their street addresses, and whenever I wrote a story about one I included such information. At first the soldiers weren't too cooperative, or they teased me, poking my press card and saying things like, "Well, I pressed but nothing happened." But once they'd seen an issue of the *Daily Star*, they changed their tune, and some of them bought extra copies to send to friends and relatives back home. I wasn't the only one getting rich; the whole economy of Stay More was surging, and even Lola Ingledew's old store, hardly ever patronized any more, was selling out its dusty remaining merchandise.

It was during Willard's shift patrolling the south road at Piney Gap that he detected the first far-distant sound of some big machine one evening after supper. I was on my way to relieve him when he came running hard and didn't even pause when he panted at me, "They're coming!" and I tried to keep up with him as he ran all the way to the samurai's bivouac.

McPherson and his men were ready to go, as they had been for days. Ever since the arrival of Major Evans and the engineers, who had brought along a good supply of K rations for them, they had abandoned their pleasurable habits of dining with the Stay Morons and had remained in their bivouac, where Sergeant Harris, who had had to tell poor Miss Jerram he couldn't see her again until the fighting stopped, led them in constant calisthenics, judo practice, the alertness drills, whatever. Now they were all dressed in Japanese combat uniforms, complete with those funny Jap caps and *amiage kyahan*, laced leggings. They didn't need any commands, spoken or signed, to move out.

Because they didn't want to pass through the village, Willard and I led them on a shortcut that crossed Dinsmore Hill east of the hermit Dan's place and then crossed Banty Creek at a spot where stepping-stones kept your feet dry, and gained the Banty Creek road to move westward to its intersection with the Swain road south. At that inter-section, McPherson thanked us but told us we couldn't go any further with them. He put his hand on my shoulder and said, "If I have my way about it, there won't be any of this that you'll be able to watch. But you'll hear it. Go find yourself a good seat. The front porch of the hotel would be the best place." And then they were gone into the gathering dusk.

Willard and I moseyed over to the porch of the Ingledew house that had been the hotel and was now headquarters for Major Evans, who was sitting in a rocker after supper smoking his fancy briar pipe with a couple of his staff, a sergeant and a corporal. Our old friend Lieutenant Bosco was also there. "Hey, Japs," Major Evans said to Willard and me. "What's up?"

"Nanimo," I said: nothing, and Willard also said *"Nanimo"* although he didn't quite pronounce it correctly. We sat on the porch too; there were plenty of chairs. We watched the lightning bugs coming out, and I considered telling the major that those were mosquitoes with flash-lights, but decided he didn't have any sense of humor at all. After a while, I said, "We were wondering, could you tell us, since all the am-munition is fake and doesn't hurt anybody, how does the umpire know when one of the tanks is hit by a shell or something that would have blown it up but didn't *really* blow it up. I mean—"

"A good hit," said Major Evans with exaggerated patience, "will leave a temporary yellow mark if it's antipersonnel, and a temporary red mark if it's antimateriel. Does that make any sense? Instead of real bullets or shells, there's some soaplike stuff with colored dye in it."

"Yellow if it hits people, red if it hits tanks?" Willard said. "Okay, but how does a grenade know whether it's hitting people or tanks?"

"Different kinds of training grenades," the major said. He was slouched in his rocker in a bored attitude. But suddenly he snapped into an upright, alert position. "Speak of the devil! Was that a *grenade?*" He looked at his men.

"Sounded like one, sir," the sergeant said. "Far off."

All of us listened, and slowly but increasingly other sounds drifted out of the distance through the gloom. "Browning fire," the major said. "And another grenade. Rifles. Was that a bazooka? Hey, mortar!"

We were all looking toward the south, and the sky down that way, or rather the mountainside, was illuminated by the light of a flare. And then another flare. It was spectacular, almost like watching fireworks exploding in the sky. Not that I had ever seen fireworks. But I had watched meteor showers.

"Jesus!" the major said, and then his ears really perked up and he said, "Do you hear tanks?"

"Yes sir," said the sergeant, and the corporal nodded too, and Willard and I both nodded also. Not that I had ever heard tanks, but Willard had, earlier this night.

"Get the jeep!" the major said, and the corporal ran around behind the hotel and returned with the jeep. The soldiers piled into it and took off down the south road. Bosco stayed behind.

"I sure do wish we could mosey down thataway too," Willard said.

But we just had to sit there, for a long time, listening to all of that gunfire and the explosions and the rumbling of the tanks. The noise had alerted everybody in Stay More. The whole platoon of engineers were out of their tents, Doc Swain was on his porch, and kids were approaching from every direction, along with Miss Jerram and many others.

Sammy Coe ran up, asking, "Has it started?"

"Sounds like it," Willard said. "But it's still a long way up the road yonder. I thought it was supposed to happen right here in the village."

"McPherson ambushed 'em," I said, with more exultation than I'd felt in a long time. "He wouldn't let 'em get anywhere near the village."

My analysis, I was pleased to discover and to report in the next day's

Daily Star, was right on target. McPherson's samurai had indeed ambushed the whole convoy of tanks, jeeps, and trucks coming from Camp Chaffee, the elite troops of the 715th Tank Batallion, 16th Armored Division.

When all the shooting stopped, the jeep returned to the hotel. Major Evans was swearing obscenely as he got out of the jeep and just stood there in the road with both of his hands on his hips as if somebody had stolen his favorite toy.

"Who won?" Willard had the audacity to ask.

"Won?" Major Evans said. "It's still top of the first inning, and the score is already twelve to nothing, Japs."

Another jeep pulled up, and a captain got out. He saluted the major and said, "They caught us by complete surprise, sir. We couldn't get a shot off. That wasn't in the script."

"Fuck the script!" said the major. "If this were really Kyushu, Stoving, your whole outfit would be wiped out. The Japs won't take prisoners. At least McPherson was nice enough to take prisoners. Here he comes."

Another jeep pulled up, driven by our friend Corporal Rucker, with the lieutenant in the back. I assumed they had commandeered the jeep from the enemy.

McPherson jumped out, saluted the major (with a Japanese salute) and then offered his hand to the captain. "Good game, Burt. Kind of short, but I like them that way."

"Fuck you, Mac," Captain Stoving shot back. "The game hasn't started. That was just a warm-up, and you haven't scored a point yet."

Major Evans said to Captain Stoving, "I'm afraid he has. Quite a few points. In fact, according to the rules, you are so dead you'll have to wait two days for replacements."

"That's not fair, sir!" Captain Stoving was nearly whining. "If I'd had any idea we'd get waylaid before arrival, I'd have sent scouts on ahead. And if I'd used my scouts, there's no way Mac could have taken us."

"Let's do it over again," McPherson suggested, "and you can use your scouts this time."

"We're already *here!*" Stoving said. "We've finally arrived to start the exercise, which is all we were trying to do! Do you know how many days it took just to *find* this place? If the visiting team is arriving for the game, you don't send out the home team to beat them up while their bus is coming into town!"

Major Evans said, "Gentlemen, you're both forgetting this isn't a game. You can't do anything over again. This is *war*. And as in love, all is fair."

A long column of soldiers was coming across the Banty Creek bridge, their hands raised behind their necks while McPherson's men with rifles escorted them. Dozens of them. No, hundreds. Corporal Rucker turned his jeep so its headlights illuminated their arrival. Most of the prisoners had blobs of yellow on their uniforms, which meant they were dead, or wounded, or at least captured, one and all. Sergeant Harris stopped the column in front of the hotel, and ordered them to stand at attention in rows with their hands still raised. Some of those guys looked really scared, as if their captors actually were Japanese. Sergeant Harris certainly looked like a terrible vicious *rempei gakari gunso* in his uniform. He gave McPherson the Japanese salute and said, "One hundred eighty-three POWs sir. What shall we do with them?"

McPherson turned to Major Evans. "When we invade Kyushu, sir, the Japanese will take no prisoners."

"That's what I've been trying to tell Burt," Major Evans jerked his thumb at Captain Stoving.

"Okay, Sergeant," McPherson said. "*Jusatsu suru.* Shoot 'em." Sergeant Harris summoned his BAR man, Corporal Quigg, and they prepared to mow down the rows of POWs. "No, wait," McPherson said. "Burt, I'll make you a deal. How about a pack of cigarettes per hostage."

"Aw hell, Mac," Captain Stoving said. "Even if you shoot 'em all, I get 'em back tomorrow, don't I, Major Evans sir?"

I had never seen Major Evans smile before, and what he was wearing now was more like a smirk. But he said, "Day after tomorrow, according to the rules. And when you get 'em back, they're not these men, who are dead, but 'replacements.' And you lost every one of your fucking tanks, didn't you?"

"He didn't hit my M-7," Stoving pointed out, but he was hanging his head.

"Excuse me," Major Evans said. "You lost *eleven* out of your *twelve* tanks. Take your two dead companies and bury 'em, and when you get 'em exhumed, tell 'em a thing or two about defense."

"Better luck in the second inning, Burt," McPherson said. "I'd invite you up to my place for a sip of Chism's Dew, the best whiskey on earth. But you won't *ever* find my place."

"Wanna bet?" Stoving said, and turned on his heel and got back into his jeep. Then he noticed his one hundred and eighty-three dead men, still standing with their hands behind their necks. He turned to Major Evans. "Can I have my men back? Is the exercise over for tonight?"

"A pack of cigarettes per man, is it?" said Major Evans.

Later McPherson told me that actually he and Captain Stoving were pretty good friends. They'd known each other for more than a year, and had once roomed together in BOQ at Camp Chaffee. BOQ, he said, stood for Bawdy Oldmen's Quonset, but when I asked if I could quote that in tomorrow's *Daily Star* he said actually it just stood for bachelor officers' quarters. McPherson and Stoving had started out together as second lieutenants, but Stoving had been promoted to captain because he was a "brownnose." I didn't know that word, and wondered if the brown was like the red or yellow marks used in fake ammunition. Stoving was from Arkansas; his father owned an insurance company in Little Rock. That ought to have made me proud of him, as I was proud of all the Arkansas soldiers that Ernie Pyle had mentioned in his columns. But I was a Jap and Stoving was a Yank and I was rooting for McPherson's samurai to win the exercise that they were supposed to lose. The company of engineers, who had been making bets among themselves on the outcome, with the odds heavily in favor of the Yanks and their tanks, were so overawed by McPherson's ambush of the Yanks' arrival that they were now betting on the Jap rangers. I posted the betting odds in my daily.

Actually, the exercise was not exactly in the singular, McPherson explained to me; it wasn't to be thought of as a single battle won or lost. Rather, it was a series of "problems," and he was careful that I understood that a problem is not necessarily a difficulty but a question to be solved, as in a math problem, just as "exercise" is not necessarily calisthenics but an engagement between two opposing teams in a war game. The ultimate problem for the Yanks, and the final inning of the game, was to find and destroy the Japs' bivouac. But before then, the Japs had to defend the village not just once but repeatedly, from each direction of the compass, and during the night as well as in broad day, and also in the middle of a hard rain, if we could only get one. It had been dry for a long spell.

Larry Duckworth was having fits of glee because the Yanks had chosen for their bivouac the broad meadow across the road from the Duckworth's house, south alongside Swains Creek. It had once been the site of an Osage Indian camp, and in the days before we became Allies and Axis we had played cowboys and Indians in that big meadow. Now the field, which had already had its first mowing of hay, was the home for two companies of the 715th Tank Batallion under Captain Burton Stoving. There were twelve enormous tanks parked there, mostly M-4 Shermans, some of them with howitzers in tow, but also a huge M-6, and the peculiar M-7. There were also jeeps and trucks and a few motorcycles. There were three dozen tents, and latrines, and everything. During the two days that they were required by the umpire's rules to remain dead or regroup or whatever they were supposed to do, those two companies of armored troops had built themselves a little city on the south edge of Stay More, and all of us kids, Yanks and Japs alike, spent a lot of time watching them in wonder. That first day we watched them give their tanks a bath in Swains Creek to wash off the red marks that indicated they'd been hit and destroyed by grenades, mortar, or the bazooka.

Before the next problem was due to start, which was an assault on the village from the south by the battalion of the Yanks and their tanks, Captain Stoving met with Major Evans and Lieutenant McPherson to protest the Japs' use of the bazooka. He claimed that the Japanese did not yet have the bazooka in their arsenal, and therefore if McPherson wanted to be strictly "realistic," he could not use a weapon that the Japanese did not possess. McPherson claimed that the bazooka was his "handicap" against the vastly superior forces of Stoving's tank companies. But Major Evans ruled in Stoving's favor, and McPherson was required to stow the bazooka and give his champion bazookamen, Privates Nilson and Hewes, the Japanese .80 antitank rifles instead. McPherson told me an extra reason he was peeved by the decision: the bazooka had got its name because a radio comedian of the 1930s, Bob Burns of Van

Buren, Arkansas (not far from Camp Chaffee), had had a weird musical instrument of that name and shape. "It may not be Japanese," McPherson said, "but it certainly is *Arkansas.*" I quoted those words in my editorial in the next issue of the *Daily Star* in which I protested Major Evans' decision, and I titled the editorial "Japs Unfairly Deprived of Best Weapon," and I made sure that Major Evans got a copy of that issue.

With the total population of Stay More now running close to four hundred, with all the soldiers, I had a rough time printing enough copies of my paper to meet the demand. One "press run" on a gelatin board could not exceed fifty copies before it started dimming out. But sweet Ella Jean solved the problem by simply making duplicates, or rather quadruplicates, of each of the hand-lettered purple master sheets. That was a lot of extra work for her, and, since we were now rolling in loose change from the sale of all those copies, I insisted on paying her a salary.

"I don't need ary salary," she said, unmindful of the rhyme. "But I sure could use a kiss."

I was stunned. No, at first I just thought she'd said something hilarious, and I laughed uproariously, but then, when I determined she was serious, I was speechless with the wonder of it. I stared at her. There was nothing on earth I'd rather do than kiss her. I had never kissed a girl before, but I had imagined it, I had dreamed of it, I had even licked a couple of my fingers and pretended they were lips and pressed my mouth against them. Now here we were, in the newspaper office, nobody else around, Latha somewhere out on the porch, and all I had to do was do it. "Are you all right?" a voice asked me, and I had to shake my head to clear it to realize that a real voice hadn't spoken, it was just good old Ernie Pyle taking care of me again.

"Do you mean *me?*" I stupidly asked Ella Jean.

She ought to have said—she had every right to have said—something dismissive, like "No, I was just a-talking to myself," or "Actually I was thinking of Cary Grant," or even "I'd druther kiss a frog than you." But she did not speak at all, which was the beauty of it. She simply gave her lovely head the slightest but clearest of nods.

And I could have compounded my stupidity by continuing to babble

something like, "That's a swell idea, honeypot," or "Okay, if you insist," or "Well, ready or not here I come," but I was inspired by her example to say nothing, to let silence have its eloquence as a setting for a
head movement. I moved my head close to hers. I took a keen look at
her mouth. Just being that near to it shook me. When I could still the
tremble of my head I had to consider how to hold it. It would not be
seemly to tilt it so much to get our noses out of the way of bumping. I
should keep my head proudly upright but somehow in moving my
mouth forward I should allow the noses to pass.

Then as we made contact—hers were mildly pursed, mine were
not—I was hit with the uncertainty of how long I should maintain the
contact. It did not occur to me just to wait and let her break the contact
after a suitable duration; that, I assumed, was my responsibility. But I
didn't know what to do. I think she did, though. She had put her two
hands on the sides of my two arms, as if to pull me closer to her. She
held me like that, with our lips mashed together, as if she couldn't let
go, for a very long time.

CHAPTER
22

When the defense of Stay More began, I had a ringside seat, as McPherson had said I would. Not only that, but the evening before the battle he attempted to give me a private lesson in just what I would be watching, so I could understand and even appreciate the various things I would see. Using blank pages of my Indian Chief, he drew maps with arrows and symbols representing tanks and troops and his own arsenal of weapons, and rectangles representing the various buildings of "downtown" Stay More, and squiggles representing the two creeks and their confluence. I tried to pay attention. Not only did I have great difficulty grasping terms or concepts like *displacement* and *retrograde operation* and *point targets* but also many of the words he used were

neither English nor Japanese but French—*echelon, defilade, abatis, melee*—
and I didn't bother to ask him what they meant, not because I didn't
want to expose my ignorance but because I truly didn't care. I simply
could not concentrate because my mind was elsewhere, namely, the office of the *Daily Star* during the long moments of that kiss. "Are you all
right?" McPherson asked me, and I realized I must not have been paying close attention. "Do you understand this flanking maneuver?"

"I guess so," I said.

"I realize it's confusing," he said. "I'm not sure my men understand
it, and we've rehearsed it a dozen times." He took out his cigarette
lighter and set fire to the sheets of the Indian Chief on which he'd made
his maps. "But trust me, it's the only way to keep the tanks out of the
village, and I'm not at all sure it will work."

"How are you doing with Annie?" I suddenly asked.

Did I detect a blush? "I didn't realize you knew about me and
Annie," he said.

"I didn't realize you knew about me and Ella Jean," I said.

He studied me for several moments. Then he smiled and said, "I
didn't. But it doesn't take much to guess. So. How are you doing with
Ella Jean?"

"I asked you first."

"As a matter of fact," he looked at his watch, "in just a little while I'm
supposed to take my pal Burt Stoving over to meet her."

"He must really be your pal, if you're doing that," I said.

"I was being a bit sarcastic," he said, and reached out and rumpled
my hair. "You're my only pal. But Burt and I are not simply rivals on
the battlefield, we're also competitors in the game of life. At Camp
Chaffee, he was always parading his dates in front of me. So now I'm
giving him a good look at mine. I think I'm really falling for that girl. I
wish you could tell me more about her. But nobody seems to know anything about her. Except her father. And how do I ask him? Vermonters
are notoriously taciturn, and here I am running off at the mouth again.
So tell me: how are you doing with Ella Jean?"

"I think I'm really falling for that girl," I said.

Falling, hell. I had already fallen about as far as you can get before
hitting bottom. Naturally I was just a little suspicious that the reason

she had, after all these years, suddenly taken a shine to me was because her bosom companion, Gypsy, had more or less abandoned her in favor of her brother Willard, who, ever since that famous pie supper when she'd kissed him, was allowing his keen analytic mind to be diluted by daydreams of Gypsy.

It was almost pathetic. Sammy Coe invited all his Jap friends to use the front porch of the Coe house as the grandstand to watch the great battle, because it commanded a view of downtown Stay More, and it was also safely out of the way of any stray bullets, fake and soapy though they were. All the kids were more excited than they'd ever been, except for four of them: not only were Gypsy and Willard sitting with their heads and their hands together, but also Ella Jean and I were so caught up in each other that none of us was really going to be able to play close attention to the battle. At least Willard had enough sense of the occasion to offer periodic analysis of what was happening on the battlefield, but Ella Jean and I were lost in each other. It is a wonder that I had the presence of mind to remember to save a seat for *you*, Gentle Reader.

But which, after all, is more exciting, love or war? As I sat there, scarcely noticing the tanks coming into town from the south or observing McPherson's samurai as they took cover in the old mill, behind the canning factory, or even in some of our leftover foxholes, and paying more attention to what Ella Jean was saying (she was relating some gossip about Rosa Faye Duckworth, who had been fooling around with one—or more—of the soldiers bivouacked in the Duckworth meadow), my mind was dwelling neither upon the deployment of the combat nor upon sweet Ella Jean's breathy chatter but philosophically upon the power of passion to banish one's interest in more important things, like armed conflict. Knowing him as I did, I knew that McPherson himself would much rather be walking in the woods with Annie than trying to keep a dozen tanks out of Stay More. And I suddenly realized how much Mare Coe would have preferred being with Gypsy on the banks of Banty Creek to facing the Japanese on Iwo Jima. Was fighting a substitute for loving? Or a counter for it? A remedy to it? Or what?

These profound thoughts were scarcely interrupted by the sound of the tank corps' battle cry, "Hang it in and let 'er go!" or the answering (and rhyming) battle cry of the samurai, "Mare Coe!" I reflected with

just a little pride that McPherson and his men had chosen that battle
cry after I had told them the story of our town's boy at Iwo Jima. Both
battle cries were soon accompanied by the ringing of the schoolhouse
bell, sounding its mournful "BOMB!" and "DOOM!" repeatedly. I wondered who was ringing it. That elegiac, almost pastoral chiming was
soon drowned out by the beginning of Major Evan's sound effects. He
had brought with him a recording of the actual sounds of battle, and
these were now being played at full volume from loudspeakers the engineers had set up around the village, for the sake of realism, as if all the
fake ammunition were not enough, or as if the actual tanks and guns
might be induced to sally and volley and battery by the artificial noise. I
tried to explain to Ella Jean how funny the idea was: that fake sounds
were being used to prompt fake ammunition. But I'm not sure she got
it. Or quite possibly she was so wrapped up in *me* that it didn't matter.
The schoolhouse bell stopped ringing, unable to compete with that
noise. The ringer stepped out of the building. It was Miss Jerram.

I thought of all the kids of Stay More whose fathers had gone to the
war and who had had those identical recurrent nightmares involving
monstrous mayhem and the weapons in action, things they'd never actually seen but could now watch: tanks, howitzers, missile launchers,
machine guns, mortars, if not the banished bazooka. What they could-
n't see they could hear, and between Major Evans' sound effects and
the actual implements of war they could hear enough battle noise to last
them for the rest of their lives.

As journalists, Ella Jean and I had a responsibility to report to our
readers just what happened on that day. While Ella Jean was probably
more interested in reporting the spectators' reactions, I was somewhat
interested in being able to detect just who was winning that battle and
how. When the smoke cleared and Major Evans turned off the sound
effects, I examined the notes in my Indian Chief, based more on Willard's running commentary than on my own observation of the fighting,
and discovered that I had just the bare outlines for the lead story in the
next daily: YANKS AND TANKS TAKE TOWN FROM JAPS. McPherson
had prepared me to accept that outcome, but what bothered me most
was that I didn't really seem to care. What did it matter that Japs had
destroyed two tanks in the middle of the WPA bridge so that the others
couldn't cross Banty Creek and had to shell the town from the school-

house road? Who really cared that Sergeant Harris and Corporal Rucker were both killed in the engagement? The town's own Yanks, led by Sog Alan, were overcome with the joy of victory and were acting like maniacs, while the town's Japs were despondent, but I really and truly didn't think it was anything to get excited about. After all, there were still going to be more battles, weren't there?

But dutifully I went to interview Major Evans afterward, sending Ella Jean away from me for a little while by assigning her to the story of the effect the battle had had on the town physically (her story would report that a post holding up the porch roof of the Ingledew store had suffered a direct hit from a fake grenade and had broken, collapsing the porch roof, but the engineers were already at work repairing it to better than new). Major Evans was too busy or simply didn't have time for me. His staff sergeant gave me the "casualty figures": thirty-two dead Yanks, three destroyed tanks; eight dead Japs, the remaining four taken prisoner, including McPherson. The sergeant would not give me the present score, if there was one, but he said the village was "secure" in Yank hands, and "the utter rout of the enemy more than makes up for the enemy's opening ambush." I told him he sounded like he had been rooting for the Yanks. "Well, what do you think I *am?*" he replied.

With Ella Jean's stories on the parties of the town's kids and grown-ups who watched the battle and made a picnic of it, and my story on the battle itself, we discovered that we still didn't have enough news to fill the four pages of the issue. Ella Jean put her hand on top of mine. "You can just make things up," she said, and winked at me. And so I embellished the news a bit, which one shouldn't do. I added a story about the wholesaler's truck bringing orders to Latha's store right in the middle of the battle, and the truck driver being scared out of his wits and high-tailing it out of town. Actually, the wholesaler's truck had arrived during the battle, but the driver just calmly watched the action along with everybody else on Latha's store porch.

Among the merchandise the wholesaler had sent to replenish Latha's rapidly sold-out stock (and which it remained my job to arrange on the shelves) was a box of twenty-four bars of Palmolive soap! I eagerly bought a bar from Latha with my own newly earned riches, and, since Ella Jean wouldn't accept a salary (other than kisses, in which she was now overpaid), I presented her with the bar.

"Why, Dawny!" Ella Jean exclaimed. "This is my favorite of all the soap there is!"

"I know," I let slip.

"How did ye know?" she asked.

I groped for evasion. "Well, sometimes you just smell like it," and I buried my nose in her hair.

That evening once again I made my pilgrimage to the sacred spot on Banty Creek, and my effort was rewarded: Ella Jean came down the hill to take her bath with the new bar of Palmolive. I was tempted to reveal my presence to her. After all, I was her boyfriend now. Would she mind? But I was afraid of offending her. I was glad enough, as it was, to have the privilege of the marvelous sight and the more exquisite privilege of the fragrance, and to reflect that this part of Banty Creek was remotely over the mountain from where all the soldiers were, so that none of them could ever share the sight or the fragrance.

It was hard for us to keep apart from each other, and early the next morning she came to walk with me on my rounds delivering the new issue of the *Daily Star,* the issue that had two of her stories in it. We held hands and talked. She told me the latest gossip about Rosa Faye, who had actually been seen jumping up and down after one of her "dates" with a soldier. And everybody knew what she was jumping up and down for: it was the best known contraceptive. I asked Ella Jean if she'd ever have any notion of going with a soldier. "Not as long as I got you," she said, and I was so moved I had to stop walking and give her a kiss. Walking on, a little while later, she looked at me sidelong and said, "You were watching me down on Banty Creek yester evening, weren't you?" At first I shook my head and got ready to deny it vigorously, but I saw it was no use, and I nodded. "Why didn't ye just come and jump in too?" she asked.

"Next time I sure will!" I said. And I hoped she might even want to take another bath that very night, which would have been exceptional: I'd never known her to take one more often than biweekly. Did I have to wait two more weeks before we could bathe together?

But even if she'd wanted to bathe that very night, we wouldn't have, because it was time for the soldiers to have their Night Exercise. In this part of the maneuvers, the village would be "given back" to the Japs, and the tanks would once again attack it, but this time from the west, over the pontoon bridge, and under cover of darkness. Major Evans decreed that the pontoon bridge itself could be neither "destroyed" nor blocked during the exercise. Tanks crossing it could be targets but not disabled on the bridge. Once again the town's Japs congregated in the front yard of Sammy Coe's house to watch the exercise. We couldn't see very much because it was dark, but we could hear plenty. Ella Jean caught a lightning bug and crushed it on my nose, and I caught one and crushed it on her nose, and we both had glowing noses for a while, although a squashed lightning bug is pretty stinky.

Sergeant Harris was killed again, hiding behind Miss Jerram's house, but not before he had destroyed three tanks with his *juyo tekidan*. He "expired" in Miss Jerram's arms, while Captain Stoving stopped the exercise to protest to Major Evans that none of the Japs were supposed to be on the west side of Swains Creek. Major Evans ruled that the Japs could be anywhere they damn well pleased, and, as the exercise continued, the Japs were everywhere, and this time they successfully defended the village against the attack. An occasional flare would be sent up, or in the headlights of the tanks we'd catch a glimpse of the action, although not enough to suit Willard and his analysis, so most of the civilians had to wait until the next morning's issue of the *Daily Star* to find out just what had happened. Because it had been mostly dark, I could easily follow Ella Jean's advice to "just make things up," and I embellished the stories right and left: not only Sergeant Harris' brave deeds at Miss Jerram's (five tanks instead of three) but also his dramatic death in her arms and I even gave him some last words, "I can't stay any more in Stay More." Major Evans summoned me to his headquarters after the issue appeared and protested that the casualty figures I had posted were not those his staff sergeant had given me. Only fifty-two Yanks had been killed, not a hundred and fifty-two. I told him I was glad to know that he was reading my newspaper. And then I asked him, since he liked the metaphor of the baseball game, what inning we were in, and what the score was. He said it was the bottom of the third, and the Japs were leading, eighteen to eleven. "But don't quote me on that," he admonished me. Did this mean we still had six more innings to play? I wanted to know. "More or less," he said.

I began to wonder if the *Daily Star* could continue to be interesting. The game, and the score, seesawed back and forth for several days. The town was taken and lost, and retaken. One of the big windows on the front of Latha's store got shattered, but the engineers went to Harrison to get a new piece of glass, and replaced it. A soldier nearly drowned in Swains Creek but Doc Swain revived him. A dog was hit by a fake bullet and had not been seen since. Major Evans hoped for a torrential downpour to test the troops mud-fighting abilities, but the weather continued dry and hot. One advantage the Japs had over the Yanks: the latter didn't know about the former's use of pennyroyal to prevent chigger bites and the use of Chism's Dew to cure chigger bites. The Yanks were suffering, and scratching so much they couldn't keep their tanks on track. Luther Chism had completely sold out his stock of Dew, indiscriminately to Japs and Yanks alike, and the first new corn wouldn't be ready for picking for several more weeks. Since Major Evans couldn't have the fifth and sixth innings in a downpour, as he'd hoped, he held the sixth inning with smoke bombs that obscured the battle even more than darkness could do. The smoke was so thick it nearly drowned the sound effects, and two Sherman tanks crashed into each other, wrecking one.

Every Dill offered to see if he couldn't repair the busted tank. Just as legend had it that the disease hadn't been invented that Doc Swain couldn't cure (and, now, the new legend that the tank hadn't been built that McPherson couldn't destroy), the legend was that there was no mechanical apparatus devised by the hand of man that Every Dill couldn't repair. I livened up the tedious *Daily Star* with a story on Every, whose garage was enjoying the greatest period of prosperity ever, with so many jobs servicing and repairing the various army jeeps and trucks that he had to hire Lawlor Coe, Sammy's dad, to give up blacksmithing and learn auto mechanics. I was able to report that Every successfully repaired that Sherman tank. Latha and Every both made so much money that they were going to enjoy a happy retirement.

Major Evans called a meeting between Captain Stoving and Lieutenant McPherson and reminded them that the main purpose of this entire exercise was to train both of their outfits for the invasion of the mountain country of Kyushu. "Here we are in the seventh inning stretch, and everything we've done so far has been down here in these bottomlands." Major Evans pointed at the mountains to the north and east. "So let's leave the village and get up into those hills."

"That's exactly what I have been waiting for," McPherson said. And just barely remembered to add, "Sir."

I wanted to talk with McPherson. I hadn't had a word with him since that night before the first battle, when we'd exchanged confidences about our girlfriends. We'd both spent all our free time since then in the company of those girlfriends. I missed him.

So one afternoon I decided to return to the bivouac and apologize to him for having spent so much of my time with Ella Jean. As it turned out, however, Ella Jean insisted on going with me up to the bivouac. "Just for old time's sake," she said, reminding me that the bivouac had been as much a campground or playground for her as it had been for me. I let her go with me, I held her hand along the way, but I warned her in advance that I wanted to have just some private "boy talk" with Mac.

"That's okay," she said. "While you're chawing with him, I'll just socialize with Emil."

"Emil who?" I asked.

"Polacek." She looked at me sideways. "Didn't ye know he was sweet on me?"

"I didn't even know that was his name," I declared.

As we neared the bivouac, we came to the turning in the climbing trail where it had always been our custom to look over our shoulder— which I had not been able to do the time Rosa Faye followed me because I had a washtub over my head. I glanced over my shoulder and my heart stopped when I beheld a figure behind me. Ella Jean caught a glimpse of him too before he dashed into the woods.

"Was that Sog Alan?" I asked her.

"Looked like it," she said.

"Darn. Let's not go to the bivouac then, in case he's following us."

We took a logging trail that cut off up the mountain to the south, almost toward that remote pasture where the glider had landed, and then we cut back and approached the old farmstead from a different angle, making sure that we didn't see anyone following us.

CHAPTER

23

WHEN I WAS ALONE WITH MCPHERSON, I FELT OBLIGED TO TELL him that we had been followed part of the way by Sog Alan, who, I suspected, was trying to find out the location of the bivouac so he could tattle to the Yanks—not his own Yanks but Stoving's. I said I hoped McPherson wouldn't be upset: Ella Jean and I had deliberately taken that diversionary route so that Sog couldn't follow us to the bivouac, but still he might have detected the general location of it.

But McPherson was not upset at all. I was surprised at his indifference. I wondered—but stopped short of asking him—if he was getting bored with the exercise himself and maybe even wanted the bivouac to be discovered so the exercise would be over. Or possibly his mind, like mine, had concluded that the pursuit of the opposite sex was a more worthy mission than warfare.

"I guess Annie is all that matters to you." I was just thinking out loud.

And as he had often done, he needed to study my face for a while to understand just what I was intending with what I'd said. While he was looking at me, I suddenly realized how tired he was. Unlike Captain Stoving, who could drive all over creation in one of his jeeps, McPherson had to go on foot, and his feet were tired. But out of his exhaustion he managed to smile and say, "There's no way you could have prevented Sog or one of his Yank buddies from finding the bivouac." He rubbed his forehead with his hand as if to wipe away the weariness. "But yes, you're right. I'm not thinking about much other than Annie. That's dangerous, and not fair to my men. Fighting and loving simply don't mix. Probably Mare Coe understood that when he was on Iwo Jima. I suspect that he had to put Gypsy out of his mind before he could return those grenades that were thrown at him."

His mention of Gypsy reminded me of her favorite animal. "Maybe," I suggested, "you ought to load up Jarhead and move on out of here to a different spot."

"Roger," he said. "We've got that contingency in mind. But first we want to see if the enemy is able to find us here, and, if they can, we want to defend it. It's our home, and right now we're taking a little rest in it."

"When you're done resting," I offered, "I could show you a good place to go, where nobody would ever find you."

"On Ledbetter Mountain?" he said. "The hollow with the waterfalls and bluff shelters?"

"It's so far back up in those coves you have to keep wiping at the shadows," I said, as close to poetry as I ever got. I did not tell him that I myself had been lost up there at the age of almost six. "How did you find it?"

"Macklin found it. He's my reconnaissance man. Remember he was the one who found the bodies of Ella Jean's sisters below Leapin Rock." McPherson's face became very sad once again. But it passed. "Did you know we were using Leapin Rock when we beat Stoving in that north-

223

ern assault problem yesterday? I was up there with a couple of the men firing the *juyo tekidan* and from that vantage point we knocked out five tanks."

"I wondered if you would think to use Leapin Rock," I said. "And I was about to suggest it to you, but I didn't want to remind you of—you know."

"Your Ella Jean seems to be over that," he observed. I really liked his using that "your." She was really mine.

"She's real strong and brave," I said proudly. And then I chuckled. "It didn't even bother her when we learned that you were killed yesterday!"

He laughed too. "Yeah! I stood up on the edge of Leaping Rock and a sharpshooter got me. I nearly fell off."

We both went on laughing, but I think we were both also whistling in the dark. McPherson and I often had the same kind of thoughts at the same time. So when I said what I did next, and he nodded, I knew he'd been thinking the same thing at the same moment. "But a sharpshooter might *really* get you when you invade Japan." There was of course nothing he could say to that, except to nod. "Or maybe not," I quickly added. "Maybe you guys will be lucky. And you can come back to Stay More and marry Annie!"

He hit me mildly on the shoulder with his fist. "Hey, I'd like that. And you know, maybe we will be lucky. But it's not just luck, it's also skill. Those tank guys are *good*, let me tell you. I mean, really good. They'll make mincemeat out of Kyushu." The thought made him happy, even though the "tank guys" were currently his enemy. "But one reason they'll make mincemeat out of Kyushu is that my men will soften it up beforehand. And probably we'll all be killed doing it. So that's why I can't even *hint* to Annie that I'll be coming back to marry her."

"That's the same way Mare felt about Gypsy before he had to leave her and go into the marines," I said. "But are you going to ask her to wait for you?"

"Not even that," he said, and hung his head. But then he raised his head and gave it a shake, and said, "I've got to stop thinking about her! I've got a job to do. Tonight the mountain fighting begins."

"I wish you guys didn't have to keep having battles for three more innings."

He laughed again. "You've been standing too close to Major Evans! But he's right, I guess. From now on, the Yanks will be searching for us, and we'll be defending this place against them, and then, if they take it, we'll take it back from them. And finally, we'll escape to the lost hollow of the waterfall on Ledbetter Mountain and see if they can find us up there. If they can't, the exercise is over."

"And then everybody goes back to Chaffee?" I wanted to ask, "And I won't ever see you again?" but I could not.

"Yes, but say, listen. When the exercise is all over, we'll all have a short leave before we have to report back to Chaffee. How about I borrow a jeep and we'll have a double date? You and me and Ella Jean and Annie will go to the movies in Jasper. Did you know Annie has never seen a movie?"

"I don't think Ella Jean has either."

"Okay, so let's count on that!"

"I can't wait," I said.

"*Sayonara,*" he said.

"*Sayonara.*"

Walking back to the village with Ella Jean, I told her right away what McPherson had suggested about a double date to see the movies in Jasper. I thought she'd be tickled to pieces by the idea, but she just gave me another one of those sideways looks and said, "Emil has already asked me."

"To the picture show?" I demanded. She nodded. "How's he going to take you to Jasper? He couldn't borrow a jeep like McPherson could!"

"He says he can get a jeep."

"And you're going to go with him?"

"I reckon I might."

I lost my temper. The thought of that made me really angry, not so much the idea that a grown man from some weird foreign place like the Bronx would try to take my girlfriend away from me, but the fact that she would *let* him do it. "You're just another one of these V-girls!" I yelled at her. "No better than Rosa Faye!"

"What's a V-girl?"

"Victory girl. Mac says the army camps and the cities have lots of girls under sixteen who fool around with the servicemen."

"I'd just let Emil take me to the pitcher show," she said. "I wouldn't jump up and down afterwards."

It took me a moment to realize what she was referring to. In the moment of my realizing what she meant, I couldn't avoid a mental image of her and Polacek lying together. It looked awful, and it really got my dander up. "Well—" I groped for some good words but found none. "I sure hope you sure enjoy yourself!" And then I ran away from her. I left her on that trail and went back to town by myself, and I put the next issue of the *Daily Star* to bed all by myself, without any help from her, although the fourth time I slowly hand-lettered the master sheets I was running out of energy and patience and I made a bunch of dumb mistakes. It wasn't a very good issue anyway. To fill up the increasing empty space in the daily, I'd started a "Letters to the Editor" column, but there were only two: E. H. Ingledew wrote to say he sure would be glad when these here soldiers went back to wherever they came from. And Oren Duckworth wrote to say that he was missing three dozen chickens and he wasn't going to sue the Army for them but he wanted some kind of guarantee that the Army would leave his remaining chickens alone. In a foul mood, I added, "Editor's Note: It's not your chickens you ought to worry about. It's your daughter." Good sense prevailed, and I scratched that out.

I didn't feel like hiking up to the bivouac again to cover the action of that night's exercise, so I simply asked Major Evans (or rather his staff sergeant) what had happened. "The Yanks found it, and took it," he said simply but proudly. That was, after all, what McPherson had predicted would happen but it struck me as further fuel for my foul mood. My story wasn't an important story, and I gave it a small-lettered headline: JAP BIVOUAC SEIZED BY YANKS.

With the action of the maneuvers shifting to the mountains, Stay More became practically a ghost town again, which it had been working hard at doing for all the years I'd known it. It was littered with the soldiers' cigarette butts, and with spent cartridges and casings here and there, and there were tank tracks all over the place, but otherwise you'd never have known that such hectic operations had been going on here.

It was peaceful. After cleaning up the mess, and even smoothing out those tank tracks, the engineers went fishing and swimming. Then they took down the pontoon bridge and once again Swains Creek had to be crossed by ford or footbridge.

Major Evans's staff sergeant informed me that in a bold night raid the Japs had attempted to retake their bivouac and had killed sixty-one Yanks before being totally wiped out themselves. Chui McPherson had committed hara-kiri with his samurai sword. Celebrating, the Yanks had accidentally set fire to the old farmhouse, and it had burned to the ground. Latha told me I ought to write in my Indian Chief: "(6) The Story of Long Jack Stapleton and His House." I did, but I think I was getting bored with my Indian Chief. And it was all used up.

Major Evans and Captain Stoving and the dead *chui* had an argument, in which Stoving argued that the spoils of victory ought to include the mule belonging to the Japs. The dead *chui* countered that Corporal Jarhead was not simply a necessary pack animal for the samurai platoon but also a mascot, and it would demoralize his men in the ninth inning to be without it. Major Evans pointed out that in the bottom of the ninth the home team had a chance to pull out and win, although the Japs were now so far behind it didn't look likely. He ruled that the Japs could keep Jarhead, and further that the Yanks would have to evacuate the Japs' bivouac and remain out of sight while the Japs loaded up all their gear onto Jarhead and fled to their new secret bivouac.

I was tempted to go up to that glen of the waterfall and see McPherson and his samurai in their new location. I wanted to tell him something about mules, what Joe Don had said at Old Jarhead's funeral about how mules do everything the easy way: "Horses will pull a load for all their might; mules'll only use as much of their strength as they have to, and not a pound more." Maybe that could be a lesson for McPherson's samurai in defending that lost hollow: take it easy, and let the Yanks wear themselves out. But it was so spooky up there in those woods, and I hadn't been back to them since the time I'd been lost six years before. Willard and Joe Don and Sammy wanted me to tell them where the Japs had moved, but I would not. I simply wrote a story, JAPS NOW DUG IN AT SECLUDED HIDEOUT.

We thought the Yanks would never find them. Patrols of the Yanks went out into every holler and ravine of Stay More, well beyond Butter-churn Holler in one direction and almost to Parthenon in the other direction, on foot, by jeep and by motorcycle, but the tanks remained idle. And the Japs remained concealed. There was nothing to report in the *Daily Star.* I decided that I was going to have to convert my paper from a daily back to a weekly, especially because I didn't have my assistant any more. I missed her. It was small comfort that she too did not know where the Japs were now hiding, and thus she couldn't go "socialize" with old Emil.

For the final daily issue of the *Star,* I had to make up most of the news, such as it was. The only real news to animate its moribund pages was an announcement that I picked up by listening to Latha's radio. Now that the town had reverted to its drowsy lethargy and I had no girlfriend to take up my time, I spent most of my hours at Latha's store again. I even resumed listening to my old favorite shows, *Captain Midnight* and *Hop Harrigan* and *Terry and the Pirates.* During a news broadcast, the announcer said that for the first time during the war some Americans had been killed on American soil. The War and Navy Departments had disclosed that during the past several months Japanese paper balloons carrying bombs had reached the North American mainland, and although "these attacks are so scattered and aimless that they constitute no military threat," there was one reported incident of a woman and five children on an outing in Wyoming or Oregon or one of those western states who had been killed by a Japanese balloon-bomb.

So the final daily issue of *The Stay Morning Star,* with no more stories about the "occupation" of Stay More, had as its only headline, JAPANESE BALLOON-BOMB KILLS FIVE KIDS IN OREGON OR WYOMING. My editorial for that issue said that if we were all bored with the military activities being conducted around town, or rather the absence of any further military activities, we might shift our attention to the skies and start watching out for balloons.

I didn't anticipate the effect it would have on the town. Not just kids but grownups too started walking around with their eyes anxiously scanning the heavens. I even caught myself casting a glance upward, but it was infectious: if other people are looking at something, you look too.

Ella Jean showed up again, and it was her turn to be angry. "Dawny!

When I told ye just to make things up, I didn't mean *horrible* things like that!"

"I hate to tell ye," I was obliged to inform her, "but I didn't make that up. I got it off the radio!" When she threw me another one of those maddening sidelong glances, I added, "Ask Latha if you don't believe me! She heard it too."

"Well," Ella Jean said. That's all she said, but she didn't go away. After a while she added, "I reckon it's harder to believe the truth than what's made up."

"Yeah. And it's harder to *tell* the truth than make something up."

Another of her sidelong looks. "You don't believe me about Emil?"

That hadn't occurred to me. But I was quick enough to put in, "What if I don't?"

She hung her head. "I was just trying to see if I could make ye jealous," she confessed. "Emil never asked me to the pitcher show. I was just making that up."

"Why would ye want to make me *jealous?*"

"You don't have much feelings," she said. "Leastways, you don't *show* much feelings. Sometimes I wonder if you really *care* about anything."

"I cared about you," I said.

"Sometimes it was hard to tell."

"Well I don't mind saying I *still* care about you."

"I care a lot about you too," she said. "A whole lot. I would jump up and down for you."

Once again I was slow in getting her meaning, and as if to demonstrate, she jumped up and down a little bit. It was cute. It was also ardent and devoted and sexy.

All I could think to say was, "When?"

"Tonight," she said. "Would you like to share my Palmolive with me?"

"Oh, that would be fine and dandy," I said, borrowing a long-lost favorite expression of Mare Coe's, probably because I was thinking of what Mare and Gypsy had done on the banks of Banty Creek.

"You'll be there?" she asked. "You won't be hiding?"

"I'll come out of hiding," I promised.

"All right then," she said. "I can't wait."

"*Sayonara*," I said.

"What's that mean?"

"I'll be seeing you," I translated, with a stress on "seeing."

"*Sayonara*," she said.

If she couldn't wait, just think, Gentle Reader, of what I couldn't do. There were still hours to kill before twilight. I went to Latha's store and tried to sit on the porch, but I couldn't sit still. I gave the whole store a good sweeping and even tidied up the office of the *Star,* which I hadn't done for months. I arranged and rearranged merchandise on the shelves. "Dawny, you're going to wear yourself out," Latha said to me. And she observed, "You're just covered with sweat all over."

"That's okay, I'll be washing it off directly," I announced. I was almost tempted to tell her where and how I would be washing it off. All afternoon while I worked I thought of who would be the best person to talk to about my important upcoming tryst. I could really stand some advice. McPherson would have been my first choice, if he'd been accessible, but for all I knew he didn't have much experience in such matters himself. I'd never been able to ask him just how far he had managed to get with Annie. I thought about Willard, and I had every reason to suspect that Gypsy had introduced him to the mysteries and pleasures, but he was Ella Jean's own brother and I couldn't ask for advice on how to handle his sister, and besides I wasn't going to go up to his house looking for him, because that's where Ella Jean was, and I wasn't going to lay eyes on her again until we laid eyes on each other in our birthday suits. Thinking of that, I had a big doubt: what would she think when she saw me naked? I wasn't even sure what I looked like naked. I needed a big mirror. The only one I knew of was in that side room of Latha's store that had once been her bedroom when the store had still been her house too before she married Every and moved into the Dill dogtrot. So I waited until she'd gone home to start supper for her and Every and then I sneaked into that side room where the long mirror was. There I took off all my clothes and had a good look at myself, pretending I was Ella Jean . . . I mean pretending it was Ella Jean doing the looking at myself being me naked. While I had my clothes off, I suddenly had a deja vu of the previous time in that room, when I was only five-going-on-six, when Latha, before Every had come back to Stay More to take her away from me, had let me sleep one night with her, and, because she never slept with a stitch on, had let me sleep naked too. And I had told her, without even knowing for sure what the word meant, that I loved her. I really had loved her, and I still did, but now I knew that it's better to love someone your own age. Naked in that room, I remembered what Latha had replied when I'd told her that. "Oh, Dawny," she'd said, "I love you too, and if you were a growed-up man I would marry you right this minute."

Later, as dusk gathered and I headed for the sacred spot on Banty Creek, I reflected on how appropriate it was that Latha had been the last person I had seen while I was still "normal." I wished I could have told her that, and told her that I was on my way to being no longer a child.

I reached the spot on Banty Creek, the idyllic spot of hogscalds and willows and music in the rippling water, but Ella Jean was not there. I was abashed at myself for being so overeager that I'd probably got there a long time before her, although the world was certainly already enfolded in twilight. All I could do was sit down on a rock and wait for her.

Sitting there waiting and wondering when she'd come, I caught a whiff of that delectable Palmolive. My first thought was that she was coming down the hill and I could already smell it in her hand. But I waited and she did not appear. Could I possibly be smelling the remnants of Palmolive left over from her previous bath? No, nor was I simply *wishing* that I could smell it. It was in the air.

I stood up. I sniffed. I moved around, sniffing, and turned, and moved the other way. I began to follow my nose. Not far. Just a little way upstream, into a thicket of thorny locust trees, a level open place beside the bank. Where she lay. My first thought was: she's playing with me. I wanted to hold that thought, but it got entirely away.

CHAPTER
24

WHEN? *Now.* SUMMERTIME GLOAMING CREEKWATER CLEAN FRESH Ella Jean. She lies still. I call her name. She does not move. "Don't play," I ask of her. Now I see the blood on her thigh. Crickets cicadas katydids tree frogs and a whippoorwill. She has no dress. She holds the bar of Palmolive clenched tightly in one fist as if it's all she has in this world, and I think what a brave and strong girl she was to hold onto that Palmolive while she was being raped and strangled. I drop to my knees beside her, and tell myself I must touch her. She is still warm. I reach for the wrist of the hand holding the Palmolive. I have been crazy about this wrist since the second grade. I have been crazy about all of this, this whole human, since I was seven. My sweet, my secret passion. I try to feel for her pulse. Surely blood still pumps and throbs through this real strong and brave girl. But it does not. If it does, I cannot feel it. Can I never take her to the movies? *You can just make things up.* Can I make up for her a pulse she does not have? Ernie Pyle? Every Dill? Anybody? Gentle, oh *Gentle* Reader . . .

I stand. I look around, hoping to see Emil Polacek lurking in the shadows. I will kill him with my bare hands, as he has killed her with his bare hands. But he is not there. There is nobody there. I am the only one there. Crickets cicadas katydids tree frogs and a whippoorwill. *You don't have much feelings, leastways you don't* show *much feelings.* I scream. With feelings I scream. At the top of my lungs I scream, loud enough for *you* to hear me, a thousand miles away or right here beside me, wherever you are, who can only watch and listen, who cannot bring this girl back to life to me to here to now to stay more forever. I scream loud enough for everyone in my town to hear me. I scream so that McPherson in his faraway hiding place at the glen of the waterfall can hear me. I scream so deafeningly that I deafen myself. I scream and scream and scream until I can no longer hear myself screaming. I can still hear crickets cicadas katydids tree frogs and a whippoorwill but only inside my head; I cannot hear myself. Am I making me up? I have a voice, a screaming voice, but I cannot hear it. Can you? You who have listened through all this, are you listening now? Can you hear what I cannot? Can you *do* anything? Gentle Reader with your magic that can make things go away or come again, can you not at least remind me that once I said to you *When I dream of Ella Jean, either at night or whenever my conscious reveries need her, the loss of her at the end of the episode is always softened by the thought that she'll return whenever I want?* I scream because you cannot, you cannot, you can neither tell me that she'll return nor that she is gone forever.

I scream and scream, remembering Ella Jean saying *I aint skeered* as she stood up from hiding after the glider landed and they shot at her, even with blanks. My real strong and brave secret girl. Sweet potato pie, made with her own hands, even if the taste isn't my favorite. I go on screaming even though I cannot hear myself. "Every word you say I want to keep," I'd told her and now I have so few words of hers to keep, and none more to hear. Even if I could hear. *Mister we'uns aint et our dinner yit* and Polacek had poked fun at her voice. Where is the bastard?

Here he comes. I am ready for him. I will sink my fingernails into that thick neck as he has sunk his into her little neck, and I will never let go, even when it thunders, because I will never hear the thunder. Even though his thick neck is covered with a beard. How has he grown such a beard so fast? Is he trying to disguise himself as murderer? And it is a grizzled beard. And the rifle he carries is not a *shoju* but a Winchester. And the clothes he wears are not a Japanese soldier's uniform but faded denim overalls. I go on screaming although I go on not hearing myself. He holds out his hand as if to stop my scream. He helplessly motions with his hand to stop my screaming. Then he is shaking me with both hands to make me stop screaming. Finally I stop screaming not because he is shaking me but because I realize that I am continuing to scream even though I cannot hear myself. He is speaking to me. I am not hearing him. He is speaking to me over and over and I am not hearing him over and over. He looks at Ella Jean and seems to speak to her but he is speaking to me words I cannot hear. I am beginning to understand that he is not Polacek in disguise. I am beginning to believe who he is, though I have not seen him so close in longer than I can remember. I wish I could hear him, what words of comfort he seems to be trying to say with his mouth that moves but does not make any sound. Now he drops to his knees beside her and does what I have already done, lifts the frail lovely wrist and tries to find a pulse. He stands again and shakes his head and speaks to me again, and again I cannot detect any sound of any sort except all the crickets cicadas katydids tree frogs and a whippoor-will, which is only in my head. He slides the straps of his overalls down from his shoulders, unbuttons and removes his shirt. What is he doing? I ask him what he is doing but no sound comes from my mouth so I do not know if I have spoken or not. He shows me what he is doing: he is covering Ella Jean's nakedness as best he can with his shirt.

Now comes the angel to take Ella Jean's soul to heaven. But no, she only looks like an angel: it is this man's daughter, following him, not able to keep up with him as he runs to find the source of the screaming. It is McPherson's own living breathing true love, as mine is no longer living breathing. She holds both hands over her mouth as she looks at Ella Jean. She looks at me with revulsion as if I am responsible for this crime. She speaks to her father. He answers her but I can hear neither of them. Then he speaks to me again. I shake my head and whine *I caint hear you!* but do not know if I have uttered at all.

Now comes a bunch of kids I should know, but I cannot convince myself I know them—friends maybe, Dinsmores maybe. Is one of them Willard? He speaks to me, and then he too must drop to his knees and feel for a pulse. Ole Dan speaks to him. The others speak, each to each. I speak, I speak, I speak, but do I? Willard yells at me, I can tell he is yelling because of the muscles in his neck and the look in his eyes and his mouth being open enough to eat a horse. But I can only wait until he has finished all the yelling and then I can only whine again, *I caint hear you!* He puts his mouth up against my ear and yells again, and I feel the hot rush of his breath into my ear but no sound at all.

Ole Dan puts his hand on Willard's shoulder and stops his yelling and then speaks to him again. The other Dinsmore children collapse upon their sister's body. They are howling with sobs I cannot hear. Then Willard begins running, in the direction of town. I start after him, but ole Dan stops me. He tries to tell me what Willard is doing, where he is going, and finally I have enough sense returning to me to realize that in my hip pocket, folded, is a new Indian Chief tablet and in my shirt pocket is a pencil stub and I offer these to ole Dan, saying, whining *I caint hear you could you please write down whatever you're saying.*

And ole Dan takes my tablet and writes on it. He seems to write slowly as if he is having trouble making letters, but he is only trying to compose what he has to say. When he hands it back to me I am surprised at the elegance of his script. *Willard must fetch Doc Swain. We mustn't move her until Doc Swain has seen her, not that he can do anything for her, but he is the justice of the peace, after all.* I am so thrilled to see these words. I have heard nothing yet, it is almost as if these written words are speaking to me, at last. *Thank you,* I cry, *thank you so much!*

He holds out his hand for the tablet, and wants to write one more thing: *There are many questions I'd like to ask you, but I'll just wait and see if Doc Swain asks them.*

So there is nothing to do but wait. Now appears Ella Jean's mother, Selena, who is holding her hands high above her head as if to catch Ella Jean's soul before the angels can lift it to heaven.

The angels may not be taking Ella Jean's soul to heaven, but I think they have roused themselves up from whatever rest and recuperation they have been taking.

Finally here comes a car on the Banty Creek road that goes to Spunkwater. It stops, then here is the sight of Doc Swain coming down to the creek. He is carrying his black bag, as if it contains anything that could save her. He talks to ole Dan. Ole Dan talks to him, and points at me, and talks some more. Doc gives me a look, but there is no accusation or suspicion in it. Doc does not lift her wrist but uses his stethoscope, briefly. Then he comes and I give him the Indian Chief and hold his flashlight for him while he writes down quite a lot of questions which I try to answer although I cannot tell if my voice is whining or calm or pleading or unruffled or what. Then he writes that he wants me and all the others present to turn our backs for just a moment while he completes his examination of the body. He says this aloud to them after I have read it. We turn our backs and wait, a long while. He touches my shoulder to let me know the wait is over. Then he examines me. He uses his stethoscope on me, and his hands, and tries to determine if I am feverish or ill in any way. He takes a thing from his bag and pokes it into each of my ears, and looks through the thing into my ears.

It is full dark now. Annie has returned to their house and brought a kerosene lantern. More people continue to arrive. There is now a soldier there, one of the engineers, and soon two jeeps arrive behind Doc Swain's car on the Banty Creek road, and there is Captain Billings of the engineers. And Major Evans, the umpire. These men stand around talking with Doc Swain and ole Dan. A soldier covers Ella Jean completely with an army blanket, including her face. I am tired of standing and wish I could sit down but I dare not. After a while there comes another car with a flashing light atop it, and here comes Sheriff Frank Cheatham all the way from Jasper, with two of his deputies. They talk to Doc Swain, they talk to Major Evans, they try to talk to me but Doc Swain talks to them and they stop trying to talk to me.

There is a large crowd on the banks of Banty Creek. Willard is holding Gypsy while she cries, but his face is all soaked with tears too. Sammy Coe is also crying. Joe Don is asking questions of everybody. Two more jeeps come down the road, and there is Captain Stoving, and then there is Lieutenant McPherson, who rushes right to me, ignoring all the others, not saluting the major or anybody, not even looking at the sheriff, and puts his hands on my shoulders and starts talking real fast, and I would give anything to be able to hear him but I cannot. Doc Swain talks to him. I offer him the Indian Chief. He takes it and writes, *Are you all right?* I shake my head. I cannot hear my voice saying, "I am sorry I am deaf. I am so sad I caint tell you." He writes furiously on the Indian Chief, *This is terrible beyond belief. We will find the murderer and destroy him!*

"It was Polacek," I inform him.

His face is astonished. He writes, *It couldn't have been. Polacek has been with me up in the lost hollow all day and evening. He hasn't been out of my sight.*

The sheriff talks to McPherson. McPherson answers him, then yells something at Captain Stoving. Everyone is yelling, except Gypsy, who cries and cries and cries.

It is late. It gets later. I am so tired. McPherson writes in my Indian Chief, *Come on. I'll drive you home.* I am so grateful for his offer. But first I must go and kneel and pull back the army blanket and give Ella Jean a kiss goodnight, a last kiss. *Sayonara*, I whisper to her, which is the last thing I'd said when she could hear me and now I cannot even hear myself nor can she. Then I tell McPherson I don't want to go home. I don't want to see my aunt and uncle. I want to spend the night with Latha. *I'll explain to your aunt*, he writes, *and she had better accept my explanation*. In a jeep he takes me to Latha's house. Latha and Every have already heard from others, and they embrace me. McPherson says he'll see me first thing in the morning. Latha and Every put me to bed. Sometime away along in the night with no night sounds at all except the crickets in my head I finally finally finally drift into the arms of sleep.

In the days that follow, McPherson is with me often. He becomes my ears and writes in my Indian Chief everything that is going on. The exercise is over. The Yanks never have found the lost glen of the waterfall, and therefore the Japs have won by default. Major Evans has wanted to continue the exercise but McPherson has refused. Another captain has arrived from Chaffee, a Military Police investigator, with a staff of MP lieutenants and sergeants, and they are questioning every man of the Yanks, the Japs, and the engineers. Private Polacek is heartbroken. At

Ella Jean's funeral he appears with an armful of wildflowers he has picked from all over. When they sing "Farther Along" he tries to join in. I cannot hear them singing it but I know they are singing it. Even if I could hear myself singing, which I cannot, I would not join the singing because I do not believe anymore that farther along anybody will ever understand anything, that farther along anybody will ever know all about it, that any one of us will ever understand it all by and by. I watch McPherson during the singing, and afterward I say to him, "You can't believe this! Farther along we're not going to understand anything!" He takes my Indian Chief and writes, *Donny, the point of the hymn is not that we will ever have any final answers farther along but that there will be a farther along to look forward to.*

I tell him I don't believe that either. What is there to look forward to? The army investigator cannot find the murderer, the sheriff cannot find the murderer, McPherson cannot, Willard cannot, I cannot, although I have tried: at my suggestion, since I have considered that if the rape occurred in that grove of thorny locusts there was a chance the culprit got himself scratched and blooded by thorns if Ella Jean put up any sort of struggle, every man in Stay More has been examined for thorn scratches. They have examined me too, and found none. None of the soldiers have any. Sog Alan has a bad scratch on his back but there are witnesses who can testify that Sog got the scratch from a nail in his barn. McPherson himself has had a serious talk with Sog and doesn't think he's guilty. The sheriff tells McPherson that there doesn't appear to be any chance of finding a suspect among any residents of Stay More. The investigating MP captain tells McPherson that none of the soldiers can be held as suspects. So what is there to look forward to?

Nor do I have a newspaper to publish anymore. McPherson offers to help me put out an issue of *The Stay Morning Star,* at least to carry the story that the "occupation" of Stay More is about to end, that the tanks have already returned to Chaffee and that the engineers and all the other soldiers will leave soon. I remember what Ella Jean had written on my plaster arm cast: *Hope you go far with the Stay Morning-star,* and I break down in sobs, not just from thoughts of sweet Ella Jean but also because I know I will not go anywhere any more, far or near, with my newspaper. Doc Swain has examined me twice again, once with what he writes are "tuning forks," and he has written into my Indian Chief: *It seems you must have howled away your hearing.* He has told my aunt and uncle that they should take me to St. Louis to see a specialist, but they have no money for that. I am not going to be able to interview anybody, ever again. The *Star* is dead.

When I am very sad, McPherson snatches my Indian Chief and fiercely begins a new page: "(7) The Story of the Lost Glen of the Waterfall, including (a) how Bluff-Dweller Indians inhabited it for generations; (b) how Sewell Jerram was assassinated there in 1914; (c) how Nail Chism hid out there following Jerram's assassination; (d) how I myself was lost there at the age of almost six; (e) how the samurai under Chui McPherson successfully hid themselves there at the conclusion of the War Games, and (f) whatever else may yet happen there in years to come." Then on another page he writes: *You don't have to be able to hear to write about all of that! Nor do you need to have a newspaper!*

Then he tells me that he must go. The jeeps are ready, the trucks are loaded, all of the soldiers are set to go back to Chaffee. McPherson writes that all of us are probably glad, or should be glad, to see them go. *We may never know,* he writes, *if it was one of us, but it might as well have been. We are the anonymous instruments of death.* He tells me that I have been the only real friend he's ever had, and that he is going to miss me terribly, and that he will write to me from wherever he is, and that he will always hope, against hope, that he will survive the invasion of Japan and be able to come back to Stay More, where he will stay more and marry Annie and be my friend forever. Then he gives me a big hug and writes one more thing: *I have arranged for Gypsy to keep Jarhead.* That strikes me as very funny, and I laugh, the first time I've laughed in a long long time. Then he takes a stick and scratches deeply into the dirt the four figures that make up the word *sayonara* in Japanese letters. He says the word aloud, though I cannot hear him.

But I cannot say *sayonara* to him. Not because I cannot hear myself. Nor because I cannot tolerate the thought of good-bye. But because it was the last thing I said to Ella Jean, and is hers alone. So I try to smile. He salutes me, at full attention. He executes a smart about-face and is gone. Gone.

I have already decided this, I have already thought about this a lot and have made up my mind: I will watch the evacuation of Stay More from the vantage of Leapin Rock. Though I have never been atop it before, I know how to get there, where the trail is, and I go there now. Now I sit on Leapin Rock, not too close to the edge but close enough to look over and see how very far it is to the place where Ella Jean's sisters landed. I wonder which is worse, hitting the earth from this height or being raped and strangled. I open my Indian Chief and on the page where I had written "(4) The History of Leapin Rock," I write a few things, I write several things while watching the jeeps and the trucks far below like mindless bugs doing whatever they have to do, lining up to leave town. I write a note for Latha. I really have loved her more than anyone.

I flip back a page to "(3) What's the picture on Ella Jean's nightie?" written in her own lovely hand, asking the question about the Question Mark, which will always remain that, Whoever killed her, or Whoever was meant to be her lover but never got a chance. The jeeps and the trucks are moving along the road to Parthenon, heading north out of town. From this height I cannot tell which ones have McPherson and his samurai in them. I write a few things for Ella Jean on that page, and finally I answer aloud her question: "It was ME in that picture on your nightie, Ella Jean! And here I come!"

I stand up, and need only a moment to decide whether to keep my eyes open or to close them. Probably with them closed I can see her better.

Two hands clamp my shoulders and jerk me away from the edge. It is McPherson. He is talking up a storm but then remembers that I cannot hear. He shoves me into a sitting position far from the rock's lip and sits down beside me and takes the Indian Chief and begins writing. I notice there is something different about him: the silver bar on his collar has doubled. He's a captain now.

He hands me what he has written: *I suspected I'd find you up here. And it's a good thing I did, isn't it? Well, I'm sorry to interrupt you but you're needed for a few more jobs in this world. One is that you'll have to sit at the Press table during the ceremony for the posthumous awarding of the Congressional Medal of Honor to Mare Coe. It looks like I'm going to be around for several more days at least. And you're going to be around for many more years.*

"I thought all of you were gone," I say.

We almost were, he writes. *We were all set to stay no more in Stay More when the radio message came from the brass at Chaffee telling us that the big brass in Washington want us to stay more. And we're all mighty proud to do that.*

CHAPTER
25

WHEN WILL THE SOLDIERS LEAVE STAY MORE? A SECOND INVASION
will happen, not just by the army but also the navy and marines and
press corps and politicians. I will not reveal to anyone, not even Captain
McPherson, my suspicion that the memory of Mare Coe and his heroism at Iwo Jima will be given such recognition because the army will be
trying to cover up or at least apologize for its rape and strangling of a
young girl. Throughout the days of this second invasion, Captain Mc-
Pherson will give everyone to think that he is my personal *aide-de-camp*,
as he will have written yet another French military expression. He will
hardly ever let me out of his sight, not, he will assure me, because he
will fear that I would run back up to Leapin Rock, but because he will
want to make absolutely certain that my deafness will not prevent me

from knowing everything that is going on. I think he will not want me to be left alone with all of the reporters who will have come to town.

McPherson and his samurai will no longer be wearing either their Japanese combat uniforms or their army fatigues, but full dress uniforms, which will have been brought to them by a truck sent from Chaffee, the same truck which will have contained an item Captain McPherson will have obtained through calling in a favor owed him by a supply lieutenant: an Underwood upright typewriter. McPherson will spend too much of his time trying to teach me to use it, when he himself will have known only the hunt-and-peck system, whose rudiments, however, I will pick up sufficiently to pretend to be using when McPherson will set the Underwood up at my place at the Press table, facing the rostrum set up out in the schoolyard.

Other tables all along one edge of the schoolyard will be covered with the best linen tablecloths, upon which all the ladies of Stay More (and many other parts of Newton County) will have deposited innumerable sumptuous dishes, just as if it will have been a funeral feast, or at least a dinner-on-the-grounds: huge platters of fried chicken and such pies and cakes that even the sight of them will have brought to the mouth of poor starving Willard Dinsmore the first smile he will have managed since the recent tragedy. His hands will itch. But Miss Jerram will have appointed herself to the job of standing guard over the tables, with the assistance of Sergeant Rodney Harris of Wisconsin, and they will keep kids and dogs away from the tables until the ceremony will be all over.

My colleagues at the Press table will include reporters from the Jasper weekly, the dailies of Harrison, Fayetteville, Fort Smith, and Little Rock, and even one from Kansas City, as well as several photographers. Although they will have attempted to tease me in the beginning because I am so young and small, they will quickly cease their teasing when they notice how deferential the army captain standing behind my chair will be—or maybe he will have told them to lay off. Once, one of them will attempt to pass me a note with a question on it, but my captain will intercept it, and I will always after wonder if it sought to question me about Ella Jean.

My captain will hand to me a prepared typescript of the main part of the ceremony: the actual awarding of the medal. After the navy chaplain will offer the benediction, after Every Dill as the closest thing to a local preacher will offer a brief obituary of Gerald Coe, after Doc Swain will speak a few words in support of this boy's character, after United States Congressman J. W. Trimble will be introduced long-windedly by County Judge Will Jones of Jasper and will give a long speech (my captain will hand me a note: *I'm not writing any of this down for you because none of it is very important*), finally a colonel of the marines will summon Lawlor and Dulcie Coe to stand before him, and the colonel will present Lawlor with medal after medal, which my captain will explain for me: *The Purple Heart, the Presidential Unit Citation with an Iwo Jima star, and the Asiatic-Pacific Area Campaign Medal with an Iwo Jima star.* Then the colonel will hold up a medal in the form of a golden star as big as the sheriff's badge with the fanciest blue silk ribbon anyone has ever seen. He will hand it not to Lawlor but to Congressman Trimble, who will present it on behalf of President Harry S Truman and the United States Congress, while the colonel will read the citation, a typescript of which McPherson has placed before me so that I can follow it: *For conspicuous gallantry and intrepidity at the risk of his life above and beyond the call of duty . . . in action against enemy Japanese forces during the seizure of Iwo Jima . . . he boldly defied shattering Japanese machine-gun fire and knee mortars as well as small-arms fire . . .* the colonel will read on and on, covering in detail Mare's throwing back all those grenades at the enemy, *killing an estimated sixty Japanese before he was mortally wounded. . . . His dauntless initiative, unfaltering courage, indomitable determination during a critical period of action, and valiant spirit of self-sacrifice in the face of certain death reflected the highest credit upon Private First Class Coe and sustained and enhanced the highest tradition of the United States Naval Service. He gallantly gave his life for his comrades and his country.*

Squeezed into the overpopulated schoolyard, there will be a band of musicians, a small but loud marine corps band of buglers, saxophonists, and drummers, and they will strike up a rousing number that I will not hear. My captain will write for me: *It's just as well you can't hear them. They're playing some nonsense about the halls of Montezuma and the shores of Tripoli.*

Lawlor Coe will receive the fancy medal on behalf of his son, thanking Congressman Trimble and thanking the colonel. They will direct him to the microphone but he will say only a few words. My captain will write them down for me: *He was a good boy.*

A cannon will be fired—the very last shot in the occupation of Stay More. The smoke from it will take a long time to drift out of the valley.

While we all will be filling our plates at those groaning tables, my captain will hand me another note: *Excuse me a second. Burt's trying to beat my time again.* I will watch as he goes to rescue Annie from the attentions of Captain Burton Stoving, who, although his tank companies will have returned to Chaffee, will have insisted on staying more in Stay More, possibly because he will have become smitten with the hermit's daughter, or possibly will just want the challenge of taking her away from Mc-Pherson. I will not be the only one interested in watching them. Everybody will be curious because this will be the first public appearance of Annie. And of her father too.

McPherson will never get me to agree to interview ole Dan, even with his help. I will somehow not be able to banish the image of him as the first to appear after Ella Jean's death, and that unreasonable prejudice will further contribute to my fall as a newspaperman. McPherson will insist that I allow him to help me put out one more issue of *The Stay Morning Star,* devoted almost entirely to the Medal of Honor ceremony, but with a small box in one corner: IN MEMORIAM, ELLA JEAN DINSMORE, 1933–1945.

My captain will fail in his good-intentioned effort to persuade me to continue the newspaper. A journalist without ears, I will have to tell him, is like a doctor without hands. *Let others do the reporting,* he will suggest, on a final page of my Indian Chief. *You could just be the editor.* "What others?" I will want to know. "Nobody but Ella Jean was ever interested in helping out around here." Trying to cheer him up and let him know that I will not be a totally hopeless case, I will say, "Well, she once told me I ought to just make up the news. And I did, sometimes. But that's not such a good idea, is it?"

No, that's not allowed, he will write, *but nobody's ever going to stop you from writing things that don't pretend to be news. Besides, news gets old. News never lasts. Good writing stays new and lasts forever.*

And that will be practically the last thing of consequence that he will write in that Indian Chief, which will be filled up anyhow. There will be just a few other words written there, attempts to say goodbye. I will tell him how I can't say *sayonara* because that is only for her. So he will tell me there is simply *ja ne!* which means just "See ya!" *I will, you know*, he will write, *I will see you*.

But he will be wrong about that too. I will not watch the jeep carrying him away from Stay More; there is a superstition, old as the hills, that you should never watch anybody going out of sight; to do so is to doom them.

I will never see him again. He will not be killed in the invasion of Kyushu, because that invasion will never occur. I will no longer be able to listen to the radio, but I will have outgrown those silly shows, *Captain Midnight*, *Hop Harrigan*, and *Terry and the Pirates*, and will no longer have any use for the news, but if there is anything important on the air that she thinks I ought to know, dear Latha will write it down for me. It will be in her handwriting, in August, that I will learn that an incredible bomb, made from atoms, unimaginable in its power, will have been dropped on a city called Hiroshima. So many people will have been killed that, when another bomb like a deathly echo is dropped on another city, Nagasaki, the Japanese will surrender. While I will be stunned and will share with Latha her sorrow and her tears over the senseless deaths of all those hundreds of thousands of innocent civilians, I will be rapturous that the worst war in the history of mankind is finally over—and that McPherson's samurai will not be needed after all.

In time, McPherson will write to me from the Kyushu city of Kagoshima, where he will have been promoted to major and will be serving as the chief interpreter for the occupation of Kyushu. I will imagine that he will be as polite and kind to the Japanese people as he had been to us, but I will not imagine that he will meet and befriend a twelve-year-old Japanese boy who edits a newspaper. Later he will be promoted to colonel and established in the occupation headquarters in Tokyo, where he will remain for several years. He will mail to me a photograph of Yoshino Hijiya, a beautiful girl he will intend to marry. Perhaps because of his love for her, I will not hear from him much anymore after that. I will eventually get a letter from Rutland, Vermont, where he will be working for an American publisher, Charles E. Tuttle, who specializes in the printing of Japanese books and will soon be sending him to work permanently in the Tokyo office. There will be a photograph of the two children born to him and Yoshino.

One samurai will return to Stay More after the war, and one Yank. Using a map he had drawn on the flyleaf of his Bible, Rodney Harris will find his way back here to persuade Estalee Jerram to accompany him to Eau Claire, Wisconsin, to meet his family. She will argue with him over her desire to stay in Stay More, and they will spend a month here, and a month there, and a month here, before finally settling for good there. I will regret that, for throughout the sixth grade Miss Jerram will have helped me avoid being sent away to Little Rock to attend the Arkansas School for the Deaf, as my aunt and uncle will have tried to make me do. Miss Jerram will write things down for me, and make it possible for me to stay in the Stay More school. When Miss Jerram will move permanently to Wisconsin, her replacement as Stay More schoolteacher, a young woman named Jane Harrison from Valley Springs in neighboring Boone County, will write in my Indian Chief on my first day in the seventh grade, "(8) The Story of How Boone Harrison Became the First Schoolmaster of Stay More." She will write *He was my great-grandfather, and you don't have to have ears to learn the history of Stay More and write about it, and besides Estalee Jerram wrote me a long letter about you and I can't tell you how glad I am you're going to be my pupil.* Between Latha and Miss Harrison, I will learn enough to write the first story in my book called *Stay Morons*, which will never be published but will serve as the wellspring for many that will.

Burton Stoving will not be as bright as Rodney Harris, and will not have a Bible with a flyleaf map showing how to find Stay More. Just as it had taken his tank battalion forever to find us in the first place, he will get lost several times and will go back to Little Rock in frustration. But he will be nothing if not persistent, which is why he will be a rising executive in the insurance business. Burton Stoving will no longer be trying to steal McPherson's girlfriend because he will not know that McPherson will have a Japanese wife; he will only be trying to steal a girl away from her hermit father, and he will succeed, like Rodney Harris reducing the female population of Stay More by one more. Not without considerable trouble. Ole Dan will not like Burton Stoving. Ole Dan will never have liked Burton Stoving. And, now that Burton Stoving will no longer be in a captain's uniform but just civilian clothes, I will wonder why Annie likes him. He will be good-looking, and rich. He will drive a nice car. I will have to wonder if McPherson will have written Annie to tell her that he will be marrying Yoshino. As always, I will know nothing about Annie. And I will write in the Indian Chief: "(9) Why Did Annie Elope with Burton Stoving?" It will be years before I get around to learning the answer to that.

Annie will spend the rest of her life in Little Rock. But nearly everybody else in Stay More will move to California. A very few of them, like John Henry "Hank" Ingledew, will come back, but there will be so many other Stay Morons in Orange County, California, that the towns of Fullerton and Anaheim will have colonies of Stay-Morons-in-exile.

Time and the rains and the flooding creeks will fill with silt our foxholes until, in time, no one will know that we ever played here. Sometimes when it will be raining very hard and no one will be watching me or hearing me, I will let myself cry, for a little while. But once Doc Swain will catch me crying and will take my Indian Chief and write something in it, but then he will scratch it out, black it out, think better of it and delete it. Later I will hold it to the light in just such a way that I can make out the effaced letters: *You will find another Ella Jean.* Latha will tell me a little about Doc's own story, enough to suggest that he himself had once had his own Ella Jean, a girl named Tenny, whom he had lost and never again found a replacement for, and thus I will understand why he will have had second thoughts about leaving that sentence in my old Indian Chief. But before I can ever get old enough to ask him about his Tenny, he will be killed by lightning, and at his funeral I will watch him being interred beneath a double headstone beside Tennessee Tennison Swain, his long lost love. "Are you still there?" I will ask, not of either of them but of *you,* and on the spot will solemnly promise to learn their story and tell it to you, farther along, all by and by.

Among the men of Stay More who had been Our Boys Overseas and who will return after the war long enough to pack up their families and take them to California will be Ace Dingletoon, returning alive and unhurt but without medals or promotion. He will be evicted from his rent-free farm and will resume his former habit of instant evacuation, blowing his horn to summon his family into removal. Eyewitnesses will give the lie to the hoary legend about his pulling a rope tied to all their belongings but will report that it will indeed be true that the chickens will lie down with their feet in the air so that Gypsy can tie their legs. And with the help of her trophy Corporal Jarhead, they will escape a step ahead of the sheriff to some other unoccupied farmstead at a far remove from Stay More. We will miss them.

Willard Dinsmore will miss Gypsy so much that in time he will go off on a heroic quest in search of her, only to learn that the Dingletoons too will have been rumored to have joined the endless emigration of Ozarkers to the promised land of California. He himself will go to California, only to discover that California has no abandoned farmsteads because of its incredible growth and prosperity. Unoccupied farms in California are as rare as mansions in Stay More. But by persistent search, and the exceptional sense of tactics that had once made McPherson call him "General Willard Dinsmore," he will in time locate, not an abandoned farm but at least an abandoned shack out in the middle of a vast grove of orange trees near Mission Viejo, where the Dingletoons will be squatting. I will wish desperately to have seen Gypsy's face at the moment Willard will appear, but I will just have to be content in the hope that he will convey to her the message that we will all have missed her and will continue to hope that after she and Willard are married they might want to come back to Stay More on a visit out of nostalgia. But they never will.

Even my aunt and uncle will move to California, good riddance. But I will not go with them. I will rather have committed myself to the Deaf School than go with them. Latha will let me convert the office of the *Star* back to its original function: it had once been the bedroom of her daughter Sonora, who will be gone to California. The Stay More school, for lack of enrollment, will shut down and its few remaining pupils will be bused to Parthenon.

My seatmate on those yellow bus rides to and from Parthenon will be Sammy Coe. Of all the original members of the Axis and Allies, Japs and Yanks, only Sammy Coe and I will remain—and Sog Alan, the miscreant, when he will come back from a stint in the Korean War. Sammy and I will grow out of the rivalry of our childhood and become good friends. I will even take him with me when I go to explore the lost glen of the waterfall, not telling him that the place still spooks me, not look-ing for traces of the samurai but for traces of the Indians who made a community there hundreds of years before or for anything else we can find in that cornucopia of splendid stories.

You will come too. On every visit to the lost glen of the waterfall, I will find it not with Sammy's help but with yours, Gentle Reader. We will find what we will be certain is the spot where Sewell Jerram was as-sassinated in 1914, and the cavern where Nail Chism hid out with his true love Viridis Monday, as sung by the choiring of the trees. We will find the spot where I at the age of nearly six spent a night lost, haunted by lightning bugs, alone except for my dog Gumper. And we will find, although we will not yet know it as such because it will not yet have happened, the spot where ole Dan will be shot and killed by State Police Corporal Sog Alan, a story to be told in some other place, which will become one of your favorite stories.

From that moment when you watched and heard and identified with that breaking of my arm on the first page of this writing, you have kept the faith that all things of this world have become, for a while, your world too. But that while, that time, will draw now to its closing al-though the future tense of this closing will suggest that it might never end.

Just as McPherson and I exchanged all those promises and secrets when first we met, I'll need in return a promise and a secret from you, Gentle Reader, *himitsu to himitsu-ni suru*, in return for mine: you have had the privilege, throughout all of this, of sitting there silently, notic-ing everything, missing nothing, and you have unquestionably noticed things that have escaped my attention. If I could see all of this story through your eyes, with the power of your imagination, how grand it would be!

So this story, this world, if it will exist at all, will exist only in your mind, for as long as you can hold onto it. That will be your promise. Mine will be to find *all* the stories of Stay More. We will conspire: my secret to you is that you will be, as you have been, the real creator of this world. Your secret to me is that you will have known that, all along.

Ja ne!